WHAT WE WISH FOR

BOOKS BY
MELODY MAYSONET

What We Wish For

A Work of Art

WHAT WE WISH FOR

Melody Maysonet

BLACK
STONE
PUBLISHING

Published in 2024 by Blackstone Publishing
Cover and book design by Sarah Riedlinger

Printed in the United States of America

First edition: 2024
ISBN 979-8-212-63828-9
Young Adult Fiction / Coming of Age

Version 1

Blackstone Publishing
31 Mistletoe Rd.
Ashland, OR 97520

www.BlackstonePublishing.com

For God and the 441, who helped me get better

CHAPTER 1

I clench my teeth,
Hold my breath
The cry caught like a speck of dust
In a spider's web

—from "SOS" by L.F.

Maybe today's my lucky day. That's a thing, right? People have lucky days? I think today might be mine because how often do you find a twenty-dollar bill stuck in a tree? Just stuck there and waving like a crisp little flag saying, "Come on, Layla. Pick me."

The money is still in my pocket where I shoved it this morning. It stayed with me all day at school, even though I could have bought a milkshake with it. I could have bought Hostess CupCakes or a slice of pizza. But I'd rather have it in my pocket. It feels like insurance. Like, if something goes wrong, I can handle it because if there's one truth I've learned in my fifteen years on this earth, it's that money fixes things.

If only I had more of it.

The musty room where Mom and I sit is getting crowded, but we have a table up front. I made sure of that, and the fact that Mom didn't argue is a good sign. Still, I'm worried—the way she's gulping her coffee like she can't get enough—and yeah, it smells like your standard crappy coffee, but what if she spiked it somehow? It wouldn't be the first time, and maybe, if I pull her into a hug, I can get a better whiff.

Just as I'm leaning closer, though, she looks me straight in the face, and I see my own suspicion reflected in her eyes. She knows my tricks, just like I know hers, and the last thing I want is to break this fragile trust we've built.

A guy in a stained T-shirt bumps her chair from behind. Her coffee slops on the table, but she hardly notices . . . and that tells me her drink *isn't* spiked because, if it was, she'd be upset about the spill.

It also tells me how nervous she is—and how nervous I am to think she'd drink on such an important day. Her shoulders are hunched as she stares straight ahead, and I want to make her feel better, so I nudge her and say, "Hey, you got this." It's lame encouragement, but she conjures up a smile that crawls into my heart and settles there. Now I want to hug her for real, but I don't want her to think I'm sniffing for booze, so I touch her hand instead.

She flinches like I've burned her, which of course sets off my paranoia. I'm about to ask if something's wrong when she turns to me and looks me in the eye. "I'm fine, Layla."

She doesn't look fine. She's squeezing her cup so hard the Styrofoam's starting to crack, and when I take it from her hand, I notice dried blood on her nails from where she's been picking them. That just means she's nervous, though, right? It doesn't mean she's been drinking.

Normally I don't come to Mom's AA meetings, but this one's super important because, in less than an hour, she'll be picking up her thirty-day sobriety chip. And yeah, thirty days without a drink doesn't seem like much. But it is when you've caught your mom drinking before noon, when you've found empty bottles in her closet, and picked her up off the floor, and seen her lose her job and her apartment and everything that makes her a human being. When you've seen all that, thirty days is huge.

Which is why she shouldn't look so miserable. Not today of all days.

I'm about to tell her about the money I found, hoping it will cheer her up, when a hand claps my shoulder. I turn to see James Saint James grinning at me with his huge smile. Without his dreadlocks, I almost don't recognize him. He shaved them off because his caseworker said they were keeping him from finding a job. Now he rubs his hand over his scalp as he eases his oversized body into the chair next to me.

"You doing okay, girl?"

"Yeah, I'm good."

He studies my face. "You're a bad liar."

Actually, I'm a good liar. I've had to be, living with Mom.

James leans in to whisper, "She's going to be fine."

"Yeah," I say, wishing I had his confidence. Or faith, as he calls it. I'm trying to believe Mom is making good headway, but the fact is, she hasn't had a job interview since we started staying here. Plus, she keeps bending the rules—pretending to be sick when she should be going to her education classes or skipping out on her AA meetings, even though I try to make sure she goes. So far, no one's reported her, but that doesn't mean they won't. Just yesterday the girl in the room next to us got reported because someone *suspected* she was high. And yeah, she was acting weird, but she also had her four-year-old son living here, so you'd think they'd give her a second chance. Now she's on the street somewhere, and her son got taken by child services. He might be better off, but no one here thinks so since we've all heard horror stories about foster families.

Mom slouches in her seat, as today's chairperson—a smiling woman who limps when she walks—hands out laminated sheets of AA doctrine. She stops in front of our table and tries to give Mom one of the readings. Mom shakes her head. "I can't read."

Which isn't true, but the woman, who seems like a newbie at this, gets flustered. "Oh," she says. "Sorry."

Mom shrugs. "Don't worry about it."

Once the chairlady has moved on, I turn to Mom, choosing my words so I don't sound critical. "They say it helps to get involved."

"I know what they say."

"Then maybe it wouldn't hurt to participate?"

"I'm trying, okay?"

"Are you?"

Mom sighs. "You want me to be sober, and I am."

"I want you to be happy."

And I want her to find a job and save enough money for us to move out of here. I want her to be the mom she used to be, and why is it so hard? Why does she make everything so hard?

She's studying my face like she knows what I'm thinking. "You know I'm trying, right?"

"Yeah, Mom. I know."

As I reach to squeeze her hand, the chairlady bangs a gavel at the front of the room. "Okay, group, let's have a meeting!" Then she launches into the Serenity Prayer, and everyone chants along. Everyone except me.

"God, grant me the serenity . . ."

Even Mom's praying, which surprises me, but she stops when there's movement outside the door.

"To accept the things I cannot change . . ."

The door opens, and in walks this guy with red hair. My heart spikes into my throat because I know him, or at least

I've seen him. Today at school. He's a new kid. Morgan and I noticed him because, first of all, he looks like an indie rocker, which you'd think wouldn't intrigue me since I've been crushing on a jock named Felix since middle school, but this guy emotes cool. Plus, he's new, which automatically makes him stand out, but what's he doing here? What if he sees me? Will he recognize me from school?

"The courage to change the things I can . . ."

Mom's staring at him too, and she even ghosts a smile at me, like she knows I think he's hot. His red hair is light enough that it's almost blond, and his eyelashes and eyebrows are pale. He's got sharp cheekbones, and I think his eyes are light blue or green. He's wearing a Nirvana T-shirt, which is kind of cool and also kind of ironic considering Kurt Cobain was an addict.

". . . and the wisdom to know the difference."

Once the prayer is finished, the new guy's eyes skate the room. A woman to my left waves at him and points to an empty chair beside her. She's got the same reddish hair as he does. Since she's obviously his mom, does that mean he lives here? He doesn't look like the homeless type, but then again, neither do I—or at least, I hope I don't. Maybe they're volunteers, or maybe they're doing some kind of research project on homelessness or addiction.

I shrink behind James, trying to be invisible, but the new guy's eyes land on me, and I'm suddenly self-conscious of how my emo-punk hairdo frizzes up in the Florida humidity. Maybe I *do* look homeless, and maybe I should spend the twenty dollars I found on hair gel and deep conditioner. I don't know if he recognizes me from school, but he gives me a nervous smile that I pretend not to see. If he lives here too, he'll want to keep it a secret as much as I do, right?

The chairlady introduces the topic—something about

finding peace—and I'm trying to listen because this is a good topic for Mom, but I'm distracted by the guy from my school. He's writing in a notepad, and I wonder . . . Is he taking notes for his research? He glances up, meets my eye, and I look away, embarrassed that he's seen me staring, embarrassed that he's seen me *here.*

A woman in the back starts sharing on the topic, but I'm barely listening. Mom's twisted around in her seat so she can see the woman, and the fact that she's paying attention makes the tightness in my gut ease up. Then she slumps in her chair, and the old familiar tension comes back.

Meanwhile, the guy from my school is busily writing in his notepad. At one point, he shows it to his mom, which makes me think he *does* live here and that he's writing things down that will help her, kind of like I did for Mom the first week we were here until she told me she needed to do this herself. *His* mom looks interested, though. She keeps glancing at his notebook and nodding. Obviously, she's getting something out of it, unlike my mom, who's concentrating on picking apart her Styrofoam cup. At one point, he looks over at me with his light-colored eyes, and yeah, he's definitely noticed me. What if he tells people at school I live here? Not even Morgan knows my secret, and I intend to keep it that way.

The meeting goes long, and Mom becomes more and more fidgety. Finally, five minutes after the meeting was supposed to end, the chairlady starts wrapping up. Mom picks at her nails as someone behind me reads the "Promises" from a laminated sheet. Her leg starts bouncing.

"Stop," I whisper, because she's making the whole table squeak and a woman keeps turning around to give us dirty looks.

Mom doesn't stop.

James nudges me. "Ain't that your mom's caseworker?"

He's looking toward the door where a tall Black woman with big glasses is peering inside. She catches my eye and points at Mom, then at herself. She wants Mom to come to her office. Maybe she has news about a job, and maybe this *is* my lucky day. I nod at Claudette to let her know I got the message. She disappears, and I wonder if Mom told her she's picking up her thirty-day chip. Probably not.

"It's that time," says the chairlady. "Can I get a volunteer to do the chips?"

While James lumbers to his feet, Mom grips the edge of the table. I whisper to her, "You got this," and she tries to smile.

Meanwhile, James is grinning like he's playing Santa as he scoops up a handful of different-colored poker chips from the chairlady's desk. "Hey, y'all. They call me James Saint James, and I'm what you call a real alcoholic." His voice is huge like the rest of him, a low rumble that reminds me of gravel crunching beneath tires. "Here in AA, we got a chip system to show how long we been sober. We use poker chips to show we're gambling with our lives, and it all starts with a white chip." He finds a white chip in his open palm and holds it up. "Anyone want to give up the fight and pick up a white?"

No takers. Mom picked up a white chip our first day here, but I refused to get excited because, over the years, she's picked up enough white chips to tile a floor.

James lays the surrender chip on the desk and taps it with his finger. "It's here in case you're shy." Then he holds up a green chip, and my heart gets tight and tense because this is Mom's big moment and I'm scared she'll do something to ruin it. Scared she'll embarrass me in front of the guy from my school. Scared.

"Next we got a green chip for thirty days." James grins right at Mom. She stumbles out of her chair and goes to him with her shoulders hunched and takes the chip.

James calls out, "This here's Shauna, everyone!"

Mom stays up there while everyone claps. She stays up there looking at us, and I'm wondering why she doesn't sit down.

Then she clears her throat. "I just want to say . . ." Her voice is timid, but everyone gets quiet so they can hear. ". . . how hard it's been this past year. I appreciate all the advice, though."

She pauses to look at James, who nods at her.

"And I appreciate my daughter standing by me."

And of course she points in my direction, so now everyone's looking at me, including the guy from my school. I don't know whether to feel embarrassed or proud.

"She could have let me self-destruct," Mom says. "But she didn't. She found this place, and I know I should be grateful, but the truth is, I hate it here. I hate everything about it. And most of all, I hate my life."

Dead silence in the room.

"Last year, my dad died, which was really hard, and I know I should be grateful because I have a roof over my head, but this place sucks, doesn't it?"

A few people laugh. I want to laugh too; instead I'm holding back tears.

"It's just . . ." Her voice gets choked and she bows her head. When she looks up, her lips are trembling. "I'm praying like you said to do, even though I don't believe in God, but you guys told me in AA we get to choose our own higher power, even if it's a doorknob." She sets her jaw. "So that's what I choose. A freaking doorknob. And if my doorknob has magical powers, great. And if it doesn't, no surprise."

Everyone's staring at her in stunned silence. Except the guy from my school, who's whispering something to his mom, and maybe it's him seeing me here, or maybe it's Mom standing up there so pitiful. Maybe it's the whole damn universe, but suddenly the doubt, the embarrassment, the hopelessness—all of it catches up to me, and I slump in my chair, wanting to melt into the floor, wanting so badly to add my molecules to the sticky glaze of dirt and germs.

James calls out, "Keep coming back!"

Because, yeah, she has a long way to go—and why can't she get this? Why can't she get this and be happy for more than two seconds?

Everyone's clapping as she makes her way back to me. She sinks into her chair, and I'm trying to be proud of her—I know I should be—she's come such a long way. But it's exhausting sometimes to be around her, exhausting to keep the fear at bay with positive thoughts of rainbows and unicorns and happy hopeful joy. She needs me, though, so I give her a quick hug, and I smile at her as though everything is awesome. When really there's a dark tear inside me that's opening like a zipper. A dark tear that's ripping me in half, but I can't let anyone see that.

It's best to pretend like everything's okay.

CHAPTER 2

Hope is a fickle thing
Dangling from string,
Not like diamonds, more like bling.
—from "The Problem with Hope" by L.F.

Everyone's getting up to leave after the meeting, but I stay seated because James is talking with Mom. She's nodding and looking at her feet, and I imagine he's telling her what he told me the first time I met him, when he saw me crying in the laundry room. I was freaking out because we had just moved in, and I was overwhelmed with how crappy my life had become, but he said to me, "Look at where your feet are. Right now you're safe. Right now you got everything you need." It helped.

The thing is, though, Mom *doesn't* have everything she needs. She needs a job, for one thing, which means I need to get her to Claudette's office, where hopefully she'll tell us she found Mom a job at a hair salon—no interview required—and yeah, I know that's unlikely, but that's the way hope works.

Mom is still talking with James. I don't want to interrupt because James has a way of making people feel better, and right now, she needs all the help she can get. Across the room, the guy from my school is getting up to leave, but he seems hesitant, as in, he's taking a long time to put away his notebook. I should go talk to him, find out if he lives here, and if he does, give him a few survival tips, like never assume a glass you take from the cupboard is clean, or make sure the shelves on your wall can actually hold weight before you put books on them.

I also need to ask him to please not tell anyone he saw me here, because if it gets out how pathetic my life is, the "I-don't-care-what-you-think-of-me" image I've built won't be strong enough to hide behind.

I'm about to go over, but then his mom says something that makes him follow her out the door. He glances back. Our eyes meet. And then he's gone.

And when I look back to Mom, she's gone too.

James is wiping up Mom's coffee spill from earlier. "You just missed her."

I'm worried about her. "How did she seem?"

James hesitates, then says, "Okay," which doesn't make me feel better.

He's done cleaning up the spill, and I follow him outside, waving as we go our separate ways. It's a chilly night for South Florida, and I'm hugging myself as I look around for Mom. I don't see her, so I search for her as I walk the perimeter of the Quad. That's what the people who live here call the open space in the middle of the shelter's four buildings, as if we're living on a college campus—not that I know from personal experience what a college campus looks like, but I will someday. Hopefully. I'm just not sure how.

As usual, the Quad smells like cigarette smoke laced with raw sewage. That's because everyone here seems to smoke and also because we're just down the street from the water-treatment plant. Sometimes, when the wind is just right, you'll get a whiff of flowers too because someone decided that beautifying the place with big flowerpots was a good idea. I guess they didn't realize that most of the flowers would die, or that flowerpots make great ashtrays.

Finally, I spot Mom sitting with the smokers at a concrete picnic table. A woman who looks like someone's mean grandma is talking to her while Mom picks her nails, shoulders hunched, one knee juddering. It strikes me suddenly that Mom used to take care of her nails. She used to do a lot of things before her drinking took over, and sometimes I forget what she was like when I was little—how she played with me all the time, went to my school performances, helped me with my homework. Sometimes she was a room mother for my class, and I remember taking her hand, wanting all the kids to know she was my mom. It wasn't until middle school that I noticed her drinking, and since then, it's gotten worse; although it happened so gradually, I barely noticed the escalation. I've since learned the term *functional alcoholic*. That's what she was for a long time. Then Grandpa died last Thanksgiving, and the "functional" part disappeared. It started when she lost her job at the salon. Then she sold our car and started pawning things to pay bills, but pretty soon she couldn't pay the bills either. When my cellphone got turned off, I thought that was the worst thing that could happen to me—until we got evicted from our apartment, and I guess that was her bottom because she hasn't had a drink since. I once heard in an AA meeting that bottoms have trapdoors, but surely Mom's had enough.

She *looks* like she's had enough, always with the slumped shoulders, a sigh in her gestures, and fear in her eyes. As I walk up to the picnic table, her head shoots up like a startled deer.

"What's wrong?" she asks.

I shake my head. "Claudette wants to see you."

The grandma lady blows out smoke. "Didn't I tell you?"

"Tell her what?" I ask, and when the woman doesn't answer, I turn to Mom. "Did something happen?"

"Of course not." She's trying to sound reassuring, but I don't believe her. Just like I shouldn't have believed her when she said the landlord couldn't legally evict us.

"It's probably about a job," Mom says.

"Or about kicking you out," says the woman.

Alarmed, I turn to her. "Why would you say that?"

"Because a bunch of us been getting the axe." She stubs out her cigarette on the table. "Where you been?"

"We need to go," I say to Mom, and before she can argue, I take off walking.

"Layla, slow down."

I let her catch up, my stomach in knots. "What did she mean about people getting the axe?"

"Nothing. It's just rumors."

"What rumors?"

She slaps at a bug. "Don't worry about stuff that hasn't happened."

That would be great advice if the stuff I worried about didn't happen all the frigging time. *Look at where your feet are*—that's what James would say, but right now my feet are stuck to my shadow, and my shadow looms before me like a dark specter.

Outside the door that leads to the caseworkers' offices, Mom suddenly turns to me. "I love you. You know that?"

She's afraid, I can tell, and that makes me afraid too. "Yeah, Mom. I know."

○ ○ ○

I push open the door to the caseworkers' offices, and Mom follows me into a long room crowded with tiny desks and ancient computers. The air smells musty, just like the rest of the shelter, but there's a lingering smell of burned microwave popcorn.

"Over here," Claudette calls from the back of the room.

I let Mom go first. With hunched shoulders, she leads me through the maze of metal file cabinets to where Claudette sits behind her desk looking at us from above her glasses.

"Sit down, please." She gestures to the two chairs in front of her desk.

One of the chairs has a piñata sitting on it that I move to the floor. It's shaped like a turkey, and I assume it's for the Thanksgiving Outreach thing that's going on next week—something else to worry about since the shelter will be full of volunteers (i.e., people I'll have to hide from).

Once we're seated, Claudette clears her throat. "I wanted to ask you, Shauna, if you've been in touch with your sister."

"No . . ." Mom looks wary. "Why do you ask?"

"Because of this." Claudette turns over a newspaper lying on her desk and points to the headline—MILLIONAIRE JOINS RACE FOR MAYOR—but that means nothing, so I look at the photo. A man in a dark suit and a woman with red lipstick. For a second, I don't recognize their faces, and then I do. Uncle Scott and Aunt Tanya, both of them smiling hugely and waving in front of a podium. My cousin, Celeste, hovers in the background looking bored as usual.

Mom whirls on me. "Did you know about this?"

I shake my head, too stunned to speak. Silently, I read the caption: *If elected mayor, self-made multimillionaire Scott Rockwell (pictured here with wife Tanya Rockwell) promises to combine his business savvy with family values to revive Ocean Point's economy and reputation.*

"Anyhow . . ." Claudette looks at Mom. "When I saw the photo, I did a double take. I thought the woman was you at first. You resemble her quite a bit."

"Tanya's older by a year," Mom mutters.

"Well, I suspected she was your sister, so I looked at your intake form, and sure enough, you have a sister named Tanya Rockwell. She lives close by, obviously, so I wondered if you might want to get in touch with her."

"Why would I want to do that?"

"Well . . ." Claudette starts folding the newspaper, smoothing its wrinkles and creasing the edges. "That's why I called you here. Maybe you've heard the rumors?"

"We heard people are getting the axe," I say, hoping Claudette will laugh and tell me how wrong I am.

Instead, she winces. "The truth is, we're having a budget crisis. Donations aren't exactly rolling in, and that means we're cutting programs, cutting teachers."

"I'm sorry to hear that." Mom's tone is brisk. "But if you're looking for a donation from my sister, you're barking up the wrong tree."

"That's not what—"

"My sister and I don't talk."

"I didn't mean to imply—"

"She and her husband don't even know we're here, and if they did, they definitely wouldn't help."

"Well, it's something to think about," says Claudette. "But that's not why I called you here."

I shift in my chair, trying to relieve my nervous tension as Claudette opens a drawer on her desk and pulls out a file folder. Mom's intake photo is paper-clipped to the front, a blotchy-faced woman with gray roots staring at the camera with huge eyes.

"When you came here," Claudette says, "we agreed to give

you sixty days—unless, of course, you found a job and contributed a percentage of your income. Then you can stay for up to a year."

"Right," says Mom. "I know this."

"But since you arrived . . . And it's been, what? Almost a month? You haven't had a single job interview, which, according to the board, doesn't show sufficient progress."

"What does that mean?" I ask, already knowing the answer and desperately hoping I'm wrong.

Claudette takes off her glasses. "The board had a meeting, and they voted on some new policies. Basically, Shauna, you need to find a job in the next ten days, or we have to let you go."

This can't be happening. "No!" I say. "Please!"

"If it were up to me . . ."

"She's doing what she's supposed to, applying for jobs, working in the cafeteria . . ."

"None of that matters," says Claudette. "The board's decision is purely monetary. In fact, the only new residents we're accepting are those who can already contribute financially."

I'm holding back tears. "So that's it?"

Mom puts her hand on mine. "I'll figure something out."

"Really?" I fling her hand away. "We were lucky to find this place, or don't you remember?"

"Layla—"

"No, you probably don't, because I was the one who found it, and that's only because we got lucky. Have you thought about what will happen? Because I have. You and me wandering the streets with our stuff in a garbage bag, nowhere to shower, nowhere to go to the bathroom. And when we get hungry, what are we going to do? Hold up a cardboard sign and ask people for money?"

"I won't let that happen," Mom says.

"Right. Because you're so on top of things."

Claudette clears her throat. "The fact is, Shauna still has ten days to find a job. A lot could happen in ten days, and I do have a bit of good news." She pulls a paper from Mom's file and hands it to her. "I got you an interview."

Hope stirs in my chest, until Mom frowns as she looks at the paper. "This is for a receptionist job at an insurance firm."

"I'm aware of that."

"Are you aware that I know zilch about insurance? Or about being a receptionist?"

"Try to be positive." Claudette opens a drawer on her desk and scoops out a handful of metal tokens. "Half the job is looking the part, so I thought you could use some extra clothing vouchers. The interview's tomorrow, so in the morning, go get yourself a skirt and blouse from the donations wing. Shoes too. Maybe a new handbag."

Mom looks dazed as Claudette pours the clothing tokens into her hand, so many that they overflow and spill to the floor like winnings from a jackpot. "Sorry," says Claudette, and I don't know if she's apologizing for spilling the tokens, or for setting up a job interview that's almost certainly destined for failure.

Ten days. I haven't been this scared since we got evicted, but maybe I can fix this. If Scott's running for mayor . . .

I point to the newspaper on Claudette's desk. "Can I borrow that?"

"Of course." She looks me in the eye as she hands me the paper, and I take that to mean, *Do it. Save her if you can.*

o o o

They say everyone has a talent. Some people, like my best friend, Morgan, are awesome singers. I like to write, and I used to think I could be a poet until I realized most poets don't make money, and that's one of my fears—that I'll be poor all my life. Plus, Mr. Kidd, head of my school's English department, basically told me my poems sucked when I submitted them for his school anthology. Since then I've decided my real talent is getting Mom to do what I want.

And what I want is for her to call Aunt Tanya.

We're sitting in our tiny room with its mustard-colored walls. The metal-framed bunk beds take up most of the space, and the rest is pretty much filled with the stuff we were able to carry from our apartment after we got evicted—clothes and kitchen stuff mostly, but also some keepsakes, including a framed photo of my dad. I have the newspaper, and I'm sitting on the concrete floor in front of Mom. She's hunched on the bottom bunk hugging a limp pillow.

"If I call her," Mom says, "you know what Scott will do."

I know what Scott threatened to do. Last year at Grandpa's wake.

Grandpa was a Vietnam veteran, but he didn't want a military funeral, and he also didn't want anything fancy. Still, the wake ended up being this big over-the-top affair, all because Scott decided to pay for it, even though he refused to pay for a bone-marrow transplant that could have saved Grandpa's life. Scott and Tanya invited all their friends, so the only people I knew were Mom, Morgan, and some of the ladies Mom worked with at the hair salon. Morgan whispered that everyone was looking at her as if she was in the wrong place. Only then did I notice all the rich white people stealing glances at the one Black person in the room. My heart went out to her.

All of us family members were lined up beside Grandpa's casket, and I felt shabby next to Celeste, who is older and beautiful and, of course, rich, so the Vera Wang dress she was wearing put my Walmart skirt to shame. Scott wore a black suit that made him look all *GQ*, and Tanya was decked out in a tailored black skirt and jacket. All these people I didn't know were coming through looking at Grandpa's body and hugging us. At first Mom cried a lot, which seemed normal under the circumstances, but then she started hanging on people as she told them how much Grandpa would have hated all this fuss. That's when I knew she was drunk, even though she'd promised not to drink that day.

"Embarrassed" doesn't begin to describe how I felt.

I could tell Scott was embarrassed too. He took her arm, but she jerked away from him, snapping, "Don't touch me!" Loud enough for people to hear. Scott walked away, his jaw tense, and Celeste wrinkled her nose like we were fouling up the place, which I guess we were. Only Tanya seemed oblivious, too busy fluttering around her rich friends to notice.

"Mom," I begged her, "please calm down."

"He wanted a closed casket."

"I know, but there's nothing you can do about it."

"It's not right, how Scott took over."

"He wouldn't want you acting like this."

She started sobbing. "How do you know what he'd want? You think you know things, but you don't!"

Morgan helped me lead her to one of the sofas in the front row, but after a few minutes of silent weeping, Mom made a dash for Grandpa's casket and tried to close the lid. Scott took her arm, and this time, Mom didn't fight him. She didn't even seem aware of him. As he calmly led her from the room with me trailing behind, I looked back at Morgan. Her eyes were wide. She mouthed the words, *Do you need help?* And I shook my head, my cheeks on fire.

As soon as the door to the viewing room closed behind us,

Scott jerked Mom forward, practically dragging her to the alcove where the restrooms were. I could tell he was hurting her arm, but I was so frustrated with her that I didn't stop him.

"Listen," he hissed. "I don't know what you're trying to pull, but it stops right now."

"Or what?" Mom swiped at her tears. "You going to hit me?"

"Don't tempt me."

"Do it then. No one's watching."

Scott looked around like he was checking to see if that was true. Then he chuckled. "I won't let you bait me, Shauna."

"Since when?"

"You're drunk."

Mom lifted her chin. "That's never stopped you before."

"Screw you!"

"You'd like that, wouldn't you?"

"Goddamn you!" In one angry motion, he shoved her against the wall.

That's when I leaped forward, ready to claw Scott's eyes out, but I froze when Mom started laughing like a crazy person.

Scott let go of her, wiping his hands on his pants as if by touching her they were somehow tainted. "I'm done letting you embarrass me," he said. "Starting now, you *will* stay away from me."

"Gladly," said Mom.

"And stay away from Tanya too. I don't want you anywhere near my family."

Mom pointed a shaky finger at him. "You don't control me."

"Don't test me." Scott got right up in her face. "If you so much as call my wife, I'll have you arrested."

"For what?"

"I'll think of something."

He started to walk away, but Mom called after him. "She's my sister! You can't stop me from talking to her!"

He turned back. "Maybe not, but I can make you regret it."

"You can't hurt me," Mom said, but I heard the tremor in her voice.

"One phone call." He shoved his finger in her face. "With my connections? One call, and *poof!* Your daughter gets taken away from you."

Mom's face paled.

"Don't listen to him," I said. "He can't do that."

"No?" His head swiveled toward me as if noticing me for the first time. "Your mom's a drunk, and I know a lot of powerful people. So unless you want to live in the system . . ." He paused to straighten his tie. "I'd keep her the hell away."

○ ○ ○

So that was Scott's threat, that Mom would lose custody of me if she ever tried to contact Tanya. Which is why Mom didn't ask Tanya for help after we lost our apartment—and I didn't want her to. But things have changed, and it's now my job to make Mom see that.

"He's running for mayor," I say. "He won't do anything that makes him look bad."

She squints at me from the bottom bunk. "And taking you away from me makes him look bad?"

"Us being homeless makes him look bad. He's talking about family values, so the last thing he wants is to look like a hypocrite for not helping his family."

"What if you're wrong?" Mom asks. "What if he calls child services and has me thrown in jail?"

"He can't throw you in jail."

"You don't know him like I do."

"I know we have to do something."

"I still have ten days to find a job."

"And you really think that's going to happen?"

Her eyes drop. "I guess not."

"Mom, I didn't mean . . ."

"It's okay."

"All I meant was . . ."

"I know what you meant."

I sit beside her on the bunk and open the newspaper to the picture of Scott and Tanya. It's only been a year since I saw them at Grandpa's funeral, but they look so different, like people you'd see on TV. Even Celeste, looks like a stranger, despite the fact that I see her every day at school.

Mom glances over. "They look happy."

"We can be happy too."

A laugh catches in her throat.

"If you won't call them, I will."

She stares at the pillow in her lap. "Pandora's box. That's what this is."

I roll my eyes. "Whatever, Mom. You're being dramatic."

"You may be smart, Layla, but there's a lot you don't know."

I take her hand, squeeze it. "Please. Call Aunt Tanya. Do it for me."

After a long sigh, she pushes the pillow off her lap. "Fine. But don't say I didn't warn you."

CHAPTER 3

The slightest smile my way
I absorb and hold dear
And linger upon for days.
I'm made of stone, but I can feel . . .
—from "Statue" by L.F.

Helping Hands Homeless Shelter is actually more than just a shelter. It's an outreach center that helps homeless people transition back into society. That means it provides not only food and housing but also church services, AA and NA meetings, basic education classes, job skills training, and community building. In theory, it's cool . . . until you live here and get to experience firsthand all its stupid rules and shady people. And yeah, there are nice people here too—people like James—but mostly it's a lot of recovering drug addicts and people with seriously questionable social skills. Still, I know we're lucky to have gotten a room here since normally there's a long waiting list.

If Morgan knew I lived here, she'd say it wasn't luck that brought us here. She'd say it was God working in our lives and how everything happens for a reason. When she talks like that, I picture some old man fumbling with our puppet strings, laughing as he makes us stumble just so he can yank us to our feet and show us how lucky we are.

Not that I don't feel lucky when I think about where we *could* be. We could be begging for money on the street, so in a way, this place feels like paradise. Since we got here, Mom and I have been staying in the family unit, which is separate from the other rooms. The good thing is, there are no creepy men living down the hall from us. The bad thing is, it's super noisy, since the walls are paper-thin and the family unit is mostly made up of moms with toddlers whose favorite pastime seems to be screaming and yelling. Another good thing is, the families who live here get their own common area, which is kind of like a living room with chairs and a couch and even a TV. There's also a little kitchen attached, which doesn't have a stove, but it does have a communal phone mounted on the wall next to the fridge.

The phone is where Mom and I are headed, and suddenly it hits me what we're about to do.

One of the things that's made our homeless situation tolerable is that no one outside the shelter knows how far we've fallen. But now that we're about to call Aunt Tanya, all the feelings of shame and inadequacy I've been fighting since we moved here come rising to the surface. Probably because Tanya once used the word "pathetic" to describe a woman we saw panhandling. I was pretty little, but it's one of my most vivid memories. Tanya had taken me and Celeste out for a day of fun, and we saw a woman in a Santa hat outside the toy store asking people for money. I'd found a quarter, and I tried to put it in her jar like Mom always did for the Salvation Army people, but Tanya pulled me away with a hiss. "Don't give that to her. She'll just waste it."

"You mean she'll buy toys with it?" I asked, thinking maybe she worked for Santa.

"Hardly," said Celeste, with all the authority of a girl two years older than me. "She'll buy drugs and alcohol. Right, Mom?"

"Right," said Tanya. "We don't give to people like that."

"Dad says they're a waste of space," said Celeste.

"That's a little harsh," said Tanya, "but they are pretty pathetic."

"What's that mean?" I asked.

"It means they're not worth anything," said Celeste.

Tanya squeezed my hand as she led me into the toy store. "Mostly it means they're weak."

o o o

Usually the TV is on in the common area, but it's getting close to curfew, so the place is empty when we walk in. Or at least that's what I think until I step into the kitchen and see the guy from my school leaning into the open refrigerator. So that confirms it. He lives here, and I hate to admit it, but that makes him less enticing. I know I'm being unfair—he's not responsible for his mom's actions—but it's hard not to see him as somehow less-than for living here, maybe because that's how I see myself.

He's wearing headphones, so he doesn't hear Mom and me come in. I didn't notice before how tall he is—around six feet—and his faded Levi's are a little baggy, but they look good on him. From here I can see a tattoo peeking from under his left sleeve, but I can't make out what it is. As he moves things around in the fridge, I get the feeling he's lost something in there.

Suddenly he turns and pulls off his headphones. "Sorry, did you say something?"

"No, I—"

"Hey, nice shirt."

I glance down at my poetry shirt, a white T-shirt splattered with lines from my favorite poems, each one written in my best handwriting with a different colored Sharpie. I wear it probably once a week as part of my anti-trendy camouflage designed to fool people into thinking I'm comfortable in my own skin. He takes a step closer. "You go to Flagler, right? I noticed you during lunch."

He noticed me?

"You and your friend."

Ah, of course. He noticed Morgan.

"That's one of my favorites, by the way." He's gesturing to where my hand partially covers my sleeve. "*And what rough beast, its hour come round at last, slouches towards Bethlehem to be born?*"

Goosebumps sneak up my arms, but whether from the chill in the air, the eeriness of the lines, or the fact that he can quote Yeats's "The Second Coming," I don't know.

Meanwhile, I try not to notice that Mom is looking around the room like she's lost. Taking a step closer to him, I gesture at the fridge. "Just so you know? You have to write your name on whatever you put in there. If you don't, it disappears."

"Good to know."

"And also, you have to put a date on it. Anything without a date gets thrown out. Also anything older than three days."

He cracks a smile. "So you're saying you really like it here?"

"Exactly. That's exactly what I'm saying." And then I smile back, and it feels good. To smile.

"Layla," says Mom, "the phone's gone."

"What?" My smile disappears, and I look to where the phone used to hang, but now there's a handwritten sign tacked to the wall.

NO MORE FREE PHONE CALLS!

LOCAL CALLS NOW COST $1 AND

MUST BE MADE FROM OFFICE!

Now what? And then I remember the money in my pocket, although I hate to break the twenty just for a phone call. Still . . . I pull it out and show it to Mom. "Let's go to the office."

"Where'd you get that?"

She's staring at the money like maybe I stole it, so I'm about to tell her how I found it in a tree at school, but the new guy taps my elbow. I turn to see him holding out what looks like an old cassette tape that's actually his phone case. "Thanks," I mutter, and as I take it, our fingers touch, something I'm very aware of.

"I'm Gabriel, by the way."

"Layla."

Now I see his eyes are pale gray, not blue or green like I thought.

"Cool name," he says. "I love that song."

"Me too."

"Most people haven't heard of it."

"Yeah, well, I'm not most people."

Ghosting a smile, he zeroes in on my poetry shirt. "Yeah. I can see that."

o o o

Gabriel goes back to his room to give us some privacy, and now that Mom and I are alone, the anxiety I've been swallowing starts gnawing at my stomach. I sit beside her at the little table and slide Gabriel's phone over to her. "You remember their number?"

Her face is pale in the bright light of the kitchen. "What if Scott answers?"

"Then you ask to speak to Tanya."

"He'll recognize my voice."

"So? If he threatens you, tell him you'll go public."

"With what?"

"With the fact that he refuses to help his family."

She shakes her head. "I don't know about this."

I don't know either. Scott could still make good on his threat, but if we do nothing, chances are I'll still end up in the system.

With a sigh, Mom punches in the number. I'm sitting near enough that I hear the phone ringing on the other end. After four rings, the answering machine picks up. Tanya's voice. "You've reached the Rockwell residence. Please leave a message after the tone."

Mom hangs up. "They're not home."

"Why didn't you leave a message?"

"And say what?"

"Tell her you're sober but you're in trouble. Tell her you need to talk to her."

Again, she makes the call. Again, no answer. The answering machine picks up.

"Tanya," says Mom. "It's Shauna. I'm in trouble, and . . ." She pinches the bridge of her nose. "I need to talk to you, but I don't really have a number where you can call me back, so I guess I'll try some other time." She ends the call.

"Some other time? Mom, you have to tell her! And you forgot to say you're sober."

"Does it matter?"

"Yes. You sure you don't remember her cell?"

"I'm sure."

"Then call her back."

"You can't be serious."

I take the phone and hit *redial.* While it rings, my heart starts pounding. What if Mom's right and this ends in disaster?

I press the phone to my ear as the answering machine clicks on. Tanya's voice, but it sounds like Mom. "You've reached the Rockwell residence. Please leave a message after the tone."

"Aunt Tanya, it's Layla. Mom forgot to mention she's sober. She's been going to AA and stuff, so if you help her, it's not like she's going to buy alcohol or anything." Mom's wincing as she listens to me, which isn't helping. "Anyway, we really need your help. We know about Scott running for mayor and . . ." Crap. Now it sounds like I'm blackmailing them. "We know about Scott, but that has nothing to do with . . ." I take a breath. "We've been living in—"

There's a beep, and at first, I think someone's picked up on the other end, but the beep is followed by a dial tone. I lower the phone.

"That went well," says Mom.

"At least she got the gist of it."

"Enough to think we're lunatics. You sure you don't want to call her back and make it official?"

I shake my head. "We'll call again in the morning."

"Great," she says. "Something to look forward to."

o o o

I wait until Mom closes herself inside our room before knocking on Gabriel's door. Number thirteen, the room where the drug-using mom and her little boy used to live before they got kicked out. He opens right away, still with the headphones around his neck and a quiet smile that makes him seem shy.

"Thanks." I hold out his phone.

He takes it, and once again his fingers touch mine. "Everything okay?"

"I think so."

"Well, if you need to borrow it again . . ." He holds up his phone.

"Thanks. There is something I wanted to ask you."

"Is it juicy?"

"Juicy?" I laugh. "Who says that?"

"I do, but people call me weird."

"I can relate."

"But it's a good thing, right? Being weird?"

"Depends on who you ask."

"I'm asking you."

"Then yeah, I suppose it is."

It strikes me suddenly how easy it is to talk to him, unlike with Felix where I measure every word.

He leans against the doorjamb. "So what'd you want to ask?"

This could get awkward, but I plow ahead. "Please don't take this the wrong way, but no one at school knows I live here."

"Okay."

"And I'd like to keep it that way, so . . ."

"So you're asking me not to tell anyone?"

"If you don't mind."

"Sure. No problem."

"And I won't say anything about you either."

He shrugs. "I'm not hiding it."

"That's . . . brave."

"No, but I learned my lesson about keeping secrets. Plus . . ." He meets my gaze. "I try not to measure myself by what other people think of me."

I drop my eyes. "You must think I'm shallow."

"No."

"If you knew the kids at school . . ."

"I get it. People are douchebags."

"Some more than others. But yeah." I bite my lip. "Thanks."

"No problem. And thanks for the advice."

"I didn't—"

"About the refrigerator?"

"Oh. Yeah."

"Maybe tomorrow you can"—he scratches his nose—"tell me about the laundry room?"

"Sure."

His smile turns shy again, and I wonder what it would be like to kiss him. Not that I have anyone to compare him to—unless you count my imaginary kisses with Felix—and why the hell am I thinking about kissing when my life could blow up at any second?

He points behind him. "I should get back." Through the half-open door, I see his mom sprawled on the bottom bunk reading a paperback. She doesn't look like an addict. Maybe she's been in recovery for a while.

"Yeah, me too."

We turn to go at the same time, and I resist the urge to look back at him. Was he flirting? It seemed like he was flirting, but it's hard to tell because Morgan is the one who gets flirted with, not me. Still, I'm grinning as I open our door, and it's only when I see Mom picking at her nails that I remember how much is at stake.

CHAPTER 4

My laugh rings in my ears and reverberates
Somewhere inside my head.
I cringe and smile again
And light comes in
To shine and shine as I smile.

—"As I Smile" by L.F.

I'm lying in bed, trying to sleep, while Mom snores softly in the bunk below mine. Through the thin walls, I hear a kid crying, but that's not why I'm awake. I'm awake because I'm thinking about a girl named Darla Whitman and how maybe I wouldn't be such a coward if I'd never met her.

Darla came to our school in the middle of seventh grade—shy, scared, dressed in a faded Fifth Harmony T-shirt. Morgan and I liked her instantly. After a few weeks of hanging out, Darla told us she lived at a homeless shelter. Remembering from Tanya that *homeless* equals *pathetic*, I swore I'd keep her secret.

Kids at school found out anyway.

They started calling her "Hobo Girl" and "Trashcan Darla." They'd ask her if she got her clothes from the donations bin or if her room at the shelter was made of cardboard. One time in the lunch line, a girl named Gigi asked Darla if she was on welfare, and when Darla said she didn't know, Gigi laughed and said, "Isn't it about time you stopped being a leech?"

Morgan asked, "What's that supposed to mean?"

Gigi looked at us with her wide blue eyes and said, "Don't you realize she's a drain on society? Who do you think's paying for her lunch?"

"Does it matter?" Morgan asked.

"Of course it matters," said Gigi. "When it comes out of other people's taxes, it matters."

As if Gigi paid taxes.

"Ignore her," I told Darla, and we started to walk away, but Gigi stopped me by putting her hand on my arm.

"I just realized . . ." She wrinkled her nose at my lunch tray. "You get free lunch too."

"No, I don't." But of course I did.

"You're lying."

"Like you would know," said Morgan.

"I do know." She pointed at my tray. "I can tell because you have vegetables, and no one gets vegetables unless it comes with their free lunch."

Was that even true? Morgan always had vegetables—and never ate them. Did that mean her lunch was free too?

I'd never thought about it, but suddenly that's all I thought about: Who got free lunch? And what did that make them?

It made them a leech, according to Gigi.

"And I know about leeches," Gigi said, "because my mom's a tax lawyer and she sees it all the time."

Morgan rolled her eyes. "Whatever."

But when the three of us—Darla, Morgan, and I—sat down with our trays of free lunch, Morgan started crying, and Darla pointed out that Gigi (whose real name is Gianna Jordan) was shallow and stupid and not even that pretty, even though all the boys stared at her and all the girls wanted to be her.

Morgan called me after school that day to ask me if I was worried about hanging out with Darla.

"What do you mean?" I asked.

"People hate her."

"That's because they're stupid."

"But aren't you afraid they'll hate us too?"

And once she said it . . . suddenly I *was* afraid. And every day at school, I got more afraid. Because kids stopped talking to us. They started giggling when we walked by.

One day I watched from my locker as Gigi cornered Morgan in the hallway and asked if she lived at the shelter too.

"No!" Morgan cried.

"Are you sure?"

I marched up to them. "Yes, she's sure. Why would you think that?" I honestly thought there was some kind of tell—like having vegetables on your tray.

Gigi smirked. "Why else would she hang out with Darla Whitman?"

"Because she's my friend," said Morgan.

"Maybe you should make new friends."

"And maybe you should mind your own business," I said.

"I make it my business when people like you mooch off of people like me."

"I'm not a mooch!" I yelled.

But somehow I felt like one.

After Gigi walked away, Morgan had tears in her eyes. "She thinks we're homeless," she said, and I said, "Who cares?"

But the thing was, I did care. I cared so much that it kept

me awake at night, and it kept me from wanting to hang out with Darla Whitman.

I don't know when it happened—I think it happened gradually—but Morgan and I stopped being friends with her. And then one day, I realized she wasn't at school anymore, and it bothered me that I didn't know what happened to her—it still bothers me, which is why I can't sleep.

Now I lay in the darkness, trying to quiet my mind. Before we turned off the light, I saw a roach crawling up the metal frame of our bunk beds. Mom smashed it with her flip-flop, but I know there are hundreds more scurrying in the baseboards with their spindly legs and quivering antennae. I want to turn on the light, but I don't want to disturb Mom. She needs a good night's sleep for tomorrow. For her job interview. For talking to Aunt Tanya.

Sleep isn't coming, and after a while, I give up. Now that we've called Tanya, it really does feel like we've opened Pandora's box—just a crack, but that's enough. Whatever's going to happen, I've already set it in motion, and I'm still wondering if we've done the right thing. But what choice did we have? Mom isn't likely to find a job in the next ten days, so unless some miracle happens in the form of Scott and Tanya coming to our rescue, Mom will be living on the street, and who knows what'll happen to me? At least here, I have Mom, and at least here, she's trying to stay sober. If she's living on the street, she'll have already lost me, so what's to stop her from sinking even lower?

Something tickles my hand, and I bolt up, my whole body shuddering. Even in the darkness, I see the roach's glossy body skittering over my skin. Frantically, I shake my hand—*have to, must get it off*—until I hear the roach hit the floor with a *snick*. I peer down, but I can't see it.

It's there, though, and I try not to think of Mom as I imagine it lying on its back, legs kicking, trying with all its might to set itself straight.

○ ○ ○

"Layla?"

Someone's shaking me awake. I open my eyes to see Mom's ghostlike face peering at me in the darkness. "What's wrong?" I ask.

She takes a step back from my bunk. "I've been thinking."

"Okay . . ."

"I don't think I should call Tanya back."

"Mom—"

"I could get this job today, so why risk it?"

Because her getting a receptionist job is wishful thinking, and she knows it. If I didn't have to leave for school, I could go with her when she calls Tanya, but as it is, I have to trust her.

"It's a risk," I say, "but we're running out of time. As soon as the office opens, you *have* to call her, and if she doesn't answer, you *have* to tell her where we're staying and leave the main number so she can call you back. Then you need to take your clothing tokens over to the donations wing."

"I know all this, Layla."

"Get yourself a dress," I say. "Heels too. You have your bus card?"

"In my purse, but . . ." She drops her eyes.

"What?"

"You haven't given me the money."

For the phone call, she means, and it's true. I've been delaying because I don't *want* to give her the money. I like knowing I can buy something if I really want it.

Mom won't look at me, but I think she might be crying, and suddenly I feel bad for being selfish. I know this is hard for her. "Listen," I say, climbing down from my bunk. "Use the leftover money to get yourself some coffee after your interview. Buy one of those donuts you like."

I pull the twenty from my backpack and offer it to her, but when she doesn't take it, I lift her hand and place it in her palm.

She stares at it. "You never told me where it came from."

"I found it. In a tree, if you can believe it."

Slowly, she nods, her fingers closing around the bill. "I guess it's fate then."

Fate. Chance. God. Who can tell? All I know is, today, no matter what, our lives are going to change.

o o o

Every morning, on my way to school, I have to cross the parking lot of the homeless shelter, which doesn't sound like a big deal, but it is when all the homeless people have just been let out of the transitory unit. That's the part of Helping Hands where people living on the street can sleep as long as the beds don't run out.

A tall black gate separates the parking lot from the shelter's checkpoint. As soon as the gate closes behind me, an overly tan woman with brown teeth steps up to me. "Got any loose change?"

I shake my head, thinking how Celeste would call her a waste of space.

"How about a cigarette?"

"I don't smoke."

Keeping my head down, I hustle across the parking lot, hugging myself in the chilly November air. Suddenly an old guy with a scraggly beard steps into in my path. I veer around him, but he follows me. "Where'd you get that rucksack?"

I don't answer.

"Bet you don't know where it's from."

He's talking about my backpack, which Grandpa brought back from Vietnam. It's army green and ugly as hell, but I carry it as a way to honor him. Plus, it boosts my counterculture image, which now—seeing the pain on the old guy's face—suddenly feels disrespectful.

"I still smell the bodies," he says, and I stop, feeling like I owe him that courtesy. "Torn up and filled with maggots. You'd think all that rain would wash away the smell, but it never did. The blood neither. You see that there?" He's pointing to a dark smear on the backpack that Grandpa told me was blood from when his friend got shot.

I nod. "My grandpa was in Vietnam."

"Still alive?"

I shake my head.

"Good for him. Wish I wasn't."

I'm fumbling for what to say when James appears at my side looking like a bouncer ready to crack heads. The old guy takes one look at him, mutters, "I ain't bothering her," and slumps off.

"You okay?" James asks.

"Yeah."

"Let me walk you to the bus stop."

"You don't have to."

"It's no trouble. I'm going that way myself."

Now I notice he's wearing khakis and a button-down shirt. "Where you off to so dressed up?"

He thumps his chest as we walk. "Got myself an interview."

"That's awesome! I hope it works out."

"Me too. Guess you heard about the budget crisis?"

I nod. "Mom has nine days to find work. What about you?"

"Same. But the way I see it, a lot could happen in nine days. And right now?" He points at his feet as he walks. "Right now I'm on my way to a job interview, so life is good."

"Mom has one too. An interview, I mean."

"Really? I just saw her, and she didn't mention it."

"She's probably distracted."

"I'll pray for her." He nudges me as we walk. "For you too, girl."

"Thanks," I mumble, and I do appreciate him, but right now, I wish he wasn't with me. It's bad enough having to ride the city bus to school with the other poor kids, but what if he's on the same bus as me? And what if the other kids hear us talking and figure out I'm living in a shelter, that my mom is a drunk, that everything about me—from my emo haircut to my punk-grunge mishmash of clothes—is a façade to hide my embarrassment, my shame, my fear that I'll never amount to anything?

A dark blue car pulls up beside us and stops. I don't recognize it, but I do recognize the driver.

Gabriel.

The window goes down, and Gabriel calls out, "You need a ride?"

James narrows his eyes. "You know this guy?"

"He goes to my school."

"That don't mean you know him."

"He's fine."

James is scowling at Gabriel, who could have scowled back, but instead offers a polite nod. I like that about him. After a few seconds, James nods back. "Okay then. Guess I'll be seeing you."

"Yeah, and thanks, James. Good luck today."

Suddenly I'm nervous as I circle around to the passenger

side. I've never been in a car with a boy before. When I open the door, Gabriel smiles shyly, his red-gold hair still wet from a shower. I smile back, hoping he thinks I'm cool, smart, pretty, but who am I kidding? My hair is short, my eyes are plain brown, I don't wear makeup, and my figure barely has curves. Morgan's the one who gets all the attention from guys, especially since she got all these new clothes last summer. I'm the one with the "interesting" look, the weird one who wears thrift-store clothes and doesn't care what people think of her.

If only that were true.

The fact is, I do care. And I care even more what Gabriel thinks of me. This is a guy who wears Kurt Cobain shirts to an AA meeting, who can quote poetry, and whose eyes are obviously checking me out as I slide into his car. I keep my face neutral, trying to play it cool.

Trying to be the person I wish I was.

"Sorry about the mess," he says.

Now I see that his back seat is filled with overflowing boxes. Clothes. Books. Kitchen stuff. Mostly books. "That's okay." I buckle my seat belt. "At least you have a car."

"It's actually my mom's." Which might explain the Celtic music playing in the background. "She works nights, so I get it during the day."

"That's cool." Feeling awkward, I pick up the books lying at my feet. T. S. Eliot, Maya Angelou, and a book called *Crank*. There's a bookmark stuck in the middle of it.

Gabriel glances over as he drives. "Have you read that?"

I shake my head.

"It's really good. You can borrow it if you want."

He likes to read. Another check in his favor. "You're done with it?"

"No, but this is the third time I've read it. In fact, go ahead and donate it to the shelter library when you're done. The more people who read it, the better."

And he's altruistic? "I hate to break it to you," I say, "but I've been at the shelter for a month, and nobody's checked out books except me."

"Yeah, I noticed. Yours is the only name on the list."

I shove the book into my backpack while watching him from the corner of my eye. He keeps his eyes on the road, one hand on the steering wheel, the other—the one closest to me—resting on his thigh. Today he's wearing a Prince T-shirt. He must be into music, but the Celtic music playing on the stereo doesn't seem to jibe with the indie rocker guy sitting next to me. I wish I knew more about music. I wish I was wearing something cuter than the oversized flannel shirt I found in the donations bin.

"Have you heard this?" Gabriel turns up the stereo, and along with the eerie guitar and sad violin, there's a woman's lilting voice.

"Is that . . .?" I squint at him. "Emily Dickinson?"

"The song's called 'Because I Could Not Stop for Death.'"

"It's pretty. Beautiful, actually."

"I thought you of all people would recognize it. There's actually a lot of songs out there that quote poetry. That's why I have those, by the way." He gestures to the books in my lap. "I'm trying to write songs."

"So you're a musician?"

"I play, mostly, but I'm trying to write lyrics."

Should I tell him I write poetry? "What do you play?"

He shrugs like he's embarrassed. "Piano? Also guitar, violin, trumpet. And I was learning the drums, but I don't have a drum set anymore." He pauses. "Or any of my instruments."

"You lost a lot, huh?"

His voice drops. "Almost everything."

We're quiet for a second while the music plays in the background.

"At least your mom's getting better," I say.

When he doesn't answer, I look over. He has a sick look on his face.

"Sorry. She seemed okay during the meeting."

"Yeah."

"You probably noticed my mom's hanging on by her fingernails."

Now he glances over. "That must be hard."

"And frustrating. I get so sick of it, you know?"

He doesn't answer.

"I don't mean to talk trash about her. She's been through a lot, and I guess she's making progress. It's just . . ."

"You're tired of her screwing up."

"Yeah."

"Sometimes to the point where you don't want anything to do with her."

I nod.

"But you stick with her because you love her."

"And she's a good person. A good mom. Or she used to be." Suddenly I'm embarrassed. "I shouldn't be boring you with my problems. It's just . . . so insane."

"What is?"

"The fact that she keeps going back to drinking, even though it's ruined her life."

We're sitting at a stoplight. Gabriel's hands are tense on the wheel. "Have you ever thought that maybe she does it because she's an addict?"

I snort. "Sounds like an excuse."

"Not an excuse. A reason."

I look over at him. "I think you're more forgiving than me."

"No."

"You are. I mean—"

Suddenly he speeds up. I brace myself against the dashboard.

"I'd rather not talk about it," he says. And with that, he turns up the stereo. The music is no longer soft. Now it's some kind of heavy metal. Loud and brash. I guess he has eclectic taste.

And it's bordering on being rude.

Whatever. This is a guy who lives in a homeless shelter—not that he can help where he lives any more than I can, but still, it's not exactly a turn-on. Not to mention the fact that he doesn't care who knows he's homeless, so I have to be cautious. If kids at school see us hanging out—or riding to school together—they might put two and two together. I'd love to be like Gabriel and not care what people think, but I'm not that brave.

We talk a bit more on the way to school, and I find out he's sixteen and a junior. He used to live in Jacksonville, and so far, he doesn't have an opinion on Flagler High.

I assure him it sucks.

By the time we arrive, I'm feeling better about him, like maybe I imagined his rudeness. "Thanks for the ride," I tell him.

"No problem. I can take you home if you want."

"Um . . ." I'm distracted by Gigi Jordan and her friend Kendra who are staring at us as we exit his car. Normally it wouldn't bother me, but Gigi was one of the main people who made Darla Whitman's life a living hell just because she was homeless.

Gabriel follows my gaze. "Or not," he says.

"No, it's just—"

"Don't worry. I get it."

"What do you get?"

"That you don't know me." He looks away. "And maybe it's better if you don't."

With that, he takes off walking, his backpack slung over one shoulder. I watch him go, a little stunned and a lot confused. Mom would say he's moody. Morgan would say he's damaged. I would say he's both of those things, but it's understandable, right? Especially because I'm the same way.

CHAPTER 5

I wish I could show them
How I really feel.
I am fake;
They think I'm real.
—from "Self-Portrait" by L.F.

After Gabriel and I go our separate ways, I wait for Morgan in our usual spot, at the banyan tree on the outskirts of the schoolyard. It's the same tree where I found the twenty bucks, and something about it feels comforting to me. For one thing, it *looks* really cool, its roots boiling from the ground like sea-monster tentacles, its trunk all gnarled and twisted like it's been wrung dry by a giant's hands. From far away, it reminds me of a huge umbrella, and when I'm sitting beneath it, like I am now, I'm able to see all the insects and lizards that depend on it for food and shelter—and not one of them cares about clothes or jobs or what the rest of the world thinks of it.

If only I could be the same way. And yeah, I pretend not to care what people think of me, but it's all an act, even with Morgan, who used to be poor like me until last summer, when her mom married a dentist from her church. Now, all of a sudden, Morgan has money—not a ton of money, but enough to get new clothes, enough to get Invisalign for her teeth. And suddenly she's in drama club making all these new friends, and she's talking about going away to college to major in theater. I'm happy for her. Honest. But I'm jealous because I've dreamed of going to a university since I can remember, and I have no idea how I'm going to swing it. I haven't told her I'm jealous. I haven't told her much of anything since she moved out of our neighborhood and into Phil's suburban palace, but I've wanted to.

The thing is, I'm afraid . . .

Afraid she'll hate my mom.

Afraid she'll be ashamed of me.

Afraid I'm not good enough.

So I keep lying to her, pretending everything's fine, wishing I could be honest and hating that I can't because I'm so afraid of losing her.

I hear her laughing in the distance, and I look up to see her and Josephine Young walking toward me—Josephine with her thespian awards and perky ponytail, who Morgan's been hanging out with more and more and who always makes me feel awkward with her over-the-top personality. They're smiling and obviously talking about something exciting, but when Morgan glances up and sees me watching, her smile fades, a reminder of the growing tension between us. After waving goodbye to Josephine, she heads toward me, and I can't help noticing her new outfit—white shorts that show off her long legs and a white jean jacket over a pink tank top. Recently, she started letting her hair go natural, and now it's blowing in the wind, a gorgeous cloud of dark curls.

Her smile is back as she flops down beside me on the bench. "Good news! We found out what musical we're doing." *We*, as in Josephine and her. "You want to guess?"

"*Grease*," I say, because it's the only musical I can think of. Plus, it used to be our favorite movie.

"I knew you'd get it. Josephine wants me to try out for Frenchy, but I was thinking Jan."

"Wait a second. Does Jan even have a solo?"

"No." She brushes a leaf off the bench. "But I don't think I'm ready for that."

I gape at her. "Are you kidding me? You are *so* ready."

"Plus," she murmurs, "Jan's supposed to be pudgy."

"Morgan, you're not pudgy."

"I'm a little pudgy."

"No, you're not. You're curvy. And you should totally try out for Frenchy."

"Maybe. As long as Gigi's not trying out for her. I heard she's skipping the play this year."

"Speaking of Gigi . . ." I gesture to where Gigi and Kendra are cutting across the courtyard. Gigi with her sleek black hair and big blue eyes, who all the guys drool over and who was voted "best body" in Flagler High's unofficial polling. Today she's wearing a really short miniskirt, stockings that go over her knees, and librarian glasses that I'm guessing are fake. She's sucking on a red lollipop that's doubling as a fashion accessory.

"Oh crap," Morgan says. "They're coming over here."

"Are they?"

"What do you think they want?"

Probably to ask about Gabriel, but I don't tell Morgan that.

Gigi stops in front of us with Kendra at her elbow. "Hey, Layla." Gigi nods at me but doesn't even look at Morgan. "What's up?"

I shrug, trying to act nonchalant. "Not much."

She waits, as if expecting me to say more, and when I don't, she nudges my sneaker. "So what's up with the new guy?"

"What do you mean?"

"I mean, what's his story?"

I squint up at her. "You'd have to ask him."

"But you know him, right? We saw you getting out of his car."

Morgan gives me a puzzled look. "When did this happen?"

"This morning," I say, feeling sick that I'll have to lie to her about how we met, but at least this part will be true. "He saw me walking and offered me a ride."

"Right," says Gigi. "But what do you *know* about him?"

"I know his name's Gabriel."

"That's him," says Kendra. "Now I remember his name."

"You know him?" I ask, hoping I sound casual, even though my heart is pounding. If she knows him, she could know where he lives.

"Not really. But I heard some things about him."

"Oh."

Gigi smirks. "Don't you want to know what she heard?"

I do, but I'm scared about where this conversation could go, so I look up at her and shrug. "I'm not big on gossip."

She stares at me for a second, blinking behind her fake glasses. "Never mind then. Guess you'll find out."

While I'm wondering what she means by that, she and Kendra walk away.

Morgan pops up from the bench. "Gigi, wait!"

Kendra keeps walking, but Gigi turns back, clearly annoyed. "Yes?"

Morgan hugs herself. "I wanted to ask you about *Grease*."

"What about it?"

"I just wondered if you're trying out."

Gigi looks her up and down. "Don't tell me *you* are."

Morgan drops her eyes. "I'm thinking about it."

"Don't you usually do scenery or something?"

The whole time they're talking, my mind is whirling. What did Kendra hear about Gabriel? If she knows he lives at the shelter, does she suspect I live there too? Since he gave me a ride?

"It's just I heard you weren't trying out," says Morgan.

Gigi is talking, but I'm not paying attention. Even if Kendra does know Gabriel lives in the shelter, that doesn't mean she thinks I do. Plus, how would she know anything about who lives there? She probably recognizes him from somewhere else. So obviously I'm being paranoid because if they did suspect I lived at the shelter, Gigi would be sure to bring it up.

My secret is safe.

"Anyway," says Gigi, "I have no interest in taking part in the most overproduced play in the history of high school." She points her lollipop at Morgan. "But you go right ahead."

When Morgan joins me on the bench, she's almost crying.

"Don't listen to her," I say. "She likes making people feel bad."

"What sucks is, she's actually talented."

"Who cares? Apparently she's too talented for *Grease*."

Morgan fiddles with a button on her jacket. "You think she's telling the truth?"

"It doesn't matter because you're *so* getting that part."

"What if I don't?"

"You have to. If only to rub it in her face."

"No pressure," she mutters.

I nudge her. "Hey, I believe in you."

"Thanks." She nudges me back. "So tell me about the new guy."

"There's nothing to tell." Still not a lie. Not exactly.

"He just asked if you wanted a ride?"

She's looking at me like she knows I'm holding something back, and I wish for the millionth time I was brave enough to tell her what's really going on.

"Like I said, we talked yesterday."

"Just out of the blue?"

"Is that so hard to believe?"

My voice is sharper than I intended, and Morgan blinks. "Of course not. I keep telling you you're pretty. If I were as tiny as you, believe me, I'd be in heaven."

"What you call tiny, I call scrawny. My bra could be an eye patch."

She laughs, but it sounds forced.

"So when are play tryouts?" I ask.

"Next week. I was hoping you'd help me practice after school."

The fact that she's asking me, instead of Josephine . . . That's huge. But getting together outside of school is always a sticky issue. When we lived in the same apartment complex, I had to make sure she only came over when Mom was at work, so Mom wouldn't embarrass me with her drinking. Then, after Mom got fired and stayed home all the time, I had to think up excuses—I was sick, or Mom was sick. Eventually Morgan stopped asking to come over, and we only hung out at her apartment. Then that ended too, when she moved in with her stepdad last summer.

"Sure," I say. "But we have to do it at your place."

She sighs. "Don't tell me your mom's still sick."

"It's that cough," I lie. "It won't go away."

"Well, we can't practice at my house. Phil's got the week off, remember?"

"Right. And we know how Phil likes a quiet house."

"Don't blame me," she says.

"I'm not blaming you."

"Really? Because it sounds like you're blaming me for something I have no control over."

"Morgan, I'm not. And if it sounded like I was, I'm sorry."

"Okay." She bites her lip. "I'm sorry too."

The bell rings, and we join the herd of kids shuffling toward the school.

"Why don't we go to Starbucks," says Morgan. "Neutral ground."

"Where the coffee costs five dollars? Sure."

"I'll get your coffee. Don't worry about it."

"I haven't paid you back for last time."

"It's not a problem. Really."

Maybe not for her, but I'm tired of being a mooch.

"And if it bothers you," she says, "don't get anything. Just come with me and help me practice."

"I will," I say, wishing I hadn't given Mom that twenty bucks. Wishing I could tell Morgan the truth. Wishing, most of all, for a normal mom and a normal life.

CHAPTER 6

When I was blonde,
I had an unaware, crooked-toothed smile,
And I never thought that laughter might be hard.
—from "William Blake" by L.F.

It's lunchtime, and I still haven't heard from Mom, even though I told her to call the school and leave me a message after she talked to Aunt Tanya. I'm sitting in the cafeteria by myself, trying not to worry, but it's hard when I'm alone with my thoughts. Usually Morgan's here by now, so what's going on? For the millionth time, I wish I had a phone. Maybe I should go look for her. At least then, I might run into Felix, who usually eats his lunch outside.

There's a squeal at the table behind me, and I turn to see Joshua Burman pulling my cousin, Celeste, into his lap. Her shiny blonde hair reaches almost to her waist, and the peach sweater she's wearing is probably Gucci or Chanel or some other brand that costs way too much. For about two seconds, her chalk-blue eyes meet mine, which is weird considering she hasn't acknowledged me once since the beginning of the year. We used to be friends (sort of), but that was when we were kids, and I haven't actually talked to her since Grandpa's funeral.

Flustered, I turn back to my food. My stomach growls, so I nibble at the cookie that came with my lunch. Still no sign of Morgan, but Gabriel, I notice, is sitting two tables over. Most people would be self-conscious about eating by themselves, but he seems perfectly at ease, sitting there reading a paperback while taking absent-minded bites from his meatloaf. I wish I were as comfortable in my own skin, but here I am making sure Gigi and Kendra aren't around before picking up my tray and going over.

I stand at his table, feeling awkward. "Mind if I join you?"

He looks up with a smile, says, "Sure," and closes his book. *No One Here Gets Out Alive*, which is a biography of Jim Morrison, lead singer of the Doors. I know this because I read the same book—literally—as in, I recognize the torn cover because I'm the one who accidentally tore it after borrowing it from the homeless shelter's library.

"Good book," I say.

And then I realize—shit—I wrote a poem in that book, which I know isn't kosher, but anyone who's had to scrounge for paper knows that books sometimes have perfectly blank pages in them. When I was little, I'd tear them out, but when I got older, I started leaving them intact, so whoever read the book next (and maybe it wouldn't be for twenty years) would come across my poem and wonder: *Who is this "L.F." person?*

So what poem did I write in *No One Here Gets Out Alive?* I can't remember, and I hope it wasn't embarrassing. Ever since Mr. Kidd dissed my poems (*Overly dramatic! Too filled with teenage angst!*), I've been afraid to show them to anyone. It doesn't help that every poetry contest I've entered has given me "honorable mention," which someone once told me is the equivalent of a participation award. Maybe Gabriel won't know who "L.F." is. Or maybe he'll never see it.

But part of me wants him to see it. Wants him to see me.

"Don't tell me the ending," he says, and I think he's kidding because there's this whole mystery surrounding Jim Morrison's death.

Suddenly Morgan is flopping down beside me with her sack lunch. "Sorry I'm late." She flashes a smile. "Who's your friend?"

Before I can introduce him, Gabriel holds out his hand. "I'm Gabriel."

"And I'm Morgan." She shakes his hand. "So how'd you guys meet?"

I have a moment of panic where I think Gabriel's going to spill my secret, but he glances my way as if to reassure me. "Let's just say, poetry shirts make great conversation starters."

I laugh. "You're, like, the only person on the planet who'd say that."

He quirks a smile. "That's because I'm supremely cool."

Damn, I do like this guy.

"Hey, is that a tat?" Morgan points at Gabriel's arm where the sleeve of his Prince T-shirt is partially covering his tattoo. Now that I'm closer, I see what looks like a dragon's tail in the shape of a U. Inside the U is a date in May from more than a year ago.

"Yeah, my friend did it," says Gabriel, covering it with his hand. "It's kind of stupid."

Morgan leans closer. "Can I see?"

Reluctantly, he pulls up his sleeve. The tattoo is a phoenix, purple and black, with wings outstretched as though lifting from the ground. There's a green banner behind it with two words. *I Rise.*

Like Maya Angelou's famous poem.

"Wow," says Morgan. "What's it mean?"

His eyes flick to me, and he holds my gaze. "It means I'm an addict."

An addict? Him?

"Heroin," he says, still looking at me. "I'm not proud of it."

I drop my eyes because what the hell? He couldn't have told me earlier?

Morgan reaches across the table. "May I?" And when he nods, her fingers graze the date. "This is when you got clean?"

"Yeah, I—"

"That is so cool!"

"Not really." He leans back, pulling down his sleeve at the same time.

Morgan looks flustered. "Unless you're still . . . you know . . ."

"Using?" He shakes his head. "I'm not."

"Then yeah, it's cool." Morgan nudges me. "Don't you think so, Layla?"

"Yeah, it's great."

"Layla doesn't like tattoos," says Morgan. "She'd rather write on her shirt than her skin."

"Probably a better idea," he mutters.

"I just think it's really brave," says Morgan.

"Thanks." He glances at me. I look away, hurt, flustered, disappointed. Mostly disappointed.

Morgan offers him a pretzel from her sack lunch, and he takes it. She starts giving him the lowdown on everyone sitting within two tables of us—who's dating who, who's cool, and who he should stay away from. She mentions that Celeste is my cousin but also puts her in the who-to-stay-away-from category.

Morgan tries to pull me into the conversation, but I just can't join in. I keep telling myself it doesn't matter that Gabriel's an addict because he's been clean for more than a year.

But I can't erase the image of him crouched in a corner, cooking heroin in a bent spoon, his eyes rolling up as he sticks a needle in his arm.

○ ○ ○

If I were writing a five-hundred-word essay explaining why English is my favorite class, my three-part thesis would look something like this: English is my favorite class because (a) I really like studying literature, (b) it feels good to write poetry (even though my poems basically suck), and (c) I get to sit next to Felix Burman.

Felix is the younger brother of Joshua Burman—the guy who Celeste has been all over lately—but in my opinion, Felix is a lot cuter. And definitely nicer, but I doubt that matters to Celeste, who makes out with Joshua every chance she gets. Felix walks into English class and sinks into the desk next to mine. He's dark, like his brother, and muscular and lean at the same time, with lashes so thick you could paint with them.

Oh, and he has a killer smile.

"Hey." He leans toward me, and my heart goes bouncy. "Did you finish your poem yet?"

He's talking about our assignment. We have to write a poem in iambic pentameter, and normally I would be freaking out that I had to show a poem to a teacher, but even if Mrs. Chapman hates it, I don't think she'll rip me apart like Mr. Kidd did. Plus, no one said it had to be a reflection of my deepest self.

"I haven't even started it," I tell him.

"Really?"

He sounds disappointed, and I'm wondering why.

"You do know we have until after the weekend, right?"

"Yeah, but—"

The bell rings, cutting him off. Mrs. Chapman gets up from her desk. "All right, class. Settle down. We have a lot of ground to cover."

For the past week, we've been studying *Macbeth*, which is a cool play, but hard to understand because it's mostly written in iambic pentameter. Yesterday we talked about Lady Macbeth—how she slipped into madness and kept trying to wash out an imaginary bloodstain on her hands because she felt guilty about her part in King Duncan's murder. Mrs. Chapman has been trying to get us to relate Lady Macbeth to our own lives, which is no problem for me because, with all the lies I've told Morgan, guilt is something I can relate to.

Like usual, Mrs. Chapman has to repeat the page number a few times. Felix is one of the kids who doesn't seem to hear, no matter how many times she repeats it. He leans over and whispers, "What page?"

"Sixty-nine," I whisper back.

To which he smiles and waggles his eyebrows. I can't help grinning. So juvenile.

Mrs. Chapman goes to the board and picks up a marker. "So how do the three sisters in *Macbeth* influence what happens to the other characters?"

Before anyone can answer, the intercom clicks on with a static-filled voice. "Mrs. Chapman?"

She turns to face the speaker. "Yes?"

"Please send Layla Freeman to the office."

The class rolls out these *ooohs* like we're all in grade school, which might be funny, except all I can think is: *It must be Mom calling. Maybe it's good news.*

But then I think about all the things that could have gone wrong.

Felix leans over to whisper, "Hope you're not in trouble," and I make myself smile, even though my stomach is in a knot. She was supposed to leave a message, so why are they pulling me from class?

Someone else calls, "Good luck!" as I shoulder my backpack and saunter from the classroom like this is no big deal.

Like getting called to the office isn't the opening act for my own Shakespearean tragedy.

o o o

The office secretary is a wrinkled old lady who looks like she'd make a good grandma. She creaks to her feet when she sees me. Her mouth opens. No words come out. The knot in my stomach gets tighter.

"I'm Layla Freeman. Is there a message for me?"

"Have a seat."

"Did something happen?"

She doesn't answer.

"Why am I here?"

"Sweetie." She won't meet my eyes. "I'm not the one to tell you that."

"But—"

"She's not going to tell you."

The voice comes from behind me, and I turn to see Celeste of all people sitting in a chair against the wall. She's hugging her knees while twisting her long blonde hair into a rope. "Believe me, I tried."

"It's not my place," says the secretary.

I turn back to her. "Is my mom here? Did something happen?"

"I—"

Behind her, the principal's door opens, and a woman bursts from the room. At first, I think it's Mom, but it's not. It's Aunt Tanya. She's dressed in workout clothes, and her face is perfectly made up.

Celeste stands up. "What's going on?"

"Not here." Tanya brushes past us on her way toward the door.

"Wait," I say. "Where's my mom?"

She doesn't answer, just keeps walking. Celeste and I exchange a look before following her to the hallway.

That's where Celeste stops, planting her wedge heels on the floor. "Mom, what's going on?"

Tanya looks around. The hallway is empty. She steps toward me, and the look on her face is full of pity. "Honey," she says, burying me in a bony hug. My body stiffens—she hasn't hugged me since I was little—but I allow my cheek to be pressed against her shoulder. I allow it because I don't want to know what's happened. For two seconds, I don't want to know.

Then I pull back. "Is my mom okay?"

She grips my shoulders. "Your mom's in the hospital."

"What?" I shake my head. "Why?"

"Apparently she overdosed."

"Overdosed?"

"On heroin."

Slowly, what she's telling me sinks in, and all I can do is shake my head.

Tanya peers at my face. "Are you okay?"

I meet her gaze. Brown eyes like Mom's. Like mine. Everyone says we have doe eyes, but right now, I'm like a deer caught in the headlights. "That's . . . Are you sure?"

"Yes."

"Holy shit," says Celeste.

"Is she okay? What are they saying?"

"I don't know anything yet. We're going to the hospital now."

She starts walking, but I don't move. Maybe I'm in shock.

Tanya comes back for me and hustles me down the hallway. I hear Celeste behind us, trying to keep up in her heels.

"It doesn't make sense," I say. "Where would she get heroin?"

"You tell me."

"There's no way. She couldn't . . ."

I was about to say she couldn't afford it, but then I see myself pressing twenty dollars into Mom's hand. Mom saying it was fate that I found money in a tree.

"Layla?"

I blink. Maybe I'm dreaming. But no. I'm standing in the school parking lot next to a silver Mercedes. Tanya is on the other side of the car with her door open. Celeste is already in the passenger seat.

"Get in," says Tanya. "It'll be okay."

I shake my head, still not believing.

"We have to go. Don't you want to see your mom?"

No, I think. *No, I don't.*

Yes, I think. *Of course I do.*

I get in the back seat. Tanya hands me a tissue.

How could Mom do this?

Why? What was she thinking?

The car starts. Tanya checks on me in the mirror before pulling out of the space.

I stare at the crumpled tissue.

The car jerks forward.

So stupid! What is wrong with her?

A lot. She might be dying.

"I'll try to hurry," says Tanya.

She might be dead already.

And if she *is* dead . . .

Please don't be dead, Mom.

But if she is . . .

If she's dead . . .

Where does that leave me?

CHAPTER 7

How dismal seeing Mother time and time
Be tossed about like wailing ships of war
With all emotions fighting for the door
. . . I think the door is shut.
—from "To Mother, From Me" by L.F.

The ER waiting room is decorated for Thanksgiving with dozens of kids' drawings taped to the wall. Pilgrims, Native Americans, and lots and lots of turkeys, the kind you make by tracing your hand. All the turkeys have crayon faces, and every single one of them is smiling. Don't they know they're about to be slaughtered?

I don't know how long we've been here. Waiting. Not knowing. Anxiety shrinking my gut. Celeste has disappeared into the bathroom for the millionth time. Aunt Tanya is pacing as she talks to Uncle Scott on her phone. He's pissed. I can hear him yelling, even though the phone is pressed to her ear.

"Dammit, Tanya! What this could do . . ."

My leg jitters up and down. I'm trying not to think. Trying to keep my mind blank.

What if she's dead?

An ache rises in my throat. I swallow it down, and now

it's a knife in my stomach. If I hadn't given her that twenty dollars . . .

Here's what we know from the paramedics: A woman who works at the shelter found Mom behind the transitory unit. By the time the paramedics got to her, she was convulsing and frothing at the mouth. The paramedics gave her Narcan to counteract the heroin.

Tanya paces in front of me. "Of course I didn't know, Scott. If I'd known . . ."

Claudette was the one who called Tanya, and that's how Tanya found out where we've been living. In the car on the way to the hospital, I spilled the whole story—how Mom lost her job, how we got evicted, how we've been living in the shelter for four weeks. Apparently, Tanya's tried to reach Mom several times over the past year, but Mom's ignored her.

So when Tanya asked me in the car why Mom didn't ask for help sooner, I told her what I thought she already knew. "Uncle Scott threatened her."

"How?" Tanya asked. "What did he say?"

"At Grandpa's wake, he told her if she ever—"

"Wait." Tanya held up a hand, the diamond from her giant ring catching the sun. "I don't want to know."

I get it. It's easier not to know the bad stuff. That way you can ignore it.

Now I watch her pace the ER waiting room with her blinged-out phone glued to her ear. Her sneakers are the same hot pink as her phone, as her workout clothes. Did she do that on purpose? She probably has shoes and a phone case to match every set of workout clothes she owns—which is probably a lot because she's obsessed with the gym. The huge bag on her shoulder is splattered all over with the Louis Vuitton logo. I wonder if she realizes the money she spent on that bag could have paid our rent for three months.

Celeste comes out of the bathroom finally. Her hair was down when she went in, but now it's in a thick braid. And she's wearing lip gloss. She flops into the chair beside me. "Any word?"

"Not yet."

"This is taking forever."

I glance away, wondering if she still thinks homeless people are a waste of space. "Sorry to inconvenience you."

Tanya walks past us. Scott's still yelling through the phone.

"It won't get out," Tanya says, her voice a harsh whisper. "It won't get out because we won't let it."

"I didn't mean it like that," Celeste says.

Tanya pinches the bridge of her nose. "I know, Scott. I *know*. But if Marty has a plan, we have to trust him. He knows what he's doing."

As I'm trying to figure out who Marty is, a woman in blue scrubs steps into the waiting room. Her badge says she's a nurse, and she looks tired as she glances at her tablet. "Freeman?"

I jump up.

"The family of Shauna Freeman?"

"Scott, I have to go," says Tanya.

I feel like I'm in a dream as the three of us follow the nurse through the door that leads to the back. As soon as the door closes behind us, she turns to us. Her eyes are sad, but she's smiling faintly, and I don't know what that means.

She takes a breath. "Shauna's okay."

I don't process the words until Tanya says, "Oh, thank God!" and my eyes fill with tears. "I was so afraid she'd be in a coma. I watch this show called *Intervention* where—"

"Mom, let her talk!"

The nurse nods. "Shauna's not in a coma, but you need to understand how serious this is."

"She could have died," I whisper.

"She was lucky," says the nurse. "Has she ever overdosed before?"

Tanya shrugs. "Not that I know of, but I'm not the one to ask."

Now everyone's looking at me, and I shake my head. "No. Never."

"You're sure?" asks the nurse.

"She doesn't do drugs," I mutter. Plus, she was getting better, which is why it didn't occur to me that giving her twenty dollars for coffee might be dangerous.

The nurse makes a note on her tablet. "Is it possible she's been doing drugs without your knowledge? How well do you know your mom?"

I know her tricks, her hiding places, but this . . . I feel betrayed.

When I don't answer, Tanya says, "What now? How long will she be here?"

"Normally, we'd be able to release her, but she hit her head when she passed out, so we're keeping her overnight to make sure there are no complications. She suffered a minor concussion."

"But she's okay?" Tanya asks.

"It depends on what you mean by okay." The nurse makes a point of looking at me. "Heroin is highly addictive, so after we release her, she'll need long-term help."

"You're talking about a rehab," says Tanya.

The nurse nods. "I'll have the staff give you a list of local facilities that specialize in heroin addiction. Most of them take insurance, so it's just a matter of—"

"Mom doesn't have insurance."

Again she looks at me, and her eyes get judgy as she takes in my worn sneakers and too-big flannel shirt. "Some of the centers are free to people in need. If you want, I can—"

"Can we see her?" Tanya's frowning.

"Of course. This way."

My mind stays numb as we follow the nurse down the hall. She stops at a curtain and peeks around it.

"Shauna?" Her voice is cheery. "You have visitors."

With a flick of her wrist, she sweeps the curtain aside. I don't want to look. I don't want to see her. But Mom's right there in front of me, sitting up in bed with wires attached to her, a thick white bandage taped to her forehead.

"I'll give you some privacy," says the nurse as she pulls the curtain closed.

And now it's just family. If that's what you call us.

Shame pulls at Mom's face as she meets my eye, and I know I should feel compassion. This is my mom. She almost died. But seeing her like this, seeing what she did to herself . . .

Anger. That's what I feel. Anger like a live wire to my nerves. To my mouth. "What did you do, Mom?"

"I messed up."

She looks small in her cocoon of white sheets. There's blood in her hair. Still, all I feel is anger.

Her eyes find mine. "Layla . . ."

"Don't," I say. "Don't even."

"I'm sorry."

Of course she is. She's always sorry. How many chances have I given her? How many times has she said she'll do better?

"What is wrong with you?" I whisper. "Why do you keep doing this?"

"Hey." Tanya touches my arm. "Now's not the time."

I whirl on her, this woman who looks so much like my mom but isn't. "Don't tell me you're not thinking the same thing. Don't tell me you're not wondering how she could be so stupid."

"Maybe you should go," says Tanya.

"Where?" I say to no one in particular. "Where the hell am I supposed to go?"

"I don't blame you for hating me," Mom says.

I don't hate her, but I can't look at her. I turn, almost knocking into Celeste as I blunder out of there. I'm not looking where I'm going, but I manage to find my way back to the ER waiting room.

That's where Tanya finds me—collapsed in a chair and crying into my fists. She puts a hand on my shoulder. "I know you're upset, but we need to go." Celeste stands behind her, twisting her braid, and I get the feeling she'd rather be anywhere but here. Not that I blame her.

"What about my mom?"

"She'll be fine. And you don't have a choice. You need to come with me."

"Why? Where are you taking me?"

"For now, I'm taking you home. Scott wants to talk to you."

"Is he mad?"

She doesn't answer, and she doesn't have to. Of course Scott's mad. What Mom did makes him look bad, and if everything Mom says about him is true, he'll want to punish her.

Unfortunately, the best way to do that is through me.

CHAPTER 8

Poverty devours my Ego.
Because I want.
Because I cannot have.

—from "Want" by L.F.

The city of Ocean Point is built around the Intracoastal, which is a long stretch of water that runs up Florida and connects to the Atlantic Ocean. It has its poor neighborhoods (like the one I grew up in), but rich people flock there because the houses along the water are huge, and most of them have their own docks where they can store their fancy boats. Ocean Point is where Scott and Tanya have lived since before I was born. They don't live close enough to the water to have a dock, but they do have a huge three-story house with a pool out back. Whenever I come here, it's hard not to feel inferior.

Tanya told me to wait in the living room, so here I sit on Scott and Tanya's white leather couch, staring at their white marble floor, wondering if anyone knows how to play the white baby grand that sits in the middle of their sunken living room. The piano is new, or at least it wasn't here two years ago, back when Mom and I sat on this same couch begging Scott and

Tanya to pay for Grandpa's bone-marrow transplant. Scott refused, and of course, Tanya does whatever Scott wants.

Now Scott and Tanya are in the dining room arguing about what to do, how to protect Scott's run for mayor because, apparently, Mom's overdose could have huge repercussions for his campaign. I can't hear most of what they're saying, but Scott is definitely pissed. I hear the words *child neglect*, *jail*, and *child services*.

"Layla?"

Startled, I look up. Tanya is standing by the piano, somber, her arms crossed. "Come on. Scott wants to talk to you."

I feel like a criminal going before a judge as I follow her to the dining room where Scott sits like a king at the end of a long table. His hair is grayer than it was at Grandpa's funeral, and I don't remember his teeth being so white, but his eyes are the same icy blue. He's wearing a polo shirt and khakis, like he just got back from a round of golf.

"Go ahead and sit down," he says, pointing to the chair on his left.

I sit, my stomach in knots. Tanya takes the chair opposite me. Celeste is at the other end, fiddling with her hair.

I keep my eyes down, but I'm hyperaware that everyone in the room is watching me. My leg jitters. Should I say something?

As the silence drags on, I remember an argument I once overheard between Mom and Aunt Tanya. "How can you stand him?" Mom asked, referring to Uncle Scott. "How can you be with someone who treats you like that?"

"He treats me fine," said Tanya. "And you don't understand him."

"I understand he gets off on controlling people," Mom said. "It makes him feel powerful."

"Well, maybe he needs to feel powerful."

"Because his dad wasn't nice to him? Boohoo, get over it."

"He's trying," said Tanya. "If you knew him the way I do . . ."

I remember losing interest in their argument, but maybe if I'd stayed to listen, I'd know how to deal with him. Groveling seems like my best bet, but given how pissed he is, even that's probably a longshot.

When he finally speaks, my heart gives a jump. "Your mom," he says, "has been a thorn in my side for years, but you probably know that, don't you?"

I nod, keeping my eyes down.

"Everything about her rubs me the wrong way. The way she looks, the way she talks . . ."

I want to point out that Tanya and Mom look and sound a lot alike, but I let him keep talking as I stare at my hands.

"So knowing how much I dislike her," Scott says, "why should I help her?"

My head shoots up. Does this mean . . .?

"Answer the question."

"Because it's the right thing to do?"

"Is it? The way I see it, she'll learn best by helping herself."

"Yeah, but . . ."

"What?"

"Addiction is a disease." The words sound lame, even to my own ears.

"So you're saying she can't help it?"

"No, but . . ." I glance at Tanya, who gives me an encouraging nod.

"What?"

"She's family."

"So?"

"And you're running for mayor."

A slight smile. "Go on."

"Which means you might look bad if you don't help her."

"Finally!" He glances at Tanya. "Tell me the truth now. Was this Shauna's plan all along?"

"No, she wouldn't do that." Never mind that I would.

"Didn't I tell you?" says Tanya.

Scott nods. "Maybe you're right. Maybe Shauna's not that smart. But even if she didn't plan this, she's still causing problems. You know what happens when my opponents go digging around?"

He's looking at me, so I shake my head.

"They find *her*, and they'll blame me because she's living in a shelter—as if I'm responsible for my wife's screwed-up sister because I have money."

The cellphone sitting next to him blips with a text. He glances at it, then back to me. "Here's how this is going to work. You and Shauna will keep quiet about where you were living, and in exchange, I'll pay for Shauna's rehab. Thirty days, no more."

"That's . . . Oh my gosh. Thank you!"

He seems embarrassed by my gratitude, which is weird because, according to Mom, he lives for impressing people. "By the time she's out of rehab, the election will be over, and if I'm the new mayor, that's good for her. Celeste . . ." He points across the table. "Tell her why."

"Because the mayor's family shouldn't be homeless."

"That's right. And what about if I lose?"

"You don't have to pretend to care."

Scott laughs. "I wouldn't exactly put it that way, but yeah." He turns to me. "You understand how this works?"

I nod.

"Good. Now let's talk about you."

Tanya starts to speak, but Scott shushes her. "Let her ask."

Again, all eyes are on me. It's hard to look at any of them, so I drop my eyes. "What happens to me?"

"Can't you guess?"

I can, but I shake my head.

"My wife says you're smart."

"She gets good grades," says Tanya.

Scott turns to Celeste. "Did you hear that? She's homeless and she still gets good grades."

Celeste rolls her eyes.

"Well, I think it's wonderful," says Tanya. "Who says poor people can't succeed? All it takes is a little gumption. Right, Layla?"

I nod, still with my head down.

"Look at me," Scott says, but then his phone rings.

"Is it Marty?" Tanya asks.

He lifts his phone. "A potential donor."

"Well, you have to take it."

The phone rings again, and he stands up. "I guess you can tell her," he says.

Tell me what?

As Scott leaves the room, Tanya turns to me. I meet her gaze, trying to be brave, but inside, I'm a shivering mess. Wherever they send me, I won't cry. I'll suck it up and deal.

"You probably think we have plenty of room," she says. "And yeah, I guess we do, but this house is crowded with big personalities. You get that, right?"

I nod miserably.

"So if you stay here, it's important that you . . ."

Wait. Did I hear her right?

". . . follow Scott's rules. Which is why . . ."

I rewind my brain. *If you stay here.* She said I could stay here.

Now she's talking about clean sheets on my bed, helping myself to whatever's in the kitchen.

For some reason, I'm remembering when I almost drowned

in Scott and Tanya's pool. My head was underwater, my arms flailing. I remember the blind panic, how my eyeballs seemed to pop inside my head, how my throat wanted to burst.

And then Mom's arms around me, pulling me to the surface. Me coughing up water and Mom's terrified face as she hugged me to her chest. "You're okay," she kept saying. "You're okay. You're okay."

Tanya touches my arm. "Are you okay?"

The relief I feel . . . like Mom holding me close. I try to speak, but as Tanya puts her arms around me, it's all I can do not to sob.

CHAPTER 9

And all of my life, the hope's come and gone.
When it's here I am glad and carefree.
But when it expires, I burn with a fire
And flee from the flame that is me.
—from "Self-Destruct," by L.F.

When Tanya pulls away from me, it's brisk, like she made a mistake by hugging me. She clears her throat and turns to Celeste. "Why don't you show Layla where she'll be sleeping."

"Can't you do it?" Celeste asks.

"I need to hit the gym."

"Of course you do." Celeste motions for me to follow her, and we leave Tanya sitting at the table, rubbing her forehead.

I'm pretty sure Celeste doesn't want me here, so I don't try to make conversation as I follow her up the stairs. On the second floor, we pass through what Tanya calls the "family fun room," and I swear that's the same Harry Potter puzzle that was here years ago, sitting half-finished on the coffee table. Celeste leads me down the hallway, past where her room is, past the guest room, and on to another door that opens to a spiral staircase leading up.

I forgot about this part of the house.

She starts up the steps, and I follow, wood creaking under my feet. The passage is so narrow and the steps so steep that I hang onto the wall to keep my balance.

Celeste turns to look at me, her face hidden in shadows. "Remember when you used to be scared of these stairs?"

"I'm still scared of these stairs."

There's a door at the top that opens to the third floor. Most of the house looks new on the inside, but not this part. Up here, there's actual wallpaper on the walls, probably from fifty years ago, and the wooden floor is scarred and scuffed. It's still nice, though. It smells like wood.

Celeste leads me down a narrow hall where there's a tall window and a window seat built into the wall. "Remember this?" She tucks herself into the cubby, her knees hugged to her chest.

"Actually, I've never been up here."

"Really?"

"You told me there were ghosts."

She smiles. "I was kind of a bitch, wasn't I?"

Um . . .

"Anyway, Dad said to put you up here, not in the guest room."

"That's fine."

"You haven't even seen the room."

"I'm sure it's nice. The whole house is nice."

"Nice—that's my mom's favorite word."

"Sorry."

"Just saying." She rises from the window seat, stretching like a cat. "I actually like this part of the house. It's the only part that hasn't been remodeled in my mom's image."

With that, she leads me down the hall where there are two rooms across from each other. "I think this was the servants' quarters back in the day, but only one of these rooms has a bed in it." She opens the door on the right and disappears inside.

I slip in behind her, half expecting to see shackles built into the walls, or at least a bare mattress on the floor, but it's actually very cool. Bigger than the bedroom I grew up in and definitely bigger than our room at the shelter. Even so, most of the space is taken up by the bed—because it's not a cot or a twin, but an actual queen-sized bed with huge pillows and a thick flowered comforter. Next to the bed is a nightstand with a shelf and a drawer, and across from the bed is a tall wooden dresser. The floor is wood too, and the walls are wood panel with sections of candy-striped wallpaper. There's a closet on the left and a door on the right that Celeste opens to reveal a bathroom. I can hardly believe it. My own bathroom.

"It's kind of small," she says.

"It's great."

"I guess it would be after where you were living."

"About that," I say. "Please don't tell anyone at school."

"Why would I? Your secret's safe."

Secrets.

Morgan.

Crap.

I scan for a clock. "Do you know what time it is?"

She checks her phone. "Almost five."

"Shit, I was supposed to meet a friend after school."

"So text her."

Again I look around. "Is there a phone I can use?"

She lifts her brows. "You seriously don't have a phone?"

Embarrassed, I don't answer.

"Jesus." She hands me hers. "I hope you know her number."

I do. From all the times I've called it using other people's phones.

Celeste watches me tap in the number. "Don't look so stressed," she says. "It's not like you don't have a good excuse."

"But that means I have to tell her."

"So?"

"And I haven't told her anything."

"Jeez, you must be close."

Her sarcasm cuts, a reminder of how much my friendship with Morgan has suffered.

"If she's your friend," Celeste says, "you have to tell her something."

I nod, staring at Morgan's number on the screen. Part of me wants to tell her everything, but Scott doesn't want it getting out that we lived in a shelter. Plus, at this point, does it matter if I don't tell her? It's not like I'm still living there. I do need to explain why I stood her up, though, and yeah, I could make up some excuse, hide the fact that Mom OD'd, but this is my new beginning, and it'll feel good to finally open up.

Taking a deep breath, I hit the call button and wait for it to ring.

Celeste makes herself comfortable on the bed as I listen to Morgan's phone. One ring. Two. Morgan won't recognize the number. If I'm lucky, she won't pick up and—

"Hello?"

"Morgan, it's Layla."

Silence. I'm not surprised she's pissed.

"Listen, I'm really sorry for standing you up. My—"

"Honestly, Layla? I'm tired of your excuses."

"But—"

"Do you know I waited for an hour? And of course, I can't call you because you don't have a phone. So I'm thinking . . . she'll call me, right? She'll borrow someone's phone or—"

"Morgan, my mom's in the hospital."

"What?"

"They took her to the emergency room."

"Oh my God. Is she okay?"

"I think so, yeah."

"What happened?"

Here's my moment of truth. "Please don't get mad, but I've kind of been lying to you about my mom."

"What do you mean?"

I glance at Celeste, who's looking around the room as if bored. "I know you've noticed her drinking," I say. "But it's gotten worse. Like, out-of-control worse."

"How out of control? Oh gosh. Was she driving?"

It occurs to me that Morgan doesn't know Mom sold our car. "No, she wasn't driving. She . . ." *Say it, Layla!* "Overdosed on heroin."

"Oh my God!"

"And now she's in the hospital because she almost died."

"Is she okay? Are *you* okay?"

"I think so." A sob breaks my voice. "She has a concussion, but they say she'll be all right. My aunt and uncle are sending her to rehab. Thirty days, so after that, she should be good."

"What about you? Where will *you* go?"

"My aunt and uncle are letting me stay with them." I run my hand over the soft comforter. "That's where I am now."

"Is that a good thing?"

"Yeah, it's good."

She pauses. "Even with your uncle being a dick?"

I look around at my room. *My own room!* And lower my voice. "He's not that bad."

"Well, I'm glad your mom's getting help. You sure you're all right? Maybe I can get Phil to drive me over."

"That's okay."

"I should come."

"No, don't. My uncle might not like it."

She's quiet for a second. "The same uncle who's not a dick?"

"Please don't, Morgan."

"Fine, but can I ask you something, and you promise not to get mad?"

I brace myself. "Sure."

"Why didn't you tell me about your mom?"

For some reason, I bristle at the question. "It's not like you could have helped."

"That's not the point."

From the bed, Celeste lets out a huge yawn.

"I didn't set out to lie to you," I say. "I just didn't want you judging me."

"Why would I judge you?"

"Because my mom's an alcoholic."

"That's not your fault."

"No, but I was afraid you'd ditch me."

Silence for about two seconds.

"Why would I ditch you?"

"Because you were making all these friends, and you had all these new clothes . . ."

"God, Layla. You really think I'm that shallow?"

"No, but . . ." I glance at Celeste, who's now examining her nails. "I guess I was embarrassed."

"Because your mom's an alcoholic?"

"And because of how poor we are."

"You do realize I've been poor since you've known me."

"You're not now, though."

"Technically, I am. It's Phil's money, not mine."

I almost point out that she's Phil's stepdaughter now, so it's not like the money will get snatched away.

"Is there anything else you want to tell me?" she asks.

Want to tell her? No. *Should* tell her? Absolutely.

I should tell her the whole story—about Mom losing her job, the eviction, living in the shelter. It's not like she'd tell anyone, and it'd be a relief to come clean.

I should tell her.

I open my mouth to do just that, but then I catch Celeste watching me with her chalk-blue eyes. Scott said not to tell anyone, and if I go against him, I'm putting everything at risk.

"Are you still there?" Morgan asks.

"Yeah. Sorry."

"You didn't answer my question."

Celeste is still watching me, and it occurs to me that she and Scott have the same eyes.

"No, Morgan." I hold Celeste's gaze and make sure to speak clearly. "There's nothing else to tell."

CHAPTER 10

Death is prone to hiss at me
Always in the night
Or maybe that's a memory,
Squelched but still with bite.
—from "Grandpa's Wake" by L.F.

Slow violin music swells from hidden speakers; the notes are beautiful yet wrong. For some reason, I'm the only one here among the rows and rows of pews, feeling awkward in my skirt, feet hurting in heels that are too small. Despite my tottering walk, my shoes make no noise on the deep blue carpet as I approach the open coffin. The closer I step, the more I smell the rot. Something squirms around my feet, and I look down to see I'm walking on a carpet of maggots.

The music stops.

And I find myself staring at the shell of Grandpa's body.

I can't look at his face, though. Not yet.

Grandpa's body is too big for his casket. It's like he's hunching his shoulders to fit inside. His hands are clasped in front of him, his head raised by a small pillow. Silky and white.

Lace on the edges.

I remind myself he's dead—this isn't him!

And force my eyes to his face.

Waxy skin, the color of dried glue. Jaw stiff as stone. Frown lines carved deep, like cuts from a knife.

And a bit of blush on his cheeks to make him seem alive.

But he's not alive, so why pretend?

"You like pretending."

Grandpa's voice, but that's impossible. Am I going crazy?

I turn to leave, but there's a noise from his casket that sounds like a rattlesnake.

So I look back.

And there's Grandpa sitting up in his coffin.

His head swivels toward me. His eyes blink.

And in his hand, a bottle of pills. He shakes them.

shakeshakeshake

"The doctor gave me good ones for the pain," he says, his mouth moving like a ventriloquist's dummy.

"I thought you were dead," I say.

No answer.

"Were you pretending?"

Again, no answer. He's too busy spilling pills into his hand. With a slow wink, he pops the pills into his mouth. Crunches them like candy.

"Open your eyes," he says.

"They're open."

"Open your eyes, Layla."

Grandpa, they're open!

. . . And they are.

I'm awake, my head resting on a soft pillow, my body warm beneath a flowered comforter.

My heart is pounding, but I'm safe.

I try to remember my dream, but it's already fading. Something about Grandpa and his pills.

I push the dream away. Thinking about Grandpa hurts, and I don't want to hurt. Right now I'm in a soft bed in a clean room. Right now I'm safe.

It feels good to be safe, but the feeling doesn't last long.

Because Mom's still in the hospital.

Because Mom's still sick.

And yeah, I have hope she'll get better, but what if she doesn't?

What will happen if she doesn't?

o o o

Claudette was nice enough to bring over some of my clothes from the shelter, so today I'm wearing my poetry shirt, which Tanya obviously doesn't like, but it feels good to be sitting in Scott and Tanya's sunny kitchen on a Saturday morning where everything around me is clean and new and bright. Unfortunately, Claudette didn't bring anything besides clothes, so the one picture I have of my dad is still at the shelter.

"Aunt Tanya?"

She doesn't hear me over the hiss and grind of the coffee maker. I wait until she sets down a cup of steaming cappuccino in front of me—white ceramic cup overflowing with thick froth and a cinnamon stick on the side. It smells incredible.

"Thank you," I say.

"You're welcome." She slides a sugar bowl toward me. The spoon is tiny, delicate. Probably real silver. I don't touch it.

"Try the coffee."

I do, taking a careful sip. Strong and smooth. Perfect, in fact.

"Good, huh?"

"This is the best coffee I've ever tasted."

"Yeah, well . . ." She waves a hand. "You don't want to know how much that machine cost."

"I bet it was a lot."

"Four thousand and change."

I almost choke.

"But I got tired of going to Starbucks every day, you know?"

I don't, but I nod anyway. Four thousand dollars for a coffee maker?

She sits at the counter next to me, her back perfectly straight. Mom would be slumping on the stool. "Listen," she says. "I've been wanting to talk to you alone."

"Okay."

"I know you think Scott is a bad guy."

"I don't."

"Well, Shauna certainly does, and I'll admit he can be overbearing at times, but truth be told, you two have a lot in common."

"Because he grew up poor?"

"I'm not saying he lived in a shelter, but he didn't have an easy childhood. His dad was an alcoholic."

"Is that why he hates my mom?"

"He doesn't hate her." She sees the look on my face. "He doesn't."

"Okay."

"Anyway, Scott's father was abusive on top of being an alcoholic, so Scott grew up very unsure of himself. You wouldn't know that by looking at him, would you?"

"No."

"He's come a long way, but he's still insecure—don't tell him I said that—which is why he works so hard to be successful. And it's why he lashes out sometimes. His anger is a cover for his insecurity."

I want to tell her that sounds like an excuse, but I sip my coffee and keep my mouth shut.

"That's why he's running for mayor. Because it's not enough to have started a multimillion-dollar business. He still feels the need to prove himself. And that's why, if he loses, it would be a huge blow to his self-esteem."

"I guess I can understand that."

"Good." I feel her eyes on me. "Scott can be difficult, but you'll learn to cope."

"I'm good at coping."

"I know." She pats my hand. "I'm glad we got to talk."

"Me too."

She stands up. "So we need to get you some clothes."

"I have more at the shelter."

"Okay, but—"

"And if we go there, I can pick up the picture of my dad."

She furrows her brow.

"It's the only picture I have of him."

"Oh." She straightens the big diamond on her finger. "The infamous Blaine Hornsby."

"What was he like?" I never knew my father—he died before I was born—but I still feel a kind of loss when I look at his picture—a muscular guy with mirrored sunglasses and a dark goatee, gripping the handlebars of a Harley and grinning at the camera. "Mom doesn't like to talk about him."

"He rode a really loud motorcycle," Tanya says.

"Anything else?"

"He cussed a lot."

"Oh." I didn't know about the cussing part.

"I don't think you're missing much, Layla. From what I understand he was a really bad alcoholic."

I stir my coffee with the cinnamon stick.

"And he was drunk when he crashed his motorcycle," she says.

"Mom told me."

"He could have killed someone."

"Instead of just himself."

"Yeah, well, motorcycles are dangerous, especially when you're drunk."

"I know. I still want his picture."

She nods. "I guess I can understand that. We'll make sure you get it."

I could see her forgetting, but if she does, I can always ride the bus there. Or ask Gabriel to grab the photo before it ends up in the dumpster. And then it occurs to me that Gabriel doesn't know what happened. For all he knows, I'm still living there.

Tanya sighs. "I didn't know my dad very well either."

The hurt on her face surprises me. "Mom told me he was pissed after you married Uncle Scott."

"That's one way of putting it. He basically disowned me."

"I'm sorry."

"Don't be."

"It's sad."

"I guess, but I'm over it. You get over a lot of things, given time. You'll see."

And suddenly it hits me again. Mom almost died, and here I am sipping coffee like everything's fine. When it's not. It's so not. There's a lump in my throat I have to swallow before asking, "Is my mom going to be okay?"

"Yeah, of course."

"How do you know?"

"Because we're sending her to the best rehab money can buy. Did I tell you the name of it?"

I shake my head.

"Serenity Solace. Isn't that a great name?"

"I like the alliteration."

Her brows go up. "Such a big word."

"Sorry."

"Don't apologize for being smart."

My smile is faint. "Mom tells me that too. I miss her."

"I know."

"Thank you again for paying for her rehab."

"Hmm, you don't look too happy, though."

"I am. It's just . . ." I fiddle with my cup. "I should have been nicer to her at the hospital."

"You were upset. She understands."

"Can I see her before she goes?"

"Not today."

"But—"

"Scott doesn't think it's a good idea."

"Why not?"

"Because . . ." She sighs. "You have to understand something. Scott's a dealmaker, and he's presenting your mom with a deal. She has to agree to keep quiet about living at the shelter before he'll pay for Serenity Solace."

"But why can't I see her? Is he threatening her with something?"

"What do you mean?"

"'Do what I say or I send Layla to child services'?"

"Listen," says Tanya. "Scott and I need to talk to your mom. That's all you need to know. And while we do that, Celeste will take you to the mall."

"Okay, but I still want to see her."

"And you will, but not today." She points at my poetry shirt. "You obviously need new clothes."

In her world, if you need something, you go buy it. "You know I don't have money, right?"

"Of course I know that. That's why I'm giving Celeste my credit card."

"For new clothes?"

"And whatever else you need." She studies my face. "What's wrong?"

"Nothing! I'm just . . ." I can't remember the last time I had new clothes. "Really grateful."

"I know you are. Celeste could take a lesson from you."

"You think she'll be okay with taking me?"

"Why wouldn't she be?"

I twist my cup in its saucer. "I don't think she likes me very much."

"She likes you fine. She acts like that with everyone."

"Oh."

"And plus, she's been grounded since she totaled her car." Her white convertible, which she used to drive to school. "This will give her an excuse to get out of the house. Believe me, she'll be thrilled."

If I weren't so worried about Mom, I'd be jumping up and down, and suddenly I wonder how my life would have been different if Aunt Tanya had been my mom. As soon as I think it, I feel like a traitor, like I'm looking to trade Mom in for a better model.

Tanya sees me frowning. "Is something wrong?"

"No, it's just . . ." I shake my head. "I know you don't want me seeing my mom until you've had a chance to talk to her, but will you give her a message?"

"Of course."

"Tell her . . ." And then I can't think of what to say.

Tanya watches me closely. "I'll tell her you love her. How's that?"

"She might not believe you."

"Don't say that."

"Not because I don't love her. It's just . . . not something I'd normally say."

"How about I tell her you're thinking about her?"

"And rooting for her. Definitely tell her I'm rooting for her."

"I will." She points to my coffee cup. "You should finish that before it gets cold."

She's right. Already the warmth of the cup is fading. I lift it to my lips, fill my mouth with cappuccino. It's lukewarm, but it's still the best coffee I've ever had. I gulp it before it gets colder. I gulp it too fast and coffee dribbles onto my poetry shirt. Shit. Onto Langston Hughes's "Dreams."

Tanya wets a paper towel under the faucet and hands it to me. I rub at the spot and the spot fades, but the paper towel is disintegrating, and Langston Hughes's words will never be the same.

Hold fast to dreams

For if dreams die

And then a big coffee stain.

I feel like Lady Macbeth as I keep rubbing at the spot.

Tanya's hand closes over mine. "Layla, stop."

"It's my favorite shirt."

"Really? That's . . . sad."

It is. No one likes this shirt. No one except me and maybe Gabriel.

"Look on the bright side." Tanya plucks the paper towel from my hand and tosses it in the garbage. "Once we buy you nice clothes, you won't have to write on your shirt to feel special."

CHAPTER 11

I can't be
Materialistic
Never want to be
Materialistic
I have to
Must break away.

—from "Fifteen" by L.F.

As Tanya predicted, Celeste is fine with taking me to the mall, even though she has strict instructions not to buy anything for herself and not to see "that boy," who I'm guessing is Joshua Burman. Before we left, Tanya made me change out of my stained poetry shirt, so now I'm wearing borrowed clothes from Celeste: American Rag shorts, Gucci sweater, and Tory Burch sandals. Everything's big on me, but I don't mind. Anyone who looks at me won't judge me for being poor, and that's something I haven't felt since I was little.

Even better, the whole mall is decorated for Christmas, which normally would stress me out, but now it feels festive to have giant ornaments hanging from the ceiling and holly jolly songs playing in the background. Mom has always liked

Christmas music—she says it reminds her of *her* mom, who died when she was a teenager. I never thought much about it before, but now I realize how hard that must have been for her. Was it just yesterday that *she* almost died? The world suddenly feels surreal, like a giant hand plucked me from my old life and dropped me into this new colorful cosmos.

Celeste stops in front of a map display of the mall. "Before we do anything, we're picking up your phone."

"Wait. What?"

"You do need a phone, don't you?"

"Yeah, but . . ." She's walking fast, and I jog to keep up. "Your mom didn't say anything about buying one."

"She already bought it. All we're doing is picking it up."

"Like, a real phone?"

"What, you think she's buying you a pretend one? What I don't get is how you survived this long. I mean, who doesn't have a phone?"

By now we're entering the Apple Store, and I'm trying not to get my hopes up, but twenty minutes later, a salesguy hands me the latest iPhone and I feel like a kid in a Christmas movie who gets the present she's always wanted, a present Mom could never get me. Aunt Tanya even arranged it so I'm on her family's cellular plan, as if I'm actually part of their family. "It's got some charge," the guy tells me. "You can use it now if you want."

As we're leaving the store, I turn to Celeste. "Thank you so much."

She shrugs. "It's not like I bought it."

Mom would be happy for me. And Morgan . . . "Can you hold up for a second?"

I snap a selfie, and she rolls her eyes, then peeks over my shoulder at the picture. "Don't tell me you're posting that."

"No . . ." I add a new contact with Morgan's name and number. Then I type:

Guess what I got?

And text her the picture.

Celeste looks amused. "You about done?"

"Yeah. Sorry."

"Can I ask you something?"

"Sure."

She points to my backpack. "Is that really from the army?"

It takes me a second to readjust my brain. "Yeah, I found it in Grandpa's stuff."

"Can I see it?"

Reluctantly, I hand it over. Grandpa's backpack is one of the few things I have left of him. A woman once offered me ten dollars for it, said her daughter would love it. What if Celeste wants it for herself?

She examines the bloodstain on the front, then traces her finger over the ink stamp that says *US Army*. "This was his from Vietnam?"

I nod.

"It's funny." She lifts the bag to her nose. "I didn't get anything of his."

I'm surprised by the hurt in her voice. Sometimes I forget that *my* grandpa is her grandpa, that he doesn't just belong to me.

"There wasn't much to get," I say. "Just his clothes and a few cassette tapes. Old stuff. Nothing you'd listen to."

"How do you know what I listen to?"

"I don't, but . . ."

She takes off walking. I hurry to catch up.

After a few seconds, she says over her shoulder. "I know you blame my parents for not paying for Grandpa's operation, but the chances of it doing any good were pretty small."

I don't say anything.

"And it's not like he ever talked to them."

"No, but he was family."

"So?"

"Family's supposed to mean something."

Celeste snorts. "If you think that, you're in the wrong family."

o o o

Abercrombie & Fitch is in the same wing as the Apple Store, and that's where Celeste takes me next. While she roams the tables, I trail behind her, too shy to pick out things on my own.

She holds up a maroon T-shirt with the Abercrombie logo emblazoned across the chest. "This would be cute if it didn't turn whoever wears it into a walking billboard."

Which is exactly the point, but I don't say that.

She wrinkles her nose at me. "You like it. Don't you?"

"It's okay."

"You're such a liar." She drops the shirt on the table. "Get it if you want."

I pick it up, check the price. Forty dollars for a T-shirt? I put it back.

Celeste looks over her shoulder at me. "Aren't you at least going to try it on?"

"It's too expensive."

"Oh please." She tosses it to me.

With the T-shirt clutched to my chest, I head to the clearance section in the back. Meanwhile, Celeste wanders the store, draping everything she likes over her arm. At one point, a salesgirl comes over and puts all her clothes in a dressing room.

Celeste comes up beside me. "What'd you find?"

I show her some jeans that are 40 percent off and a T-shirt that's marked down to fifteen dollars.

"Go try them on. I already got you a dressing room."

Once I'm in the dressing room, I see all the clothes she was carrying were for me. Everything I try on is cute, and how am I ever going to decide which things to get? Celeste has me come out and show her everything, which I wasn't expecting, and it's kind of intimidating (she's hypercritical) but also kind of fun. It feels like we're friends. When I'm finally done, she scoops up the entire pile, except for one pair of jeans that neither of us liked.

She isn't buying all that, is she?

Oh my God, she is. I follow her to the counter.

"Celeste, wait."

"What?" She seems annoyed.

"Nothing."

The salesgirl starts ringing everything up, saying things like, "This is cute" or "I love this top," folding each piece like it's this amazingly precious thing and tucking it into a huge Abercrombie shopping bag. The total is more than five hundred dollars, but Celeste doesn't bat an eye as she whips out Tanya's American Express. When it's all rung up, she hands me the bag.

I take it, feeling its weight. Is this really happening?

We hit some other stores, and Celeste has no problem buying me whatever she thinks looks good on me. By my count, I have at least six pairs of shorts, four pairs of jeans, and nine tops, which—considering I've never owned more than three pairs of jeans in my life—is kind of staggering. I actually feel selfish, like maybe I should donate some of them, until I remember Mom and I are pretty much the same size, so when she gets better, she'll have a new wardrobe too.

We stop at one of those mall rest areas so Celeste can check her phone.

"Any word from your mom?" I ask.

"Why would I hear from her?"

"I just thought maybe she'd have an update on *my* mom."

"Oh. You want me to call her?"

"That's okay." No news is good news, right? I check my phone too. No reply from Morgan.

I send her another text.

Can't wait to show you what I got!

And just in case she doesn't realize it, I follow up with:

This is Layla, btw. And this is my new number. 🙂

Celeste puts away her phone. "You ready to hit the big stores?"

"You just spent, like, thousands of dollars."

"What do you care?"

"I'm worried your parents will care."

"Mom told me to get you clothes."

"But . . ."

"Are you coming or not?"

I like that I don't seem to have a choice.

○ ○ ○

Next we hit Bloomingdale's, and I can't help cringing at how ridiculously expensive everything is. The sky-blue sweater Celeste plucks off the rack has a price tag of $195, which almost makes me choke.

She holds the sweater up to me. "What do you think? It's cute, right?"

I shake my head. "You can't buy that."

"What's wrong with it?"

"Did you see how much it costs?"

She doesn't even glance at the price tag. "Don't worry about it."

Is that even possible? I guess it is, if you live in her world.

She drapes the sweater over her arm and moves to another rack.

An hour later, I'm kind of shell-shocked. All the clothes are insanely expensive, but that didn't stop her from buying me more, including the nearly two-hundred-dollar sky-blue sweater. I think maybe I should pinch myself.

We stop in the cosmetics section to redistribute our bags. I know it's stupid, but I want people to see that I'm carrying the Bloomingdale's "Big Brown Bag," so I put some of my smaller bags inside it. Celeste checks her phone. I do the same. Still nothing from Morgan.

Celeste sends off a text. "Before lunch, we need to get you a new bag."

She's eyeing Grandpa's backpack, and I shake my head. "I like this one."

"Layla, it has *blood* on it."

"So?"

"That's, like, unsanitary."

"The blood is fifty years old. I think by now it's disease-free."

"Whatever. It's gross."

I never thought of it that way. I just like carrying Grandpa's memory.

She starts walking, and I follow her, limping a little because of the blister on the back of my foot from the Tory Burch sandals.

"Is it Grandpa's blood, or someone else's?"

"Someone else's. His friend's."

"He told you that? I thought he didn't like talking about the war."

As if she would know what Grandpa liked to talk about. I was the one who played checkers with him every night, who listened to Steely Dan and Led Zeppelin with him. I was the one who found his glasses whenever he lost them and made sure he ate something besides peanut butter and saltines.

"Listen." Celeste waits for me to catch up with her. "I know you want to carry it as a way to remember him or honor him or whatever. But people talk."

"What do you mean?" I dodge a woman with a stroller. "Who talks?"

"My friends. Josh asked me—"

"Joshua Burman?"

"Yes, Joshua Burman. He knows you're my cousin, so he asked about it."

"He asked about my bag? Why?"

"Because apparently it smells."

"What?"

"That's what his brother told him."

"Felix Burman said my bag smells?"

She manages to look sympathetic. "Like a wet dog."

I feel like I've been slapped.

"Honestly, I don't smell wet dog," Celeste says. "I mean, yeah, it smells old, but maybe you left it out in the rain one day? Anyway, the only reason I'm telling you this is because we're meeting some friends in the food court in, like, a half hour, and . . ."

Her voice trails off, but she doesn't have to say it. She wants me not to embarrass her. A memory shoots up of Celeste's eighth birthday party. Aunt Tanya sent me an invitation, but as soon as Mom saw the theme—*Princess for a Day*—she told me it wouldn't be fun. I was six years old, though, and couldn't imagine a birthday party that wasn't fun, so I cried and begged until Mom agreed to take me.

She made sure to dress me in my back-to-school dress, so I'd look nice. Unfortunately, she couldn't afford to buy me new sandals until next payday, but she used a staple gun on my old ones to keep the broken straps from flopping around.

When we got to the party, Celeste and her gang of girlfriends were sitting in these giant massage chairs, getting their toenails painted. I remember Celeste wearing a pink cast on her arm, covered in brightly colored signatures. I was jealous. I wanted a cast too.

Mom held tight to my hand. "Come on. Let's go wish her happy birthday."

With Mom at my side, I stood at the foot of Celeste's massage chair and waited for her to notice me, but there was another girl who had arrived just before us, and Celeste was hugging her with her one good arm. It wasn't until the girl moved aside that Celeste noticed me standing there.

"Oh," she said. "Now there's not enough chairs."

The woman who seemed to be in charge of the pedicures pointed at the other girl. "You wait," she said, and then she gestured for me to get in the chair.

Celeste got this panicked look on her face. "Layla, you don't want a pedicure, do you?"

And of course, I shook my head and said no.

Mom crouched beside me. "Are you sure?" I couldn't answer because I thought I might cry.

I spent most of the party standing against the wall, holding tight to Mom's hand, listening to Celeste and her friends giggle and tell each other how pretty they looked.

When Mom and Aunt Tanya went off to put candles on the cake, Celeste and her friends started pointing at me. "Ask her!" they said. "No, you ask her!"

Whatever it was they wanted to ask, I knew it wasn't good. So I was already wary when a girl with a glittery headband smoothed down her dress and walked over to me. "Excuse me," she said. "Did you know your sandals have staples in them?"

I looked down. "I think they're supposed to be like that."

Her eyebrows shot up. "Because you got them from the dumpster?"

Even now, I still remember how warm my face got. It must have been bright red.

Now I'm imagining a similar scenario with Celeste's friends. Only this time, there won't be enough chairs at the food court table, and Celeste will ask if I don't mind standing while they eat. They'll stare at my bag. Someone will sniff the air and say, "What's that smell?"

Celeste stops walking and hands me a twenty-dollar bill. "For lunch," she says.

"I don't think your friends want me hanging out with them."

"Come on, Layla. I'm grounded, so Josh and I haven't gotten to spend any time together. This is our one chance, so—"

"Go without me. I don't have to be there."

"Yes, you do. I already told Josh you'd keep Felix company."

"Why would you tell him that? It's not like Felix and I are friends."

"That's not what Felix says. He says he knows you from English."

"Yeah, because my bag smells."

"Whatever. He says you're smart. He says he wants to talk to you."

"Now I know you're lying."

Felix may be friendly to me in class, but I can't remember him ever talking to me outside of class.

"Look," Celeste says. "All I'm asking is that you keep him company while Josh and I hang out. We won't even be that long."

She says this like I owe her, and yeah, maybe I do.

I look around and realize we're standing in the purse section. "Why would Felix want to talk to me?" I ask.

"Is that so hard to believe?"

Considering this is real life, and not one of my fantasies, yeah, it's hard to believe.

"It's not like you're ugly," she says, while unhooking a purse that's hanging above the counter. The purse is Coach. The price tag says *$449.00*. "What do you think?"

I think, if I carry it instead of Grandpa's bag, no one could ever accuse me of smelling like wet dog.

Celeste holds the purse out like a peace offering, and even though part of me doesn't want to, I let myself take it.

CHAPTER 12

Just once, to be with you
I'd suffer long and fast and hard.
Yearning fills my lungs,
Ending my day with a pent-up, desperate sigh.
—from "Crushed" by L.F.

The adrenaline of seeing Felix through the crowd makes me feel like I've tumbled off a cliff. I know he doesn't like me, not in the way I want him to, but I still let myself imagine . . . Maybe he *could* like me. Maybe he'll see me in my Gucci sweater and American Rag shorts and think, *Wow, she looks good.* Or maybe—just maybe—he'll see beneath the surface to the real me, and maybe he'll think, *Yeah, there's something about her, something cool and deep, something other girls don't have . . .*

He and Joshua are sitting at a table in front of Dairy Queen. They're laughing and pegging each other with sugar packets, and it strikes me how much they look alike with their ink-black hair, dark brown eyes, and dusky skin. They're so obviously brothers, but Felix's eyes are kinder, his smile friendlier.

Joshua sees us first and lifts his chin as we approach. He

nudges his brother, and I hold my breath, waiting for Felix to notice me, but Felix's eyes are on Celeste—and why wouldn't they be? How could I think he'd ever be interested in me?

Celeste dumps all her bags by their table and shakes out her arms. "God, I'm so tired of shopping!"

Felix laughs. "Looks like you bought the whole mall."

"And took your time doing it," says Joshua.

"Yeah, well . . ." She glances at me. "It couldn't be helped."

At least she doesn't say I'm a charity case.

Joshua stands. "You ready to go?"

"God, yes." She takes his hand.

"Wait," I say. "You're leaving?"

Joshua sneers at me. "Get a grip. She's coming back."

"We won't be long," Celeste says. "We're just going to talk."

I watch them walk away. I watch until the crowd swallows them. And now I'm alone with Felix, aware that he's studying me, aware that I'm standing by his table like a groupie.

Slowly, because I'm trying to think of something to say, I place my shopping bags under the table and sit across from him. Grandpa's backpack is tucked away in one of my bags, and my new Coach purse sits in my lap. I can smell the new leather.

Felix leans closer to me, which gets my heart racing. "You know what they're doing, don't you?"

"Um . . ." I go for a casual shrug. "Having sex?"

He snorts a laugh. "That too. But no. 'Talking' is code for . . ." He mimes smoking a joint.

"Really?" I peer through the crowd like I expect to see them lighting up in the mall.

"Every time they get together," says Felix. "Personally, I think it's stupid."

"Yeah, me too."

He smiles. "I knew you were cool."

My breath catches. Maybe he *does* see beneath the surface.

"I heard about your mom," he says.

And suddenly I'm on high alert. "What did you hear?"

"That she's in the hospital. Is she okay?"

My heart is beating a mile a minute as I try to figure out how much he knows. The last thing I want is for Felix to feel sorry for me.

"She's getting better," I manage to say. "She's getting . . . you know . . . proper treatment."

"That's good. My brother said you're staying with Celeste's family until she's better."

I nod.

"Until yesterday I didn't know you guys were cousins."

"Oh . . . Well . . . we don't usually hang out."

"Yeah, you seem pretty different."

Someone bumps my chair from behind. I scoot in and accidentally touch Felix's foot. He doesn't pull away, and neither do I—which means our feet are down there, touching.

"By the way," he says, "you look nice."

Flushing, I drop my eyes. "Thanks."

"So you want to get something to eat?"

"Sure." I try to look casual as I unsnap my stiff new purse and pluck out the twenty-dollar bill Celeste gave me. As if me having twenty dollars isn't a huge deal. As if me pulling money out of my more than four-hundred-dollar Coach purse is completely normal.

He stands. "You want to save the table? I can get the food."

"Sure." I hold out the twenty, but he waves it off as if money isn't important.

"Be right back."

As soon as he's gone, I let out my breath. Even if he doesn't like me—which he probably doesn't, he's probably just being nice—there's a chance that he *could* like me once he gets to know me.

Plus, he said I looked nice.

I watch him weave his way through the crowd. Most of the jocks at school are so blown up with muscle their necks disappear. Felix is built like a baseball player. He *is* a baseball player. Muscular, but lean, with a chest shaped like a V. I like how his butt fills out his jeans. I like how he walks—not a strut exactly, but confident. He looks back at me and points to McDonald's. I give a thumbs-up. He smiles, and something flickers in my chest.

And then my phone lets out a chime. It's Morgan, finally texting me back.

Glad you're having fun.

How's your mom?

Her text throws cold water on my face, and just like that, the gnawing, twisting worry is back. I send my reply:

Doing better.

Which isn't a lie, since Mom's surely doing better than she was. I keep typing.

She's going to a really good rehab.

Yeah, you told me.

My stomach is in a knot. I don't want to talk about this anymore. So I change the subject.

Did I tell you I'm having lunch with Felix Burman? 😍

I'm waiting for her reply when Felix slaps down a tray full of cheeseburgers and fries.

"Thanks," I tell him, making sure my phone is face down.

"No problem." He unwraps one of the burgers and starts chowing down, checking his phone as he eats.

I pick up a single fry and make myself nibble, even though I want to cram a whole fistful into my mouth. I haven't had McDonald's fries in a long time. They're hot and salty and amazingly good.

"So," he says, swallowing. "Should I bring up *the poem*?"

I like how he says it, as if our poetry assignment is an undertaking we both have to survive. "We still have a few days," I remind him.

"Iambic pentameter." He shakes his head as he chews. "I don't even know what that is."

Part of me wonders how he can't know what it is, since we've been studying *Macbeth* for the past week. Another part is glad he doesn't because it gives us something to talk about.

"It's the beat of the words," I say. "Five beats per line." And I start spewing lines to show him, ticking off the beats on my fingers. "Today I laugh and skip and sing and dance. Because it makes me want to go to France."

"God, that's great! You just made that up, didn't you?"

"Well, yeah, but—"

"Can I steal it?" He peels a napkin from the stack he took from the McDonald's counter. "You can write it on this."

"Yeah, sure." Once again, I unsnap my purse, but this time, I take out a pen. I have a mini notebook in there too, but I don't want him seeing all my poetry scribbles.

Felix holds the corners of the napkin while I scratch out the lines. When I'm done, I hand him the napkin. "It's not very good," I say.

"Are you kidding? It's great." He reads it over before tucking the napkin into his pocket. "If I'm lucky, the hurricane will give us a few days off, and I won't have to finish till after Thanksgiving."

"Wait. There's a hurricane? Since when?"

"Well, it's a tropical storm, but it could become a hurricane. It's all over the news."

Now I remember hearing about a storm somewhere in the Atlantic, but tropical storms crop up all the time, and most of them don't affect us. This one was supposed to turn north. "How close is it?" I ask. "Are we in the cone?"

He nods. "So far, so good. Unless it veers away, it'll hit us by Tuesday."

"So no school on Tuesday?"

"That's what I'm hoping. If we're extra lucky, it'll become a hurricane, and we'll get Monday and Wednesday off too."

"Let's hope," I say, but I can't help thinking about Gabriel and James and all the other people at Helping Hands. Everyone who lives there knows what happened last year when Hurricane Randy blew one of the roofs completely off. No one died, but a few people got hurt by flying debris.

Felix finishes his second burger and crumples the wrapper into a ball. After wiping his hands on a napkin, he pulls out his phone and starts scrolling. Maybe he's checking the storm status.

I pick up my phone too, surprised to see that Morgan has texted me back.

Forget Felix! What about Gabriel?

Seeing Gabriel's name in print is weirdly intoxicating, but the truth is, he scares me—and it's more than him being an addict. Gabriel isn't afraid of who he is, whereas I hide behind this mask I've created.

He makes me feel like a coward.

He makes me want to be brave.

I'm sipping my Coke, still thinking about what to text Morgan, when Felix catches my eye. He smiles, just for a second, before going back to his phone.

Was he smiling at me? It was probably something on his phone.

My screen goes dark. I wake it up (*my own phone!*) and read Morgan's words again:

What about Gabriel?

And finally I type my reply:

Too much baggage.

Her reply comes fast:

Seriously?

I think for a second, then type:

One addict in my life is enough.

As soon as I hit *send*, I regret it because the truth is, I'm drawn to him like a magnet, and it's more than physical.

Felix puts down his phone. "I think they've had enough time, don't you?"

He's talking about Celeste and Joshua. "I guess," I say. "How long does it take to get high?"

"Not long."

"Plus, they have to screw," I say.

"That doesn't take long either. Not if I know my brother."

"Eww," I say.

He grins as he lifts his phone to his ear.

"You're calling him?"

"He won't mind."

I hear Joshua's voice on the other end. "Dude! What the hell?"

"It's time to go," Felix says.

Joshua is talking, but I can't hear what he's saying.

"I did eat," says Felix. "I want to go home."

Not, *need* to go home. *Want.* So does that mean he's been bored this whole time? I look away, sipping the watery remnants of my Coke.

"Yeah, she's still here," says Felix. "We talked . . . Yeah, I said we talked . . . Whatever, dude. I'm coming out there in five minutes." He ends the call and slides his phone into his pocket.

"Were they done?" It's the only thing I can think to say.

He grins. "They are now. I'm meeting Josh at his car."

"Oh." I avoid his eyes. "Okay."

His chair scrapes back. "Thanks again for the help."

"No problem."

He stands, scratches his arm. "See you around."

"Yeah, see you."

This time I don't watch him walk away. Instead I stare at the remnants of our lunch while shoveling the last fries into my mouth. They're cold now, and soggy with grease, but I still choke them down. Mindlessly. Because I'm thinking about Felix and trying to swallow the hurt.

While I'm chewing, Celeste sends me a text.

> Can you bring the bags? I'm waiting
> in the car.

Like a princess, I think, but that doesn't stop me from doing what she asks.

CHAPTER 13

Funny how getting what you need
Quickly turns to Maslow's hierarchy of greed.
—from "Entitlement" by L.F.

I join Celeste in the car. No weed smell, but she has a distant smile on her face, and her eyes look a little glassy. "Are you okay to drive?" I ask.

Her eyes narrow. "Why would you ask that?"

"Felix told me—"

"Felix should mind his own business."

She puts her mom's Mercedes in reverse and starts backing out. All of a sudden, my body jerks forward as she slams on the brakes. I look behind us. There's a car driving by that she missed by inches.

"Don't say it," she says.

"Maybe we should call an Uber."

"I'm fine."

The car behind us roars away, and she continues backing out.

"Aren't you worried?" I ask.

"About . . .?"

In my head, I'm ticking off all the things she should

be worried about. Wrecking her mom's Mercedes, getting pulled over, becoming an addict. "You know addiction runs in families," I say.

"Oh my God, are you really going to lecture me?"

"No." A flush creeps up my neck.

"Good." She turns up the radio. Nirvana. Not something I'd peg her to like. With Kurt Cobain belting out the incomprehensible words to "Smells Like Teen Spirit," I remember Gabriel in his Nirvana T-shirt. Gabriel with his red-gold hair and pale lashes, who thinks it's cool that I like poetry.

Gabriel, who's a heroin addict, who lives in a homeless shelter.

The song ends, and Celeste turns down the sound. "You can't tell my parents."

"Yeah, okay."

"I'm serious. If they knew I saw Josh . . ."

I look over at her. "I take it they don't like him?"

"It's not that. Well, it kind of is. My car got totaled, and they blame him."

"So he was the one driving?"

"No, but I snuck out to see him, and that's when it happened."

I want to ask if she was high when it happened, but I don't want to get yelled at.

"So that's why I'm grounded," she says. "For sneaking out to see Josh."

"Not for wrecking your car?"

"Yeah, well . . ." Her smile is faint. "They're trying to keep that quiet."

And not doing a very good job, I think, since the rumor mill at school was where I first heard it.

"Anyway," she says. "You can't tell them about Josh."

Or about getting high, I assume, although she doesn't say that. It's like, if she doesn't say the words, it didn't happen.

○ ○ ○

It's not until we're almost back to the house that I start thinking about Mom. What if she told Scott to go screw himself? Or what if something happened and she's not getting better? What if she died while I was off buying clothes, not even thinking about her?

Celeste glances over as we pull into the driveway. "You okay?"

"Yeah, just worried." Before I forget, I hold out the twenty she gave me.

"What's that?"

"Felix bought my lunch."

"Okay." She seems confused.

"So I'm giving this back."

"Keep it."

Before I can argue, she shoves open her door, leaving me twenty dollars richer. I remember how lucky I felt when I found that money in the tree. But now my luck has turned, and it feels wrong to keep Celeste's cash, so I leave it in the cupholder of Tanya's car.

Celeste helps me gather up the shopping bags, and we go inside. Tanya is waiting in the foyer.

"God, Mom. Hover much?"

"Take up Layla's things. I need to talk to her."

"Is something wrong?" I ask.

Instead of answering, Tanya leads me to the kitchen where she takes an Evian from the fridge and offers it to me. I shake my head. "You sure? It's really good water."

"I'm okay."

She gestures to the round glass table, and both of us sit.

"Is everything okay? Is my mom—?"

"She's fine."

"But something's wrong?"

"No. I mean, no real damage from the concussion, and of course, she agreed to keep quiet about where you were living, so that's good."

I want to be relieved, but . . . "How is she, though?"

"She seemed fine. Hopeful. Once she's done with rehab, things should go back to normal."

I'm not sure what *normal* means. "What if she can't find a job right away?"

Tanya sips her water. "Is that what you're worried about?"

"That, and she won't have a place to live."

"We're not going to let her be homeless, honey."

If Scott wins the election.

"Can I visit her tomorrow?"

"That's what I wanted to tell you. She'll be in detox starting tomorrow, and they don't allow visitors."

"Oh."

"But once she goes to Serenity Solace, we'll schedule something, okay?"

"You mean I can't just see her when I want?"

"Well, no." Tanya picks at the label on her water bottle. "Even though it's a luxury rehab, it's very regulated. I don't think they allow people to visit until at least a week has passed, and even then, you have to schedule it."

"What about Thanksgiving?"

"She'll have to spend it in rehab, but we both agreed that's the best place for her, since, you know, our dad died on Thanksgiving." She fiddles with her water bottle. "I guess it's a trigger."

"That makes sense."

"She also mentioned her things at the shelter. I told her I'd have them set everything aside, but she made me promise not to bother."

"What about the picture of my dad?"

"Well, I mentioned that, and she said she'd get you another copy."

"Did she say how?"

"No, but it's probably backed up on the cloud."

I don't think Mom knows what the cloud is. "Can't I just get the original?"

"She made me promise to get rid of everything."

"Please, Aunt Tanya. That photo is the only thing I have of him."

"That's . . ." She shakes her head. "Really sad."

"It's in a frame, so it should be easy to find."

"Okay, we'll get it."

At that moment, Celeste walks into the kitchen. "How's Aunt Shauna?"

"She'll be fine," says Tanya.

"Well, that's good." Celeste opens the pantry. "Did you go food shopping?"

"Not yet."

"God, Mom, the cupboards are, like, bare."

Tanya rubs her forehead. "I've been a little busy."

"At the gym?"

"Exercise relieves stress. Plus, I've been dealing with your aunt. I'll get groceries after church tomorrow."

"Church again? Please say I don't have to go."

"You do, so set your alarm."

While Celeste argues with her, I'm thinking about what new outfit I can wear to church. I haven't been since Morgan took me more than a year ago.

"If you don't like it," says Tanya, "take it up with your dad."

"You mean, take it up with Marty," says Celeste. "Whatever Marty says, Dad does."

"Yeah, well, Marty knows what he's doing."

"You sure about that?"

"What's that supposed to mean?"

"It means he keeps changing his strategy, or haven't you noticed?"

"That's how this works," says Tanya.

"Whatever." Celeste opens the fridge. "I'm just sick of living under a microscope."

"You're not living under a microscope."

"How would you know?" The fridge door bangs shut. "You don't know anything about me."

"I know you're spoiled."

She sniffs. "I prefer the term 'entitled.'"

While Tanya rubs her forehead, I'm thinking about how I should have picked out a dress at the mall. If I'd known we were going to church . . .

"It's not fair," Celeste says. "Layla doesn't have to go."

Wait a minute. What?

Tanya waves her hand. "That's because Layla's not . . ." And then she stops herself.

"Part of the family?" Celeste asks.

"I didn't say that," says Tanya. "And Layla doesn't want to go anyway. Isn't that right, Layla?"

Suddenly, I see eight-year-old Celeste looking down at me from her massage chair. *Layla, you don't want a pedicure, do you?*

I shake my head. "Church is pretty boring."

"Especially our church," says Celeste. "You don't know how lucky you are."

CHAPTER 14

My shadow self before me stands
To whisper soft and reach her hands,
To quell my shake, to keep me still
And feed me lies to live until
My moisture fades into the ground
And I can never hear a sound
Except the echoes of my tears
That fade away amid my fears.

—"Alternative Facts" by L.F.

It's Sunday, and I'm sitting at the kitchen counter eating one of Tanya's organic frozen dinners while reading that book *Crank* that Gabriel loaned me. It's written in verse, which is surprisingly easy to read, and it's about a girl hooked on meth.

Everyone else is at church. I've showered and I'm wearing my new PacSun T-shirt and jeans. It feels good to wear new clothes, but it also feels like a waste because I'm not going anywhere. I wish Morgan were here. I wish I had someone to talk to.

I know she's at church, but I send her a text anyway.

Mom's in detox till Wednesday.

Call me when you get this?

Then I hear Scott's BMW pull into the garage, and I'm suddenly shy to have them see me eat their food. Car doors slam. Muffled voices. A key rattles in the lock, and Scott comes in while I'm throwing away my garbage. He frowns like he forgot I was here, then heads toward his office, or "man cave," as Tanya calls it. When we were at the mall, Celeste told me Scott's Internet marketing business pretty much runs itself, so now he spends most of his time reading news stories and posting stuff on social media.

"How was church?" I ask as Tanya lays her purse on the counter.

"Boring," says Celeste.

Tanya flits a hand at her. "Just go upstairs. I need to talk to Layla."

My stomach sinks. Did Scott change his mind about letting me stay? I try to get a clue from Celeste's face, but she ignores me as she flounces from the kitchen.

Then it's just me and Tanya. She watches me wash my fork in the sink. "You know we have a dishwasher for that."

At the shelter, we had to wash our dishes as soon as we were done with them. Old habits die hard. Plus, I thought it would be polite. "Sorry."

"No need to apologize. Come sit."

Nervously, I join her at the table. "Did I do something wrong?"

"No, nothing like that."

"Is Mom okay?"

"She's fine. This is good news."

"Okay." Then why does she seem nervous?

She takes a breath. "Scott's decided to make a donation to the homeless shelter."

"Okay."

"A sizable one, as it turns out. Plus, his campaign manager made arrangements for us to volunteer at their Thanksgiving event."

The Big Thanksgiving Outreach. It's supposed to be like a party for homeless people where they get stuff to help them out, including a hot meal. When I lived there, I planned on hiding out, so none of the volunteers would see me.

"You said *us*," I say. "Does that mean me too?"

"Of course it means you." She touches my arm. "You're part of this family, aren't you?"

Am I? I'm painfully aware they didn't want me going to church with them.

"You don't look too happy," says Tanya.

"No, it's just . . . I thought we were keeping it secret that Mom and I lived there."

"We were. We *are*. But this is Marty's backup plan."

"And Marty's his campaign manager?"

"Exactly. And before you say anything, you should know that Marty ran a state senator's campaign. He knows what he's doing."

"Okay."

"And yes, he's changing strategies. It's called 'pivoting' in the world of politics, and it happens all the time."

"So the new strategy is for Scott to be a friend to the homeless?"

Tanya frowns at me. "Like I said, this is a backup plan. Marty wants us to volunteer at the shelter *in case* word gets out that you and your mom lived there. That way, if word *does* get out, Scott can show how he's aware of the homeless problem, how we're donating, not just money, but also our time."

"Okay."

"Plus," says Tanya, "you can pick up that picture of your dad."

As much as I want the picture, this feels like a bad idea. And it doesn't make sense. If Scott really wants to keep it secret that we lived at Helping Hands, he won't want me showing up there as part of his family, not where people will recognize me as someone who lived there. But maybe that's what he wants, for me to be his poster child.

"Will reporters be there?"

"Of course," says Tanya. "The check Scott's presenting is—"

"So Uncle Scott's planning to tell them about me."

"No." She looks taken aback. "Why would he do that?"

"To show the world how he's helping his poor, homeless niece."

For a second, she doesn't say anything. Then she sighs and looks me in the eye. "Layla, I swear to you. That's not what this is about."

"Then I don't get it."

"Marty has a plan, and all you have to do is play your part, okay?"

"Okay."

"And don't look so worried. I know you don't want to go back there, but it's not like we're dropping you off to stay. We'll volunteer in the morning to get it over with, and then we'll all come back to the house for our own Thanksgiving dinner. Everyone says my turkey's the best. And my candied yams—they're fresh, not from the can." She touches my arm. "Have you ever had pumpkin cake?"

"Mom makes it every year."

"Well, mine's homemade."

"Hers is too. Her mom's recipe."

Tanya looks surprised. "*Our* mom's recipe. Your grandma's.

Anyway . . ." She lays her hands flat on the table. "We'll have a nice Thanksgiving. I promise."

Sudden tears fill my eyes as I remember last Thanksgiving when Mom and I ate turkey and candied yams with Grandpa. He couldn't get out of bed, so we ate in the living room, next to his cot. Everything seemed good until I went to clean up and overheard them arguing.

"Get away from me," he told her. "I can't look at you."

Then waking up the next day to see him lying on his cot, his fingers curled like claws. His mouth was open, his head sloped back, and I thought maybe he was having a nightmare, but he wasn't moving.

". . . She was always into the holidays," Tanya says, and I realize she's been speaking for a while, but I haven't been listening. "If only she could join us, it'd be the perfect Thanksgiving."

She's talking about Mom. "You actually want her here?"

"I think it'd be nice, don't you? Believe it or not, your mom and I used to be close. Before your grandma died, when Shauna and I were kids? Our mom used to sit us at the table, and we'd all make these elaborate Thanksgiving decorations. Mom—your grandma—had a gift for that kind of thing. For making things beautiful."

"I didn't know that."

"Shauna doesn't talk about her much, does she?"

I shake my head. "I know she died of cancer when you and Mom were teenagers. I know Mom took it hard."

"We both did." Tanya looks at her hands. "But Shauna especially. After that was when she started partying. She got pretty wild, to the point where . . ." Now she fiddles with her ring. "Anyway . . ." She looks up. "Shauna has always had a wild streak, but her heart's in a good place."

"She always liked Thanksgiving," I say.

"I know." She smiles to herself. "When we were kids, she

looked forward to making Thanksgiving decorations, but she never had the patience for it. She always ended up with glue and glitter everywhere."

I laugh. "That sounds like her."

Tanya peers at my face. "I don't suppose you want to help me with the decorations this year?"

"Yeah," I say. "Sure."

"Really? Celeste never wants to help."

"It sounds like fun."

I picture Tanya and me sitting across from each other at the kitchen table. The two of us cutting strips of ribbon, stringing together cranberries, spraying fake snow onto gilded pinecones. All while we're breathing in the smell of homemade pumpkin cake. There's Christmas music playing in the background, and Uncle Scott comes in and nods at me. As if I belong in their kitchen. As if I belong in their family.

"I almost forgot." Tanya pulls her purse closer. I watch her dig around inside. I watch her pull out a key. The key is topped with a yellow smiley face.

She hands it to me, and I take it, but I don't know what it's for or why she's giving it to me. I want it to be what I think it is, but I don't want to get my hopes up. So I stare at the smiley face and force myself not to hope, but the hope creeps up, making it hard to breathe.

"It's a house key," she says.

"For me?"

"I figure, if you're going to be staying with us . . ." She peers at my face. "Honey, are you crying?"

"No." The word comes out as whisper. I stare at the key. It's blurry from me not crying.

"This doesn't mean we're forgetting about your mom. You know that, right?"

I nod. I wasn't even thinking about Mom.

"She *will* get better, and when all this is over—when she's better and can actually take care of you—well, then . . ." Tanya taps the key in my hand. "Then you can return the key."

I don't want to return the key. Not ever. But, of course, I don't say that. If I say that, it'll be like I don't want Mom to get better, and that's not the case at all.

It's not.

I open my palm. The yellow smiley face beams up at me like it's welcoming me to a happy new life, and it's true. That's what I have, even if it is only temporary. A happy new life until either Scott loses the election or Mom gets better.

CHAPTER 15

I'll glitter at you with my smile,
and you'll see my gleam and
maybe you'll love me
and I'll try—
oh, how I'll try—
to love me too.

—from "Gleaming Girl" by L.F.

It feels surreal to get dropped off at school in a Mercedes—surreal in a good way, even if Celeste does completely ignore me as we get out of the car. It's like she's embarrassed to be seen with me, even though I'm wearing one of the outfits she picked out—faded Guess jeans and that super-expensive sky-blue sweater from Bloomingdale's. Never mind that the sweater has a loose thread on the sleeve that's tickling my wrist. I'm afraid to pull it, afraid it will unravel, so I ignore it and head toward the banyan tree where Morgan should be waiting.

A few people stare at me as I cut through the crowd, probably wondering who I am because, yeah, I look different in my new clothes. I *feel* different, and I really want Morgan to see this new version of myself.

Layla 2.0, that's what I'm calling it. The version of myself that's normal like everyone else, that doesn't need pity or prayers, which (based on my phone conversation with Morgan yesterday) is clearly how Morgan sees me.

When she called, I was in my room, taking the tags off my clothes, hanging them in the closet, planning my outfits for the entire week.

I put her on speaker when I answered. "Hey!"

"You okay?" Those were the first words out of her mouth. Not "What's up?" Not "How's it going?"

"Yeah, I'm good."

"You sure?"

I heard voices in the background. Lots of them. "Where are you?" I asked.

"Church."

"Still?"

"I'm helping put up shutters."

"Did it turn into a hurricane?"

"No, but we're being cautious. You want to come help? It might be a good distraction."

I thought of all the reasons why going to her church would be a bad idea. First and foremost, her mom would ask about my mom, and then her mom would give me all this advice and tell me she was praying for me and generally make me feel anxious and uncomfortable.

"Hard labor doesn't sound very fun," I said.

"I knew you'd say that." Morgan sounded disappointed. "What about Open Mic tomorrow night?"

"That's still happening?"

Her church's youth group does this Open Mic thing where anyone can get up and perform. According to Morgan, most people sing or play an instrument, but she's been trying to get me to recite one of my poems. I told her no way. The last time I tried to read one of my poems aloud—in English class last year—I got choked up, which was really awkward. Plus, who wants to hear a poem recited? That's, like, torture according to *The Hitchhiker's Guide to the Galaxy*, especially when the poem was written by an amateur like me.

"We do it every Monday," said Morgan.

"Even with a hurricane coming?"

"It's only a tropical storm. And it's not supposed to hit till late Tuesday, so I think we're safe."

"Yeah, well, I don't think my aunt will let me go. She's pretty worried about the storm." Which was a lie. As far as I knew, she hadn't mentioned it once.

"Yeah, okay." Morgan sounded disappointed, and there was an awkward silence while I unfolded my sweater from Bloomingdale's. "You asked me to call," she finally said. "Is there something you wanted to tell me?"

I wanted her to call because I was lonely, but if I told her that, she'd want to talk about everything wrong in my life, when all I wanted to do was forget, at least for a while. "I wanted to tell you what I got," I said, rubbing the expensive sweater against my cheek to feel its softness.

"You mean your new clothes?"

"I got, like, a whole new wardrobe."

"That's great, Layla. I'm happy for you."

"Are you?"

"Of course. You know I've been praying for you, right?"

"Yeah, I know."

"And for your mom. We actually started a prayer circle at church."

The sweater slipped from my hand. "What do you mean?"

"It's where a group of us pray for the same person."

"I know what a prayer circle is, but, Morgan . . ."

"What?"

"You told people? About my mom?"

"Just people at church. She needs help, so . . ."

"It's none of their business!"

"Layla, she has a problem. It's not like they're judging her."

"Of course they're judging her. They're judging me too, and I'm tired of being judged!"

She got quiet for a second. "I've said this before, but I'm not judging you, and I wish you'd just talk to me."

"I *want* to talk to you, but not about my mom. Can you just . . . honor that?"

"Sure," she said, her voice flat, and that's where we left things.

Now I'm excited to show her my new Guess jeans and way-too-expensive sweater, and I'm hoping she'll be excited for me. I can already see she's not waiting at the tree, so where is she? I look around, and that's when I spot Gigi at one of the picnic tables in front of the school. Not her usual spot. She's with Kendra, and I swear that's a script they're huddled over. Does that mean she's trying out for *Grease*? If she is, Morgan will want to know.

Normally I'd be too insecure to approach them, but this is Layla 2.0.

Kendra sees me first and nudges Gigi, who blinks up at me with her long-lashed eyes. No fake glasses today. "Can I help you?" she asks.

The loose thread on my sleeve feels like a bug crawling on my hand as I gesture to the sheaf of papers she's holding. "Is that a script?"

She makes a point of glancing at it. "Clearly."

"I thought you weren't trying out."

"Layla . . ." Her smile is so sugary it's fermenting before my eyes. "Are you stalking me?"

"No!"

"Because it seems like you're stalking me."

Kendra giggles, which makes me want to slap her.

"Forget I asked." I start walking away.

Behind me, Kendra says to Gigi, "Was she wearing new clothes?"

"I know, right? Maybe she stole them."

"You're so mean," says Kendra, but she's laughing as she says it. Gigi laughs too, and their laughter sticks to me like gum on the bottom of my Prada sneaker.

I reach the banyan tree and still no Morgan. My phone bleeps with a text.

Got hung up. See you at lunch. 😗

I check the time. Five minutes till the bell rings. I start to brush leaves from the bench, but the loose thread on my sleeve taunts me with every move. I know I should wait for scissors, but screw patience. I take the thread between my teeth and rip it off.

Which is clearly a mistake since now I have a tiny hole in my super-soft sweater. Not that anyone will notice except me.

○ ○ ○

Lunchtime, and the cafeteria is half-empty because, even though the tropical storm isn't supposed to hit until tomorrow, parents have been coming to school all day to pick up their kids. Everyone's talking about how the storm is moving faster than expected, and how glad they are that school will be closed tomorrow, and I guess I am too, but no school means I don't get to see Felix. Or Gabriel. I look around for either of them but don't see them.

I'm not hungry, but I go through the line for my free lunch and carry it to my usual table to wait for Morgan. Shouldn't she be here by now? Maybe her stepdad picked her up early. But wouldn't she have told me? I check my phone. No messages. I shoot her a text.

Are you here?

No reply.

What is up with her? Maybe she's paying me back for standing her up at Starbucks.

A shadow falls over my table, and I look up to see Gabriel standing there with his tray. I haven't seen him all day, and my heart stutters at the sight of him. He's wearing black jeans and a Linkin Park T-shirt. His headphones are around his neck. "Hey," he says. "Mind if I sit?"

His tattoo peeks out from his sleeve, and all I can think is *heroin addict*, which makes me think of Mom and how stupid she was to shoot up, and for what? So she could escape her problems for a few hours? Don't addicts realize that life will be waiting to slap them in the face when they come down from their high?

He's still waiting for me to answer him.

"No," I say. "Go ahead."

I watch as he settles himself across from me. I know it's not his fault, what Mom did, but it's hard to look at him without a tiny bit of anger. I want him to be better than he is.

Or better than he was. I remind myself he's clean now. And he's probably wondering why he hasn't seen me at the shelter.

Or maybe he heard already, how Shauna Freeman overdosed on his drug of choice.

"Hey, I'm sorry about your mom."

And just like that, my anger melts away. I drop my eyes, swallowing hard against the lump in my throat.

"Is she okay?"

"She will be."

"She's in treatment?"

I nod, still not looking at him. "Three days of detox. Then a month of rehab."

"Does she *want* to go?"

Now I lift my head. "Yeah, of course."

"Good. Some people don't, and that makes it harder."

I watch him for a second. "Did you?"

My question seems to take him off guard. He stirs his corn, puts down his fork. "It depends on which time."

So he's been to rehab more than once. Another strike against him. The smell of my fish patty is turning my stomach. I push away my tray.

"That guy James is worried about her," he says, like he's trying to change the subject. "About you too."

"I'm fine."

"Are you?"

"Yeah, I'm good."

"I'm glad. I was worried too."

He was?

"I didn't expect to see you at school," he says. "I thought you'd be . . . I don't know . . ."

"Living with foster parents?"

"Something like that."

"Yeah, well, that's the good part. My aunt and uncle are letting me stay with them."

"You're lucky then, huh?"

"Yeah, lucky." I laugh, which makes him smile, and I notice how his one dimple makes his smile look innocent.

He's not innocent, though. Far from it. And anyone who takes a drug they know is highly addictive is either stupid or crazy or so lost they don't give a shit. Which is he?

And which is Mom?

He starts eating his lunch, chewing with his mouth closed and actually using his napkin. If he hadn't told me, I'd never know he's an addict, but there's obviously a whole other side to him. Maybe he can answer a question that's been bugging me.

I take a breath. "Can I ask you something?"

"Sure."

"Is twenty bucks enough to buy heroin? Enough to overdose on?"

He chews carefully, wipes his mouth. Nods. "Yeah. Heroin's pretty cheap."

So that confirms it. If I hadn't been so stupid . . .

"Why do you ask?"

"Because I was the one who gave my mom the money."

He looks confused. "But not to buy dope."

"No."

"But you're blaming yourself?"

"I should have known better."

"Layla . . ." His eyes find mine—so light gray they're startling. "If an addict wants to get high, nothing short of locking them up will stop them." He looks down. "Believe me. I know."

"Did they lock you up?"

"I wanted to be locked up."

It's obvious that talking about this is hard for him. He looks so vulnerable and tormented that the urge to touch him, to comfort him in some way, is almost irresistible.

I resist. "You said before, you went to more than one rehab."

"Yeah, I should have told you sooner."

"You don't have to tell me anything if you don't want."

"I know, but it's bad for me to hide things. It's part of my recovery to be . . . you know . . . honest."

"Okay."

"So can I be honest about something?"

"Sure."

I have no idea what he's going to tell me, but by the look on his face, I know it's serious.

"When we first met," he says, "I let you think my mom was the addict."

I nod. This much I know.

"I wanted to tell you," he says, "but it's not something that's easy to bring up. I'm not proud of it, you know? But I knew I should tell you, and when Morgan asked about my tattoo, it seemed a natural lead-in."

"That makes sense," I say. "But if you're not proud of it—proud of your recovery, I mean—why'd you get a tattoo with your sobriety date?"

"Because I *was* proud, but I was also stupid. I thought I had it."

"Oh."

"I've relapsed since then. And there's something else . . . Full disclosure."

My heart is pounding as he comes to my side of the table. I have no idea what he's going to tell me or why he has to be close to tell it, and I have this sudden fear that he's going to take my hand and confess to being the one who sold Mom the heroin. But no. He's pulling up his shirt, showing me his stomach.

Showing me his scar.

A burn scar that covers his ribs on one side and disappears

into the waistband of his boxers. Red and puckered. A horrible swath of melted skin.

I suck in my breath. "What happened?"

He lets his shirt fall. "Our apartment caught fire. It was my fault."

Now I get it. "Because you were high?"

He nods as he rubs his tattoo. "Five weeks after getting out of treatment, I relapsed, left a candle burning—a candle I used to cook my dope. It lit up my curtains, and I was so wasted I didn't even realize. My mom was the one who got me out. She got hurt too. Smoke inhalation and third-degree burns because she saved my life."

Part of me is horrified he could let something like that happen, and another part wants to grab his hands and tell him it's okay.

"So it's my fault we're homeless," he says. "My fault that my mom got hurt. Even though she's technically healed, she's still in a lot of pain, but she doesn't complain. I know she's more worried about me than herself."

Tears flow freely down his cheeks. I wish I could make him feel better. "She sounds really brave."

"Yeah." He takes in a breath. "My mom's the bravest person I know. And yet . . ." He drops his eyes. "I let you think she was the reason we're homeless. What's that say about me?"

"Nothing. You were ashamed, like you said."

He shakes his head. "So much pain I caused her, and not just physical pain. We lost everything in the fire. Almost everything. There was a load of laundry in the washer, and those are basically the clothes we have. Most of them were mine, unfortunately. Plus, we owe thousands of dollars in hospital bills, and even though she still has her job, we can't afford the first and last month's rent on an apartment."

I could remind him of what he told me when I was complaining about Mom—that with addiction, you don't have a choice, but I have a feeling he doesn't want to hear that. "At least you're doing the right thing now," I say.

"I'm trying. I'm looking for a job too."

"And you're helping me by telling me all this. Like, now I understand more of what my mom's going through."

His smile is faint. "If you ever want to talk . . ."

"I have a phone now," I say.

"Great. Let me give you my number."

I pass him my phone, hoping he doesn't notice that my list of contacts is only three people long. He types in his name—Gabriel Connelly—and as he's typing, I watch his fingers, wondering what it would feel like to have those fingers touch my face.

He looks up. Our eyes meet, and both of us look away. Did he know what I was thinking?

"Now yours," he says and passes me his phone.

My cheeks feel warm as I type in my name and number. As soon as I'm done, his screen lights up with a text.

See you tonight!

From Morgan. And now it's like this wall comes crashing down between us. Are they seeing each other? When did they exchange numbers?

I hand back his phone. "Someone texted you." It's too painful to say who it's from, but it all makes sense. He can talk to Morgan about normal things, stuff that has nothing to do with addiction or being homeless. He feels comfortable with her, probably because she's not afraid of being found out if she's seen with him.

He glances at the text. "I assume you're going tonight?"

"What? I don't . . ."

"To Open Mic. Morgan was going to invite you."

"She did, but I'm not going."

"No?"

"It's not really my thing."

"Even with Morgan singing?"

He's right. I've been so focused on my own problems and insecurities that I forgot to be supportive of my friend. What a douche I've been! All those times I said no . . .

But does he really want me there, or is he being polite? Maybe he'd rather spend the time alone with Morgan. I wouldn't blame him, but it still hurts. Because I want him, despite him being homeless, despite his addiction. I want to talk with him. I want to laugh with him. I've never met anyone who gets me like he does.

"If you're worried about getting there," says Gabriel, "I can pick you up."

"That would be great. Thanks."

"Layla!"

The shout comes from across the cafeteria, and I turn to see Celeste standing at the entrance.

"My mom's here," she says. "Get your stuff."

I turn back to Gabriel, but his eyes are on Celeste.

"Your cousin?" he asks.

"Yeah." I stand so abruptly that my hand knocks into his phone. Both of us try to catch it before it falls. Both of us fail, our hands colliding. The phone lands on my seat with a dull *thunk*.

"Sorry." My cheeks are burning. "Is it okay?"

He picks it up. "Yeah."

"You sure?"

He turns it on. A new text from Morgan lights up the screen.

Layla says she's not coming so . . .

He pockets the phone, almost like he's hiding the text. "Yeah, it's fine."

"Layla, come on!"

What did Morgan mean with that ellipsis?

Layla's not coming, so we get to be alone?

Layla's not coming, so we don't have to worry about making her jealous?

Layla's not coming, so let's have fun without her?

"You should go," Gabriel says.

I nod.

He says something else that doesn't register because I'm walking away, flustered, trying not to trip over my own feet. It's only when I'm following Celeste down the hall that I rewind my brain.

Be careful out there, he said.

Because there's a hurricane coming, or something close to a hurricane. And what if Tanya and Scott don't let me leave tonight?

Then Morgan and Gabriel will spend the evening alone, and maybe that's what they want. Maybe they only invited me so I wouldn't feel left out.

CHAPTER 16

I'm told you're always true to what you say,
So welcome me before I fade away.
—from "In Search of God" by L.F.

Turns out, Scott and Tanya have no problem with me going to Open Mic, as long as they don't have to drive me. Tanya even makes a point of flaunting it in Celeste's face, as if to say, *See? When you're good and follow the rules, you don't get grounded.*

I thought Gabriel was going to pick me up, but it's Phil's Infiniti waiting in the driveway. Apparently, Morgan's stepdad doesn't like the idea of Morgan riding with a boy, but he does like the idea of her being involved in the church's youth group, so he sacrificed his valuable time to drive us to what he sees as a wholesome church-related activity.

I know all this because he tells me as soon as I get in the car, and when he's done telling me and I've thanked him profusely, we lapse into awkward silence. Morgan and I are both riding in the back seat, but it's me Phil keeps glancing at in the rearview mirror while Morgan shrinks into her seat as though she's trying to be invisible.

When he clears his throat, it startles me. "I heard about your mom. How's she doing?"

"Good. She's actually detoxing right now. Then she goes to treatment."

"She's in our prayers."

"Thank you."

Another awkward silence. Beside me, Morgan stares at her feet.

"Let me ask you something." Phil adjusts the mirror so he can see me better. "Is that why you came out tonight? Because you're worried about your mom?"

"What do you mean?" I glance at Morgan, but she won't meet my eye.

"Morgan tells me she's been trying to get you to this Open Mic thing for a while. Sounds like you had an epiphany, like you've finally come around to the fact that God helps those who believe in Him."

"Uh, sure. That's . . . exactly what happened."

"Young lady, is that sarcasm?"

Morgan speaks up. "She didn't mean it like that, Phil."

"I know exactly how she meant it. Sarcasm is for the weak-minded. Did you know that, Layla? But it's okay if your mind is weak. That just makes you more dependent on God. Isn't that right, Morgan?"

"Yeah," she whispers.

"Morgan would know," says Phil. "Her mind tends to be weak."

I glance at Morgan whose jaw is rigid. Maybe she can't speak up, but I can. "You know what's weird?"

"What?" Phil asks.

"You saying Morgan has a weak mind, because Morgan's one of the strongest people I know."

Beside me, Morgan grabs my hand, squeezes. I squeeze back.

For the rest of the ride, Phil blares his gospel music, which isn't that bad except he's the one playing it, so every song grates on my nerves. Finally, he drops us off in the church parking lot, and once I'm free of him, I breathe a sigh of relief.

Morgan and I stand there in the darkness watching the Infiniti pull away. "Is he always like that?" I ask.

"Most of the time."

And here I was thinking how lucky she was.

○ ○ ○

Gabriel's car isn't in the church parking lot, and there's no sign of the tropical storm. They're both still coming, though. Gabriel texted us to say he's on his way, and the weather update on my phone says the outer wind bands will reach us some time in the middle of the night. Now that we're here, I'm excited. Excited to see Morgan perform, excited to cheer her on.

As we walk in, the church feels strangely dark because all the windows have been boarded up. Morgan leads me past the chapel to a room at the end of a hallway. From the other side of the door, I hear laughter and music. Bright light seeps from under the door, and when Morgan pushes it open, it's like we're going from black-and-white Kansas into Technicolor Oz.

The room is filled with kids our age, all of them talking, laughing, and shouting to be heard in the general mayhem. One kid is banging out "Bohemian Rhapsody" on the piano. Another is tuning a guitar. One kid is standing on a folding chair playing the trumpet while a girl smiles up at him, holding her ears. A pretty girl with long, straightened hair is handing out sodas, and when she sees Morgan, she runs over to give her a hug. "You made it!" she says. "And you brought your friend."

Morgan turns to me. "Layla, this is Jasmine. She's our youth-group president. Jasmine, this is my friend Layla, the one I told you about."

"The poet!" Jasmine hugs me too, which I wasn't expecting, so my body stays stiff. "I'll put you on the lineup."

"What? No!"

Jasmine leans closer. "Can I tell you something?"

"Sure."

"For the longest time, Morgan was too shy to perform, but when she finally came out of her shell, she blew us away."

"And now they can't shut me up," Morgan says.

"Not true! We love to hear you sing." Jasmine nudges me. "Just so you know, this isn't about us judging you. It's about having fun and appreciating each other's efforts."

"Okay."

"And I'm sure you're an amazing poet."

"I don't know about that."

"Anyway, I have to go. Good luck tonight."

After she's gone, Morgan takes my arm. "Sorry about that. She can come on strong, but she means well."

"It's fine. No worries."

"Really?" Morgan turns to look at me, a huge smile on her face.

"Yeah. No big deal."

"I'm so glad to hear you say that." Morgan pulls me further into the room and starts introducing me to people, all of whom make me feel welcome. I try to remember names, but it's hopeless, and I'm starting to feel out of place, maybe because I'm one of the few white faces in the room, but I'd like to think it's because I don't know anyone besides Morgan.

Just as I'm wondering if Gabriel will ever get here, I see him standing in the doorway. He seems nervous as he searches the room. "Over here!" Morgan calls, and when he sees her, he smiles and comes over to join us.

"Sorry I'm late. Got a little lost."

"You're right on time."

He's looking across the room. "Wow, nice piano."

"I told you we had one."

"You didn't say it was a Steinway."

"Donated by the congregation. We like our music."

Gabriel smiles. "Maybe I should join your church."

"You'd be welcome. You know that." Then she turns to me. "You too, Layla."

A sharp whine pierces our ears, and all of us turn our attention to the front of the room where Jasmine is lifting the microphone from its stand. "Welcome, everyone, to our Monday Night Open Mic!"

The room erupts with cheering, and people start taking seats on the folding chairs. Not by choice, I end up in the first row. Gabriel is seated between Morgan and me.

"As I'm sure you know," says Jasmine, "there's a tropical storm coming, but we aren't going to let that stop us, are we?" More cheering, louder this time. "Especially because tonight we have some new faces. So let's show them how to have fun, okay?"

Now the room goes crazy. Cheering, whistling, stomping. I glance at Gabriel. He looks as shy as I feel, clapping but with an uncertain smile.

"First up we have Demetrius, who's singing and playing guitar."

We all clap as a stocky guy with a guitar strapped over his shoulder makes his way to the front of the room. He looks terrified as Jasmine passes him the microphone. "I always get nervous," he says. "So thanks for letting me go first."

Then he fits the microphone into its stand, hoists his guitar, and begins to play "All of Me" by John Legend. Honestly, his guitar playing is much better than his singing, but it doesn't matter because everyone's cheering and smiling. When he's done, he grins and takes an elaborate bow. Jasmine replaces him at the front and says into the microphone, "Thank you, Demetrius. That was awesome. Next up we have Michael, who, as always, is reciting a poem for us."

My ears perk up. I wonder if he's any good, but it turns out, he's not reciting his own poem. It's a sonnet called "Yet Do I Marvel" by Countee Cullen. Unlike Demetrius, Michael doesn't look nervous, but I bet he would be if he recited his own poem. He's stoic up there, and even though he's not a great performer, I can tell the poem means a lot to him.

It means a lot to me too.

I'm not sure why. I'm not even sure I understand it—something about not comprehending God—but the words are so beautiful they bring tears to my eyes, and when he says the rhyming couplet at the end, I sit there swallowing a lump in my throat while everyone around me claps.

Morgan leans over. "You should do your poem about God and all your doubts."

It's one of the few poems I've let her read, but no way could I compare to Countee Cullen, and no way am I going up there, especially not after that. Some of the lines from "Yet Do I Marvel" still echo in my head.

"*I doubt not God is good, well meaning, kind.*" And "*What awful brain compels his awful hand.*"

Michael's still up there, his head bowed. Praying, maybe? To the God he doubts? What kind of church is this?

Morgan nudges me. "You okay?"

"Yeah, I'm good."

Now she smiles. "I'm really glad you came, Layla."

"I'm glad too."

Jasmine replaces Michael at the microphone. "Next up is Morgan, who we all know and love."

Looking over at her, I can tell she's nervous. "You'll do great," I tell her.

"Thanks." She bites her lip.

While everyone cheers, Morgan makes her way to the front where Jasmine hands her the microphone.

"Most of you know I can't play an instrument," Morgan says, "so this is going to be karaoke-style." She signals someone behind her, and the music starts. I recognize it immediately. "Helpless" from *Hamilton*. A song about falling in love.

I've heard Morgan sing lots of times. I know she's good. But tonight she's incredible. Her voice is sweet and clear, soft yet powerful. How does she do that? As I watch her up there performing, acting out the words like she's onstage, I get goose bumps, and when she hands the microphone back to Jasmine, I'm clapping like mad, so proud of my friend, so in awe of her talent. They'd have to be crazy not to give her a part in *Grease.* I hug her as she joins us. Gabriel hugs her too, and I'm so happy for her that I'm not even jealous. Not until they smile at each other. Was the song about them?

Shutting down my jealousy, I turn to Gabriel. "Someone has to follow that."

"I know, right?" He winces. "Hope it's not one of us."

"Wait. What?"

He doesn't hear me. I turn to Morgan. "Did you put my name on the lineup?"

"Huh? No, you did."

"What?"

"You told Jasmine you'd do it."

"No, I didn't."

"Yeah, you did. She was trying to convince you and you said 'okay.' She even told you good luck."

"I thought she was talking to you."

"If you don't want to do it, you don't have to," Morgan says.

I don't. I definitely don't. But what am I going to say when Jasmine calls my name? That I chickened out? Maybe I can get up the courage. What's the worst that could happen?

More people get up to perform, but I'm not paying attention. My stomach is twisting and turning, and I think I might throw up. If I get up there, I'll humiliate myself, not just in front of Morgan's church friends, but also in front of Gabriel. So I have to say no when Jasmine calls my name, and so what if everyone here thinks I'm afraid? They'd be right, so it doesn't matter. Nothing matters except getting through this night with the least amount of embarrassment.

I'm staring at the floor, but my head snaps up when Jasmine calls my name.

Morgan touches my leg, which is bouncing up and down. "You don't have to," she says.

But everyone's cheering, Gabriel included. And the way he's looking at me, like he's proud of me. Slowly, I drag myself to my feet. Maybe I can do this.

Sweat trickles down my back as I walk to the front. It's like I have blinders on. The only thing I see is what's right in front of me. Jasmine hands me the microphone, and I grip it with both hands, trying to look at ease but swallowing back panic. What poem do I do? One of my good ones, but who says they're good? No one, that's who. My so-called good poems are the ones that make me cry when I read them, and I definitely don't want to cry.

"You can do this!" someone yells.

No, I can't. I open my mouth. No words come out.

"Come on, Layla!" Morgan's trying to encourage me, but it's actually doing the opposite. Now I feel like a little kid who's too afraid to go on the swing.

The cheering has stopped. Dead silence. I hear myself breathing into the microphone, feel my heart beating in my chest.

Finally, after what seems an eternity, Jasmine relieves me of the microphone. "It's okay," she whispers. "Maybe next time."

I can't look at her. My face is on fire as I walk to my seat. At least I don't have far to walk. I hunch in my chair. Why didn't I say something? Anything? I could have done a real poem, something from Maya Angelou or William Blake. I could have done a dirty limerick, and it would've been better than standing up there like a deer caught in headlights. Gabriel has switched places with Morgan, and she takes my hand. I don't pull away, but after a few seconds, I let go so I can pretend to tie my shoe. I can't even look at Gabriel, but I know he and Morgan are exchanging looks behind my back.

There's another performer, a girl singing an upbeat song called "Every Praise." By the time she reaches the end of the song, I feel a little better. No one's looking at me anymore. If I'm lucky, no one will remember me either.

"Thank you, Mariah," says Jasmine. "Our last performer of the night is Gabriel, and this is his first time here, so let's give him a big welcome!"

Morgan's clapping and whistling. I'm clapping too, but my knee starts bouncing as he settles himself at the piano. Is he any good? I want him to be good.

"This is a song I wrote." He adjusts the microphone. "It's called 'Torn.' I hope you like it."

As soon as he begins to play, I'm drawn into the song. Lonely chords set off by a tinkling melody. He doesn't look up from the keyboard, and when he starts to sing, his voice is raw with pain. The song has a pretty melody, but the chords make it unsettling, and I think that's the point because, as I follow the words, I realize it's a song about addiction, about wanting the drug and hating it too, about the war inside him, the pain he's caused, the wounds . . .

Drawn to you
Reel me in
Make me numb
Make me sin.
Run from you
Let me be
Leave my head
Free what's me.

His voice is deep and clear. At one point, he lifts into falsetto, and even though it's hard for him to reach those high notes, it doesn't take away from the song. If anything, it makes the song better because he sounds so vulnerable. As the song ends and I'm clapping along with everyone else, I glance at Morgan. Her eyes are glued to Gabriel. Her heart may be too.

o o o

When it's time to go home, it's hard to watch him hug her goodbye. He hugs me as well, but with minimal contact.

"You were brave," he says to me.

"No, I wasn't."

He and Morgan exchange a look. I know, at some point, they're going to have a long conversation with me as the topic. I shouldn't let it bother me. I know they mean well, but I hate that they pity me.

Gabriel leaves, and as we're waiting in the parking lot for Morgan's mom to pick us up, Morgan turns to me. "Gabriel's right, you know. You were brave up there."

"If you say so."

"I mean it."

"Thanks."

"And I feel horrible that you were put in that position."

I shrug. "It wasn't your fault. It was a misunderstanding."

"Still . . ."

I try to change the subject. "You were really good, though. Amazing, actually. So was Gabriel. You two are great for each other."

She gives me a weird look. "You know Gabriel's not interested in me, right?"

Whatever you say, Morgan. That's what I'm thinking, but I say out loud, "It doesn't matter."

"Why wouldn't it matter?"

"Because I don't like him like that." If I say it enough . . .

"Hmm," she says. "Could have fooled me."

Annoyed, I turn to her. "You do realize, the last thing I need in my life is another addict."

"Okay. Sorry."

What is wrong with me? Why am I snapping at her when she's only trying to be nice? "Morgan, I'm sorry."

"Don't worry about it."

"I'm being a bitch."

"I get it. You're under a lot of stress."

"That's no excuse."

"Are you mad at me?" she asks. "If you are, tell me what I did."

"No, I'm not mad." If anything, I'm mad at myself, but I can't tell her that. She'll want to know why, and then I'll have to tell her I'm hiding things from her. Or else make up another lie.

"Then talk to me," she says.

I open my mouth, not sure what to say, but at that moment, her mom pulls up—not in Phil's Infiniti, but in her old blue Hyundai.

"How was it?" her mom asks as we get in the car. She's wearing pajama pants, and her hair is under a scarf.

"Good," says Morgan. We're both sitting in the back seat. "I got to perform."

"Were you the best one?"

"Hardly."

"She was," I say.

"And how about that boy? Did he show up?"

Morgan groans. "His name's Gabriel, Mom, and yeah, he was there."

Mrs. Lawrence finds me in the rearview mirror. "Should I be worried, Layla?"

"About Gabriel?"

"Morgan keeps going on and on about him, but she tells me he's a drug addict."

"I also told you I wasn't interested in him."

"But Layla is?"

"No, Layla isn't," I say.

"Well, that's good. Addicts can be . . . Well, I don't have to tell *you,* Layla."

Silence fills the car. Morgan looks at me and rolls her eyes. I give her a tiny smile.

"So how's your mom?" asks Mrs. Lawrence.

The question takes me off guard, even though it shouldn't. "Good," I tell her. "Still in detox, but Wednesday she starts rehab."

"It's a shame. Most of these rehabs are revolving doors."

They are? Why is she telling me this?

"But your mom's going to be okay. I have faith."

"Thanks," I mutter.

"And you know we're praying for her, right?"

"Yeah."

"But I can't help thinking Morgan's right."

"Mom, she doesn't need to hear this."

"Right about what?" I ask.

"That maybe it's a good thing your mom almost died, since that's what got her in treatment."

I whirl on Morgan. "Did you really say that?"

She winces. "Not exactly in those words."

"So it's a good thing my mom almost died?"

"I didn't mean it like that."

"Of course she didn't mean it like that," says Mrs. Lawrence. "Don't be so sensitive, Layla."

Is that what I'm being? I slump in the seat. Morgan reaches out a hand, but I pretend not to see it as I stare at the floor. After a few seconds, she takes it away, and we spend the rest of the car ride in silence.

CHAPTER 17

The wind blows hard, the storm a drowning bath.
Yet in this house I'm safe from nature's wrath.
But not from tension, not from taunts or jeers.
Inside I'm sinking low from angst and fears.
—from "Sonnet of the Storm" by L.F.

Celeste once told me no one ever uses their family room, but when I wake up on Tuesday morning in the middle of a tropical storm, that's where Tanya is watching storm coverage on TV, so that's where all of us gather. It's not even noon, and normally Scott would be in his office, but now he and Tanya are holding hands on the big leather couch. Celeste, still in her pajamas, is curled up in one of the overstuffed chairs, and I'm sitting stiffly on the loveseat, thinking about how I've never gone this long without seeing Mom. I hope she's okay; I hope she *wants* to get better, and while I'm trying not to worry, I'm also trying not to think about Gabriel and how he looked last night while singing and playing piano. I'm trying not to think about Morgan and how we left things, me barely saying goodbye when her mom dropped me off.

As we watch the storm coverage on TV, I'm struck

by how strange this is—the whole family gathered together, everyone getting along . . . It feels peaceful, even while there's a tropical storm raging outside. Last year during Hurricane Randy, I was terrified, but that's when Mom and I lived in our apartment with no hurricane shutters. Scott and Tanya's house is old, but Tanya keeps talking about how it has a new roof and how it even has impact-resistant glass on all the windows, the bonus being that we can look outside and actually see the storm.

Tropical Storm Victoria is moving fast. That's what they keep saying on the news, and compared to Hurricane Randy, it's a baby, but they're still saying how dangerous it is and how everyone should take it seriously. Here in Ocean Point, we're not in its direct path, but we're still getting the kind of wind gusts that could knock out power lines and blow down trees. It's pretty amazing, actually, to look out the window and see the rain sheeting sideways, the palm fronds blowing at right angles.

"What we need is popcorn," says Tanya, "but I'm too lazy to get up."

I jump up, wanting to be useful. "I'll make it."

Tanya turns to Celeste. "See how helpful she is?"

Celeste sniffs. "Why is it okay for you to be lazy and not me?"

Scott laughs. "She's got a point."

In the kitchen, the wind sounds louder, but as soon as the popcorn starts popping, I'm able to tune it out. Three minutes, the directions said, and I'm standing close to make sure it doesn't burn.

Over the blare of the TV, I hear Scott say something that makes Tanya laugh. Is he only an asshole when it comes to Mom?

The popcorn's almost done. A few more seconds and—

Whoosh. The house seems to deflate as the power goes out. Suddenly, I'm standing in near darkness, and the only sound is the howling wind of the storm.

"Layla!" Tanya calls from the family room. "Grab the flashlight! It's on the counter."

I look around in the dim light until I spot a silver flashlight sitting by a jug of water. I grab it, turn it on. Nothing.

"Did you find it?" Tanya calls.

"It's not working," I call back.

"Shit." This from Scott.

I back against the counter as Scott comes barreling into the kitchen with Tanya right behind him. He takes the flashlight from me, flips the switch a few times. Still nothing. He turns to Tanya. "Tell me you got batteries."

She points. "They're in the drawer."

He opens it, starts rummaging around. "I don't see any."

"They should be in there."

"Well, they're not."

"Are you sure?"

"AAs, Cs, and nine-volts. No D batteries." He slams the drawer shut. "Didn't you stock up?"

"I thought we had plenty."

"Well, you thought wrong. How long have we known about this hurricane? A week? And you didn't think to get more batteries? What is wrong with you?"

"It's not—"

"I'll tell you what's wrong." He jabs a finger at her face. "It's that goddamn sister of yours. For the past week, you've had your head up your ass."

"That's not true!"

"Then where are the batteries? Where are the lanterns?"

"In the garage," says Tanya. "The lanterns are in the garage."

"Where we can't find them because it's too goddamn dark and we don't have a flashlight," says Scott.

I almost point out that we all have flashlights on our phones, but I don't think Scott would see it as me being helpful.

Tanya is amazingly calm as she points to where I'm standing. "Candles are in that drawer, Layla. Right behind you."

Relieved to have something to do other than watch Scott yell at her, I turn and start rummaging through the drawer.

"It's always like this," Scott says. "Shauna has a problem, and you drop everything to deal with it."

"I haven't dropped anything," says Tanya.

"No? Then what do you call no batteries during a hurricane?"

The drawer I'm searching is full of junk, but I don't see any candles. Do I interrupt to tell them?

"First of all . . ." Tanya takes a breath. "It's not a hurricane. It's a tropical storm. And second of all, you're saying I drop everything to deal with Shauna, but you're the one who chose to be in the public eye."

"What's that supposed to mean?" His voice is low, dangerous. If I were Tanya, I'd back off.

"It means, if you weren't running for mayor, Shauna's problems wouldn't be an issue."

He barks a laugh. "So it's my fault we have to pay for your sister's rehab? It's my fault we have to take in her stray?"

My back stiffens. Is that how they see me? The whole time they've been arguing, I've been rummaging through the drawer, but now I shut it. Carefully. Quietly. And I turn.

Both of them are looking at me.

And all I want is to disappear.

"There's no candles," I say.

"Are you kidding me?" Scott hurls the flashlight into the sink where it lands with a crash.

For a second, no one moves. Then Tanya says, "Jesus, Scott."

I turn to go.

"Layla, wait," says Tanya.

But I'm already slinking away.

Like a stray.

I creep upstairs, Scott and Tanya's argument fading behind me. When I get to the third floor, I can't hear them at all, but the storm is louder up here. Spookier, especially with the lights out and the floorboards creaking under my feet.

I don't want to sit by myself in my room in near darkness, so instead I fold myself into the third-floor window seat. Here I can watch the storm, and maybe it will distract me from thinking because right now I really don't want to think.

"*Look at where your feet are.*" That's what James would say. "*Right now you're safe. Right now you have everything you need.*"

The storm's hitting hard now, rain coming down in huge sheets and slapping the window with the force of a bug splattering a windshield. The rush of the storm is like white noise turned up to maximum volume, punctuated by groaning whooshes and teakettle whines. I hug my knees and watch the trees bow under the storm's force while my own quiet breath fogs the window. This slab of glass is all that's protecting me, and I feel safe, yeah, but I'm also feeling very small.

Small and alone.

I want to call Morgan, but what do I say to her? How do I break the ice? And what if she doesn't answer? What if she's deep in conversation with Gabriel? Gabriel, who's probably sitting on his bunk at the homeless shelter hoping his roof doesn't blow off. I send him a text.

Some storm, huh? You doing ok?

So far so good. U?

Power's out, but yeah . . .

Then my phone rings, and I think it's Gabriel until I see there's no name attached to the number. I answer it.

"Hello?"

"Hey, it's Felix."

Felix? My heart starts pounding so hard I can feel it in my throat. Why is he calling me, and how did he get my number? "Oh, hey," I manage to say.

"So what do you think of this storm?" he asks.

Is that why he's calling? To talk about the storm? Maybe he's leading up to something else. Maybe he's actually into me. All these thoughts run through my head in an instant while my heart continues to pound.

"It's pretty wild," I say, marveling at how normal I sound. "Our power went out."

"Bummer. You think we'll have school tomorrow?"

"The storm's supposed to be over by this afternoon, so yeah. Probably." Hopefully. So I can see him. I picture what he's doing right now. Maybe he's lounging around in pajama pants. Maybe he's fresh out the shower and his hair is still wet.

"That's what I think too," he says. "Stupid Randy." He's talking about last year's hurricane, how it closed schools for, like, a week and all the parents were pissed. "I still haven't finished my poem," he says. "What about you?"

"Not yet, but it's sort of in my head."

"Really?"

"That sounded weird, didn't it?"

"Not really, coming from you."

I'm not sure how to take that.

"I hate to ask this," he says, "but maybe you can help me finish mine? I still don't get this whole iambic pentameter thing."

My heart sinks. This is the reason he called, and why did I let myself hope for anything else?

"If I don't get at least a B on it, I'll get a D for the semester, and if I get a D for the semester, Coach is going to bench me, and if Coach benches me—"

"That's a lot of ifs," I say.

"Yeah, well, you know what they say . . . Ifs make the world go round."

"Do they actually say that?"

"Of course they do. Ask anyone."

I laugh. "What have you got so far?"

"Heh, that's the thing. I have those two lines you helped me with."

A beat of silence while I digest this. "You aren't seriously asking me to write your whole poem, are you?"

"Hey, would you?"

I don't say anything.

"Come on, Layla. You know you want to help me."

"Help you, yeah. But . . ."

"Did I mention how kind you are? How kind and beautiful and smart?"

"Okay, you can stop with the flattery."

"It's not flattery if it's true."

I know, for a fact, he doesn't think I'm beautiful, but that doesn't mean he thinks I'm ugly. The me in the window is hazy, just a shadow of who I am, but maybe, just maybe, there's something there to like.

"Fine," I say. "Just give me a minute to think."

It takes me about ten minutes to "help" him get the required fourteen lines, me dictating while he jots it down. I even put a rhyming scheme on it that turns it into a Shakespearean sonnet. I make him read it back so I can check the meter. The poem is kind of funny and definitely juvenile, but technically it works, and somehow it suits him.

"Now all you have to do is think of a title," I say.

"Yeah, no problem."

At least he's doing that much. And now that he's got his poem, I expect the next words out of his mouth to end the conversation.

"So let me ask you something," he says.

"Okay."

"How close are you to Celeste?"

"Uh, not very?"

"Does she ever talk about my brother?"

"What do you mean?"

"Does she ever talk bad? Does she complain about him?"

"Not that I can think of."

"Oh." He sounds disappointed.

And then it hits me. He's into Celeste. He wants to know if he has a chance with her.

"She can be kind of a bitch," I say.

"Wow."

I try to backpedal. "All I meant was, she can be hard to deal with."

I try to think of what to say after that, but I'm distracted by a bright light piercing my reflection. I turn to see Celeste hovering above me with a halogen lamp in her hand. Did she hear me call her a bitch? The glow from the lantern makes her face look eerie.

"For your room," she says, setting the lamp on the window seat beside me.

"Did you say something?" Felix asks.

I almost tell him it was Celeste who spoke, but she's already padding down the hallway, back the way she came.

"No. I didn't say anything."

"I should probably go," he says.

And I knew this was coming, but I still feel used. "Yeah, me too. I need to write my poem."

"Good luck," he says. "Not that you need it."

Yeah, because good luck follows me around.

Once he hangs up, my heart is still pounding. If only I were prettier, cooler, more popular. If only I hadn't sounded like a bitch, throwing my cousin under the bus.

If only I lived here permanently, maybe I'd have a chance.

But that's a lot of ifs.

I lean closer to the window, trying to see if there's something in my reflection to like, but the glow of Celeste's lamp is too bright. It's hard to see anything except the surging storm on the other side.

CHAPTER 18

And after that she turns and walks away.
Since after that there's nothing left to say.
—from "Aftershock" by L.F.

The power came back on some time during the night. Now the sun is shining bright, and Celeste and I are in the kitchen grabbing breakfast before Tanya drives us to school.

"I can't believe it's actually open," Celeste groans. "Why couldn't they just give us the whole week off for Thanksgiving?"

I eat my Lucky Charms and don't say anything because, actually, I have good reasons for wanting school to be open. First of all, Mom gets transferred to Serenity Solace today, and school gives me an excuse to not go with Tanya to get her settled. Not that I don't want to see my mom, but I've come to realize that seeing her will only make me worry. Because what if I find out she's one of those people Gabriel talked about who doesn't *want* to go to rehab? What if she freaks out? It's better if I don't know, so by the time I *do* visit her, she'll have some recovery under her belt.

Also, I need to talk to Morgan, like, face-to-face. I know I overreacted when she said it was a good thing Mom overdosed, since it got her into rehab. We haven't talked or even texted since then, and I need to tell her I'm not mad at her. Also, I realized this morning that I don't even know when the *Grease* tryouts are. That's how self-absorbed I've been. I can't tell her about living at the shelter, but I'm determined to repair things between us. I keep telling myself: So what if Gabriel likes her? He's a heroin addict. And so what if her prayers feel like pity? I know she means well.

And then, of course, there's Felix, who I still want to see, even though I know he likes Celeste. Today I'm wearing faded cutoffs and a Banana Republic T-shirt. The T-shirt is tight enough that it actually gives me a shape, and I know Felix only called last night to get help with his assignment, but he could *grow* to like me, right?

By the time I've thought all this out, I'm almost done with my Lucky Charms, and I'm so intent on spooning up the last soggy marshmallows that I don't notice Tanya has come into the kitchen until she clears her throat.

I look up. Her mouth is set in a tight line, and I know something's wrong.

Even Celeste notices and puts away her phone. "What happened?"

"Nothing. Just a slight change of plans."

Tanya's looking at me as she says this, and I know it's about Mom. My heart sinks. "Tell me."

"Well . . ." She takes her time sitting at the table. "I just got off the phone with Serenity Solace, and apparently their sewage is backed up. I guess the storm caused some flooding? Anyway, they can't take new patients until it's fixed."

"So what does that mean?" I ask. "What happens to Mom?"

"Well, that's the thing." Tanya kind of laughs. "She'll have to stay here for a few days."

Her and Scott in the same house? That's a disaster waiting to happen. "Can't she stay at the hospital?" I ask.

Tanya shakes her head. "The hospital's releasing her at noon, and no other rehabs can take her on such short notice."

"What about Uncle Scott? Does he know?"

"He does," says Tanya.

"Don't tell me Dad's fine with her coming here," says Celeste.

Tanya keeps silent, but I know what she *wants* to say—that Scott *has* to be fine with it. Because he's running for mayor, and that means he can't put her out on the street.

"Look on the bright side," says Tanya. "This means she'll be here for Thanksgiving."

Celeste snorts. "What could go wrong?"

At that moment, Scott walks into the kitchen. He doesn't look at any of us as he grabs a mug from the cupboard. While he gets his coffee, I creep to the dishwasher and put my bowl inside. I try to slip away without him noticing me, but when I turn around, I almost run into him.

"If your mom knows what's good for her," he says, "she'll keep out of my way."

And then he walks out.

And I can breathe, but just barely.

Tanya gives a nervous laugh. "Don't mind him. He hasn't had his coffee yet."

As if all Scott needs is a shot of caffeine and everything will be fine.

Celeste whispers to me as she brushes past, "This is going to be fun."

o o o

You'd never know by looking at the crayon-blue sky that we just had a tropical storm, but the streets and neighborhoods we pass on the way to school tell the story. Branches and leaves litter the flooded streets—there's even a few trees down—and cops are directing traffic where some of the stoplights are out. With all the tension about Mom, the ride is uncomfortably quiet. Finally, Tanya pulls up in front of the school.

Joshua is waiting for Celeste on the sidewalk, and as soon as she exits the car, he lassos her arm. She tries to shrug him off. "Don't."

"Come on. We need to talk."

"We talked last night. I'm sick of talking."

If Felix were around, he'd be glad to hear them arguing, and just as I'm thinking this, there he is, stepping out of the crowd. Today he's wearing a white T-shirt and blue baseball cap turned backward. He's smiling as he comes right toward me.

My own smile feels huge. "Hey," I say. "Did you think of a title for your poem?"

"Huh?" His smile wavers, and I realize he wasn't smiling at me. He was staring at Celeste, who's right behind me, and I'm literally standing in her shadow.

Joshua pulls Celeste away from the curb, and Felix stops beside me to watch them. His cologne smells good, but it's too strong. I try to think of something to say, something to talk about other than the stupid poem, but my brain doesn't seem to be working.

Joshua and Celeste stand face-to-face, inches apart. Joshua is pleading and gesturing. Celeste is frowning and shaking her head.

"My brother's such an asshole," Felix mumbles.

"What'd he do?"

Without answering, he brushes past me. Did he not hear me?

Suddenly all I want to do is find Morgan. Morgan will tell me I'm better than him. She'll tell me he isn't worth it. I weave my way through the crowd, and my foot snags on a fallen branch. Suddenly, I'm pitching headfirst, my arms flailing for balance. I manage not to fall, but my cheeks are on fire. I look around to see who might have seen—

And that's when I see the tree.

The banyan tree lying on its side, its giant roots splayed toward the sky like a snarl of dead wires.

I stare at the wreckage, almost crying, which is stupid, but how many times did I get comfort from this tree? It showed me a world where life thrives without worrying about wearing the right clothes or saying the right thing or being the right person. And now it's gone. Wrecked. Dead.

Someone has already roped off the area with yellow caution tape. I see Gabriel and Morgan on the bench, and God, they're holding hands. I start to walk the other way, but now they've seen me, and now they're coming toward me.

No longer holding hands, but I saw.

Morgan manages to look sympathetic as she wraps me in a hug. "Are you okay? I knew you'd take it hard."

She's talking about the tree, not them. I extract myself from her hold and look at my feet. My brand-new Coach sandals are covered in wet leaves and dirt, and the Band-Aid over my blister is soaked through with blood. "It doesn't matter," I say.

"Yeah, it does. You loved that tree."

My eyes bounce between her and Gabriel, and I can't keep the pain out of my voice. "So you guys are together now?"

When they exchange a look, a storm of jealousy rips through me.

Gabriel takes a step back. "I'll, uh . . . let you guys talk."

Morgan takes my arm and turns me around so I'm not facing the fallen tree. "You're upset," she says.

I can barely look at her. "Wouldn't you be?"

"You said you didn't like him."

I don't answer. Because it's true. I did say that.

"And if it makes you feel better—"

"How can you fall for a drug addict?"

She gives me a strange look. "Because I don't judge people for their past mistakes."

Which is such bullshit. Everyone judges.

"And he doesn't do it anymore," she says.

"But he could," I say. "That's why they call it addiction."

"Layla, I think you're blaming him for what your mom did."

"Is that what I'm doing?"

"It seems like it."

"And suddenly you're an expert?"

"No, I just . . . see you acting weird."

"Weird how?"

"You're like a different person sometimes."

"Whatever, Morgan." I start to walk away.

"At least he's honest," she calls.

My heart is pounding as I turn back. "What's that supposed to mean?"

"He told me about the shelter."

Shit.

"He told me everything."

After he promised he wouldn't. "Morgan . . ."

"What?"

It's hard to unstick my tongue. It's even harder to look at her. "I was afraid of what you'd think."

"About the shelter?" She waves a hand. "I don't care where someone lives."

"Tell that to Darla Whitman."

Morgan drops her eyes. "That was a long time ago."

"Not that long."

"And if I remember right, you abandoned her too."

"Is that supposed to make me feel better?"

She shakes her head. "Why am I letting you sidetrack me? We're talking about Gabriel here, not you."

"So what you're saying is, I'm not important."

"Don't put words in my mouth."

"But you think I'm pathetic."

"I never said that! And I don't know where this is coming from!"

I stare at her confused face, and for a second, I'm just as confused as she is.

And then it hits me. She doesn't know. Gabriel told her about the shelter, and I assumed that meant he told her about *me* living at the shelter. But he didn't. He told her about himself, about his own circumstances. My secret is still safe.

"It's nothing," I say. "Forget it."

"I don't think you're pathetic, Layla. Why would you say that?"

"I don't know."

"Oh my God, you're so full of shit."

"Whatever. Can we please talk about something else?"

"I don't want to talk about something else. I want to know why you're lying."

I throw my head back and groan at the sky. "God, Morgan, stop!"

"What am I doing?"

"You're being a bitch!"

She lowers her voice. "And you wonder why people don't like you."

"Yeah, well . . ."

"Look in the mirror, Layla."

My eyes tear up because I know she's right. No matter where I live, no matter what I wear, I'm still a piece of crap. I jab my finger at her face. "Fuck you, Morgan."

Startled, she blinks, and I'm about to tell her I'm sorry—I

didn't mean it. But I don't get a chance before she points a shaking finger at my face.

"No," she says. "Fuck you."

Her words are barely a whisper, but they cut to the bone. Before I can think to say anything, she turns and walks away.

"Morgan!"

She keeps walking, and I know I should go after her—I should tell her about the shelter, about everything I've been hiding from her—but I'm too jealous, too afraid, too ashamed.

Suddenly, Josephine appears from the crowd and links arms with her. I watch them walking arm in arm—their heads close together, Morgan smiling at something Josephine says—and I knew this was coming, but it still hurts to lose your best friend.

Especially when you brought it on yourself.

° ° °

My morning classes pass in a blur. Spanish, history, trig, and art. Then it's time for lunch, and since I don't want to see Morgan or Gabriel, I hide out in the bathroom and torture myself by wondering what they're doing. Maybe they're in the cafeteria talking about me, Gabriel saying how I seem cool, but obviously I have issues, and Morgan agreeing and saying how this past year has been hard on me, what with my mom and everything, but she's trying to be understanding, even though it's hard because I've been such a bitch.

Or maybe they're not talking about me at all. Maybe they're off somewhere making out.

Right after lunch, I have English, where at least I'll get to see Felix, but after this morning, I'm wondering if he'll even acknowledge me.

He's already there with his laptop open when I sit down next to him.

"Hey, I thought of a title," he says.

"Yeah?"

"I'm calling it 'I'm the Bard.' You know, because Shakespeare's known as the Bard?"

"Oh."

"You don't like it?"

"It's fine, but maybe you should call it 'Layla's the Bard.'"

"Heh, good one."

The bell rings, and Mrs. Chapman rises from her desk and announces that we all should have turned our poems in to Google Classroom, and if we haven't, she'll give us until the end of the day until they're considered late. "You can thank Victoria for that bit of mercy," she says. Victoria being the name of the tropical storm. A few kids laugh.

"And since it's the day before Thanksgiving break," she says, "I thought we'd do something fun."

"You're letting us go home?" Felix asks.

Mrs. Chapman smiles. "Not quite. I'm going to take volunteers to read their poems aloud, and if we don't have volunteers, then we'll go right into our study of the metaphysical poets."

A few groans from the class, which Mrs. Chapman ignores.

"So who wants to go first?"

I like the way my "Sonnet of the Storm" turned out, but there's no way I'm reading it in front of the class.

Felix's hand shoots up, and my stomach tenses. *Please don't read it aloud.*

Mrs. Chapman points at him. "You had a question, Felix?"

"I want to read my poem."

His poem, not mine. So it doesn't matter if no one likes it. They won't know it was me.

"Oh." She blinks. "Of course. You can read it from your desk. Or, if you're feeling particularly brave, you can stand in front of the class."

"I'm feeling brave," he says, bringing his laptop to the front. "It's called 'I'm the Bard.'"

Mrs. Chapman nods. "Whenever you're ready."

With a theatrical clearing of his throat, he begins:

There was a day when all was going fine,
When all I had to do was eat and sleep,
A day where nothing much could make me
whine,
A day where nothing much could make me weep.
But then I went to English and I viewed
A teacher standing stiff and frowning hard.
(I didn't mean that last line to sound lewd,
But sometimes words slip out. I blame the Bard.)
This teacher, though her kindness is well known
Did wreck my day by giving me a chore
To write a poem in meter set in stone
That leaves the listener always wanting more.
So in my humble home I cracked a beer
And wrote this wondrous poem for all to hear.

Throughout the reading, kids are cracking up, and Felix is hamming it up with sweeping hand gestures and exaggerated facial expressions. When he's done reading, everyone claps, a few people whistle, and Felix takes a bow.

"Thank you, Felix," says Mrs. Chapman. "I'm sure you worked very hard on that."

I'm clapping too, but I'm kind of in shock because, wow, they really liked it, and how did that happen? At the same time,

I'm swelling with pride, and as Felix flops into his chair, I look over at him, hoping he'll make eye contact.

"Do we have another volunteer?" asks Mrs. Chapman.

No response.

"Come on," says Mrs. Chapman. "I know some of you want to share your poems."

Finally, a hand goes up and she points. "Okay, Kieran. You're up."

As Kieran's making her way to the front of the class, my phone vibrates from my pocket. I fish it out. A text from Felix!

Think she'll give me an A?

I stare at the words. Not even a thank you?

Meanwhile, Kieran's reading her poem in a breathy whisper.

When last you spoke to me and ruined my life
I felt my heart would burst with pain and
strife . . .

I can feel Felix's eyes on me, so I look over, and he lifts his brows as if to say: *Well?*

I read the text again and think about how pathetic I am. All he has to do is flirt with me, and *poof!* I do what he wants.

Well, screw that.

Sure. Unless she hates your
crappy title.

My finger hovers over the *send* button, but before pressing it, I delete the second sentence. No sense in cutting off one of the few friends I have left.

CHAPTER 19

That was me,
Cupping sand between small hands.
My chest was flat, like my hair,
Bangs cut like crooked gift wrap
And pasted to my forehead.
—from "William Blake" by L.F.

Thank God the school day's over, but it's not like going back to Scott and Tanya's will be any better. That's because Mom's there. And yes, I want to see her—I want to make sure she's okay—but right now, after the day I've had? I don't think I can handle anything else going wrong.

"So your mom's all settled in," says Tanya, as soon as Celeste and I are in the car. "I put her in the other bedroom on the third floor."

"Has Dad seen her?" Celeste asks.

"I don't expect him home till later," says Tanya.

"How does she seem?" I ask.

"Fine. A little sad, but that's to be expected."

When we get to the house, Mom is sitting by the pool out back, her bare feet dangling in the water, which is littered with debris from the storm. Tanya leaves me alone to talk to her. At first, I just stand in the living room, watching her through the sliding-glass door. She's sitting very still, staring at nothing, almost like she's in a trance, which is how she was sitting when I caught her staring at Grandpa's empty pill bottle the morning I found his body.

Gently, I took it from her hand. Oxycodone. The one he took for pain. A cold thought whispered in my ear.

"It was already empty," Mom said, as if she knew what I was thinking. "I was planning to pick up his refill today."

I nodded, wanting to believe her, and any doubts I had were later dispelled when the medical examiner said Grandpa died due to complications from his blood disease. Basically, his heart gave out.

Remembering how we comforted each other that morning makes me want to hug her. I open the sliding-glass door and step outside.

"Hey, Mom."

She looks up and smiles. A sad one, but I'll take it. "How you doing, kiddo?"

She hasn't called me that in a long time. "Good. What about you?"

"Better."

"Really?"

"Yeah."

Relieved, I slip off my shoes and sit beside her. The water is warm when I dip my feet in.

"So how is it?" she asks.

She means living here. "Good."

"Scott's not being a dick?"

"No."

"Small miracles, huh?"

She's never talked to me about miracles, although I know it's a big topic in AA. *You are a miracle*, and all that.

I stir my feet in the water. "Did Aunt Tanya tell you what he said?"

"About keeping out of his way?" She nods.

"Are you going to do it?"

"Of course. The last thing I want is to screw things up for you."

I can tell she means it, but saying and doing are two different things.

Mom plucks a twig floating on the water and tosses it aside. "Tanya told me she got you a phone, a bunch of new clothes."

"Yeah."

"You know I wish I could do those things for you, right?"

"I know, Mom."

"And I wish . . ." She closes her eyes.

I wait for her to finish her thought, but she doesn't.

"Hey, Mom?"

"Yeah?"

"Are you happy about going to rehab?"

"Happy?" She kind of laughs. "I wouldn't say that."

"What I mean is, do you *want* to go to rehab?"

"Sure, but I think the place they're sending me to is a crock."

I hold back a sigh. "Why would you say that?"

"Because it's one of those fancy-pants places. You know that, right?"

"I know it's expensive."

"Which means it has to be good, according to Tanya."

"It *is* good. Did you look at their website?"

"I did, and it looks really snobby."

"But you have to go."

"I know that."

"You have to *want* to go."

"Who says?"

I'm gripping the edge of the pool. "Tell me you're not going to ruin this."

"I'm not going to ruin this, okay?"

"Okay."

We sit in silence. A gnat flies between us. Mom bats it away.

She looks over. "So everything's fine?"

I nod.

"I ask because you look a little stressed."

I shrug.

"Because of me?" she asks.

Of course because of you! That's what I want to say, but I've already burned too many bridges today. And to be honest, it's not just her.

Even though it all traces back to her.

"No," I say. "It's stuff at school."

"What stuff?"

"Nothing you need to worry about."

"Layla, I'm your mom. It's my job to worry."

She's not going to let this go. "Fine," I say. "Morgan and I are fighting."

Her brow furrows. "About what?"

I don't answer. Answering would be way too complicated. And really, it's none of her business.

"About me?" she asks.

"No, Mom."

She looks doubtful, and I don't blame her. I didn't sound very convincing.

"I don't want to talk about it," I say.

She stares at the water, all the debris from the storm floating on top. "Since your grandpa died, I haven't been a very good mom."

I don't say anything.

"But I'm trying to do better."

"I know."

"Will you please just talk to me?"

"Why? It's not like you can help."

"You don't know that."

Again I keep quiet.

"Whatever you and Morgan are fighting about, I'm sure it will work out. Have you tried talking to her?"

"Of course I've tried talking to her."

"Well, maybe you should try again."

"Wow, that's great advice, Mom."

She ignores my sarcasm. "Sometimes when you think you're communicating, the conversation is actually one-sided, so it's important to—"

"Did you learn that in detox?"

"I learned it in life."

I pull my feet out of the water. "Stop, okay?"

"I'm just trying to—"

"I know. But stop trying to be a good mom."

She flinches like I've slapped her. I try to take her hand, but she pulls away.

"I don't blame you for hating me," she says.

"I don't hate you."

"It's okay if you do."

"I said I don't hate you, so please stop feeling sorry for yourself."

"I'm not," she says. But she's sulking.

I hold back a sigh.

"I know I'm not a good mom," she says.

"Christ!" I stand up because I can't sit here anymore. "This is exactly what I'm talking about!"

She squints up at me with teary eyes. "I'm sorry, okay? I'm sorry for being a horrible mother."

Another apology, and God, I'm sick of hearing it. "If you want to be a good mom," I say, "you might try getting your act together."

That one hits home. I can tell because her mouth is open, but no words come out.

Which is fine with me because I'm already stomping toward the house. The sliding-glass door is heavy enough that I can't slam it, even though I want to. And when I'm on the other side—when I see her out there by herself—I think I should feel guilty, but I don't.

Because what I said is true. She needs to get her act together and stop feeling sorry for herself. She needs to know she's running out of chances.

○ ○ ○

Some time while I was outside, Scott came home, so I head up to my room to keep out of his way. I hope Mom will do the same when she's done moping outside.

Once I get to the third floor, I'm surprised to see Celeste huddled in the window seat, her head resting against the glass. It's just getting dark, but she's dressed for bed in a T-shirt and pajama shorts. She doesn't hear me at first, but when the floorboards creak under my feet, she lifts her head, and her eyes are filled with tears.

I stop, kind of shocked. Because she's not the type of person who cries. Or at least I didn't think she was.

"What do you want?" she asks.

"Nothing."

"Good." She turns back to the window. Her reflection in the glass makes it seem like there are two girls sitting there. One real and one ghostlike.

"Are you okay?"

"Don't act like you care, Layla."

"I do care."

"Well, do me a favor and go away."

"Did something happen?"

"Does it matter?" She turns to face me, tears still wet on her face. "Why are you so interested in me all of a sudden?"

"I'm not. I mean, I am. I always was."

"Because I'm such a nice person?"

I open my mouth to say something, but nothing comes out.

"Yeah, that's what I thought," she says.

"Maybe if you talked to someone . . ."

"Like you?"

"I'll listen."

She makes a face. "I think you have enough problems, don't you?"

Does she work at being mean? I think she does.

"I guess you're right," I say, and before she can insult me further, I take off walking.

She calls after me. "I heard when you called me a bitch."

That stops me. I turn around, start to apologize, but she interrupts me.

"It's not like it isn't true. Why do you think I don't have friends?"

She has friends, doesn't she? I always see her hanging out with Joshua—and other guys—but now that I think about it, I can't remember seeing her with any female friends.

"My mom says I'm spoiled. She says I should be more like you."

"Yeah, well, I'd be spoiled too, if I lived here."

"You do live here."

"You know what I mean."

"Yeah." She rests her head against the window. "Sometimes I think she hates me."

"She doesn't hate you."

"Easy for you to say. She's actually nice to you."

"Only because I'm a guest."

"No. Because you're good."

I think of what happened with Morgan today. What I said to her. And what I said to Mom. "I'm not good, Celeste."

"Better than me."

I step closer. "You do remember I called you a bitch, right?"

That gets her to smile. Faint, but still . . .

"At least your mom likes you," she says.

I almost laugh. "If we're comparing dysfunctional moms, I'm pretty sure I have you beat."

"Yeah, I guess you have a point."

I think of how Mom called me *kiddo* today, how normal that felt, even though she hasn't called me that in a long time.

"She's had a hard life," I say.

"I know."

"After Grandpa died, she went a little crazy."

"Crazy seems to run in the family."

"Grandpa wasn't crazy. He had PTSD from fighting a war, but—"

"I'm not talking about Grandpa. I'm talking about my dad."

"Oh."

"Who's that guy in the story who drinks the potion and turns into a monster?"

"Dr. Jekyll and Mr. Hyde?"

"Right. My dad's like that. Great out in public, but behind closed doors, watch out. Any second he might explode. You're lucky you haven't seen that side of him."

"I've seen it. Believe me."

"You haven't seen anything."

"I've seen the way he treats my mom."

She turns back to the window. "You're not hearing what I'm saying."

"Then what are you saying?"

"I'm not supposed to talk about it."

"Then how am I supposed to understand?"

She sighs and turns back to me. "Remember when I had that broken arm?"

At her eighth birthday party. I nod. "You fell off your bike."

"Well, that was the cover story."

"So, you're saying your dad . . ."

"Broke my arm, yeah."

My mouth drops open. "Celeste, I had no idea."

"Why would you? We never told anyone."

"Does he still . . .?"

"Abuse me?" She shakes her head. "After the broken-arm incident, Mom made him go to anger management classes. He also sees a therapist, like, every week. But he's still majorly FUBAR."

She means "Effed Up Beyond All Recognition," a phrase Grandpa taught us from his days in the army.

"Celeste, if I'd known . . ."

"Don't worry about it, okay? I shouldn't have brought it up."

"I'm glad you did."

"Why? So we can bond?"

"No. So I don't think you're a bitch."

She snorts a laugh. "I should probably thank you."

"For what?"

"For getting me out of myself."

I want to ask why she was crying, but I don't want her to yell at me.

"Hey," she says. "You want to get high?"

"What? No!"

"Don't freak out. It's just medical marijuana."

"As in, you got it from a doctor?"

"I got it from someone. Who got it from a doctor."

"In other words, you got it from a drug dealer. I don't do drugs, Celeste."

"Fine. I'll do it by myself."

"Isn't marijuana a depressant?"

"Oh my God, you sound like a textbook. It helps relax me, okay?"

"But aren't you afraid of getting addicted?"

"It's not like it's heroin. Doctors prescribe it to help people."

"To help people in pain," I say.

"You don't think you're in pain?"

"Not that kind."

She shrugs. "I'm not going to pressure you. I was just offering it as a friend."

"You said you don't have friends."

"Well, maybe I was wrong."

Which kind of makes me feel good—that she considers me a friend. Or potentially a friend.

"Will you at least keep me company?" she asks. "Sometimes I get paranoid if I do it alone."

"Yay, paranoia. You realize you're not helping your case."

Her face brightens. "So you're saying you will?"

"I didn't say that."

"But you're coming to my room."

"To keep you company."

"Right." She smiles. "Come on."

o o o

I let Celeste talk me into it. Because she wants me to. Because I've never done it before. Because right now I really need a friend.

And bonus—medical marijuana comes in the form of chocolate.

Like a candy bar, I swear. She breaks off a chunk and offers it. "Just a few bites is all it takes."

It even tastes like real chocolate. We're sitting cross-legged on her bed, waiting to feel the effects. "Are you sure we ate enough?" I ask.

"For now. See how it affects you. Then you can take more."

I fidget. "I don't think it's affecting me."

"It will."

"This is crazy."

"No, this is normal. I can't believe you've never gotten high. Have you ever drank?"

"Once. Morgan and I shared a beer. It wasn't that good."

She bursts out laughing, which maybe I should be offended by, but deep in my gut, I feel something stirring. A tingling that wants to burst forth.

Celeste is still giggling.

"What's so funny?"

"You."

"Why me?"

"You can't split a beer with someone and expect to get drunk."

"Who said I wanted to get drunk?"

"Why else would you drink?"

"To taste it."

"You don't drink to taste it. You drink to feel it." She frowns. "Or not to feel anything."

For some reason, that strikes me as incredibly deep. I look around her room. "Do you have a pen?"

"Why do you need a pen?"

"What you just said—I want to write it down."

"Oh my God, you're such a dork." Celeste opens the drawer on her nightstand and rummages around. "No pen," she says, "but I found some peach schnapps."

"Why do you have peach schnapps in your nightstand drawer?"

"Because it's a good hiding place."

"No, it's not."

"You're right. I have much better ones." She opens the bottle, takes a drink. "Want some?"

"No, thanks."

"You sure? It's good."

"I thought you didn't drink it for the taste."

"I don't, but it helps."

She's rummaging around in a dresser drawer now, and I hear what sounds like a plastic grocery bag.

"What's that?" I ask.

"Munchies."

"Another hiding place?"

"Not my best one. But look!" She holds up a pen.

I have a vague recollection of wanting a pen, but now I don't remember why.

She tosses it to me, and I watch it come toward me in slow motion. I watch as it bounces off my lap.

"Wait. I wasn't ready."

She snickers. "You want me to do it again?"

Laughter bubbles inside me. Laughter I can't stop. We stare at each other laughing. Cracking up. Tears coming out of our eyes. And it feels good. To laugh. To let go. To not care.

"You should see your face," she says.

"You should see yours."

We point at each other and laugh some more while the room and everything in it fades to the background like a hazy dream. Right now, life is good because all I am is this moment where nothing is wrong, and nothing can *be* wrong because nothing else exists . . .

THUD THUD THUD

Until there's a knock on the door.

"Layla?"

Mom's voice—shit! And now I'm in a dream where I can't move. I try to force myself awake, but everything feels slowed down, and it's hard to get my thoughts straight.

Another knock. "Celeste? Is Layla in there?"

Celeste clutches her own throat to stop herself from laughing. "No, Aunt Shauna. I haven't seen her."

"You sure? I thought I heard her."

"Yes, I'm sure."

We wait. I strain my ears, willing her to walk away. She can't see me like this. She can't know.

Both of us are quiet, listening to her receding footsteps.

"I think we fooled her," Celeste whispers.

"This isn't funny."

"It kind of is."

But it's not. It's so not. All my talk about Mom needing to get her act together, and here I am getting high.

"She can't know what we're doing," I say.

"You think I'm going to tell?"

"But what if she knows?"

"That's you being paranoid."

"I don't think so."

"Believe me. I know what I'm talking about. When this wears off, you're going to realize everything you're afraid of right now is just an illusion. And speaking of illusions . . ." She picks up the chocolate from her bed and offers it to me. "You want another piece?"

She's smiling as she says it, so I know she's kidding, but I still shake my head. "I don't like this feeling."

"Yeah, neither do I." She tosses the chocolate onto her bed. "Remind me not to invite you next time I get high."

CHAPTER 20

I'm caught between the flow,
And water's creeping up
To drown me,
And my cries could cut through stone.
—from "Drowning Girl," by L.F.

The rain is beating on the roof, and I'm scared, even though Mom tells me it's fine.

"No, it's not," I say. "It's so not."

Because we're back in our room at the homeless shelter, and I think this can't be real, but I look around and it is. Our tiny room with its metal bunk beds and dank smell of mold.

Look at where your feet are. That's what James would tell me. *Right now you're safe.*

But I'm not safe. My feet are planted on cracked tile while water drips from the ceiling onto my head.

Drip.

Wet and cold.

Drip drip.

The room shakes like we're having an earthquake, but it's not an earthquake, it's a hurricane. The wind is rattling the walls.

"Mom, I'm scared."

"Don't be," she says from the corner where she's putting on pantyhose for her interview. The pantyhose are ripped, but she doesn't seem to notice.

The rattling gets worse. Mom puts on her high heels and tries to walk, but it's like she's drunk, stumbling around.

Above me, the roof groans. Plaster falls around me, pelting my shoulders, striking my feet, and suddenly there's a great ripping sound, and I look up as the roof peels off like a scab, and the sky above is gray and wet and falling.

The wind takes my breath and slams me against the wall. "Mom!" I cry, looking for the door, but I can't find it, and water's creeping up, and the water's up to my waist, and Mom can't hear me. She can't hear me, even though I'm screaming as loud as I can, my mouth stretched open, water up to my chin, filling my mouth, making me choke. Spluttering for breath. Drowning.

o o o

I wake, gasping for air.

A dream. It was only a dream.

o o o

It's too early to get up, but it's hard to go back to sleep when your mind won't turn off. Grandpa had this trick for falling asleep where he'd count backward from a thousand. When he stayed with us for those two weeks before he died, he was always waking in the night, shouting and panting from his cot in the living room.

Nine hundred ninety-nine, nine hundred ninety-eight . . .

One time after his cries woke me, I sat with him on his cot and asked him how long he had to count before he fell asleep.

"It ain't about the number," he told me. "It's about forgetting."

"Forgetting the numbers?"

"No." He poked a finger at my temple. "Forgetting what's in your head."

Right now it's hard to forget what's in my head because today is Thanksgiving, the one-year anniversary of Grandpa's death.

Nine hundred ninety-seven . . .

And also, today I have to volunteer at the homeless shelter. The thought of walking through that gate . . .

Nine hundred ninety-six . . .

. . . and seeing all those people . . .

(slumped shoulders, proud but desperate faces)

The thought of smelling all those smells . . .

(mold and sweat and cigarettes)

All I want is to hide under the blanket until the day is over.

But I can't do that.

And yes, I'll get through this, and yes, it'll be over soon, but it's not like the rest of the day will be any better.

Nine hundred ninety-five . . .

Mom eating Thanksgiving dinner with Uncle Scott.

Nine hundred ninety-four . . .

Mom pissing him off just by breathing.

And what happens when she pisses him off?

Dr. Jekyll and Mr. Hyde.

I don't want to think about it, and I'm trying not to.

Nine hundred ninety-something . . .

But Grandpa's trick of counting backward isn't working.

So I throw off the covers and get out of bed and look at where my feet are.

Right now I'm safe.

o o o

Hunger drives me downstairs, and I'm surprised to see a light on in the kitchen. Whoever it is, they're trying to be quiet, but I still hear cupboards opening and closing, dishes clinking. It's probably Aunt Tanya getting a head start on Thanksgiving dinner. I walk in, intending to offer my help, but it's Mom standing there with a carton of eggs that she almost drops when she sees me.

"God, you scared me," she says. I'm about to apologize, but then I see the mess she's made. Flour and sugar on the counter, dirty dishes in the sink, every ingredient known to man cluttering the island. I used to tease her that she's the Jackson Pollock of cooking, but now it's not funny. If Scott sees this . . .

"Mom, what are you doing?"

"I couldn't sleep."

"So you decided to destroy their kitchen?"

"Very funny. I'm making my pumpkin cake."

She raps an egg against the edge of the mixing bowl. Too hard. The egg crumbles in her hand, dripping egg white down the side of the bowl. Before I can grab a paper towel, she's wiping her hand on the Ralph Lauren T-shirt she borrowed from Aunt Tanya.

Above us, the light fixtures rattle from someone walking around upstairs. And then the pipes clunk as whoever it is turns on the shower.

"We have to clean this up," I say.

"I will when I finish the cake. Now that you're up, do you want to make it together?"

"Come on, Mom. If Scott sees this . . ."

Her face falls. "Yeah, okay."

For a few minutes, neither of us speaks, me rinsing dishes and placing them in the dishwasher, her wiping up the spilled egg and putting away ingredients.

Upstairs, the water is still running, but it could turn off at any second.

I finish with the dishes and start sweeping the floor—all the flour and sugar she spilled. Meanwhile, she's wiping down the counters, but it seems like she's moving in slow motion, and when I look up from my sweeping, I catch her staring at me.

"What?" I say.

"Nothing."

"Just say it, Mom."

"I was looking for you last night."

I shrug like this is news to me. "I was around."

"I know." She steps closer. "I heard you in Celeste's room."

I keep sweeping, not daring to look up because I don't want her seeing the guilt on my face.

"What were you doing in there?" she asks.

"What do you mean?"

"Why were you hiding from me?"

"I wasn't hiding. I was avoiding."

She sighs. "Is it really that hard to be around me?"

Upstairs, the pipes squeak as the water turns off.

"Mom, we don't have time for this."

"I know you'd rather I wasn't here," she says. "I just thought . . ."

"What?"

"I thought we could talk before I go away."

"It's not like you're going to prison."

She sniffs. "It kind of seems that way."

"Right." It's hard not to roll my eyes. "Because swimming pools and private chef equals prison."

"You know I won't fit in."

I sweep the last of the flour into the dustpan and stand up. "You don't have to fit in, Mom. You just have to get sober."

"I am sober."

"Just like you were sober for thirty days and then decided to shoot heroin?"

"That was different."

"How?"

She doesn't answer.

"How was it different, Mom?"

"I hadn't hit my bottom."

"And now you have?"

"I think so."

"You *think so*?" The urge to throw all the crap from the dustpan into her face is really tempting. "We were homeless," I say. "But I guess that wasn't low enough for you. Then you almost die from heroin, and you're still not sure you hit bottom?"

"Layla . . ."

"What?"

She shakes her head. "Nothing."

"Tell me, Mom."

"It's nothing. Addiction is hard."

"Clearly."

"And you know how sorry I am."

"Please stop apologizing."

She thrusts out her chin. "Then what do you want from me?"

"I want you to go to rehab."

"I never said I wasn't going."

"And I want you to leave so I don't have to look at you."

Too late, the words escape my mouth, and I realize they're an echo of what I overheard Grandpa saying to her the night he died.

I can't look at you.

"Mom . . ."

I reach for her, but she's already walking away, heading for the stairs.

"Mom, wait!"

I go after her, but I forget I'm holding the dustpan, and the next thing I know, all the mess I've swept up is spilling down my legs, scattering over the floor, sticking to the bottoms of my feet.

Shit.

And then I hear voices on the stairs.

Tanya and Mom, their voices so alike, but Mom's is sadder. I hear them talking, but I can't make out what they're saying.

Until Mom says, clear as day: "It's best if I go to my room."

"Are you sure?" asks Tanya.

I strain my ears, listening for Mom's reply, but I don't hear anything, and a few seconds later, Tanya comes into the kitchen.

"Happy Thanksgiving," she says, glancing first at me, still holding the empty dustpan, then at the mess on the floor.

"Sorry. I was just . . ."

"Making pumpkin cake? Your mom told me."

"Oh."

"I told her she could finish it, but she said she was tired."

It's hard to look Tanya in the eye. "I guess she had trouble sleeping."

"Because apparently the air mattress I gave her has a leak in it," says Tanya. "Maybe you and her can share a bed tonight?"

"Yeah. No problem."

Tanya points at the dustpan. "You want help with that?"

"No, I got it."

I bend and start sweeping. By the time I'm finished, Tanya is wearing an apron over her silky blouse.

She hands me an apron too. "So I guess it's just you and me now, huh?"

"I guess."

As I tie on the apron, I'm picturing Mom in her room, hunched on top of her flat air mattress. Knowing I'm down here making pumpkin cake with Tanya instead of her.

Thinking I don't want her around.

"So . . ." Tanya peers into the mixing bowl. "What have you done so far?"

"I'm not sure."

Tanya picks up the bowl. "Then I think it's best to start over, don't you?"

"Sure," I say, and watch as she dumps all of Mom's work into the garbage.

CHAPTER 21

Shake me and move me to that song
while I listen carefully and
try in vain to contour
myself to the correct shape.
—from "Gleaming Girl" by L.F.

By the time we arrive at the homeless shelter, my stomach has twisted and turned so much that it's tied into a knot. My worst fear is that Tanya lied to me and some reporter is going to do a story on how mayoral candidate Scott Rockwell rescued his niece from the dregs of society. My second worst fear is that someone who lives here recognizes me and calls me out in front of a reporter.

"It's nothing like I pictured," says Celeste. She's sitting beside me in the back seat of Scott's BMW.

"Yeah, well, it doesn't usually look like this."

The building's the same—squat yellow stucco with tiny windows—but music is blasting from hidden speakers and the people milling around the parking lot aren't homeless. They're volunteers. Some of them are teens, but mostly they're adults, all of them piling out of church buses and vans, all of them with smiling, happy faces. The parking lot is so crowded that Scott parks his BMW on the street.

Tanya looks around as we get out of the car. "You think it's safe?"

"It's fine," says Scott. "Let's get this over with."

Scott leads the way, the music getting louder as we approach the gate. Tanya grabs Scott's arm to steady herself on the uneven pavement. Scott's wearing khakis and a blue polo, but Tanya dressed up, wearing a silky blouse, black shiny pants, and heels so high she's stumbling her way across the parking lot. As I follow behind her, I remember what she told me about Scott being insecure, and I think maybe—since she spends so much time and money trying to look good—she has a bit of insecurity too.

Somehow that makes me feel better for having spent way too much time deciding what to wear today. I finally settled on a loose pair of Guess jeans, my metallic Prada sneakers, and the Abercrombie T-shirt Celeste says makes me look like a walking billboard. I figure, if I'm wearing pricey clothes, people won't mistake me for someone who lives here.

The gate stands open, and as we pass through it, I think of the inscription on Dante's entrance to hell: *Abandon All Hope Ye Who Enter Here*. There's a folding table set up just inside the gate. Two old ladies sit behind it, checking off volunteers as they come in. Scott goes right up to them and introduces himself as a special guest of the director.

"You must be the mayor," says one of the ladies. She's wearing a pink tracksuit. Her nametag says *Maureen*.

Scott laughs. "Not yet, but I'll take it."

The other lady (*Freida*, according to her nametag) has a shawl draped over her thin shoulders. "I heard of you," she says. "You're the one who says he's going to clean up the streets."

"That's right," says Scott.

"How you plan on doing that?"

"By creating jobs, mostly. So all these people who don't have a place to live can pull themselves up by their bootstraps."

Maureen chuckles. "Bootstraps. I like that."

Freida squints at Scott through thick glasses. "You too handsome to be a politician."

Scott gives her a wink. "You're not so bad yourself."

"Oh, you full of it," she says, but I can tell she's charmed. This is the first time I've seen Scott in politician mode, and it strikes me how good he is at it.

Tanya loops her arm into Scott's. "Be sure to vote next week, okay? December fourth. Don't forget."

"I won't," says Maureen.

"I'll think about it," says Freida.

Scott and Tanya step aside to wait for Lester Thomson, the director of the homeless shelter. They're here to present a ten-thousand-dollar check, not to actually do any volunteering. Celeste and I give Maureen our names, and she checks us off her list. She wants us to help at the kiddie corner, but Celeste insists on working the snow cone booth.

"Both of us," Celeste says, as if we're a package deal.

Maureen eyes us skeptically. "Snow cone–making is hard work."

"I think we can handle it," Celeste says.

And maybe because Celeste has the same last name as the charming mayoral candidate, Maureen gives in. "It's back there." She points toward the corner of the Quad where the women's dorms are.

"Thanks," I say, and we head out, leaving Scott and Tanya to shake hands with Lester Thomson, who's just come out to greet them. I've never met Mr. Thomson, but I've heard him speak at the shelter's weekly "township" meetings. He's kind of a legend at Helping Hands because, twenty years ago, he used to be homeless too. But through God's grace (his words), he kicked his drug habit, got a job cleaning toilets, and went to night school, eventually becoming director of the very same shelter he used to live in. I know Scott's heard that story because he and Tanya were talking about it on the way here. Scott was saying how Lester Thomson's background makes him a great ally for his campaign. "Plus, he's Black," Tanya said, to which Celeste looked at me and rolled her eyes.

Celeste and I don't speak as we make our way across the Quad, and that's fine with me because I'm on high alert for anyone who might give me away. At the same time, I'm amazed at how the shelter has been transformed. Music is pumping and people are laughing and kids are running around with balloons and face paint and cotton candy. There's a bounce house set up in front of the family wing, and all around the perimeter, there are booths with striped awnings. One booth is giving away stuff like shampoo and toothbrushes. Another is offering free shaves and haircuts. Near the education wing, there's a bunch of tables piled high with used clothes, like something you'd see at a yard sale. A sign written on cardboard says everyone can take three items, and tons of people are milling around the tables.

I stop walking.

Because one of those people is Gabriel.

He's with his mom, and they're both rummaging through the pile of used clothes. I watch him pull a pair of jeans from the bottom of the heap. His mom takes them from him, looks them over, and stuffs them into a plastic grocery bag. They both go back to digging.

Why didn't it occur to me that I might see him today? Maybe I thought he'd hide in his room like I was planning to do. Should I avoid him? And if I don't avoid him, what should I say to him?

He's dating my best friend. My former best friend. The friend who probably hates me and wants nothing to do with me. I'm sure she's told him all about our fight. And he already knows I'm lying to her, so maybe he wants nothing to do with me either.

Celeste turns around. "What are you looking at?"

"Nothing."

She follows my gaze, but there are so many people, she can't possibly know who's caught my attention. "The guy with the red hair?"

"How'd you know?"

"I saw you at school with him. He's cute."

"We're just friends."

"You sure about that?"

"Whatever, Celeste. I'll see you in a few minutes."

"Don't take too long."

Gabriel doesn't see me as I move toward him. He's wearing the same Linkin Park T-shirt he wore the other day, and I remember what he told me, how most of his clothes burned up in the fire. As I step up to the table, his mom tosses him a T-shirt that he catches one-handed. He looks at it, shakes his head, and tosses it back. That's when he sees me.

"Layla." He looks confused. "What are you doing here?"

"Volunteering."

His mom frowns at me, and I want to tell her I'm on her side. On Gabriel's side. Because she's looking at me like I'm a danger to her son.

"So how long are you here?" he asks.

"Just a few hours. Did I tell you my uncle's running for mayor?"

He shakes his head.

"That's why I'm here. He thought it'd be good for his campaign if his family was seen helping out."

"Oh."

"Anyway . . ." I'm distracted because his mom is still frowning at me. "I just came over to say hi."

"Hi."

"And I won't keep you."

"Actually, I'm glad you came. Do you have time to talk?"

He probably wants the inside scoop on Morgan, on how great she is.

And she *is* great—smart, funny, the best person I know.

So that's what I'll tell him. It's the least I can do after I told her to eff off.

I point behind me. "I'm actually supposed to be helping my cousin make snow cones. You want to walk over with me?"

"Sure."

Before we go, he kisses his mom on the cheek. "Find something for yourself," he says, trading his empty plastic grocery bag for her full one.

Now I see the burn scars on her hands from where she saved Gabriel from the fire. That must be tough for him. Every time he sees her hands, he's reminded of his guilt.

We start walking, Gabriel matching his much-longer stride to mine as we weave through the crowd.

"How's your mom?" he asks.

"Okay, I guess."

"You guess?"

"She was supposed to go to rehab yesterday, but they got flooded, so now she's staying at my aunt's house until they can take her."

"At least you get to spend Thanksgiving with her."

I make a face.

"Should I not ask?"

"No, it's fine. It's just, her and my uncle hate each other. Thanksgiving dinner is going to be interesting, to say the least."

A gray-haired woman I vaguely recognize is coming straight toward us. I avoid eye contact, but she grabs my arm as we pass.

"Hey, Layla. How's your mom?"

"Good."

"Tell her I said hi."

"I will."

Gabriel glances over as we walk. "Her name's Edith, by the way."

"Oh."

"But I only know that because she's friends with my mom."

And she's obviously friends with my mom too, but I didn't bother to know that.

"Speaking of your mom . . ." I'm trying to change the subject. "She seems nice."

Gabriel nods. "She is."

"But I don't think she likes me."

"Why do you say that?"

"She was giving me the evil eye."

He laughs. "She's just protective. She'd like you if she knew you."

"I bet she likes Morgan, though, right?" Inside I wince, hating that I sound so jealous.

"Well . . ." Gabriel dodges a guy in a wheelchair, and our arms touch. Just barely, but the warmth of his skin was like a flash of sunlight. Did he feel it too? Suddenly, I'm wondering what it would be like to kiss him, to have him pull me close, run his fingers through my hair.

Stop this! Gabriel's with Morgan, and if there's one thing I won't do, it's steal my best friend's boyfriend. Even if she isn't my best friend anymore.

And it's not like Gabriel would have me anyway.

"She knows *of* her," says Gabriel, bringing me back to our conversation.

"And probably likes her," I say. "Everyone likes Morgan."

"Morgan's a nice girl." I feel him looking at me. "But so are you."

I'm not fooled. That's what you say to someone you want to be friends with.

"Speaking of Morgan." He switches the bag of clothes he's carrying to his other hand so now it's a barrier between us. "There's something I've been wanting to tell you."

Does he think I don't know already?

"What you saw yesterday . . . us holding hands . . ."

I swear there's a fist gripping my heart, squeezing as hard as it can. "It's none of my business."

"That's not what I mean. What I mean is—"

"Layla!"

I recognize Celeste's voice, but it's hard to spot her with so many people lined up for snow cones.

"Is that your cousin?" Gabriel points with his bag of clothes, and finally I see her, not ten feet away, standing behind the snow cone booth. She's wearing plastic gloves, and she's squirting blue syrup onto a lopsided cone of ice. The syrup splatters her face, and she laughs. A hand reaches out and wipes it from her cheek.

And my heart stops. Because the hand belongs to Joshua Burman. Which is bad enough. But standing behind him is the one person I absolutely don't want seeing me here. Not where all the Ediths walking by could give me away.

Felix grins at me as he bites into a red snow cone. "Hey, Freeman. What took you so long?"

CHAPTER 22

Surround her soul, the claws, the grasp, the gasp.
The girl dives deep, her shadow self to mask.
—from "Shadow Self" by L.F.

For a few seconds, I'm too stunned to say anything, my brain catching up to the fact that Felix is here, that maybe he knows I used to live here. Maybe Celeste told Joshua and Joshua told Felix and now Felix knows.

But the way he's smiling as he slurps his snow cone . . . Maybe he doesn't know.

Because Celeste said she wouldn't tell, and there's no reason why she would, especially when Scott said he didn't want it getting out.

"Hey." I try to act casual, even though my heart is beating out of my chest. "I didn't expect to see you here."

Felix tosses his half-eaten snow cone into the garbage behind the booth. "I'm here," he says, "so they can have their alone time."

They, meaning Celeste and Joshua. Now I get it. Felix and I are their stand-ins.

Celeste manages to look guilty as she peels off her plastic

gloves. "Don't tell my parents, okay? Since I got grounded, this is the only way for Josh and me to see each other."

"Okay, but . . ."

"We won't be long."

Joshua lifts a lock of her hair and smells it. "You do realize you insult my manhood every time you say that."

She bats him away. "All we're doing is talking, remember?"

"If you say so." He grabs her hand and leads her away. All the people in line for snow cones watch them go.

"So . . ." Felix hands me the box of gloves. "It's just you and me."

And that would be awesome if we weren't *here* where someone could give me away at any second. We both step up to the booth, and after the first few customers, we fall into a rhythm. I scoop ice into paper cones, and he adds the syrup. I keep my head down and let Felix do all the talking. So far I haven't seen anyone I know, but my hands are shaking, and not from the ice.

After about the fifth customer, Felix nudges me. "I think you lost your stalker."

"Huh?"

"The kid hovering around with his bag of clothes."

Gabriel. Shit. How long did I leave him standing there? Why didn't I at least tell him I'd talk to him later?

I was distracted by Felix, that's why. Felix and my fear of being found out.

Felix hands a little girl her snow cone. "He goes to our school, doesn't he?"

"Yeah, he's new."

"So you know him?"

"He's not a stalker, if that's what you're saying."

"But it's weird, you know?"

Sweat trickles down my back. "What's weird?"

"That someone from our school actually lives here."

I don't say anything. My hands are freezing, but they're clammy beneath the plastic gloves.

Minutes go by. Long minutes. The more I think about Gabriel, the worse I feel. Maybe I should leave and go find him. Can Felix work the booth by himself?

"Hey, Felix. I hate to—"

"Layla? Is that you?"

The voice comes from someone in line, and I look up to see Claudette, Mom's caseworker. The lanyard around her neck says *Staff.*

"It's good to see you volunteering. How you been?"

"Good," I mumble. My hands are trembling as I grab a paper cone.

"How's your mother?"

"Fine."

"I'm glad to hear that." And then she lowers her voice. "She gave us all a scare."

Instead of handing the cone to Felix, I pump the syrup myself. Anything to keep my head down. But when I'm done, it's not like I can hand it to Felix to give to her, so I give it to her myself.

"Thanks, and here's my card." She holds it out. "When you get settled, let me know how you're doing."

"Yeah, okay." I pocket the card and go back to scooping ice.

"Someone you know?" Felix asks. He looks amused.

"Sort of."

"She works here, doesn't she?"

I nod.

"So you must volunteer here a lot."

"Yeah."

"You okay?"

"Yeah, I'm good." This could have ended in disaster, but it didn't.

"Anyway . . ." Felix takes the cone of ice I hand him. "I'm glad you're here now."

"Really?" We're close enough that our arms are touching. "Why's that?"

"No reason. Can't a guy be glad to see you?"

"Yeah, but usually you want something."

He laughs. "That's harsh."

I risk looking out at the crowd to see if Celeste is on her way back. That's when I see Scott and Tanya in the distance. They're heading my way, and someone's with them. Not Lester Thomson. Whoever it is, he's young and white. Dressed like a hipster.

"Well, now that you mention it," says Felix. "Mrs. Chapman gave me an extra-credit assignment to help bring up my grade. I wanted to ask you about it."

Tanya spots me and points me out to Scott, who in turn points me out to the hipster guy they're walking with. He has a camera around his neck, and it's not the kind everyday people use. This one looks professional. Which means . . .

Felix is still talking as he makes the snow cones. "She wants me to do this *Macbeth*-themed essay on I-don't-know-what. It doesn't make sense to me."

It means the hipster guy is a reporter. And now, just as I suspected, I'm about to become Scott's poster child. I imagine my picture in the paper. Mayor candidate Scott Rockwell's poor little niece who he rescued from the homeless shelter.

And then I imagine Felix standing by while the reporter takes my picture, while the reporter asks me questions about what it was like to live here. I wish I was braver. I wish I was more like Gabriel, but I'm not.

I have to get out of here.

A girl steps up to the booth and asks for a blue snow cone. Felix waits for me to hand him the ice, but I don't move.

He nudges me. "Freeman, wake up."

I drop the scoop in the bin. "I have to go."

"What? Why?"

"I don't feel good."

"You can't just leave me by myself."

I barely hear him as I back away, bumping into people left and right as I blunder toward the parking lot. I steal a glance back. Scott and Tanya are easy to spot. The reporter too. They're still heading for the snow cone booth, but I don't think they see I've disappeared. I keep shoving my way through the crowd. The gate is just ahead.

And then I spot Celeste and Joshua coming through the gate. They'll pass right by me, so I duck my head, hoping they won't see me.

"Layla, where are you going?"

Should I ignore her? A hand clamps down on my shoulder. Startled, I turn to see James Saint James smiling at me.

Joshua is suddenly between us. "What do you think you're doing?"

He's talking to James, who backs away, arms up like he's surrendering. "I ain't done nothing."

"You ain't done nothing?" Joshua mocks. "You put your hands on her!"

"It ain't like that. I know her."

"Bullshit."

James turns to me. "Tell him, girl."

I open my mouth, trying to think of what to say, how to get out of this without Joshua finding out the truth.

But no words come out.

"Come on, girl. Tell him you used to stay here."

My heart sinks because now I have no choice. If he hadn't said that, if he hadn't said I lived here . . .

The words are hard to get out, but I say them anyway. "No." And I hate myself for saying them. "I don't know him."

Joshua points at James's face. "This is why you people get a bad rap."

"Calm down." Celeste lays her hand on Joshua's shoulder, her mouth close to his ear. "Obviously he thought she was someone else."

"Obviously he should get his eyes checked."

Celeste and I exchange a glance. I know she won't give me away, but maybe it's too late. "Come on." She tries to lead me back the way I came, but I shake her off.

"I'll wait by the car."

As I slink away, James's wounded eyes look back at me. I try to tell him with my face how sorry I am, but I don't expect he'll ever forgive me.

I wouldn't if I were him.

CHAPTER 23

Silent you come with your roots grasped to mine,
Stalking my soul when my future seems fine.
—from "Family Tree" by L.F.

The tension inside Scott's BMW feels charged, just like the storm looming on the horizon. Low dark clouds press in on us while thunder rumbles in the distance. Scott drives with his jaw locked, eyes staring straight ahead, hands clutching the steering wheel like any second the car will hurl itself out of control.

Turns out, the guy with the camera wasn't a reporter. He was Marty, Scott's campaign manager, and Scott and Tanya weren't bringing him over to get pictures of me for the news. They were bringing him over so he could say hello.

So now Scott's mad because I made him look bad by not being where I was supposed to be. Seated in front of me, Tanya keeps glancing at the back seat, a frozen smile on her face, but she's not looking at Celeste or me. She's looking at the stuff Mom and I had at the shelter—pillowcases stuffed with clothes, cardboard boxes of kitchen stuff, plus a laundry basket heaped with odds and ends. Mom told Tanya she didn't want anything from our past life, but someone at the shelter saved it for us anyway. Now it's all piled in the back seat because Scott's trunk is filled with campaign signs and pamphlets—all the stuff he's taking to his campaign rally tomorrow. Somewhere in one of these boxes is my dad's photo. His picture is the only thing in here I want, but Mom should want some of it, shouldn't she? It worries me that she doesn't.

Scott whips around a car, and all our belongings slide toward me.

Tanya flips on the radio. "Who wants Christmas music?"

No one answers, but she fiddles with the dial, finally settling on a country version of "I'll Be Home for Christmas."

From where I'm sitting, I have a perfect view of Scott's scowl. When Tanya starts singing the chorus, he reaches for the radio and snaps it off.

Lightning blinks on the horizon. The storm is still a long way off, but it's supposed to pour later today.

"So what I want to know," Scott says, his voice making me jump, "is, why the person I'm letting stay in my house couldn't do the one thing I asked of her?"

Tanya's perfume, combined with all the sudden stops and starts, is making me carsick. Plus, the back seat is so crowded I'm getting claustrophobic. "I thought Marty was a reporter," I say, "and I didn't want to be in the news."

Scott finds my eyes in the rearview mirror, glaring at me with icy stillness. "Since when does it matter what you want?"

Never, I think, but that doesn't stop me from wanting.

"This is my fault," says Tanya. "I thought it'd be better if we didn't tell her."

"Tell me what?"

Tanya turns to face me. "We weren't just bringing Marty over to say hello. He was there to get pictures of all of us volunteering."

"One big happy family," Celeste mutters.

Tanya ignores her. "We wanted the pictures in case it gets out that you and Shauna used to live there."

All this political pivoting is making me dizzy. "First you said I wasn't supposed to tell anyone, but now it seems like you *want* it to get out."

"Not at all," says Tanya. "But in case it does, Marty wanted to send pictures of us volunteering to the press, proof that we aren't ashamed of you having lived there. Because here we all are, the whole family giving back to the very place that took you in."

Scott veers around a car. "Of course you screwed that up. I shouldn't have expected anything less from Shauna's daughter."

"Scott, watch out!"

Tanya clutches the dashboard, and Scott slams on the brakes to avoid hitting the SUV in front of us. The car behind us blares its horn.

Scott glares at me in the rearview mirror as if it's my fault. "I don't think you realize how close to the edge you're walking," he says.

I do, but I don't argue with him. All I want right now is to get through this day with no more arguments.

But that's probably wishful thinking.

In fact, I know it is. Just thinking about him and Mom sitting at the same dinner table makes my stomach hurt.

After a few minutes of silence, Tanya must think it's safe to turn on the radio again. At first, it's so low I can't hear it, and then she turns it up—some dude singing "Do You Hear What I Hear?" and Tanya straining to sound cheery as she sings along.

o o o

When we reach the house, Scott tells me to get all my junk out of his car. Tanya tells me to stack it in the garage, so that's what

I do. After dinner, I'll dig through it to find Dad's picture, but right now, I need to check on Mom.

Her job while we were gone was to get the pumpkin cake out of the oven and baste the turkey every hour. I'm hoping she didn't screw it up, and I guess she didn't because when I come in from the garage, the kitchen smells amazing.

Tanya smiles at me from the sink where she's peeling potatoes. "You want to help?" She's wearing her apron again, and her high heels are gone.

"Sure, but . . . have you seen my mom?"

"I just gave her my laptop. She's up in her room."

Mom's not the type to be on the computer. "Any idea what she's doing?"

"She said something about AA chat rooms. Anyway, go see if she wants to make the icing for the cake."

"Good idea. I need to check on her anyway."

Up on the third floor, Mom's door is closed. I knock. "Mom, it's me."

"Just a second."

Could she be drunk? We left her alone in the house, but any store that sells liquor is too far to walk to. Plus, she has no money. Plus, Tanya told me this morning that she poured out all the wine in the house. "What are you doing?"

The door opens. Mom's standing there in Tanya's clothes. Her hair's a mess. "Nothing," she says.

I step into the room, look around, but there's nothing to see. Just the air mattress on the floor, half-inflated. Blankets piled in the corner. Tanya's laptop.

"Did you find those chat rooms?"

"What? No. I didn't find any."

"You want me to help you look?"

"That's okay."

"You sure?"

She hugs herself, gives a quick nod. "Yeah."

I brush past her, look down at the computer. The lid is closed.

"Layla?"

I look up to see her crying. "Mom, what's wrong?"

"I'll be okay."

"Is this about the pumpkin cake? Because Tanya—"

"It's not about that."

"Well, if it is, I'm sorry for yelling at you earlier. I freaked out because I didn't want Scott seeing the mess."

"It's okay."

"No, it's not." I take a step toward her. "I need to be more patient with you."

She shakes her head. "You've always been a good daughter."

Have I? I remember how I held her the morning I found Grandpa's body. I held her while she sobbed, and I tried to comfort her, but I was sobbing too.

And then I remember what today is. Why today is so hard for her.

I close the space between us, take her hand. She tries to pull away, but I hold on.

"I know you're thinking about him," I say. "I am too."

She turns her face away. "What are you talking about?"

"Grandpa. Today's the anniversary."

Now she does pull away, and I let her. "Actually, it was yesterday," she says. "The date of Thanksgiving changes every year, so it was one year ago yesterday that he died."

"Oh."

"I asked Tanya to take me to the cemetery, but she said she was busy."

"She has a lot going on. All the Thanksgiving stuff and Scott's campaign rally. Maybe we can go tomorrow."

"Maybe," says Mom.

"Aunt Tanya thinks Serenity Solace will be open by tomorrow, so maybe we can stop at the cemetery on the way."

She nods. "Why did you come up here, Layla?"

"To talk to you."

"But why?"

"To see if you want to make the icing for the pumpkin cake."

"I don't."

"You sure? I thought maybe we could make it together."

"Just call me when dinner's ready."

"Okay," I say, thinking it'll be less stressful with just me and Aunt Tanya—but after the door clicks shut behind me, it's not relief that follows me downstairs. It's guilt.

CHAPTER 24

Family
Undone
By
Artificial
Revelry

—"Thanksgiving FUBAR" by L.F.

Two hours later, after helping Tanya make stuffing, green bean casserole, and candied yams—after I've helped her set the table and listened to more Christmas songs than I knew existed—it's time to get Mom. Should I remind her she needs to be on her best behavior? If I do, it'll start an argument.

"Mom?" I knock on her door. "Food's ready."

"Be down in a minute."

"You want me to wait?"

"No, Layla."

So I leave, creeping down the stairs like I've done something wrong.

When I get to the dining room, everyone is seated. Scott at the head of the table, Tanya and Celeste flanking him. There's a place for me next to Celeste, and Mom will sit across from me, next to Tanya.

I slide into my chair, and Tanya frowns at me. "Where's Shauna?"

"She's coming."

But the food is getting cold while we wait. The turkey sits on a platter in the center of the table, already carved with the bones sticking out, so it looks more like a carcass than something I want to eat.

Scott looks at Tanya. "Aren't you forgetting something?"

Glancing at me, Tanya gets up, goes to the kitchen, and comes back with a bottle of wine, already uncorked. "Don't worry," she says to me. "It's been locked in Scott's desk."

"But I thought . . . with Mom being here . . ."

"I know, honey, but wine with Thanksgiving . . . it's kind of a tradition."

"And we're not changing the way we do things just to accommodate Shauna," says Scott. He holds out his goblet (which wasn't there when I set the table), and Tanya pours. I stare as wine glugs from the bottle, dark and rich like blood.

When Tanya's done pouring, Scott lifts his glass to his nose and breathes deeply before sipping. As though he's some kind of wine connoisseur. Tanya pours herself a glass too, and I can smell it from where I'm sitting—pungent, tempting, even for me. If I can smell it from across the table, Mom will surely be able to smell it too.

Thunder rumbles outside.

"How long are we going to wait for her?" Scott asks.

"Let's just start," says Tanya.

Scott unfolds his napkin, and that's our cue to begin. The serving dishes get passed around. I add a bit of turkey to my plate. Gravy, stuffing, and a big helping of candied yams because Tanya's so proud of them.

Other than the clatter of silverware, we eat in silence, and with every bite, my stomach gets more and more tense until it feels like a trap about to spring.

What is Mom doing?

Should I go get her?

Maybe it's best to leave her alone.

And then she comes clomping down the stairs. At first I think she's making so much noise because she's in a hurry, but then she yells, "I'm coming!" and my heart sinks because I know that voice. That too-loud voice. A voice that tells me she's drunk.

Everyone stops eating as she plops into the chair next to Tanya. For the briefest of seconds, Mom's eyes meet mine, and I think I see something there—regret, shame, an apology—but then she glances away, says to Tanya, "Sorry I'm late."

"You're fine," says Tanya.

But she's not fine. Can't Tanya see that? Her hair is tangled, her eye makeup smeared like she's been crying. Only right now, she's grinning as she reaches for a roll.

"Wow," she says. "This looks good."

"Thanks," says Tanya.

"But I'm not surprised," says Mom, "since it's always about how things look for you."

Scott snorts a laugh. "Amen to that."

"Not funny," says Tanya with a rigid smile.

Am I going crazy? Don't they know she's drunk?

But looking around the table, I don't think they do. Scott has the same pissed-off look he always has when Mom's around, only now he's sipping wine between giant bites of turkey. Tanya, meanwhile, is still smiling as she ladles a huge spoonful of yams onto Mom's plate. "We have to fatten you up," she says, and then she laughs, and that's when I realize she *does* know. Because it's a nervous laugh, sharp and tight. She knows, but she's trying to cover it up.

So that's the game, and I guess I'll try to play it, but I don't have high hopes for how this will turn out.

Neither does Celeste, judging from the way she's staring at her plate. Staring but not eating. Her fork isn't even in her hand.

"So," says Mom, shoving a wad of bread into her mouth, "you cook like this every year?"

"Of course," says Tanya.

"Just for the three of you?"

Tanya shrugs. "Thanksgiving is special."

"That's what I thought too," says Mom. "Until last year when Dad was dying and you didn't even invite him over."

Tanya lowers her eyes. "That was a mistake."

"You think?" asks Mom. "Considering he died that night?"

"Probably from your cooking," says Scott, and then he laughs, so I do too. Loud enough so he'll notice—anything to distract him from Mom.

"They don't know what he died from," says Mom.

Tanya takes a careful sip from her water glass. "I thought they said his heart gave out."

"It did," says Mom. "But they don't know *why*."

"I think it was a blessing," says Tanya. "He was suffering, after all."

Mom spears a piece of turkey. "How would you know?"

"Because you told me."

"Did I tell you I took him for blood transfusions every two days?"

"No, you never told me that."

"Probably because you didn't return my calls," says Mom. "And now you won't even visit his grave."

Tanya puts down her fork. "Well, it's not like he wanted anything to do with me."

"And whose fault is that?" asks Mom.

"His," says Tanya. "I should be able to marry who I want without my dad disowning me."

"But you never even tried to talk to him," says Mom.

"I did."

"But Scott wouldn't let you?"

Scott looks amused as he sips his wine.

"Did I tell you he wore diapers?" Mom asks. "That he shit himself on a regular basis?"

Celeste has been staring at her plate this whole time, but she finally lifts her head. "Can we please talk about something else?"

"It's okay," says Tanya. "I need to hear this."

"I don't," says Celeste. "I don't want to talk about Grandpa."

"Of course you don't," says Mom. "No one in this family does. Not even my own daughter."

"Mom . . ." I meet her eyes, and inside I'm pleading with her. *Please just stop. Please please please.*

"It's too late now," Mom says. "Everything's been leading up to this."

"To what?" Scott asks.

"To you losing your shit."

Scott flings aside his napkin. "Are you drunk?"

"Of course not," says Mom. "There's no alcohol in this house, right?" And here she looks directly at Celeste.

"Nothing except what's on the table," says Tanya.

"So how could I be drunk? I think you're imagining things, Scott."

"Get out," Scott says.

"I'm not done eating."

"I don't care. I don't want you at this table."

Mom grins. "You sure about that? Because once upon a time—"

Scott slams the table. "Shut up, or I swear to God . . ."

"You going to hurt me?" Mom asks. "You going to make me pay for my sins?"

"Mom, stop!"

"Be quiet, Layla! This isn't about you."

"Don't tell her to be quiet," says Tanya.

"And don't tell me how to treat my own daughter."

"It's not like you're taking care of me," I snap.

Now Mom turns to me, a slow swivel of her head. "Finally! Finally you acknowledge that."

"We all acknowledge it," says Scott. "That's why she's living here."

"And are you happy?" Mom asks.

She's talking to me, but I can't answer. All I can say is, "Why are you doing this?"

"Because I really want to know," says Mom. "Are you happy living with this self-centered prick and his Stepford Wife?"

"Enough!" Scott stands so suddenly his chair tips over.

Tanya's up too, grabbing Scott's arm. "Please," she says. "Please, can we just make this nice?"

"Nice?" Mom says. "I'll show you what's nice." She reaches across the table and grabs the bottle of wine. "This is what's nice. Wine on Thanksgiving." And then she upends the bottles and chugs. So fast it's dribbling down her chin. I make a grab for the bottle—Tanya does too—but Mom backs away from us and keeps guzzling, not stopping until it's empty. She lowers the bottle, looks right at Scott, and slams it on the table.

"Nice vintage. Got any more?"

For a second, the scene freezes. And all I can think is, *Wait. Maybe I'm dreaming.* And then the scene starts up again, only now it's in HD with digital surround sound.

Scott lunges. Tanya screams. And I stand helpless, watching my worst nightmare come true.

CHAPTER 25

The pressure underneath
Is pulling me away
To drown me,
And the pool is plagued with tears.
—from "Drowning Girl" by L.F.

Plates of food crash to the floor as Scott grabs Mom by the hair and drags her across the table.

"Scott, let her go!" cries Tanya.

He doesn't, even though Mom's kicking and clawing at his hands. Celeste is staring with glazed eyes at the candied yams dripping onto her lap. Tanya's screaming and pulling on Scott's arm. And me?

I'm standing frozen, watching spit fly from Scott's mouth as he shakes Mom like a ragdoll. Mom's eyes are shut, her mouth twisted in pain. Tanya tries to peel Scott away from her, but he shoves her so hard she falls to the floor. I try to move, but I'm trapped in my nightmare, trying to wake up.

Scott's dragging Mom to the foyer, and Mom's whimpering and struggling, and Tanya's picking herself off the floor, and Celeste is still rigid at the table, but now her face is streaked with tears. Scott's cursing and yelling, and Mom's feet are scrabbling while Scott drags her to the door, and I'm trying to move, but I can't. Trying to say something through the lump in my throat, but all that comes out is a sob.

Mom's limp now, like all the fight's gone out of her. Scott's gripping her by the hair, by one arm, and he kicks open the front door. Tanya's trailing him, begging him to stop, to think about what he's doing. To think about his campaign. But she might as well be mute.

Like me. Why can't I speak?

Scott keeps spewing. ". . . sick of you, waste of space . . ."

Why can't I help her?

"Stupid bitch . . . throw you out on your ass . . ."

And that's what he does. Scott throws Mom out like a sack of garbage, and I catch a glimpse of her skidding over the walkway, her hands splayed as she tries to break her fall. Her sharp cry of pain cuts through me, finally unfreezes me, and I hurl myself at him, but Tanya catches me around the waist, her arms surprisingly strong. The last thing I see before Scott slams the door is Mom limping away, hurrying, like she has somewhere to be.

o o o

I'm kneeling in the foyer with Tanya's arm around my shoulders. She's crouched beside me, trying to calm me with words, but I can't hear her through the roar in my head. Mom is out there somewhere, and I feel like I'm in shock, like this can't be happening. Did she get herself kicked out on purpose? It almost seems that way, but if so, why? Maybe, by her screwed-up logic, she thought she was helping me, or maybe she couldn't stand the idea of going to rehab.

What I do know is, she's out of options, and yes, she brought it on herself, but I feel responsible. If I'd been nicer to her . . . If I'd shown her I wanted her here . . .

I squint at Scott through my tears. He's leaning against the door, chest heaving, sweating, hair plastered to his forehead. God, how I hate him. This is his fault too.

"You can't just leave her out there," I say.

When he turns to look at me, he seems surprised I'm still here. "The hell I can't."

"She has nowhere to go!"

"Not my problem."

Tanya helps me stand. "Let her stay one night, Scott. One more night, and first thing tomorrow, I'll drive her to Serenity Solace."

"Are you out of your mind? You think I'm shoveling out thousands of dollars so Shauna can have a vacation?"

"Don't think of it as helping her. Think of it as helping your campaign."

"You mean the campaign she's hell-bent on ruining? Is that the one you mean?"

"She won't ruin it. Not unless you let her. Think of what Marty would say. I'll call him right now. He'll say—"

"I don't care what Marty says. I'm sick of listening to him. I'm sick of listening to you."

"Scott, she's my sister."

Scott gets right up in her face. "I put up with this shit from my father, but I'll be goddamned if I put up with it from her."

I wait for Tanya to say something—she's always so good at calming him down—but all she does is lower her eyes.

Which seems to satisfy him. He turns to walk away, and I know I shouldn't make myself a target, but all I can think about is Mom wandering the streets with no money, no ID, and nowhere to go.

"She's your family," I tell him, "whether you like it or not."

He stops mid-stride, swiveling his head to look at me, and

I start to say something about Thanksgiving being a time for families, but all I see is the blur of his anger rushing toward me.

"Scott, don't!"

He stops, takes a breath, then keeps walking. Celeste presses herself against the wall to let him pass.

As soon as he's gone, Tanya turns to me. "You shouldn't provoke him."

"Did you see what he did to her? We have to go after her."

"We can't. At least not yet."

"When?"

"After Scott calms down. He won't change his mind until after he calms down."

Celeste goes to the window and peers between the blinds. "Maybe we can catch her and give her some money without Dad knowing."

"Not a good idea," says Tanya.

"Why not? At least then, she could get a room somewhere."

"Or buy heroin," says Tanya. "Never give an addict money."

I hate to admit it, but she has a point. "Do you see her?" I ask Celeste. "Is she out there?"

Celeste peers out the window again, then shakes her head.

She can't have gone far, though. "What about your credit card?" I ask Tanya. "If she had your credit card—"

"She'd buy more alcohol."

Celeste crosses her arms. "So you're going to do nothing?"

"I told you. We need to—"

"Wait for Dad to change his mind? That's stupid."

"It's not stupid. It's—"

"I think you're afraid," Celeste says.

Tanya glares at her. "So what if I am? You're not the one who has to deal with him when he finds out I helped her."

"He doesn't have to find out," I say.

"But he would," says Tanya. "That's how he is."

"It's not like he hasn't hit you before," Celeste mutters.

Is that true? Tanya's the one who's always able to calm him down.

Tanya glares at her. "I need you to be quiet, Celeste."

"Why? Because you don't want Layla to know he hits you?"

"It has nothing—"

"You know what I think?" Celeste asks.

"I don't care."

"I think you're afraid he'll divorce you."

"I'm not—"

"And if he divorces you, this cushy life you have suddenly goes up in smoke. You call me spoiled—"

"Celeste, I'm warning you."

"But you're the one who doesn't want to give up her *nice* things."

"I said shut up!"

"Does the truth hurt, Mom?"

Tanya pinches the bridge of her nose. "Please just go to your room."

"Gladly." Celeste brushes past me on her way to the stairs. "Happy Thanksgiving, Layla. Hope your mom's okay."

When she's gone, there's a gaping silence. Mom's out there with no money, not even her bus card, and there's a storm about to explode. Where will she sleep tonight? What if she ends up raped or dead in a ditch somewhere?

I turn to Tanya. "Let's call the police."

"And say what?"

"Report her missing."

"Absolutely not. The last thing we want is to draw attention to this."

I don't even try to keep the bitterness out of my tone. "All for Scott's campaign?"

"That and other reasons."

So maybe Celeste is right. Maybe she's afraid he'll divorce her.

Thunder rumbles in the distance. I go to the window and peer out. No sign of Mom, but the first drops of rain are splattering the walkway.

Tanya comes over and puts her hand on my shoulder. "She'll be okay."

"You don't know that."

"I know my sister."

"No, you don't." I shrug away from her. "Maybe you used to, but you don't now."

"Fine, maybe you're right, but it's not like she's a child. She can take care of herself."

But she can't. That's the whole point. Never mind that she doesn't have a place to sleep. What happens if someone feels sorry for her and gives her money? Will she buy heroin? Will she end up dead?

"I have to find her."

"And do what? You can't bring her back here."

"I'll figure something out."

"And what happens when Scott finds out you went after her?"

"All I need is to get her settled somewhere. After that—"

"He might not let you come back."

A chill goes through me. "You think he'll kick me out?"

"The way he is now? I think it's a definite possibility."

"What about his campaign? Isn't he worried what people will think?"

"Right now he's not thinking straight. You have to stay."

"I can't. You know I can't."

Tanya sighs as thunder rumbles the windows. "At least let me give you something."

She grabs her purse, and I think maybe she changed her

mind about the credit card, but instead she hands me a pink umbrella, one of those tiny compact ones that's more like a doll's umbrella than the real thing.

Her smile is sad. "Sorry. It's the only one I have."

I nod my thanks. "It'll be fine."

And who knows? Maybe it will be. Even with a storm raging outside, maybe it'll be enough.

CHAPTER 26

Oh Love must rescue me.
Oh Love, a Love divine.
I'm drowning,
And I'll look to Love till death.
—from "Drowning Girl" by L.F.

As soon as I walk outside, there's a crack of thunder like a window slowly breaking, and suddenly I'm in the middle of a deluge.

I struggle to open the umbrella while gusting sheets of rain drench me. "Mom!" I call, but there's no answer. Finally I get the umbrella open, a flimsy pink shield, but somehow it gives me hope as I jog down the walkway, pausing in the driveway to see if maybe Mom's crouched beside Tanya's Mercedes like a stray cat. She's not. I lift my face to the wind. "Mom!"

All I hear is the pounding roar of rain. At the end of the driveway, I peer up and down the street. The wind turns my umbrella inside out, whips it out of my hand, and sends it rolling down the street like a pink tumbleweed.

Where is she?

I squint through the gusting rain for some hint of her passing.

The street is narrow and winding, lined with dense trees and tangled bushes. The few houses are set back from the road, screened from view by ivy-covered gates and cobblestone walls. I watch the umbrella tumble down the street and disappear around a curve, and because I have no idea which direction Mom went, I decide to follow it, as if Tanya's parting gift is somehow my guide.

The rain makes it hard to see as I run down the street, my Prada sneakers splashing through puddles. She couldn't have gotten far, but what if she did? What if she hitchhiked?

I feel like I'll never find her, not with gusting rain making it hard to see, but I keep walking, keep hoping. I turn the curve where the umbrella disappeared, and—

"Mom!"

She's walking along the side of the road with her head down and her shoulders hunched against the rain, and even though she looks miserable and lost and pathetic and even though I'm frustrated and angry and ashamed of who she is, the relief I feel when I see her is so crushing my legs almost buckle.

I watch as the umbrella whips across her path and nearly trips her. She lifts her head and squints through the rain as if to see where it came from, but even though I'm waving my arms, she doesn't notice me. There's a car racing around the corner, and she sticks out her thumb, but the car speeds past her, blasting its horn and drenching her with sheets of water.

She wipes water from her face, and that's when she sees me. "No," she says, as I close the distance between us. "What are you doing?"

"Looking for you."

"No," she says again, thrusting out her hands as if to ward me off. Her palms are scraped and bleeding from where she broke her fall on the driveway. "You have to go back! Go back right now before you ruin everything."

I gape at her. "*Me* ruin everything? You can't be serious."

She kicks the umbrella toward me, but it barely moves. "Just go back, Layla."

"I would," I say, "if I thought you could take care of yourself. Did you really need a drink so bad you had to guzzle it in front of Scott?"

"Is that so surprising? I'm an alcoholic."

"You know what I think?" I take a step toward her. "I think you *wanted* Scott to throw you out. You wanted him to throw you out because you don't want to go to rehab. Because you're afraid to live without drinking. Because you're weak and all you ever think about is yourself."

I want her to deny this, but all she says is: "Now you're catching on."

"Oh my God." I throw up my hands. "I can't take this anymore."

"Then don't. Go back to the house."

"And what about you?"

"I don't need a babysitter."

"Well tough shit," I say, "because that's what I am. That's what I've been for a long time."

Her face hardens. "What do you want, Layla?"

A crack of thunder makes both of us jump.

"I want to get you somewhere safe. So you don't die out here. So you're not sleeping under a bridge tonight."

"And then you'll go back?"

"You think I *want* to stay with you?"

When she winces, I can't help feeling gratified.

"Fine then." She waves a hand at me. "Do what you have to do."

If only I knew what that was. I pull my phone out of my pocket and hunker over it, trying to shield it from the rain.

Mom watches me for a second, then grabs the umbrella off the ground and holds it over me.

"Who're you calling?"

If I still had the twenty dollars Celeste gave me for lunch, I could call an Uber, but I stupidly gave the money back—trying to be noble, I guess—and what was I thinking? That money was no longer precious because I'd somehow become part of Tanya's family?

At least I have a phone. But I only have five contacts, and Celeste and Aunt Tanya take up two of them. Morgan is the obvious choice, but even if she could talk her mom or Phil into letting my mom stay there until I figure out what to do, I don't think she'd want to help. Not after all my lies, not after I told her to eff off.

I tap her number and wait. One ring. Two. In my head, I'm pleading with her to please pick up, but with every ring, my heart sinks lower. Finally I get her voicemail. I've heard her greeting a million times, but it's like I'm hearing it for the first time.

"Hey, it's Morgan. Leave a message and maybe I'll get back to you."

Maybe. As in, if you're worthy. Which I'm not because I've been lying to her for so long, and now, only when my back is against the wall, am I ready to tell her the truth.

"Morgan, it's Layla. There's something I need to tell you, and you're going to think I'm only telling you because I need your help, and you're right. I've been a shitty friend, but . . ."

I pause to look at Mom. She's staring at the ground, shivering as she holds the umbrella over me, but I know she's listening to every word.

"You know my mom's been spiraling downhill," I say, "but it's worse than that."

Mom shuts her eyes.

"She lost her job a while ago, and we got behind on bills and . . ."

"Just tell her," says Mom.

So I do.

"Before I moved in with my aunt and uncle, Mom and I were living in a homeless shelter. The same one as Gabriel, which is how—"

Beep!

The sound is like a slap as her voicemail cuts me off. I'm about to call back, but then my phone rings in my hand, and my heart leaps because it's Aunt Tanya, and maybe she talked to Scott. Maybe Scott's calm now, and everything's okay and . . .

"Hello?"

All I hear is rain pelting the umbrella. Then a voice.

"You have a choice," Scott says, his tone brittle. "Come back now, or don't come back at all."

The call ends just as the wind whips the umbrella out of Mom's hand. It scrapes my face as it goes, and as I watch the pink vinyl float away, it's like I'm watching the last of my hope go with it.

CHAPTER 27

I walked into the depths
Myself, by own free will
And drowning
I will weep and wail my song.
—from "Drowning Girl" by L.F.

I'm soaking wet and I'm freezing and my clothes are sticking to me and all I have to do to be safe again is walk away and go back to the house. But that would mean abandoning Mom, and as I look over at her, I know I can't do that. She's hunched into herself, teeth chattering, staring at her scraped palms like the umbrella performed some sort of magic trick and disappeared. Her hair is plastered to her forehead. Rain drips from her chin, her nose, even her eyelashes. As I'm staring at her, a flash of lightning whitens her face, and for a split second, it's like I'm staring at a ghost.

She looks at me, blinking rain out of her eyes. "Who called?"

I almost tell her, but then I picture her running back to the house to scream at Scott, making things worse than they already are. I imagine Scott grabbing her by the hair, throwing her against the wall, punching her.

"No one."

"Don't pretend, Layla. I know it was someone."

"It doesn't matter. We have to get somewhere dry."

"The closest gas station is on US 1."

I know the one she's talking about. It's kind of sketchy, like the rest of the neighborhood, but that's the trade-off for living in a really old house near the ocean.

We walk in silence, our heads lowered against the rain, and as we walk, the silence gives me time to think. About what to do when we reach the gas station, who to call, what the plan is. A passing car splashes us, but I barely notice. All I can think is, I'm homeless.

I'm homeless and shaking, and inside me, there's this black pit and I'm standing at the edge looking down and the pit is getting bigger and I want to scream but screaming won't help so I back away from the edge and keep walking.

I'm homeless, so what am I going to do? Mom broke the shelter's number one rule when she did heroin, so there's no way they'll take her back.

But maybe they will. Maybe if I explain, maybe if they see how desperate we are, they'll take pity on us.

Or maybe Morgan will call and Phil will come get us and let us stay with them until we figure out what to do.

The more I think, the harder it is to push back the fear. I feel it rolling in my gut, pushing up through my throat. The scream is so close.

Gravel crunches beneath my feet, and for some reason, I think of James, how, if he were here, he'd lay a hand on my shoulder, tell me in his deep, rumbling voice to look at where my feet are.

So that's what I do. I look at my feet in my Prada sneakers. They're soaking wet, but I'm moving forward, and right now, my feet are crossing the parking lot of the gas station, and right now, I'm opening the door to the brightly lit convenience store, and it's such a relief to be out of the rain that tears burn my eyes.

The store is empty except for a tall skinny man behind the counter. I look around. No bathroom in sight.

"Hey," I say, going up to the counter. "Do you have a bathroom we can use?"

He looks me up and down, does the same with Mom. "Yeah, but you have to buy something first."

"We don't have any money."

"Sorry. Can't help you."

"Please. We just want to dry off."

"Fine." He hands me a key attached to a block of wood. "Bathroom's around back, and I don't want to hear anything about it not being clean. Beggars can't be choosers."

We have to walk around the outside of the building to get to the bathroom, but at least there's an overhang that lets us stay out of the rain. I let Mom go in first while I fish out Claudette's business card. Was it just this morning she gave it to me?

Her phone rings for a long time, and I think I'm going to get her voicemail, but then she answers.

"Hello?"

"Claudette?"

"Who is this?"

"Layla Freeman."

"Layla? What's wrong?"

For a second, I can't speak around the lump in my throat. "Please," I sob. "Mom and I need help. We need a place to stay."

I wait for her to say something, but she doesn't.

"Is it possible to get our old room back?"

"No, Layla. You know it's not."

The speck of hope I was cradling floats away.

"But if you just need a bed for the night, there's always the transitory unit."

Hope flares again. "How does that work? We just show up?"

"Pretty much. The beds are on a first-come, first-serve basis, but I feel like I should warn you."

I brace myself.

"Anyone can stay there," she says, "so you're going to get all types. People who haven't showered in months, people with mental problems, people on drugs."

This much I knew.

"And it's not the cleanest," she says. "Sometimes there are fleas."

"I can deal with that," I say, because what choice do I have? Beggars can't be choosers.

"Thanksgiving is a busy night," says Claudette, "but I'll bend the rules and save you a bed. You have to get yourself here, though. Can you do that?"

"I think so, but . . ." There's so much I want to say—like, *What about tomorrow?* And the day after that? Like, what will we eat? And how will we change our clothes when we have nothing but the sopping clothes on our backs? I want to tell her how scared I am. I want her to fix things, but I know she can't.

"Layla, I have to go. Things are really busy here. I'll see you soon."

"Okay."

She hangs up, and when I lower the phone, Mom's coming out of the bathroom. She hands me the key. "You're taking me back to the shelter, aren't you?"

"Don't argue with me, Mom."

"I'm not arguing. I just want to know."

"We're going to the transitory unit."

"Just me, though, right? You're leaving me there and going back to Tanya's?"

"Yeah, Mom." At some point, I have to tell her Scott won't let me come back, but not now. First I have to get us to the shelter.

I think about calling Morgan again, but if she was going to forgive me, she would have called back by now.

That leaves Gabriel.

I tell Mom to stay put and shut myself in the bathroom to call him. The trapped air is moist and smells like sewage. The sink is clogged with toilet paper, and the floor is grimy and wet. To avoid looking in the mirror, I stare at my feet. They're sopping wet, but the Band-Aid on the back of my foot is still hanging on.

My phone is in my hand. It only rings once before I get his voicemail.

"Gabriel, it's Layla."

And then I think about this morning when I saw him at the shelter, how I completely ignored him after Felix showed up. Felix, who only talks to me when he wants something.

Just like I'm only talking to Gabriel because I want something.

Is that the kind of person I am? A taker? A user? It's not who I want to be.

All these thoughts go through my head in a flash, and when I start talking, I don't know what I'm saying until the words come out of my mouth.

"I'm sorry."

It's a relief to say it, and I mean it with all my heart. "I called to ask a favor, but after hearing your voice, I realize how shitty that is, to ask a favor after the way I treated you. So now I just want to say how sorry I am. I'm sorry for the way I ignored you. I'm sorry if I made you feel insignificant or unimportant or invisible. You're none of those things. You're actually really nice—also really brave and really smart—and I have no excuse for the way I treated you other than my own insecurity. I hope you know how awesome you are, and I hope . . ." I stop myself from saying *I hope you can forgive me* and say instead, "I hope you have a good life."

And then I hang up.

And I feel better—as though a weight has been lifted from me—but I still have to get us a ride. So I look at my short list of contacts to find the only other person who might be able to help me.

Plus, he owes me.

CHAPTER 28

When I was blonde,
I didn't know what that meant.
Not until the years shadowed my hair
And left me dark and shuddering,
Wondering at this bent picture of myself.
—from "William Blake" by L.F.

Felix picks up on the first ring. Maybe he thinks I'm calling to help him with his extra-credit assignment.

"Hey," he says. "What's up?"

"I need a favor."

"Okay." Already he sounds hesitant.

"I need a ride. My mom and I are stranded."

I hear him chewing. "You do know I don't have my license, right?"

"But your brother does. Can you ask him to come get us?"

"I don't know . . ."

"Please. I'm desperate, and I swear I'll help with your *Macbeth* assignment—I'll even *do* your assignment—but first I really need your brother to come pick us up."

"Then I'll owe him."

I'm suffocating in this tiny bathroom. "Don't you owe *me*?"

"Yeah, but . . ."

"What?"

"Can't you get an Uber?"

Just tell him, I think. *Tell him everything. What does it matter?*

"No," I say. "I can't."

"Why not?"

"Because I don't have any money."

"They take credit—"

"Because my mom's an alcoholic, okay? She's an alcoholic, and my uncle kicked us out of his house, and we're stranded in the rain trying to figure out what we're gonna do because we don't have any place to live."

"Wait a second. You're serious, aren't you?"

"Yes, Felix. I'm totally serious."

"Well . . ." Again with the chewing. "You can't stay with me. My parents—"

"I'm not asking to stay with you. All I'm asking for is a ride."

"But you just said . . . Wait a minute. Are you thinking of staying at the homeless shelter?"

"It wouldn't be the first time."

"Wow."

"Please just ask your brother."

"Okay . . . Yeah."

"Yeah?"

"I'll ask him."

He hangs up, and I wonder what I've just done. Maybe he'll keep quiet, but I have a feeling it won't be long before the whole school knows.

Before Gigi and all her friends know.

I can't help but think of Darla Whitman.

Hobo Girl. Trashcan Darla.

I wonder what happened to her.

I wonder if she remembers me. I wonder if she remembers what a shit I was.

I would, if I were her.

Suddenly I don't feel so good. I crack the door to get some air and catch a glimpse of Mom pacing in the parking lot, oblivious of the rain. She sees me and starts to come toward me. I hold up a finger. *Wait.* I close the door again.

Breathe.

Look at where your feet are.

Right now they're not in the best place, so I lift my head, trying to avoid the mirror, but it's hard to avoid in such a cramped space, and I find myself staring at my own reflection just as my phone rings in my hand. It sounds extra loud in the enclosed space of the bathroom. I watch myself answer it. A girl with bloodshot eyes, her teeth locked in a grimace, tendrils of wet hair sticking to her cheeks like fat slugs.

"Hello?"

"Layla, it's Gabriel."

I knew that already, but hearing his voice makes me all the more ashamed for how I treated him.

"I got your message," he says.

"I'm really sorry, Gabriel."

"You said that already."

"You don't have to forgive me."

"That's good because I'm not sure I do."

"Okay." The person staring back at me is ugly as hell, so I drop my eyes to the stained porcelain of the sink.

"But you sounded like you were in trouble," he says.

I bite my lip.

"*Are* you in trouble?"

"You don't have to be nice to me, Gabriel."

"I know that."

"You don't owe me anything."

"Just tell me what's wrong."

So I take a breath. And I look at the girl in the mirror.

(Someone scared. Someone about to cry.)

"My mom and I are homeless again."

"Shit. What happened?"

"She showed up drunk to Thanksgiving and my uncle kicked us out."

"Both of you?"

"Her first, but when I went after her, he told me not to come back."

"What an asshole."

"Part of me doesn't blame him."

"So where are you now?"

"Some gas station. We walked here."

"In this storm?"

"We're okay. Just wet, and . . ." *Scared*, I think. More scared than I was when I came home from school and found we'd been locked out of our apartment. At least then, we were able to pawn enough of our belongings to stay in a motel for a few nights. Now we have nothing, and I'm more scared than I've ever been, but I don't want to say it out loud. Somehow that will make it more real. If I can keep my fear at a distance, like it's happening to someone else, then I can deal.

"You still there?" Gabriel asks.

"I called my mom's caseworker, just in case we could get back into Helping Hands, but of course, we can't, not after Mom's heroin incident."

"So what are you going to do?"

"Claudette said she'd save us some beds at the transitory unit, so at least we'll have somewhere to sleep tonight. Then tomorrow . . ." I swallow hard. "Tomorrow I'll try to find Mom a rehab. Somewhere free because we don't have insurance."

"I might be able to help with that."

"Really?"

"The rehab I went to was based on your income."

"That would be great."

"But what about you?" he asks.

"I'm not sure. I was going to ask Morgan if I can stay with her for a few days, but . . ."

"What?"

"You probably know we got in a big fight. I wouldn't blame her if she never wants to talk to me again."

Gabriel's quiet for a second. "You don't think your uncle will take you back?"

"I think it would be a miracle if he did."

"What about child services?"

"That might be my only option, but I'm not sure how it works."

"Me neither."

"I guess I'll find out. But I'm not going anywhere until I get my mom somewhere safe."

"What can I do? Do you need a ride to get back here?"

"Um . . . Maybe?"

"What does that mean?"

"This guy Felix—"

"The guy from the snow cone booth?"

"He's going to ask his brother to come get me."

"And you haven't heard from him?"

"Not yet."

Gabriel sighs. "I'll come get you."

Relief floods through me. "Gabriel . . ."

"What?"

"I didn't want to ask because I don't want to be, like, the only time I talk to you is when I want something."

"I don't think that. And even if I did, this is kind of extenuating circumstances, don't you think?"

"I guess."

"So text me the address."

"I will. But, Gabriel?" I'm almost afraid to ask, but I have to know. "Do you think you'll ever forgive me?"

He laughs a little. "I think I already have."

CHAPTER 29

Though I can never do my part
Remain to take my fears
And hold my tears
With love, for future years.

—from "Statue" by L.F.

As Gabriel pulls into the Helping Hands parking lot, I'm thinking about how drastically my circumstances have changed since this morning. This morning I was here as a volunteer, and now . . .

Don't think about it.

Now all volunteers have gone home, and the parking lot is empty except for a few cars and a few people with matted hair and ragged clothes wandering around like lost souls. These are the people waiting to get a bed for the night, the ones I'll soon be joining.

Don't think.

In the back seat, Mom's eyes are closed like she's tuned out, and I wish so bad I could do the same—close my eyes, curl into a ball, and make this disappear. But I can't. More than ever, Mom needs me.

Gabriel shuts off his car. "You ready?"

I take in the yellow building with its tiny windows and scraggly palm trees. "Not really."

"I know it's hard," says Gabriel. "It sucks, but you're not alone."

You're not alone. People say that all the time in AA, but I don't think it applies to me. I guess it applies to Mom, though. Once she finds out I'm staying with her in the transitory unit, once she finds out I can't go back to Tanya's, I'm hoping she'll be grateful she's not alone.

"Mom?"

She lifts her head from the window and opens her eyes.

"We're here."

"Yeah, okay."

I study her as she reaches for the door handle. I'm pretty sure she's sober by now, but she looks like a drowned rat. So do I, come to think of it, and part of me is mortified that Gabriel is seeing me like this, but I know that's stupid. He's with Morgan, for one thing. And I have bigger things to worry about.

At least it's stopped raining. As we walk toward the gate, Gabriel drapes the lanyard that IDs him as a resident around his neck. He doesn't have to show it, though, because James Saint James is on guard duty and opens the gate as soon as he sees us.

Gabriel gives him a fist bump as we pass through. "Hey, James. How you doing?"

"Can't complain. How about you?"

"Hanging in there," says Gabriel.

"That's all we can do, brother."

I try to catch James's eye, but he won't look at me. Not that I blame him. A few hours ago, I did nothing while Joshua shamed him and shoved him—when James's only crime was to try to talk to me.

James looks past me to where Mom is picking her nails. "It's good to see you, Shauna. Good to see you alive."

Mom's reply is a mumble. "Good to see you too."

"Don't be scaring us no more, you hear?"

Mom nods.

James holds out his arms. "You know I got a hug if you want one."

Mom goes to him and lets him wrap his arms around her, and I know it's stupid, but I'm jealous.

"Get yourself well," James says. "We're all praying for you."

"Thanks." Mom's eyes are shiny with tears as she pulls away.

"James?" I'm hoping he'll look at me, but he acts like he doesn't hear. "James, I'm really sorry for—"

Quickly, he steps toward me, and I think for a second he's going to hug me too. But then he brushes past me to close the gate, and it's like I've bitten my own tongue. It hurts, but I know I brought it on myself.

Gabriel touches my elbow. "Come on," he says, and because I don't know what else to do, I let him lead me away.

The transitory unit is to the left, and Claudette's office is to the right, but we're going straight, cutting across the Quad toward the family units.

"Shouldn't we check in with Claudette?" I ask.

"Not yet. I thought we could talk in my room first. Figure stuff out."

I know enough about the rules around here to know he's not supposed to have outsiders in his room. I also know James should have called someone from the office before letting us in.

"Won't you get in trouble?"

Gabriel doesn't answer. By now, we've reached the family wing. He pulls open a scarred wooden door, and we enter the common room with its old refrigerator and beat-up couches.

Sometime while I was gone, they decorated for Christmas. A scraggly tree stands in the corner—no ornaments—and on the floor there's a plastic nativity scene next to a menorah. The TV is showing *Miracle on 34th Street*, and a bunch of kids are crowded in front of it. It's the scene where Susan is telling Kris Kringle she won't believe in him unless he gets her a house for Christmas.

"She's spoiled!" yells one little girl, and all the moms on the couch burst into laughter.

I recognize some of the moms. I know their faces but not their names. Not one of them acknowledges me, though, and why would they? When I made absolutely no effort to get to know them.

Gabriel calls from the hallway. "Layla, you coming?"

"Just a second."

Before joining him in his room, I take a last look around, knowing that, after I check into the transitory unit, this part of the shelter will be off-limits. I never thought I'd miss staying here, but seeing how relaxed everyone is as they watch the movie, I'm envious. I wish I'd been more grateful when I lived here.

Gabriel holds open his door for me, and once I'm inside, I realize his room is identical to the one Mom and I stayed in, complete with cracked tile floor, mustard-yellow walls, and metal-framed bunk beds that take up half the space. Mom is already inside, sitting on the edge of the bottom bunk next to Gabriel's mom. Gabriel gestures me further inside. He's trying to tell me something with his eyes, but I don't know what.

"Layla?"

The voice comes from behind me—Morgan's voice—and I turn to see her stepping out from the corner beside the door. She stops a foot in front of me, staring at my face like she's not sure it's me. I look for anger in her eyes. I look for pity. But all I see is sympathy, and before I can tell her how sorry I am for everything, she throws her arms around me and buries me in a hug.

For a second, I stay stiff, not sure I deserve this, but her hug is like a warm blanket, and I let myself sink into it. I close my eyes, blacking out the room, blacking out everything except this moment where I feel safe because my best friend is here, and Gabriel was right. I'm not alone.

o o o

I forgot what it was like to let go. I forgot what it was like to not hide, to just be me without the mask. And suddenly, sitting here in Gabriel's room at the shelter, I'm glad I gave back that twenty dollars because if I'd called an Uber instead of Gabriel, I wouldn't be sitting here with my friends. It's a weird feeling, knowing I don't have to guard what I say in front of these people, knowing I don't have to keep track of what lies I told.

The five of us are crowded inside Gabriel's room. Mrs. Connelly and Mom are on the bottom bunk. Gabriel sits on the floor with his back against the bed while Morgan and I are seated on the floor facing them.

"So," says Gabriel. "Mom and I have a plan."

"Sort of," says Mrs. Connelly. I notice again the burn scars on her hands. "I called a few rehabs," she says, "but none of them answered. I guess because of the holiday."

At the mention of rehab, I half expect Mom to protest, but her head stays down. I'm not even sure she's listening.

"We'll call again tomorrow morning," says Gabriel. "It would be great if we could get her in the rehab where I got clean."

"Plus, it's free to people without income," says Mrs. Connelly. "Even if you don't have insurance."

"But we're not sure how full they are," Gabriel adds. "I got checked in right away, but it could take days before a bed opens up, maybe longer."

Morgan nudges Gabriel's foot. "How long did you have to stay there?"

"For me? Three months."

"That's a long time," Morgan says.

"Yeah, well." Gabriel glances at his mom. "Some of us are sicker than others."

Morgan reaches over to squeeze his hand, and I fight a twinge of jealousy. I wonder why they're not sitting together, probably to spare my feelings.

"They have good counselors," he says. "I did a lot of soul-searching while I was there." He turns to my mom, who's still staring at the floor. "It's a good place, Mrs. Freeman. They really helped me a lot. I'm sure they can help you too."

"I believe you," Mom says, finally looking up. She offers him a faint smile. "Does my daughter know how nice you are?"

Gabriel blushes. Our eyes meet. And in that moment—that one frozen moment where I'm looking in his eyes—I know for sure that this is a guy I could fall in love with. If only I hadn't thrown away my chance. Now he's with Morgan, and never in a million years would I try to steal him away from her. She deserves him more than me.

Morgan speaks up. "I only asked how long Gabriel was in rehab because I'm wondering . . . I mean . . ." She turns to me. "I asked my mom if you could stay with us for a few days, but Phil said no. I'm really sorry."

"It's okay."

"No, it's not. I want to help."

"You are helping. Believe me."

"But I want to help more. It's just . . ." She shakes her head.

"So unreal that you were going through all this and I didn't know."

"Because I didn't tell you."

"But I should have realized."

"You didn't do anything wrong, Morgan."

"I got so wrapped up in my own life. Mom marrying Phil. The stupid musical."

"Morgan, stop."

"Please? Just let me say this."

"Okay."

She takes a breath before speaking. "I was actually holding my phone when you called. But I didn't answer because I was mad at you. And as a way to punish you, I didn't listen to your message right away. And then, when I did listen to it, when you told me you'd been living here, I thought maybe you were playing a joke on me. So I called Gabriel to see if it was true." She pauses to bite her lip. "And when I found out the truth, I was . . ."

"Pissed?"

"No! Devastated. And when he told me he was bringing you back here because your uncle kicked you out . . . Well, it didn't seem right to call you on the phone. I wanted to be here when you got here. So I asked Phil to bring me—I told him I wanted to volunteer—and he actually dropped me off."

I've been so wrapped up in my own problems that I've been blind to hers. Now I turn to look her in the eye. "Morgan, I know your life's no picnic."

"What are you talking about?"

"I know Phil's hard to live with, not that you've complained, but I was so busy being jealous of your new house and all your new clothes that I refused to see it."

Morgan smiles sadly. "Phil can be an ass, but compared to your life . . ."

"Why do we have to compare? I should have been there for you."

She nudges my arm. "You're here now, right?"

"Always," I say.

"Me too." She lays her head on my shoulder. "Always."

Mrs. Connelly clears her throat. "I think we should talk about where Layla will go once Shauna's in rehab."

Mom suddenly sits up straight. "What are you talking about? Layla's staying at my sister's."

Dead silence in the room. Everyone's eyes are on me, Mom's included.

My mouth is dry. I thought I was done hiding the truth, but there's one more truth I have to tell. "Mom, Scott kicked me out."

Her eyes widen. "What?"

"That's who called when we were standing in the rain. He told me not to come back."

"No." She puts her hands over her ears and slowly shakes her head. "Don't tell me this."

Mrs. Connelly squeezes Mom's shoulder. "It'll be okay, Shauna. Layla seems like a tough kid and . . ." Her voice trails off because it's obvious Mom's not listening.

Her eyes are fixed on me. "This is because you helped me, isn't it? That's why he kicked you out."

"It was my choice, Mom."

"Don't say that." She holds out her hand. "Give me your phone."

"No!"

"Give it to me right now so I can call him. I swear to God, I'll *make* him take you back."

"Mom, he's not going to listen. Tanya already tried to talk to him, and you calling him up to scream at him will only make things worse."

"How can things be worse? Why didn't you just stay there?"

"I had to help you."

"Why? Can't you see I'm not worth it?"

THUMP! THUMP! THUMP!

"Gabriel?" I recognize Claudette's voice on the other side of the door. "Come on. I know you have people in there."

"That's it," says Gabriel. "We're out of time."

I'm out of time. That's what it feels like because once I leave this room, all these people who care about me will blur into the background, leaving me alone with myself, my mom, and all my many fears.

CHAPTER 30

Flames lick at the pages of our songs . . .
And then they're gone, with only ashes left over.
Our ashes, the ones we serenaded.
—from "The Reaping" by L.F.

I wake to panic, like something's pressing on my chest. My breathing comes in shallow gasps. I sit up, looking around at the darkness. Was I having a nightmare? If so, I can't recall it, but then, like an icy splash of water, I realize my real life is the bad dream.

Heart still pounding, I stare into the darkness, trying not to breathe the thick stench of twenty sour bodies packed into one sweltering room. I listen for Mom's breathing in the bunk below mine, but any sound she might make is drowned out by groans and snores and mumblings, by food wrappers crinkling, bedsprings squeaking, by whispered prayers and murmured cursing.

I can't believe I actually fell asleep. After they turned off the lights, I laid awake for hours in the dank humidity, sure the mattress I am laying on was teeming with fleas and bed bugs, convinced the giant palmetto bug I'd seen planted on the ceiling would come flying toward my face. I tried imagining I was back at Aunt Tanya's, but no matter how hard I tried,

I couldn't fool my brain into thinking I am laying on a soft bed with clean-smelling sheets. So then I tried Grandpa's trick of counting backward from a thousand, but I kept picturing Grandpa dead on his cot with his mouth open. I kept telling myself tomorrow would be a better day—and somehow, I fell asleep, because now it's tomorrow, or I think it is.

Carefully, so I don't shake the bedframe and wake up Mom, I grope for my purse where I buried it beneath the sheet, so it wouldn't get stolen. Now it's only half-hidden, but at least it's still there. It's too dark to see, so I feel around inside for my phone.

It's not there.

And it's not in my pocket either.

Or in the bed.

Could it have fallen out of my purse?

I creep down the ladder, cringing as my bare feet come in contact with the tacky floor. I left my shoes under Mom's bunk, but when I bend to get them, I see that Mom's bunk is empty.

My heart freezes.

Maybe she went to the bathroom. But no, the door hangs open, and I can see in the dim light that no one's in there.

So where could she be? Did she run away? Did someone give her money or drugs or—

The door leading outside is open just enough for me to see someone silhouetted against the rising sun. Quickly I pull on my filthy sneakers and hurry outside.

"Mom?"

She turns to face me, and she's smiling of all things. She's also holding my phone. "Good. You're up."

Is she drunk? She doesn't look drunk.

"You were sleeping so soundly," she says. "You didn't hear your phone."

"Who called?"

"Tanya."

I shake my head. "Why would Tanya call?"

"To tell us Scott changed his mind."

I gape at her. "Mom, don't get my hopes up."

"It's true, kiddo. Grab your stuff. Tanya's coming to get us."

o o o

I don't move, still refusing to believe, but Mom's still smiling, and I can tell . . . I can tell she's not making this up. Still, there's got to be a catch.

"What about you?" I ask. "Where will you go?"

"Don't worry about me." Her smile is frozen in place. "Before you go back to the house, you and Tanya are dropping me off at Serenity Solace."

"Wait. What?"

She nods.

"Scott said it was okay?"

"Only because it's already paid for, but yeah."

I blink at her, wondering if I'm dreaming. Because this is too good to be true. Isn't it? With the sun coming up on the horizon? With the sky glowing orange and purple?

o o o

Five minutes later, Mom and I are waiting in the parking lot for Tanya to pick us up. My body smells tangy, my hair is oily, and my mouth tastes like a dirty sock.

But none of that matters because the thing I didn't dare hope for is actually, really happening. Plus, the weather is gorgeous—cool, but not cold, the sky so clear that the moon's white ghost is still visible, even though the sun is shining brightly.

Tanya called to say she'd just left the house, so we have another ten minutes before she gets here. She told us she'd treat us to pancakes before we drop Mom off at Serenity Solace. Pancakes sound good. Perfect, actually. A perfect food for a perfect day.

Behind us, the gate squeaks open, and I turn to see James fist-bumping the guy on guard duty. James is wearing some kind of uniform, brown work pants and a blue striped shirt. As he turns, I see the Jiffy Lube logo on his chest. He's looking down, smoothing out the wrinkles in his shirt.

Mom calls out to him. "James!"

He lifts his head, grins at Mom, but when he sees me, his eyes go distant.

"You got a job," Mom says.

"I did. About time, right?"

"That's great," says Mom. "I'm happy for you."

"I'm happy for me too." He squints at her. "What about you? You doing all right?"

"Yeah, I'm good."

"You sure? Where you off to?"

"Rehab."

"For real?"

"And Layla's staying with my sister."

James nods, still not looking at me.

Mom doesn't seem to notice. "Layla, I just remembered . . . I want to leave a note for Claudette, to thank her."

"Okay."

The guy on guard duty lets Mom through, leaving James and me alone in the parking lot. I know he's on his way to work. I know I'll never see him again. I have about two seconds to make things right.

"James?"

Already, he's moving past me. "Gotta catch the bus."

"Thanks for helping my mom."

He stops but doesn't turn around.

"And for helping me too—you'll never know how much."

Now he turns to face me, his eyes wary.

"I don't deserve your forgiveness," I say. "I'm not even asking for it because I have no right. But I wanted you to know I appreciate your help. And also who you are."

"Who I am? I'm just an addict trying to get better."

"You're more than that."

He shakes his head.

"They call you James Saint James for a reason."

"They call me that because it's who I want to be. Someone good."

"You *are* good."

"Naw." He rubs his scalp. "But I'm trying real hard."

I take a step closer. "I wish I was more like you."

"Ain't nothing stopping you."

"Yeah, there is." I lower my head. "But I'm trying to do better."

"That's all we can do."

"I'm sorry, James. Sorry for not—" The lump in my throat won't let me talk. I want to tell him I'm sorry for acting like I didn't know him, sorry I didn't defend him, sorry for letting him suffer that humiliation. But just as I'm about to speak, Tanya pulls up in her silver Mercedes.

"That your ride?" James asks.

"Yeah, but—"

Tanya rolls down her window, eyeing James like she thinks he's dangerous. "Layla, get in the car."

"Just a second." I turn to James. "Thanks again for everything."

But when I go to hug him, he steps back, his eyes darting to Tanya.

"It's fine," I say, because I *want* Tanya to see me hugging him—and I want him to know I'm proud to be his friend. Instead of letting me hug him, though, he takes off walking, and even when I call his name, he doesn't look back.

CHAPTER 31

And when it ends, will we rejoice?
Will a new dance then begin?
Will we laugh,
And will we sing?
Will we never cry again?
—from "The Dance We Share" by L.F.

Mom and I are still wearing yesterday's clothes, the ones that got soaked in the rain. We haven't showered. We haven't even brushed our teeth, so it's no wonder the receptionist at Serenity Solace gets this panicked look on her face as we step in the door. She pops up from her desk. "Can I help you?" As though we're intruding and she's about to call security.

"Yes, you can." Tanya steps up to the marble counter like she owns the place. "I'm Tanya Rockwell, and this is my sister, Shauna Freeman."

She points at Mom, who's looking around the reception area like she's wondering how she got here. At least she brushed her hair while we were at breakfast. At least she washed off her smeared makeup.

"We have a reservation," says Tanya. As if we're in a hotel.

"Yes, of course." The receptionist turns on a smile and blinks her false eyelashes. "Welcome to Serenity Solace. Can I get you something? Sparkling water? Herbal tea?"

Tanya says something I can't hear, and the receptionist hands her a clipboard. Mom and I step further inside. There's no sign of hurricane damage. The floor is marble, like the receptionist's counter, but the walls are dark wood, and there's a posh-looking rug in the middle of the room that's surrounded by the kind of furniture you'd see in a fancy hotel. The room smells like flowers. Ethereal music plays in the background, and above our heads is a chandelier that casts a dim yellow light.

While I'm checking out the lobby, Mom drags the Louis Vuitton suitcase Tanya packed for her over the thick rug and settles in one of the overstuffed chairs. She sits on the very edge, still gripping the suitcase like someone might steal it. I try to imagine what she'll be like when we come get her a month from now. She'll be waiting in this same posh lobby, only she won't look out of place. Her eyes will be bright, and her clothes will be clean. She'll be eager to get a job, eager to get back to life. Most of all, she'll be smiling.

At the counter, Tanya is taking her sweet time filling out the paperwork. She wants to get ready for Scott's campaign rally, so I thought she'd be in a hurry, but here she is chatting with the receptionist about the weather, about the damage from the storm, about how beautiful the lobby is.

Mom's leg bounces up and down as her eyes dart around the room. Just looking at her makes me nervous, so I check my phone for the twentieth time to see if Morgan got my text about Scott letting me come back. Right now I could use Morgan's positive energy, but so far, nothing. She's probably still sleeping.

"What are you doing?" Mom asks.

"Checking my messages."

"Your email?"

"My text messages. I'm just seeing if Morgan—"

"How often do you check your email?"

"I don't know. I check it for school."

"Once a week?"

"Something like that."

She nods, her leg still bouncing.

"Why do you ask?"

"Because . . ."

I wait.

"I thought I might write you."

"While you're in here? I don't think they let you have Internet."

"Oh."

I watch her for a second. She's staring at the floor.

"Are you okay, Mom?"

"Please stop asking me that."

"It's the first time I asked."

"Then please stop staring at me like you think there's something wrong."

"Is there?"

"No!"

"Ever since breakfast, you've been quiet."

"I'm fine."

"You don't look fine."

"God, Layla! Would you please lay off?"

As if I don't have a right to be worried. I clench my jaw and twist in my chair, so I don't have to look at her. So I won't snap at her.

At the counter, Tanya is handing the receptionist her credit card. But wait a second . . .

I turn back to Mom. "Didn't you say it was paid for?"

"What are you talking about?"

"You said the whole reason Scott changed his mind was because he'd already paid for it, but Tanya's paying now."

"Well, that's what Tanya told me."

I stare at her for a second. "Are you sure you didn't call Scott?"

"Yes, I'm sure."

"Because you wanted to call him. You said you'd *make* him take me back."

She drops her eyes. "I didn't call Scott, okay?"

I want to believe her. I almost do. "If you didn't call him, why'd you sneak off with my phone this morning?"

"I didn't sneak off. Your phone was ringing, so I answered it."

"Why didn't I hear it?"

"I think it was on vibrate."

"You think?"

"It was."

"Shauna Freeman?"

The cheery voice comes from behind us, and we both turn to see a tall woman with sharp cheekbones stepping into the lobby. She's hugging a clipboard against her pink scrubs. "I'm Tish," she says. "I'm the intake nurse."

Tanya steps over to her. "I'm Tanya Rockwell, and that's my sister, Shauna Freeman."

"Nice to meet you, Shauna."

"Yeah, you too," Mom mumbles.

Tish comes over and stands in front of her. "It's time to say your goodbyes, okay?"

Mom nods. She looks miserable as she gets to her feet. I get to my feet too, and suddenly it doesn't make sense that I was sitting here arguing with her. Not when I should be saying goodbye.

Tanya comes over to stand beside me. "Good luck," she says to Mom.

"Thanks," says Mom. "For everything." And then, in an unexpected rush, she pulls Tanya into a hug.

Tanya stands rigid, but then her arms go around Mom, and I realize this is the first time I've ever seen them hug.

"Get better," Tanya says, and when Mom nods, Tanya steps back.

Leaving Mom and me alone in the center of the room. Suddenly I feel shy. I search for something to say. "You ready to do this?"

She nods, forcing a smile.

Tish touches Mom's arm. "I'm sorry, Shauna, but we can't draw out the goodbyes. It's time for you to go."

"Can I at least give my daughter a hug?"

"Of course."

Our hug is stiff. Maybe because we have an audience. I pat Mom's back and say in her ear what I think she needs to hear. "I'm proud of you."

But apparently that's the wrong thing to say. Her whole body stiffens, and it's like I'm hugging a statue. "Don't hate me too much," she whispers, and before I can ask her why in the world she'd say that, Tish takes Mom's arm and leads her away.

CHAPTER 32

Joy of a moment
Struggles in my torn heart.
The pain makes me hear.
—from "Joy of a Moment" by L.F.

Mom is safe at Serenity Solace. That's what I keep telling myself as I stare out the window of Tanya's Mercedes. They have nurses there. Counselors. They know what they're doing.

Still, there's a weight in my stomach as Tanya drives us back to the house. The radio is tuned to a Christmas station, and Tanya's going on about Scott's campaign rally, how she has to get ready, how she's not sure which earrings to wear with her new dress. I'm trying not to listen as I sit here in yesterday's clothes, but I hear her say something about making a good impression on the wealthiest people in the city, about Celeste not wanting to go, so of course, Celeste gets her way.

Tanya glances over at me. "Maybe it'll be better if she's not there."

I don't say anything.

"She has a way of making fun of me. You know what I mean? With her snide comments? She thinks I don't catch on, but of course I do."

"She does that with everyone," I say.

"What do you mean?"

"The snide comments. She does it with me, with her boyfriend."

"Her boyfriend?"

Crap, I shouldn't have said that. "Maybe he's not her boyfriend. A boy at school I see her talking to."

"Does she have actual friends?" Tanya asks. "Friends who aren't boys?"

I hesitate before nodding. "Yeah."

"You don't sound convinced."

"We don't really hang out."

"That's a shame."

While Tanya drives, I look out the side window, trying to concentrate on the passing scenery, trying not to think about Mom. I wonder what she's doing right now. Is she alone? I hope she likes her room. I hope she makes friends.

"I know you're worried about your mom," says Tanya.

I look over, and she offers a tiny smile.

"You know she'll be fine, right?"

"Yeah, I know."

"It's a really good rehab. The best money can buy."

I want to tell her she's said that already. About twenty times. I kind of get why Celeste makes fun of her.

"Are you nervous about going back?" Tanya asks.

She means to the house. "A little."

"Scott has a temper, I'll admit, but I've found ways to deal with it. You'll find ways too."

Before I can answer, she turns up the radio so all I hear is some kid singing "I Saw Mommy Kissing Santa Claus."

"I love this song," she says. "It reminds me of my mom."

I know the song. It reminds me that things aren't always

what they seem. Like, why didn't I hear my phone this morning when I know it wasn't on vibrate? Why did Mom tell me not to hate her when she's finally doing the right thing?

I listen to Tanya sing.

And even though I'm not sure I want to know, I have to ask . . .

"Aunt Tanya?"

She stops singing, her hands tightening around the steering wheel.

"Did Mom call Uncle Scott this morning? Is that why he changed his mind?"

"Not that I know of." Her brow furrows. "Did she tell you she called him?"

"No. But I thought . . ."

"You thought what?"

"That maybe she had dirt on him or something."

Tanya flicks off the radio. "Did you hear something?"

"No, but I—"

"You didn't hear anything about Scott? Any rumors?"

"Where would I hear rumors?"

"You tell me."

I heard a lot from Celeste, but I'm not telling Tanya that. "I didn't hear anything."

She nods. "Okay then."

I study my hands. Obviously there's stuff about Scott she doesn't want getting out—how he once broke Celeste's arm, how he took anger management classes. Also, Celeste said he still goes to therapy every week.

A sudden thought startles me. What if Mom knows about these things and threatened to blow the whistle if Scott didn't take me back?

I turn to Tanya. "So you're the one who talked to Uncle Scott?"

"What do you mean?"

"I'm just wondering why he changed his mind about helping us."

"Because he's basically a good person, that's why."

Somehow I doubt that, but I let it go.

"And because I had his campaign manager call him last night," says Tanya. "So I think between Marty and me, we basically convinced him he was being bullheaded, that it was best for everyone if he went on helping you. You and Shauna."

"He hates her," I say.

"I know."

"Do you know why?"

She opens her mouth, then closes it again. "I guess because she's an alcoholic. I told you about his father."

"Yeah, but I think it's more than that."

She fiddles with her ring. "You and I both know she deliberately pushes his buttons."

I guess I do know that. What I don't know is why.

Suddenly we're at the house, and Tanya's turning to look at me. "Before we go in, please know you're welcome here. But you need to stay on Scott's good side."

"I will."

"That means no rattling the cage. No poking the bear. Sometimes you have to tiptoe around him."

"Okay."

"And when he gets mad, which—I'm the first to say it, he *will* get mad—you have to find ways to deal with his temper, ways that don't make it worse. Because there are limits to his generosity." She looks at me closely. "Do you understand what I'm telling you?"

"Yes." She's saying he could kick me out at any moment, which I already knew.

"Good." She smiles and takes out her keys. "I don't know what kind of mood he's going to be in, but please . . ."

"I know." I unlatch my seat belt. "Don't poke the bear."

○ ○ ○

Scott is waiting for us in the foyer. I check his face. Is he angry? He doesn't seem to be. In fact, he seems distracted. He keeps sneaking looks at me like he doesn't know who I am.

"What is it?" asks Tanya, slipping off her shoes. "Is everything okay?"

"Fine. How'd it go with Shauna?"

"Good. We dropped her off."

"How was she?" Scott asks, which is a really strange question coming from him.

"Fine," says Tanya.

"Was she fine?" Scott asks me.

"A little sad, but yeah."

"Good." He takes in my appearance. Unwashed hair, wrinkled clothes. "What about you?"

"I'm okay."

His stare is making me uncomfortable. Maybe he thinks I'll blab to the press that he kicked me out of his house. Or maybe he just thinks I need a shower.

"She's not going to tell anyone what happened," says Tanya.

"There wouldn't be any point." He holds my gaze. "I hope you know that."

"I do."

Tanya checks her watch. "You need to change," she says to Scott. "We have to leave in an hour."

"Yeah, well, I'm not the one who has to put on a new face to make myself presentable."

"Very funny." Tanya flashes a rigid smile, but I can tell she's hurt. "I'll go get ready."

Scott watches her head up the stairs, and then he turns to me. "Is there anything you want to say to me?"

"Um, thanks for giving us another chance."

His eyes search my face, and I'm struck again by how blue they are. Finally, he nods. "You're a tough kid." He claps me on the shoulder, gives me a weird smile, and heads upstairs.

Leaving me to wonder what the hell just happened.

o o o

I take the stairs two at a time, telling myself with each step that everything's fine. That I'm worrying for nothing.

It's only when I reach my room on the third floor that I realize how jittery I am. My heart is pounding as I sit on the edge of my bed. Something weird is going on, something I'm not seeing. Maybe I'm just tired. Maybe a shower will help . . .

A shower does help. Quite a bit, actually. Wrapped in a towel and smelling like cherry shampoo, I go to my closet. I'm not leaving the house today, so it doesn't matter what I wear, but still, it's nice to have new clothes. It's nice to have a room, a bed . . .

And then I see my poetry shirt hanging in the closet. I take it off the hanger. It's been freshly laundered. Even the coffee stain is gone.

Thank you, Aunt Tanya.

Instead of putting it on, I hang it back up, and part of me feels disloyal to my own self, but I don't want Scott to see me wearing it. Not after he spent so much money on new clothes for me. Tanya said not to poke the bear.

o o o

After I'm dressed, my phone bleeps with a text from Morgan.

> THAT'S SO AWESOME!!! Call me
> when you get this.

Finally! Someone to talk to.

Morgan picks up on the first ring. "Tell me you're okay," she says. "Tell me you're calling from your aunt and uncle's."

"I am."

"Thank God! They're letting you stay?"

"For now."

"So what happened?"

I sit on my bed. "I'm not really sure. Scott changed his mind. Supposedly Tanya convinced him."

"What do you mean, *supposedly*?"

"I don't know. I was thinking maybe Mom has dirt on him."

"Why would you think that?"

"Because it's weird how he changed his mind out of the blue. Plus, he's acting weird. And so was Mom."

There's a short pause on her end. "You want to hear what I think?"

"Sure."

"I think your mom's safe. She is safe, isn't she?"

"We dropped her off at rehab this morning."

"And you're safe too?"

"Yeah."

"So . . ."

"So you think I'm worrying for nothing."

She takes a breath. "I think you need to stop worrying, at least for now. Enjoy the moment."

Maybe she's right. Maybe I'm so used to worrying that I don't know how to stop.

"I'm here to help," she says. "Whatever you need."

"Thanks, Morgan. You've been more than a friend, and I'm sorry I've—"

"Enough apologies. We're past that, okay?"

"Okay."

"Have you told Gabriel?" she asks.

"Not yet. I wanted to tell you first. Plus, I didn't . . . you know . . . want to call him."

"Why not? He's really worried about you."

"I don't want it to look like I'm trying to get between you two."

"What are you talking about?"

Her voice fades to the background as I focus instead on a muffled sound from downstairs. Scott's voice. Angry.

"Morgan, wait a second."

"What is it?"

"I'm not sure." I go to my door and open it, surprised to see Celeste coming down the hall.

"You need to come downstairs," she says.

My stomach sinks. "Why? What's going on?"

"I'm not sure, but I think your mom walked out of rehab."

CHAPTER 33

Beneath my stubborn heart,
Amid my tendons, nerves, and bones
A voice is lurking, forcing
Selfish ears to heed its groans.

—from "Denial" by L.F.

At first, I think Celeste is playing a joke on me, but then I see how she's biting her lip, how she's looking at me like I might collapse.

I lift my phone to my ear. "Morgan, I have to go."

"Is something wrong?"

"My mom walked out of rehab."

"Are you serious? Why?"

"I have no idea."

"Go," says Morgan. "Call me when you know something."

I don't remember ending the call, but my phone is off and I'm dimly aware of Celeste talking to me.

". . . left a bunch of messages, but of course, my mom didn't think to turn on her phone."

"How long?" I ask.

"What?"

"How long ago did my mom walk out?"

"Right after you dropped her off. Apparently they didn't even process her."

She must have left as soon as we drove away.

"You okay?" Celeste asks.

I nod. My face feels numb. My whole body feels numb.

"You sure?"

"Yeah, I'm sure."

And I am. Because something inside me has frozen up, some exhausted part of my mind that is too worn, too frustrated, too angry to deal with this.

After everything she's been through . . .

After everything *I've* been through . . .

And suddenly I want nothing more than to wash my hands of her. If she wants to destroy her life, go ahead. But leave me out of it.

"Let's go talk to my mom," Celeste says.

All I want is to be left alone, but I let her lead me down the steep stairs. When we reach the second floor, I hear Scott and Tanya fighting from their bedroom. Scott's yelling at her that she should have known this would happen, and Tanya's saying how no one could have predicted this, so it's not her fault.

Suddenly, their bedroom door bursts open, and Tanya walks out carrying her shoes. She's dressed for the rally in her new pink dress, but it's clear she's been crying. "It's not going to hurt your campaign," she says.

"Are you out of your mind?" Scott comes barreling out behind her. "If this gets out—"

"It won't."

Scott's face is red, his tie loose around his neck. "You," he says, pointing at me. "I thought you said she was fine."

"She was. I thought she was."

And suddenly I remember how sad Mom looked when I hugged her goodbye. And I remember what she said to me.

Don't hate me too much.

She planned this. She planned this the whole time.

Which means she's probably planning her next drink.

Or her next drug. Heroin's easy to get—that's what Gabriel told me.

My anger vanishes. A cold splash of fear takes its place. "We have to find her," I say.

Scott throws up his hands. "Great idea! Let's skip my campaign rally and go find Shauna."

"She's going to drink, or do drugs, or do *something.*"

"Not my problem."

"Listen," Tanya says to me. "I know you're worried. I'm worried too. But I've thought about this. Your mom has no money, which means she can't buy anything that will get her in trouble."

Behind me, Celeste barks a laugh.

Tanya whirls on her. "What's so funny?"

"Nothing." Celeste's eyes skate to me. "I just think you're being really naïve. If she wants to get her hands on something, she will."

"We should call 911," I say.

"Absolutely not!" Scott shouts. "She's not a child, for Christ's sake."

"But she's missing. And Celeste is right. If she wants to get her hands on something, she will."

"She's not missing," says Scott. "She's an adult who made a choice."

Tanya bites her lip. "Maybe we should still report it, though. It can't hurt."

"Are you kidding me?" Scott glares at her. "The election's in less than a week."

"I know that, Scott."

"And what do you think's going to happen when reporters find out my crazy-ass sister-in-law walked out of rehab? They'll start digging, that's what."

What's he afraid of? That Mom will tell the world he kicked me out of his house?

"That doesn't make sense," I say. "How would reporters even know she walked out of rehab?"

"Because they listen to police scanners," says Scott. "You report her missing and suddenly it's news."

Is that even true? I want to argue, but my brain feels scrambled.

"We should ask Marty," says Tanya. "Marty will know what to do."

"Fine," says Scott. "Get him on the phone."

o o o

It turns out, Marty agrees with Scott. If we report her missing, it won't be long before reporters come sniffing around, and who knows what kind of dirt they'll dig up.

Tanya breaks the news to me while putting on her earrings. Celeste and I are seated at the kitchen table. Scott is grabbing something from his office before they leave.

"Marty doesn't think she's actually missing," says Tanya. "He thinks she'll probably turn up by the time we're done with the rally."

"Marty's an idiot," says Celeste.

"Well, I agree with him," says Tanya.

"I rest my case," Celeste mumbles, but Tanya doesn't hear her. She's holding up a tiny mirror and putting on lipstick.

"So that's it?" I ask. "We do nothing and hope she turns up?"

"For now, yes." Tanya snaps the mirror closed.

"What about her suitcase?" I ask.

"What about it?"

"You packed her a Louis Vuitton suitcase. She could pawn it."

Tanya makes a face. "No one would want that old thing. It's all beat up."

I feel panic creeping up. "Do you even care what happens to her?"

"Of course I care. We all do."

At that second, Scott enters the kitchen, still tucking in his shirt. "You about ready?"

She nods, then leans in close to me. "I promise," she whispers, "as soon as the rally is over, I'll drive us around. We'll find her, okay?"

○ ○ ○

Celeste and I are still seated at the kitchen table when they leave. As soon as the garage door closes behind them, Celeste gets up. She seems nervous. "You want coffee?"

"No, that's okay."

"You sure? I'm going to make coffee."

So while she grinds coffee beans, I stare at my lap through the clear glass table. My hands are fists, my knees juddering. If only Mom had a phone. If she had a phone, I could call her.

Phone.

My phone.

Mom said Tanya was the one to call her this morning, to tell her that Scott changed his mind, but when I pull up my recent calls, I see that Mom was the one who called Tanya.

So she lied about that.

And at Serenity Solace, Mom asked me how often I checked

my email. Could she have sent me something when she had my phone? Or maybe when she borrowed Tanya's laptop?

I open my email, and sure enough . . . A message from Shauna Freeman is buried among a stack of notices from teachers. The subject line is in all caps as though she doesn't want me to miss it.

A LETTER FROM MOM

I open the email, my heart racing.

Dear Layla,

By now you're probably wondering why I did this. I did it because it's what's best for you.

Best for me? What is she talking about?

I wanted Scott to kick me out, and that's why I ruined Thanksgiving. But my plan blew up when he kicked you out too, so I had to improvise. Sorry for the confusion, but now that I'm out of the picture, I'm going to tell you a secret, and once you know it, everything will make sense.

No, Mom. This will never make sense.

When I got pregnant, Blaine was my boyfriend, but he isn't your father. Your real father is Scott and—

A moment of disbelief, and my world tilts. Everything I thought I knew—everything I thought I was—comes sliding toward me.

I can't breathe.

Scott's my father?

I can't see.

Scott's my father.

But I feel the table beneath my hands.

Solid.

And I hear the coffee brewing. I hear Celeste opening a cupboard.

And slowly I take a breath.

I'm vaguely aware that my hand hurts from gripping my phone. I make myself let go, blinking as my vision returns.

Mom's words on the screen.

> Your real father is Scott. . .

I keep reading.

> . . . and I know you probably hate me, but I want you to know, it only happened because both of us were drunk and he had a fight with Tanya (not that that's an excuse). When I found out I was pregnant, Scott had me do a paternity test, but when the results came back and it turned out he was the father, I got scared, so I lied and told everyone it was Blaine. I lied because I was ashamed and I didn't want to hurt Tanya, and plus Blaine was dead by then, so I didn't have to lie to him.

As if lying to me wasn't enough. Celeste is saying something to me, but I keep reading.

> That's no excuse for not telling you, but I honestly thought you'd be better off without Scott screwing up your life. I didn't want you growing up thinking you were some kind of mistake because you aren't. You deserve better, and that's why I can't

be in your life. I did my best to take care of you, but ever since your grandpa died, things have been so hard. I keep wanting to tell him I'm sorry, but you know how that's going.

Also, I told Scott he's your father. I had to email him the paternity test before he believed me, and I promised I wouldn't tell anyone, including you, as long as he took care of you.

So that's why Scott let me come back.

There's more to the letter, but Celeste is standing over me. "Did you hear what I said?"

I blink up at her. Her blue eyes stare down at me. Scott's eyes. My father's eyes.

I shake my head.

"I said, it's my fault your mom got drunk yesterday."

"What?"

"My peach schnapps disappeared. I thought I put it under my bed, but it's not there."

Again, she waits for my reaction, but all I can think is,

She's my sister.

"Layla, are you listening to me?"

My half sister.

"What's wrong with you?"

And my cousin.

"Seriously, you're freaking me out."

I barely hear her. My phone is in my hand. I look down at it.

Celeste looks too. "What is that?" The subject line screams in all caps. She bends closer. "Your mom sent you an email?"

"It's . . ."

I'm about to say *private*, but she takes my phone. I don't have the energy to fight her. And maybe I don't want to fight her. Maybe I want her to know.

So I watch her face as she reads. I watch how it changes, how she shakes her head as she scrolls. Finally she sits beside me. "Tell me this is a joke."

I don't say anything.

"When did she send this?"

"This morning, I think."

"This is insane." She keeps reading, her lips moving as she scrolls down the screen.

She stops, looks at me. "I think she's telling the truth."

Yeah, me too.

"I think we . . ." She stops to take a breath. "I think we need to find her."

"No. I'm done with her."

"Layla . . ."

"What?"

Her eyes lock onto mine. "You do realize this is a suicide note."

What? I take my phone back. No, she's wrong.

"She says she can't be in your life," Celeste says.

"That doesn't mean it's a suicide note."

"Are you sure?"

"Yes!"

Because she wouldn't do that.

I know she wouldn't.

I read the letter again. Nowhere does it say anything about killing herself, although she does talk about me suing Scott if he "tries to wiggle out of responsibilities."

But it's the last line that makes the hairs stand up on my neck.

> So I just want to tell you I love you. I know you probably hate me, but I hope one day you can forgive me.

Because it's an echo of what she said to me at Serenity Solace.

Don't hate me too much.

Celeste touches my arm, and I look at her face. She looks as scared as I feel.

I take a breath, say out loud what I want to be true. "It's not a suicide note."

"Okay."

Because nowhere does she say anything about killing herself.

Because she wouldn't do that.

She wouldn't.

"But maybe we should find her," I say.

"Exactly. Any idea where she'd go?"

I shake my head.

"The pawnshop? Maybe that suitcase is actually worth something."

I know it's worth something, despite what Tanya says, but what pawnshop would she go to? The one she knows, of course, the one near our old apartment, but how would she get there? Walk? Take the bus? Does she even still have her bus card?

"You want me to look up pawnshops?" Celeste asks.

I don't answer.

Something in her email . . .

Something about Grandpa . . .

I scan the letter until I find it.

> . . . ever since your grandpa died, things have been so hard. I keep wanting to tell him I'm sorry, but you know how that's going.

Present tense. As though she could really talk to him.

And suddenly I know where she went. I just hope she's still there.

CHAPTER 34

Her cries cut to the bone
and still she sits alone
waiting for the first and righteous stone.
—"Judgment Day" by L.F.

Two minutes later, Celeste and I are speeding toward the cemetery in Tanya's Mercedes. Celeste has the address plugged into her phone. She changes lanes and honks at the car in front of us.

It's been more than two hours since Mom walked out of rehab. How long would it take her to get to the cemetery? Did she stop to pawn the suitcase? And if she did, what will she do with the money?

She'll buy vodka. That was always her drink of choice.

Unless she buys heroin.

Celeste looks over. "I need to tell you something."

"Okay." But instead of speaking, she chews on her lip.

"Celeste, just say it."

"Fine. You know how your mom was in my room?"

"Yeah . . ."

"Well, I can't be sure, but . . ."

"Tell me."

"I think she might have found something."

"You mean, besides the peach schnapps?"

She nods.

"Your stash?"

She nods again.

I let that sink in.

"So what I'm saying is—"

"You're saying my mom didn't have to buy drugs on the street. You're saying she could've got them from your room."

"Could have, yeah, but I don't know for sure."

"Didn't you check?"

"Yeah, but I forget where I hide things."

Of course she does. "So what was in your room? What *could* she have taken?"

"Percocet, Molly, Oxy."

"Shit, Celeste!"

She winces. "Did she seem high to you? You were with her the whole time."

"She seemed fine. Other than being drunk at Thanksgiving. Nervous, but fine."

"So maybe she didn't find anything," Celeste says.

"Or maybe she didn't look."

But even as I say it, I know that's wrong. If Mom found peach schnapps under the bed, she would look.

A horrible thought crosses my mind. I'm thinking about the restaurant this morning, how once we were done eating, she went to the bathroom. How she was in there for a long time . . .

Tanya and I assumed she was in there cleaning herself up. And when she came out, she did look better.

But what if she hid in the bathroom so she could swallow whatever pills she took from Celeste's room?

Something cold settles in my chest.

Maybe Celeste is right.

Maybe it *is* a suicide note.

"Layla?"

I ignore her, wanting to hate her. If not for her stupid drugs . . .

My phone is in my hand, my fingers trembling as I touch the numbers on the keypad.

"Who are you calling?"

"Nine-one-one."

I lift the phone to my ear. It's ringing.

"My dad won't be happy."

"Screw your dad."

My dad.

"Yeah, screw him," says Celeste.

Finally, after the third ring, a man answers the phone.

"Nine-one-one. What's your emergency?"

I swallow. It's hard to say out loud because saying it out loud . . .

"My mom's missing," I blurt. "I think she's trying to kill herself."

Saying it out loud makes it real.

○ ○ ○

The emergency dispatcher asks a bunch of questions. I answer like a robot, distancing my mind, because if I think about it . . .

Don't think!

If I think about her killing herself . . .

Please, Mom. Please be okay.

I won't be able to function.

I tell the emergency dispatcher that Mom could have taken a bunch of pills. If she took them while we were at breakfast, they would have been starting to take effect about the time we left her at Serenity Solace.

Which means she could be dead by now.

When I end the call, the urge to panic is almost overwhelming. I told the man on the phone everything I knew, everything I feared, but once he found out Mom didn't have access to a firearm, he didn't seem all that enthusiastic about finding her. Still, he said they'd send police to look for her in the vicinity of Serenity Solace and the cemetery.

We've left the city behind. Instead of buildings, the road is lined with trees. We go through a stoplight, and the cemetery appears on our left. Celeste makes the turn, and we pass through a tall iron gate. The lot is full. There must be a funeral going on. Celeste can't find a space, so she drops me off near the grass. There's a path that leads past the main office.

I unbuckle my seat belt before the car rolls to a stop. I turn to her, point to the building. "They have maps in there."

She nods. "I'll find you."

As soon as my feet hit the path, I start running.

And pass her suitcase lying on the grass. It's open, Tanya's clothes spilling onto the ground and blowing in the wind.

I don't know what that means, but I don't slow down. The gravestones are a blur as I run. I pass a big white mausoleum, and that's when I know I'm close. Holding the stitch in my side, I slow down and squint into the distance where I know Grandpa is buried. All I see is sunlight. Flashing. Golden. I blink.

And see her. She's slumped against Grandpa's tombstone wearing a metallic gold blouse.

"Mom!" I call. But she doesn't hear me.

Her eyes are closed. She's not moving.

CHAPTER 35

Quick
and crushing,
wrenching, splattering.
Me and my insides,
painted splats
Streaked on
Grandpa's grave.

—from "Gutted" by L.F.

I call again, my voice shattering the stillness, but she doesn't move. Her head rests against the gravestone. Shadows from the trees skim her face.

I run closer, screaming, "Mom, wake up!"

Please wake up!

I reach her and fall to my knees. Afraid to touch her, afraid she'll be stiff with death like Grandpa on the morning I found him.

And then . . . A miracle. She flinches and opens her eyes.

"Mom?"

Her eyelids flutter. She sees my face and recoils. "No! What are you doing here?"

"Coming to save you."

"I don't need saving."

"Did you take something?"

"What?"

"Drugs, Mom. Did you take drugs?"

"No. Just go."

I peer at her face, trying to see her pupils, but she won't meet my eyes—which is how she acts when she's drunk.

All that fear I was holding inside gives way to relief. Drunk, I can handle. I go to hug her, but she pushes me away.

"Why are you doing this, Mom?"

She doesn't answer.

"Why'd you walk out of rehab?"

"I told you that place wasn't for me."

"You didn't even try it."

"Please, just go away!"

I'm pissed enough that part of me wants to do just that, but no way am I letting her off the hook that easy. "Not until you explain your email."

Her shoulders stiffen.

"What? You didn't think I'd read it?"

"Not so soon."

"Celeste thought it was a suicide note. But it's not, is it? It's just a note to clear your conscience."

"Please leave me alone." She gets to her feet, steadying herself on Grandpa's tombstone. Now I see a half-full water bottle lying on the grass next to a limp bouquet of dandelions. I'm sure the bottle has vodka in it. That's one of her tricks to hide it.

"At least tell me to my face," I say. "Tell me Scott's my father."

Instead of answering, she staggers away from me.

"Where are you going?"

Her only response is to walk faster.

More frustrated than I've ever been, I pick up her water

bottle and throw it at her. "Don't forget your vodka!" It thumps against her leg, but she doesn't stop to pick it up.

If it was vodka, she'd stop to pick it up.

"Mom, wait!"

She keeps walking.

Without thinking, I go after her. Something skims across my sandal. At first, I think it's a dragonfly, but it's a plastic baggie. It twitches in the wind, caught in the bouquet of dandelions. Some part of me knows before I stoop to pick it up, and like one of those tile puzzles, the pieces slide into place.

The fact that Mom found Celeste's stash. How could she not? The fact that she walked out of rehab before they even processed her.

Which means she had Celeste's pills on her the whole time.

While we were eating Thanksgiving dinner.

While we slept at the homeless shelter.

While we ate breakfast before dropping her off at Serenity Solace.

All she was doing was waiting for her chance.

A chance to be alone. A chance to talk to Grandpa.

Mom didn't swallow the pills before we dropped her off. She swallowed them sitting here at Grandpa's grave.

○ ○ ○

A million thoughts crowd my brain.

Call someone. Get help. Go after her.

Do something!

But I can't move. It's like I'm paralyzed because I don't know what to do first.

And then Celeste appears from around the mausoleum. She's looking at a map and doesn't see me.

"CELESTE!"

Her head snaps up.

"Call 911!"

The map falls from her fingers. Her phone is in her hand, and time slows to a crawl. I watch her tap her screen, watch her lift the phone to her ear as her long blonde hair blows behind her. Her mouth is moving, but all I hear is wind.

The map skitters over the grass and drifts past me. Celeste's eyes widen. She's still talking into the phone, but she's pointing, and I think she's pointing at the map, but now she's running toward me, gesturing at me to turn around.

So I do. In a daze, I turn around.

Mom is bent over. I think she's choking, but as I sprint toward her, she takes off running. Staggering, more like. I'm almost on her, close enough to hear her breathe, close enough to touch her. I grab her shirt. Pull. She stumbles, and I tackle her to the ground. She wails as we skid over the grass in a tangle of arms and legs. Then she tries to push me off, slapping at my arms like I'm trying to kill her—when all I want to do is save her.

"Mom, please!"

She's still fighting as I pin her with my body. Still struggling as I pry open her mouth and force my fingers down her throat. She gags, but nothing comes up. I jam deeper. A tiny bit of liquid seeps from her mouth, but no pills.

Celeste is beside me. "Layla, stop."

"She did it. She took your pills."

"I know, but you're not supposed to make her vomit."

"How do you know that?"

"I just do. Do you have any water?"

I think about her water bottle. If only I hadn't thrown it. "No!"

"Help me sit her up."

Her body is limp as we pull her upright. Her head lolls on her shoulders.

"She's dead!" I cry.

"No, I hear her breathing."

I put my ear close to her mouth, and yes, she's breathing, but it's coming in strangled gasps.

"Try to keep her awake until the ambulance comes."

"How long will that be?"

"I don't know. They said it's on its way."

I listen for sirens, but all I hear is shouting in the distance. I think I'm imagining it, but the shouts get louder, and when I look up, a cluster of people wearing church clothes are running toward us.

The funeral, I think.

Ready-made mourners. Like vultures in their grays and browns and blacks.

A bald man with a kind face crouches beside me, his hand on my shoulder. "What can I do?"

"I don't know! She took a bunch of pills."

"She's your mother?"

I nod.

"What's your name?"

"Layla."

"Okay, Layla. My name is Mitch, and help is on the way. Do you want to pray with me?"

I nod, snot running from my nose.

He hands me a tissue, takes my hand, and bows his head. "Dear Heavenly Father, be with Layla and her mother. Protect them and bring them comfort. Let them look back on this day and—"

Mom's eyelids flutter open.

"Mom!"

"Layla?" Her eyes are unfocused.

"I'm here. Do you see me?"

"You need to go away."

"Mom, no!"

She starts to gag. White froth spills from her mouth.

Mitch helps me turn her on her side. White liquid spills from her mouth onto the grass while the people from the funeral gather round us, their whispered voices like a chorus of ghosts.

"What happened?"

"I think she overdosed."

"Oh my God."

Celeste lunges to her feet. "Get away! Have some respect!" But none of them move, and I see why she's yelling and waving her arms. Three of the vultures have their phones out.

Recording us. As if watching Mom suffer is something to be savored.

CHAPTER 36

And when you look upon my lively dance,
I will flinch and fear for you and say:
Oh Mother,
I wish you were well today.
Dear Mother,
I long for your laugh today.
—from "To Mother, From Me" by L.F.

My world feels surreal, like my brain is amped up on twenty cups of coffee, like I'm living under a strobe light, and everything is stark and bright and cartoonish. I'm sitting in a hard plastic chair in the ER waiting room. Celeste is slumped beside me, staring at her phone. I don't know how long we've been here, but it feels like hours. No one's told us anything except, "Sit tight. We'll let you know when we have news."

So I'm sitting tight, but my leg is going a mile a minute. I'm trying not to think the worst, but I can't help it. What if they can't save her? She was unconscious by the time the paramedics got to her.

What if they did everything they could, but she was too far gone?

Or what if they took one look at her and decided she was just another junkie, not worth saving at all?

Mitch said he would keep praying for us, and I'm grateful for that. Morgan is praying too. She's trying to get a ride to the hospital, but her mom and Phil are in a movie and Gabriel's mom has his car.

Celeste sighs loudly from the chair beside me. Her earbuds are in, and she's watching a video.

"Any word from your mom?" I ask.

She shakes her head before pulling out her earbuds. "Maybe the rally is still going on."

Or maybe Tanya doesn't care.

The video on Celeste's phone is still playing. I do a double take. Is that what I think it is?

Mom on the ground at the cemetery. Me hunched over her.

My mouth drops open. "Where'd you get that?"

"One of the guys who recorded it goes to our school."

"He sent it to you?"

"I told him to."

"Why?"

"I have my reasons."

I stare at her.

"Trust me, okay?"

Strangely enough, I do.

Celeste starts the video over, and I don't want to watch it, but I can't help it. Mom's face is hidden because Mitch and I are in the way, but you can see her legs thumping the ground. Then Celeste comes on-screen, yelling at whoever's holding the camera. The sound is muted, but it's clear she's calling him an asshole. She tries to grab the camera, and the picture jerks as whoever's taking the video tries to dodge her.

The camera zooms in, and there's a close-up of Mom's face.

Her eyes are closed, and my hand is slapping her cheek. Then the camera zooms out, and you see me crying with Mitch's hand on my shoulder. The camera jerks again, and Mom's shiny gold blouse catches the sunlight. Then the picture goes dark.

"That's where I grabbed his phone," says Celeste.

"You don't think he'll post it, do you?"

"I threatened to castrate him if he did, but he also knows my dad's running for mayor."

"So this could be news?"

"Maybe."

I should probably be worried, but right now, it doesn't seem important. I keep thinking about the blouse Mom was wearing. Gold and fancy, not something she'd ever wear. Tanya must have packed it in Mom's suitcase, and for some reason, Mom felt the need to change into it. Was she concerned about how we'd find her body? Or was she dressing up for death like she'd dress up for a party?

"Freeman?"

The voice makes me jump. It's coming from a woman in scrubs who stands in the open doorway that leads to the ER. I spring to my feet. Celeste is right beside me.

The woman nods at us but doesn't smile, and I don't know what that means. Her scrubs are bright pink, which doesn't seem fair, not when she's dealing with trauma and sickness and death.

"What's happening?" I ask. "Is my mom okay?"

The nurse looks past us. "Do you have an adult with you?"

"Me," Celeste says. "I'm an adult."

I'm pretty sure the nurse knows she's lying, but she nods before gesturing us through the open door. I hesitate—maybe it's better not to know—but Celeste grabs my hand and pulls me through.

○ ○ ○

Mom is unconscious with a fat tube coming out of her mouth. I know it's there to help her breathe, but I hate how frail it makes her look. Another tube, this one skinnier and black, goes through one nostril. A monitor beeps beside her, and there are more tubes and wires attached to her arms and chest.

"I know it looks scary," says the nurse in pink scrubs, "but all these tubes and wires are here to help her."

I should be sobbing, but all I feel is numb. "Will she be okay?"

Instead of answering, the nurse starts talking about NG tubes in her stomach to pump out the contents, charcoal in the tube to neutralize the drugs. She gets really technical, and I don't understand most of what she says, but I nod as though I do.

Celeste interrupts her. "This all sounds great, but you haven't answered the question."

The nurse blinks. "What question?"

"Is she going to be okay?"

The nurse's eyes flick toward me. "We're doing everything we can."

"What does that mean?" I ask.

"It means her heartbeat is weak, so we're keeping a close eye on her. It means we've done what we can to get the drugs out of her stomach, but it's hard to know how much is already in her bloodstream. Everyone absorbs medicine at a different rate."

"So in other words, you don't know," says Celeste.

"Like I said, we're doing everything we can," says the nurse. "As soon as there's room in ICU, we'll move her there."

"Can we stay with her?" I ask. "In case she wakes up?"

"You can stay right here until she goes to ICU, but once she's there, you'll have to wait in the visitor's room until they tell you it's okay to visit."

I leap on the words *okay* and *visit*. "Does that mean she'll wake up soon?"

The nurse's smile is sad. "We hope so," she says, and then she leaves us alone, pulling the curtain around Mom's bed.

○ ○ ○

A wax exhibit. That's what I think of as I look at Mom's face. Her chest moves up and down, but that's only because the respirator is pumping air into her lungs. Outside the curtain, people are talking. I hear laughter, and it doesn't seem fair that life is going on as if nothing is wrong.

Celeste steps up beside me, so close I can smell her flowery body spray over the hospital's disinfectant. "If you want me to leave, I will."

It almost sounds like she *wants* to leave, and it hits me again—what Mom did to Celeste's family.

"No," I say. "But if you want to go . . ."

Celeste grips the bedrail, and I think this is where she'll tell me she *has* to leave because she can't stand looking at the skank who slept with her dad.

"It's not that," she says. "I wanted to say I'm sorry."

For the drugs, she means. "I'm not blaming you," I tell her, even though I was. On the way to the cemetery I was, but I'm not now.

"If I hadn't talked you into getting high, your mom wouldn't have seen us. She wouldn't have known to look in my room."

I squeeze the bedrail. "She's been planning this for a long time. She would have found a way to do it."

"You're too nice," she says.

"Yeah, well, maybe you are too."

She half-laughs. "No one's ever accused me of *that*."

Probably not, but I've come to realize Celeste isn't as callous as she pretends to be.

"I don't know why you don't hate her," I say. "Or maybe you do."

"No." She keeps her eyes on Mom. "Aunt Shauna has always been nice to me. Maybe it was out of guilt, but it still felt good not to be yelled at all the time."

I almost smile. "Remember when she used to babysit you? How she'd play hide-and-seek with us?"

"I used to wish she was my mom," Celeste says.

"Really?"

She turns to look at me. "Is that so hard to believe?"

It's not, actually. Before her drinking got so bad, she was a good mom, despite how much she struggled.

We lapse into silence, both of us watching her as the respirator pumps air into her lungs.

"So maybe now's not the best time," says Celeste, "but what are you going to do about my dad?"

"Nothing."

"Nothing?"

"He doesn't know that I know. And no offense, I don't *want* him as my dad."

"So you're just going to . . . What? Pretend it's not true?"

"Something like that."

"What about after you graduate?"

"What do you mean?"

"Once you graduate high school, you think he's going to quote-unquote, take care of you?"

"I haven't thought about it."

"Well, I have, and if you sue him, you could get him to pay for your college. You do want to go to college, don't you?"

"Yeah, but I'm not going to throw my family under the bus so he'll pay for it."

"What are you talking about?"

"Your mom, for one thing. Can you imagine how she'll feel if she finds out the truth? She'll be devastated."

"It wouldn't be your fault."

"She'd still be hurt, though, and I don't want to hurt your mom. Especially after she's been so nice to me."

Celeste snorts. "A whole week of your life, my mom's been nice to you, and you want to throw away your future?"

"I'm not throwing it away. I plan to go to community college."

"Wow, big dreams."

"Shut up, Celeste."

"Sorry."

"Plus," I say, "if Aunt Tanya found out, I don't think my mom could handle it."

Celeste is quiet for a second. "You think she'd try to . . ."

Kill herself. That's what neither of us can say.

Gripping the bedrail, I squeeze until my knuckles are white. "The only reason she told me the truth in her email was because she thought she'd be dead by the time I read it."

"Okay," says Celeste. "I get that."

"So we're agreed? We won't tell anyone?"

"Whatever you want, but I still think you might change your mind."

"I won't."

"Well, that's good then."

"Really?"

"It's not like I want people knowing my cousin is my half sister."

"God, when you put it that way . . ."

"What other way is there? Nothing says 'redneck' like a family tree that doesn't fork."

I laugh. I can't help it.

Celeste laughs too, and then her phone rings. She fishes it from her pocket. "It's my mom."

Finally, we can tell her we found Mom, but what's Scott going to say? What's he going to do?

"I'll take it outside," says Celeste. "There might be yelling."

I nod, even though I want her to stay.

Celeste steps out of the privacy curtain, and suddenly I'm alone. Unless you count Mom, which I don't, not when she's lying here hooked up to machines. She's with me, but it's like she's a nonperson. And I realize that's how she's been for a while now.

Here, but not present.

Alive, but not living.

Will she ever get better? Or is this all she is? A sad alcoholic who's only going through the motions. A miserable woman who wants to die because she thinks I'll be better off without her. I want my mom back. More than anything in the world, I want her back.

I take her hand. It's like I'm holding a slab of meat.

And suddenly I burst into tears. "Please don't die, Mom!"

Please, God, if there is a God, don't let her die.

Of course, she doesn't hear me, and I doubt God does either. Maybe if I keep talking to her, she'll know how much I need her to wake up.

So I start talking.

I tell her Morgan is praying for her. I tell her I forgive her for everything. I tell her how much I appreciate all the things she's done for me.

Despite her alcoholism, she tried to be a good mom. I could have been nicer to her. I could have persuaded her to get help; instead, I denied she had a problem—until Grandpa died and everything fell apart.

"You can be happy," I say, squeezing her hand.

And then I wait.

And I watch.

Her hand doesn't twitch, her eyelids don't move. Did I think my tears were magic?

Maybe I did, a little.

I let go of her hand, and as I do, I freeze.

Was that . . .?

I think it was.

I think as I let go of her hand, the beeps measuring her heart got faster.

So I take her hand again, lacing my fingers with hers.

Please, God. Please make her okay.

○ ○ ○

It's been at least ten minutes, and still Celeste hasn't returned. Finally, I go to look for her. She's not in the ER waiting room, but I find her outside leaning against the building. She's still talking on her phone. When she sees me, she waves me over.

"My mom wants to talk to you."

I take her phone. "Hello?"

"How is she?" says Tanya. "Any change?"

"She's still unconscious."

A short pause. "Listen . . . I can't come out to see her. At least not right now. It's too risky."

"What do you mean?"

"Scott doesn't think it's a good idea."

"Oh."

"And he wants you back at the house. You and Celeste both."

"I can't just leave."

"You have to."

"Or what?"

She sighs. "Don't test him, Layla."

"I'm not, but I can't just abandon my mom because Uncle Scott says I should."

"Well, that might be a problem if you want to live here. Scott wants—"

I hand the phone back to Celeste. I can't listen to what Scott wants.

Celeste lifts her brows as she takes it, and even though Tanya's voice is still coming through the speaker, Celeste ends the call.

"So." She pockets her phone. "I take it you're done listening to her bullshit?"

"I think she's actually trying to make things easier for me."

"Is it working?"

"Not really."

She laughs, which kind of makes me feel like we're in this together. I lean beside her against the wall. "Your dad wants us back at the house."

"I know." She glances over. "I take it you're staying?"

"I have to."

"Yeah, I figured. But Dad will be pissed."

I shrug. "What else is new?"

"I guess you're going to find out." Her smile is grim as she pushes off the wall. Watching her trudge toward the parking lot, I stop myself from asking her to stay. I want us to be in this together, but it doesn't matter if we're friends or cousins or even sisters. Whatever happens next is between Mom and me.

CHAPTER 37

Silent in her suffering,
there's beauty in her heart, crying to be seen.
If only I'd paid attention.
—from "Portrait of My Mom" by L.F.

Mom is sitting up in her hospital bed with all of us surrounding her. Me, Aunt Tanya, Celeste. Even Uncle Scott.

Mom looks happier than I've ever seen her. "It's good you all came."

"We got you something," says Scott.

"A going-away present," says Tanya.

Mom turns to me, her brow furrowed. "Am I going somewhere?"

"I don't know," I say.

Scott smirks. "Didn't they tell you?"

"Tell me what?"

He holds up a clear plastic garbage bag.

"What's that?" I ask.

"Her present," says Celeste.

"But it's empty."

"Not for long." Scott shakes the bag open.

"What are you doing?" I ask.

"What we should have done a long time ago," says Tanya.

"Your mom ruined everything," says Celeste.

"Wait!"

But I'm too late. Scott whips the bag over Mom's head and pulls it tight. She blinks at me through the clear plastic. "It's okay, Layla."

"NO!"

A bony hand shakes me awake.

"Honey?"

I open my eyes. At first I think it's Mom, but then I see it's a tiny old lady, one of the nurses from ICU. I take a huge breath. "What is it?"

"It's okay, honey." Her eyes get squinty when she smiles at me. "Your mom's awake."

o o o

Thank God for kind nurses. ICU has strict visiting hours, and they definitely don't extend to the middle of the night, but this particular nurse, whose name is Mary and who I'll never forget, knows I've been waiting out here for close to twelve hours. As I follow her through the maze of sleeping patients and beeping monitors, she explains that Mom woke up about an hour ago. She's stable, so they took out her breathing tube. Since then, she's been asking for me.

"Does this mean she'll be okay?" I ask.

Mary turns around to smile at me. "It's a good sign."

I follow her around a corner. "How is she? I mean, how does she seem?" What I really want to know is, does she seem suicidal? But I can't bring myself to say it.

"She seems overwhelmed," says Mary, and my heart sinks.

"But that's to be expected. Your job right now is to make her feel not so overwhelmed. Do you think you can do that?"

I nod, even though I'm not sure at all.

"Don't worry," says Mary, and her voice is so kind I want to cry. "You won't be alone in this. Your mom will be getting therapy, and she'll be under suicide watch for at least seventy-two hours."

"Okay."

"I hope that makes you feel better."

"It does."

"Good." She stops walking. "And here we are."

I look up to see that Mom's bed is right in front of me and that Mom is watching me with wary eyes from her cocoon of white sheets. Her bed is raised, so she's sitting up. The black tube is still in her nose, and she's still attached with wires to a bunch of machines with their blips and beeps and squiggly lines. I want to rush to her side. I want to throw my body against her and have her put her arms around me and tell me everything will be okay. But I'm afraid of what she'll do. I'm afraid she'll shrink away.

"Mom?"

She lowers her eyes.

I glance at Mary, who nods encouragingly. "I'll go now."

Mary leaves, and now Mom and I are alone, but I just stand there. Because what do you say when your mom tries to kill herself? How do you tell her how stupid that is without making things worse?

She's the first to speak, her words coming out as a croak. "I'm sorry."

And what do I say to that? Do I tell her it's okay? That I forgive her?

"You scared me," I say.

"I didn't mean to."

"Really?" A surge of anger sharpens my voice. "You didn't think trying to kill yourself would scare me?"

"You weren't supposed to be there."

"What difference—"

"I didn't want you to find me," she says, "the way you found your grandpa."

The way I found him dead, she means. The image of him frozen on his cot is stamped in my brain, but so is the memory of how Mom and I held each other and sobbed. Right now, I want to hug her, but I'm afraid to touch her. Afraid to speak. Afraid of so much.

"I need to tell you something," she whispers, and my heart sinks. Something else besides Scott being my father?

"The night your grandpa died. You remember it?"

"Yeah, of course."

"You heard us fighting."

I nod, moving a bit closer. "You never told me what it was about."

"Because I didn't want you to know."

"Know what?"

"I told your grandpa . . ." She tries to meet my eyes but fails.

"That Scott was my father?"

She nods miserably. "I wanted to tell him before he died. I wanted his forgiveness, but instead . . ." Tears fill her eyes. "His face after I told him . . . He said he couldn't stand looking at me."

"It's okay, Mom."

"He said he couldn't wait to die."

And the next morning, he was dead.

"He killed himself because of me."

"No, the medical examiner said—"

"I know what the medical examiner said. But I looked it up. Do you know what happens when you overdose on Oxycodone? Your heart gives out."

Which is how Grandpa died.

Mom is crying. Silently, her fists pressed to her forehead.

"It's okay," I say.

"No, it's not. My dad hated me."

"He was angry, but he never hated you."

She lifts her head. "Of course he hated me, and I don't blame him." Her hands grip the bedsheets like she wants to pull them over her head. "I'm so sorry, Layla. I know you hate me too."

"No."

"I lied to you your whole life."

She did.

"And I betrayed my own sister . . . Who does that?"

"I don't hate you, okay?"

Her brow furrows. "How could you not?"

"Because you're my mom."

She chokes out a laugh.

"And alcoholism is a disease."

Tears stream down her face.

"And I love you."

In a rush, her eyes meet mine. "Is that true?"

"Yeah, Mom. Of course."

But even as I say it, I wonder . . . when was the last time I told her I loved her? I honestly can't remember.

So I say it again. "Mom, I love you."

She bites her lip. "I didn't know that."

Leaning over her bed, I put my arms around her, but it's awkward with all the wires attached to her. Plus, I'm remembering all the shit she's done, how damaged she is, what a long way she has to go before things can be good.

I feel her sobbing against me, so I hug her tighter. "It's okay," I tell her.

"It's not," she says. "But I'm going to try."

And even though she's said that before—I've lost track of how many times—this time feels different. I know, at some point, we need to talk about rehab and Scott and what we're going to do, but right now, the quiet is peaceful. It feels right. So I keep my mouth shut and hang onto her words. *I'm going to try.* I feel how fragile she is—her body like a sack of bones. But that can be fixed, and so can she.

CHAPTER 38

Joy of a moment
Eases my own destruction
Letting me be loved.
—from "Joy of a Moment" by L.F.

Gabriel and Morgan picked me up from the hospital, and now we're sitting in Starbucks, the one by our school. We're sitting at a table by the window, and the sun is warm on my skin, and I know I should probably go back to Scott and Tanya's, but since Scott's already pissed that I didn't come "home" when he told me to, I figure, what's a few more hours?

And besides, I need to be with my friends.

I've told them everything. About Scott being my father, about Mom's suicide attempt . . . It's early enough on a Saturday morning that not many people are out, so we have the place mostly to ourselves, which is a good thing because I spent the first ten minutes bawling my eyes out while Morgan rubbed my back and Gabriel pressed napkins into my clenched fist.

But now the crying's done and I feel strong again, like I got this, and yeah, it won't be easy, but when is life ever easy?

Morgan and I are on one side of the table, Gabriel on the other, and as we sit drinking coffee (Morgan bought for all of us), I'm trying not to notice Gabriel's shy smile, the way he blows on his coffee before every sip, the way his hands cradle his cup as though it might shatter if he grips it too hard. I know he and Morgan are trying to spare my feelings by sitting on opposite sides of the table, but I wish they'd just come out with it already so I can get used to seeing them together.

"Listen to this," says Morgan. She's reading from her phone. "*Most states have mechanisms in place that allow paternity suits to be filed by the state at no cost to the mother who's seeking to establish paternity.*" She lowers her phone. "So that means you don't have to pay for a lawyer if Scott tries to get out of child support."

I shake my head. "He's not going to be paying child support."

"Why not?"

"Because that would mean Tanya finds out."

Morgan sets aside her cup. "Listen," she says. "I know you like your aunt, and I know you don't want to hurt her, but this is bigger than that. If Scott's your dad, which apparently he is, don't you think he owes you?"

"Maybe."

"He owes you, like, fifteen years of child support."

"But if Tanya finds out," I say, "what happens to my mom? I don't know if she could live with it. The shame, I mean. That's one of the reasons she tried to . . . you know . . ." I still can't say *kill herself* without choking up.

Gabriel lifts a finger. "Can I say something?"

"Sure."

"Your mom's a recovering addict," he says. "And as someone who knows a little something about that, I want to point out that making amends to people is one of the things we have to do to get better."

"But isn't that, like, step nine? My mom's on step one. I don't think she could handle the shame of Tanya knowing."

Morgan touches my arm. "You really think she'd do it again? Try to take her own life?"

"I don't want to take the chance."

"But what about you?" Morgan says. "I know you're afraid for your mom, but you have to do what's best for you. What if Scott kicks you out?"

"Again," says Gabriel.

"I don't know. But I do know that what's best for me is having my mom around to see me graduate high school."

"Okay." Morgan bites her lip. "Whatever you decide, I've got your back."

"I know."

And I do.

Gabriel clears his throat, but I don't dare look at him because I know he's going to say something kind or smart or supportive, and every time he does say something kind or smart or supportive, I realize how stupid I was to not see how great he is.

"I know I haven't known you very long," he says, "but I feel the same way as Morgan. Which is to say, whatever you need, I'll try to help."

I steal a glance at him as I mutter my thanks, and there he is smiling at me in that quiet way of his. Maybe I'm too vulnerable or too hurting or too something, but I want that smile for myself. Only for myself. And that's not fair to Morgan.

"You know . . ." I nudge Morgan. "It's okay if you two sit together."

Gabriel furrows his brow. "Why would we want to sit together?"

"Because you're dating. Duh. It's pretty obvious."

"Uh . . ." says Morgan.

"Didn't you tell her?" asks Gabriel.

"I tried," Morgan says, "but there was so much going on. And plus, I figured *you* would have told her."

"Told me what?"

"That we're not dating for one thing," says Gabriel.

"But I saw you holding hands."

"Because he was letting me down gently," says Morgan. "I asked him out. But not because I like him. I asked him out to get back at you." She smirks at Gabriel. "No offense."

He smirks back. "None taken."

"It was dumb," says Morgan, "and I'm really sorry."

"Wait a minute." I look at each of them in turn. "So this whole time, you guys weren't even interested in each other?"

"I tried to tell you," says Gabriel.

Did he? And then I remember him wanting to tell me something at the snow cone booth, but I was too busy trying to keep my secret from Felix.

"And then I figured Morgan must have told you."

Morgan's smiling as my mouth hangs open. "Wow, this is awesome. It's like you've been punked."

"Only not funny," says Gabriel.

"You're right," says Morgan. "You two need to talk."

"Wait," says Gabriel, but already she's leaving.

And now we're alone. Gabriel on one side of the table. Me on the other.

"Layla . . ."

I hold my breath.

Who knew my heart could hurt with hope?

o o o

Gabriel fiddles with the cardboard sleeve on his cup, refusing to look at me, which can't be good. I didn't notice before, but he's wearing a T-shirt with Amy Winehouse on it, and I realize suddenly that his T-shirts have a theme. Musicians who died from addiction.

Suddenly his hand is covering mine, and it's warm and his touch feels good, and I want to sink into it, sink my whole body into his touch and have him hold me.

I look into his eyes, and he doesn't look happy. "What's wrong?"

He hesitates, then lets go of my hand. "This. Me liking you. Wanting you."

"That's bad?"

"I can't."

I look down. "I understand."

"Do you?"

"I treated you like dirt, so yeah."

"Not dirt, exactly, but it hurt."

"And I'm so, so sorry."

"I've forgiven you, but I still can't . . ."

"Be with me?"

"Even though I really want to."

I try to keep the hurt from my face.

"Layla, I'm an addict."

"But you're sober."

"And I want to stay that way."

"And you think I'm going to corrupt you?"

"No, but . . ."

"What?"

"My sponsor says I'm not supposed to start new relationships in my first year."

"Your sponsor?"

"It's someone who helps you through the steps, who calls you on your bullshit."

"I know what a sponsor is."

"And this man. My sponsor. He's not just throwing out rules to punish me. These things he tells me, these suggestions, they go way back. He's not just pulling them out of his ass."

"Are you sure about that?"

"They're designed to help me stay sober. Because I'm apt to make bad decisions in my first year."

"So now I'm a bad decision?"

"I didn't say that."

"You kind of did."

"Layla, this isn't about you."

And that makes me stop. He's right.

"It's about my recovery," he says, "which I have to put first."

"Okay." I nod. "I get that."

"Do you? Last time I got clean, I wanted to do everything my way, and we both know how that turned out."

He pulls up his sleeve to show me his tattoo, but instead of seeing a phoenix rising from the ashes, all I see is fire and a defunct sobriety date.

"I thought I could handle one more time," he says. "But I burned down our apartment. My mom almost died. Because of me."

I think about that. The guilt he must feel.

"And I want to be with you," he says. "I want to hold your hand and I want to kiss you, like, really bad. But I can't. And it's driving me crazy that I can't."

I imagine his lips on mine, his tongue slipping into my mouth, and I've never wanted anything so bad.

"Gabriel . . ." I reach for his hand, but he pulls it away, and suddenly there's this space in my chest, empty and cold.

"I'm sorry," he says.

"Don't be."

"I wish things were different."

"So do I."

And maybe they can be. His sponsor doesn't control him.

But then I think about Mom, how if her sponsor told her to do something—or not do something—I'd want her to listen. And I'd be pissed at anyone who might get in the way of that.

I don't want to be the person who gets in the way of that.

"I'll have a year in June," he says. "Maybe we can try then. If you want to."

I know I'll want to, but what if I'm not around in June? If Scott loses the election, my days of living in his house are over. I could end up with some foster family on the other side of Florida. And what if it's better that way? At least for Gabriel.

"We probably shouldn't hang out," I say.

"Don't say that."

"I don't want to be the one who messes things up for you."

"You won't."

"You can't know that."

"I know we can help each other." He leans forward. "Can I show you something?"

"Sure."

He reaches into his pocket, pulls out a folded-up piece of paper, and slides it over to me.

"What's this?"

"I think it belongs to you."

As I unfold it, I recognize my own handwriting. And then I see it's the poem I wrote in the book I borrowed from the homeless shelter. The same book I saw Gabriel reading.

I know the words by heart, but I read them anyway.

THE FALLACY OF HOPE
BY L.F.

Hope is a wriggling organism
Dividing, multiplying
Amoeba-like, invisible to the naked eye.
But not my eyes.
My eyes wear rose-colored glasses.
My eyes see hope in the empty air.
I reach for it, touch it . . .
Only to watch it scatter
And become like the wind.

When I'm finished, I look up, embarrassed, but Gabriel's eyes make me feel safe.

"I saw that my first day at the shelter," he says. "I saw it and I thought, Who is this 'L.F.', who writes poetry in books? Where is she? I hope she's okay because she sounds like she's really hurting.' And then you introduced yourself, and I knew."

"That I'm someone who vandalizes books?"

"That you're someone I want to know. And since then . . ."

"What?"

"I've loved getting to know you. But I also realize you have your own stuff to work through."

Sadly, he's right. I'm still kind of a mess, and even though I'm no longer hiding, I'm still afraid of what might happen today, tomorrow, a year from now . . .

Because what if Mom can't stay sober? What if she dies? Or what if she spends the next ten years struggling and failing and hating herself?

Where does that leave me?

"Don't you ever get scared?" I ask.

"All the time. But whenever I'm feeling overwhelmed, whenever I'm afraid of the future, my sponsor tells me to look at where my feet are."

I smile because now of course I know who his sponsor is, and I know that James wouldn't lead him astray.

Right now he's safe. Right now we're both safe.

And right now, maybe that's enough.

CHAPTER 39

Disease has spread and caused my soul to roam.
My heart stays put; it's bitter, harsh, and dark.
And never-ending struggles for a home
Have fought with me and fiercely left their mark.
—from "Ode to Fifteen" by L.F.

Morgan, Gabriel, and I are quiet as Gabriel drives to Scott and Tanya's house. This time I'm in the front seat, my knee juddering, and Morgan and Gabriel keep stealing glances at me. I know they're worried for me. I'm worried too. What will Scott do when I show up at the house? He won't kick me out, will he? Just for staying at the hospital? Not with the election next Friday.

"I just thought of something," says Gabriel. "That poem would be perfect for Open Mic."

"What poem?" asks Morgan.

"Something I wrote a while ago. It's stupid."

Gabriel looks over. "It's actually really good."

"If you say so, but I'm *not* doing it for Open Mic."

"We should still go, though," says Morgan. "All of us together."

Gabriel nods. "I'm in."

I look at each of them in turn. "Honestly, you guys? I don't know if Scott will let me leave the house."

"Well, if he doesn't, we'll kidnap you," says Morgan.

"Or you could sneak out," says Gabriel.

"You guys are bad influences."

Morgan grins. "So we're going?"

"Sure. Why not?"

"Awesome!"

"Hey, wait a second." I turn around to look at her. "Isn't that the same day you find out about Frenchy?"

"Monday, yeah." Her mouth twitches. I can tell she's nervous.

"Who the hell is Frenchy?" Gabriel asks.

By the time Morgan's done explaining about *Grease*, we're pulling into Scott and Tanya's driveway. The Mercedes is gone, which means Tanya's probably at the gym. Celeste is no doubt asleep—it is Saturday morning, after all—and that leaves me to face Scott alone. Maybe he won't care that I stayed at the hospital. Maybe he won't notice I've come back.

Or maybe he's waiting for me to show my face.

Morgan touches my arm. "You want me to go in with you?"

"No, that's okay."

"I'll walk you to the door at least."

"Thanks."

Before I get out, I look over at Gabriel. "I guess I'll see you Monday."

He nods, and I hate that we're so awkward.

Morgan joins me in the driveway. "So what's up with you two?"

"What do you mean?"

"Are you an item, or what?"

I hesitate, not sure how to answer that. "Not really."

"What?" Her eyes widen. "Why not?"

"Because he's not supposed to start a relationship until he's a year sober."

"Are you kidding me? Who told him that?"

"His sponsor."

"Well his sponsor blows."

"But it kind of makes sense," I say.

"How so?"

"People who are new in recovery don't always make the best decisions."

"And you think you're a bad decision?"

"Maybe."

"I'll talk to him," says Morgan.

"No, don't."

"He likes you. He told me he likes you."

"I know."

"Don't you like him?"

"Yeah, but I don't want to get in the way of his recovery."

"It's just a stupid rule," she says. "If you pushed him, I bet he'd drop it."

"I don't want him to drop it. It's important." Still, my heart aches from wanting him. And knowing I can't have him. "He'll have a year in June," I say.

Morgan rolls her eyes. "So you only have to wait six months?"

"It's not about me," I say, echoing what Gabriel told me.

Morgan thinks about that, then throws her arms around me in a bear hug. "I still think you should make Scott pay," she whispers.

"Yeah, well, you know why I can't."

"I know why you *say* you can't."

"Morgan . . ."

"I know." She taps her lips. "Shutting up now."

"I'll text you," I say.

"You better."

As I watch her climb into the front seat with Gabriel, I realize how nice it is not to be jealous when I see them together. They both wave to me, and Morgan blows me a kiss. Then Gabriel's backing out of the driveway, and I'm alone.

Alone to face Scott. I'm pretty sure he won't kick me out, not after the deal he made with Mom, but I also know he's going to be pissed that I didn't come running back to the house when he told me to.

The smiley-face key turns easily in the lock. Holding my breath, I push open the door, listening for footsteps upstairs, for movement in the kitchen, but the house is quiet. Maybe I got lucky and Scott's still asleep. I lock the door behind me, wincing as it reverberates with a solid *thunk.*

I wait a second, then turn around to see Scott rising from the couch in the living room. His jaw is unshaven, his hair a snarled mess, and as he calmly walks toward me, it hits me like a door in my face.

This is my father.

"Tell me something," he says. "Did you think you'd get away with it?"

His voice sounds relaxed, conversational even, but there's a danger lurking behind it, and I remember how quickly he exploded at Thanksgiving.

"Sorry for not coming back when you told me to."

"Really?" He almost seems amused. "This is how you're playing it?"

I don't say anything because I don't want to piss him off. My head is down, but I feel him sizing me up. Maybe he's wondering if we look alike, act alike. Maybe he's wishing he could throw me back.

"Fine," he says. "Come with me."

My heart thudding, I follow him to the white living room where an open laptop sits on the coffee table. He picks it up, turns the screen to face me, but all I see is a news website. Then he presses a key.

A video starts playing. Mom and me at the cemetery.

"Look familiar?"

I stare at the awful scene. Mom on the grass, her legs kicking as she convulses. Me hovering over her, begging her to be okay. I wrench my eyes from the screen. "Why are you showing me this?"

"Because *someone* sent it to a fake news site."

Then I see the headline:

RALLY MORE IMPORTANT THAN FAMILY
FOR MAYOR CANDIDATE ROCKWELL

"Well, it wasn't me!"

"Really?" His tone drips sarcasm. "Who was it then?"

"The guy who took the video?"

Scott snaps the laptop shut and tosses it on the couch. "So you're saying this asshole just happened to know Shauna is my quote-unquote family?"

"Yeah, I mean . . . he could have figured it out. He knew Celeste."

"Did he also know Shauna walked out of rehab right before this?"

I don't say anything. There's no way the guy could have known that, so either the media picked it up from police scanners, or Celeste told him.

Or Celeste posted the video herself to derail his campaign.

Scott leans down, his stale breath in my face. "Reporters have been calling all morning."

"So tell them you tried to help her."

"You don't think I have? It doesn't matter. They're already

blaming me, saying it's my fault she tried to kill herself because I didn't cancel my rally to chase after her."

"Well, it's no secret you hate her. Maybe if you—" I was going to say, *Maybe if you visit her in the hospital*, but I remember my dream where he tried to kill her.

He sneers at me. "Maybe if I what?"

"I don't know. If you weren't such a dick?"

With no warning, his fist slams into my stomach, and I double over, gasping from shock and pain. He grabs my arm, throws me to the couch. It's hard to breathe, and as I struggle to get away, his fist rears back for another punch. Instinctively, I shield my face, but it's my torso he's aiming for. His fist lands, and there's a stabbing sharpness, like someone cracking a wishbone inside me. He grabs my hair, and I hear myself sobbing as he grinds my head into the couch.

He's snarling words, but I'm struggling to free myself and can't make sense of them. Blood from my mouth trickles onto the white couch, and like a fade-in, his words come into focus. ". . . love pushing my buttons, just like your mom . . ."

But Mom's better than me. That's what I want to tell him.

"I waste money on you, let you live here . . ."

Because unlike me, Mom doesn't want his money. She never did. All she wanted was to keep him out of my life.

Through needles of pain, I hear myself begging him to stop. But he doesn't stop. I grit my teeth, twist with all my strength. Hair rips from my scalp, and I'm able to sit up. He tries to grab me, and I scramble backward into the corner of the couch. He raises his fist, but by some miracle, he freezes. Lowering his arm, he takes a deep breath, trying to calm himself. He knows he's gone too far.

And just like that, I know what to do.

I shove him with all my strength, but my ribs are screaming pain, so there's no force behind it. Still, it pisses him off, which is what I want. He grabs my wrist, wrenches it, and just as I think the bone will snap, he throws me to the floor, pinning my arms.

"Asshole," I snarl, wanting him to hit me. Needing him to hit me. I see him trying to hold back, so I knee him in the balls, hear his little *oomph—*

Watch his face contort.

With a sharp thwack, my eye explodes in white, electric pain. For a second, I can't see, and then I start laughing. I must sound like a crazy person because slowly he gets off me.

Already, my eye is swelling up, and that's good. While he backs away, I yank my phone from my pocket.

"What are you doing?" he asks.

I don't answer as my fingers fly over keys. Scott tries to grab the phone, but I hold on tight, so he smashes my whole hand against the coffee table. Once, twice.

My hand is throbbing as a tinny voice comes through the phone. "Nine-one-one. What's your emergency?"

"I need help," I yell, just as Scott hurls the phone across the room. It lands near the foyer where the faint voice of the emergency dispatcher tells me to stay on the line.

Scott grabs my arm. "Tell them it's a prank," he whispers. "Tell them you—"

"What's going on?"

I turn my head to see Celeste walking into the living room. From the phone at her feet, the emergency dispatcher is still talking, but she ignores the voice as her eyes land on my swollen eye. "Dad, what'd you do?"

And maybe she's thinking of her own broken arm as she bends to pick up the phone. Or maybe she's only concerned for me. Whatever the case, her hands are shaking as she holds the phone to her ear and tells the emergency dispatcher to please send someone over. "Hurry," she says. "My dad is out of control."

CHAPTER 40

Kings and beggars, they end up the same
Buried in stench and rot and blame.
—from "As Long as I'm Rich" by L.F.

Scott is a smooth talker. If it weren't for my black eye, the two police officers who came to the house might have actually believed him when he told them Celeste and I were trying to get him in trouble by placing a fake 911 call. But the cops weren't buying it. After taking pictures of my swollen eye and bruised ribs, they placed a call to the Department of Children and Families, and now I'm sitting on my bed hugging a pillow as I wait for a rep from DCF to take me into protective custody.

Whatever that means. I asked the cops, but all they could tell me was, I'd probably get taken to the hospital to get checked out, and then I'd be taken to the DCF office. From there, they couldn't tell me what might happen to me.

So yeah, I'm scared. But I'm trying not to think of all the horror stories I've heard about being in the system. And yeah, I'm confused. Because I don't know if I did the right thing by calling 911.

At least Celeste is backing me up. She's downstairs talking

to the female police officer. The other one—a big, dark-haired cop named Ruiz—is waiting outside my door as if to guard me. I've been instructed to pack, but I don't have a suitcase, so all my stuff is sitting on the bed.

Including the framed photo of the man I thought was my father. It was sitting on the bed when I came in—Tanya must have dug it out of the stuff in the garage. Should I take the photo with me? If I leave it, Tanya will wonder why.

And the truth is, I don't want to leave it. Because I'm still attached to this man Blaine Hornsby. I know he was a drunk, but if he'd lived, maybe he would have gone to AA, and maybe he and Mom would have been happy, and maybe I wouldn't be sitting here with a black eye as I wait to be taken into protective custody. I stare at the man under the glass, wondering what color his eyes were. Brown like mine? Why did I never ask Mom?

And what does it matter? He's not my father.

But I want him to be.

All my new clothes are folded on my bed. My older clothes are in their own pile. I lay the photo of Blaine Hornsby on top, noticing a tiny crack in the glass that wasn't there before. It feels like a metaphor.

A knock on my door, and Ruiz pokes his head inside. "Okay if your aunt comes in?"

I know she must hate me for calling the cops on Scott—I don't blame her. But I need to face her. I nod at Ruiz.

A second later, she steps into the room clenching a big white envelope in both hands. As soon as she sees my battered face, her mouth drops open. For a second, I think she's going to rush to my side, but then her shoulders stiffen, and she turns to the cop. "I don't suppose you'd give us some privacy?"

Ruiz looks at me, and I nod. Then he steps from the room, leaving the door open.

Tanya clutches the envelope, biting her lip like she's holding back tears.

"I didn't mean to cause so much trouble," I say.

"What?" She looks startled.

"I'll be out of your hair soon. But I was wondering if maybe you have a box I can put my things in?"

"Of course."

"Unless you want to return the clothes." I gesture at the piles on my bed. "I took the tags off, but—"

"Layla, we bought those for you."

"I know, but I thought maybe you'd want to get your money back."

"Why would you think that?"

"Because of what I've done."

"What you've done?" She shakes her head. "You haven't done anything. I'm the one who should be sorry."

"For what?"

"For inviting you here, knowing what Scott was capable of. I know I can't change what happened, but I wanted to give you this." Biting her lip, she thrusts the envelope at me.

"What is it?"

"Something I've been saving for you."

The envelope is thick and heavy and sealed with a metal clip. I can't imagine what's inside, so I open it, pulling out a thick booklet and a bunch of papers. The papers are filled with pie charts and numbers, and the cover of the booklet shows a smiling man and woman and a little girl sitting on the man's shoulders. *It's Not Too Late to Save*, it says, which only confuses me more.

"It's a prepaid college plan. Only good for Florida colleges, but Florida has some good schools and . . . Layla, what's wrong?"

I shake my head, staring at the booklet. "Is this . . .?" I can't get the words out. Because if I'm wrong . . .

"It's for you." She hesitates before sitting beside me on the bed. "I started it when you were little, squirreled away money so Scott wouldn't know."

"I don't understand."

"Well, it's simple. This means you don't have to worry about college. This will cover everything."

Stunned, I search her face. "Why? Why would you do this for me?"

"Because I always thought you got a rotten break."

"But this is . . ." I shake my head. "So much."

"It's not like you don't deserve it."

"Because I get good grades?"

"No, honey." She hesitates before taking my hand. "Because I know you're Scott's daughter."

o o o

"What?" I blink at her, not sure I heard her right. Because if she knows I'm Scott's daughter, then why doesn't she hate me? Why is she sitting here beside me on the bed? Why is she holding my hand?

"I only found out yesterday," she says. "In case you were wondering."

"How?" I ask, not even sure what I mean.

"I found some papers," she says, "stuck in the frame of that picture." She's pointing to Blaine Hornsby's picture. "I didn't know what they were, so I read them. It wasn't addressed to you, but it was obviously a letter from your mom."

"Telling me Scott's my father?"

"Along with paternity papers to prove it." She kind of laughs, but it sounds more like a cry. "And just so you know, I suspected a long time ago. Before I knew Shauna was pregnant, I thought maybe something had gone on between her and Scott. Just a one-time thing. Scott and I had been in a fight, and I knew Shauna and him had gone out for drinks. They used to be friends. Did you know that? And then she got pregnant. But I never knew for sure, and I didn't want to ask because I didn't *want* to know. Some days I'd convince myself I was being paranoid, but other days . . ."

Her voice trails off, and I think back to all the times when she was cold to Mom and me. Then she'd turn around and invite us to a barbecue.

"There's something else you need to know," she says.

"What?"

"The letter to you—it was basically a suicide note."

I let that sink in, and suddenly it makes sense why Mom decided to shoot heroin back on the day of her job interview. She was trying to kill herself.

"The letter said how sorry she was." Tanya's voice is gentle. "How you'd be better off without her, that if Scott tried to deny paternity, here was the proof."

And she'd put it in the one place she knew I'd find it. Only I never went back to our room. Because instead of dying, she woke up in the hospital, and Scott and Tanya said they'd take me in as long as she didn't tell anyone where we'd been living. And so she agreed, knowing that, as long as Scott was in the public eye, he'd have to take care of me. I remember thinking how weird it was that she didn't want our things from the shelter. Because she didn't want me finding the letter.

And this whole time I was so pissed at her, wondering why she always screwed things up . . . If I'd known the heroin overdose was a suicide attempt, I wouldn't have been so mean to her. I practically drove her to try it again.

And she almost succeeded.

"Hey," says Tanya, touching my arm. "You okay?" And then she flushes, glancing at my swollen eye.

"Just thinking about Mom."

"Me too."

It hits me suddenly what Tanya must be going through.

"Why don't you hate me?" I ask.

She seems surprised by the question and takes her time answering. "I tried to. I always thought you looked like him. But slowly I realized . . ." She hugs herself. "Even if what I suspected was true, it's not your fault."

"So you started me a college fund?" It sounds ridiculous when I say it out loud.

She laughs. "Don't give me too much credit. I started it partially for selfish reasons. I figured, if Scott really was your father and you someday found out, you might come looking for money. Not that you wouldn't be justified. Then yesterday, after seeing the paternity papers, I guess it hit home. All the hurt came back, and I decided I wasn't going to give it to you."

"But you changed your mind?"

"I did."

"Why?"

"Because of how you are."

"What does that mean?"

"Because every time I do something nice for you, you're just so . . ."

"Pathetic?"

"No, honey. Grateful."

"Oh."

"And I love you for that."

"How?" I ask.

She looks startled by the question. "How can I love you?"

I nod.

"Because nothing that happened is your fault. And because you're my family."

"That doesn't matter."

"It does."

"So does that mean you don't hate Mom?"

I wait for her to say, *How could I not hate her?* But she takes a long time before answering. "I have hated her," she finally says, fiddling with her ring. "But I love her too. We were close growing up."

"Mom told me that."

"And then she started drinking and partying after our mom died."

"That happened when she was my age, right?"

"Yeah, she was fifteen."

"Mom said she was drunk when . . ." I can't bring myself to say it.

"I figured," says Tanya.

"Not that that's an excuse," I say.

"No, but I suppose it's a reason," says Tanya.

"So you forgive her?"

Again, she fiddles with her ring as she thinks. "Shauna's my sister," she finally says. "And I don't know if you know this because you don't have a sister, but . . ."

And then she stops because maybe she realizes I *do* have a sister.

She bites her lip. "I just know it's really hard to live in hate."

And suddenly I'm thinking of all the times I've hated Mom—how I basically told her I didn't want her around—and before I know what's happening, I'm bawling into my hands.

"I'm sorry," I say, because it's stupid that I'm crying when Tanya's the one whose whole life has been shattered.

"It's okay." Her hand is on my back. "None of this is your fault."

"But now your life's screwed up."

"No more than it always was."

How can she be so brave? Is she planning to ignore the whole thing?

And if she does, what does that mean for Mom? I want to ask, but somehow it seems selfish.

Outside the room, I hear Ruiz talking on his radio. Then he pokes his head inside. "The caseworker from DCF is here."

Tanya pats my leg. "You should go down. I'll put your things in a suitcase."

"Can we have another few minutes?" I ask Ruiz. "We need to finish talking."

Ruiz looks like he wants to say no, but he relents. "Sure," he says with a gentle smile. "But don't take too long."

When I turn back to Tanya, she's stuffing the college booklet back in the envelope. My heart fills up—I want to hug her—but I'm not sure she'd like that.

So I say instead, "What are you going to do? Will you tell Scott you know?"

"Maybe." She finishes with the envelope and sets it aside. "I haven't decided yet."

"Celeste knows," I blurt, because I don't want to keep secrets from her. I'm tired of keeping secrets.

"I figured. The way she was acting. Has she been treating you okay?"

"You mean Celeste?"

Tanya nods.

"She doesn't hate me. At least I don't think she does. It's hard to tell sometimes."

Tanya sighs. "I know the feeling."

"Will you tell her you know?"

"She's my daughter. It's something we need to talk about."

"And what about Mom? Is it something you need to talk about with her?"

She takes a second before answering, while outside my door Ruiz talks on his radio. "I don't think so," she finally says. "Even if I told her I forgive her, she wouldn't believe me. And if she finds out I know, I think it would destroy her."

I think so too. But I also remember what Gabriel said, how making amends is one of the things addicts do to get better.

"You disagree?" Tanya asks.

"I'm not sure. I just know Mom's been living with the secret for a long time."

Tanya nods. "So why change things, right?"

Maybe, I think, as Ruiz steps into the room. Or maybe that's why we *should* change things. Because maybe it's the secret that's destroying her.

CHAPTER 41

Stay, beautiful joy.
Make me float on crusty water,
Make the scum scatter.
—from "Joy of a Moment" by L.F.

The investigation into Scott is ongoing. Meanwhile, I've been placed in a home for at-risk kids. The home is called Circle of Hope, and the lady from DCF told me this is where I'll be staying until a court decides Mom's well enough to take care of me. I'm hoping that will be soon, but I also know she has a long way to go. At least she's no longer an immediate danger to herself—that's what her psychiatrist at the hospital told me—so yesterday they transferred her to one of those free rehabs, the same one where Gabriel went. Mom's psychiatrist said she was happy to go, especially because now she knows I'm somewhere safe.

And I *am* safe. That's the cool thing. And I'm discovering that being in the system isn't as bad as I feared. At least people have been nice. This morning, a guy named Andre who volunteers at Circle of Hope took a bunch of us in his van and dropped us off at our various schools. There's one other girl who goes to Flagler—a freshman I don't know—but we walked together from the van to the school, and she asked about my poetry shirt, which I made a point of wearing today because, even though I still have all my new clothes, it's good to remind myself of who I am.

Not Layla 2.0—just Layla.

So it's just me sitting with Grandpa's backpack at the bench where the banyan tree used to be. It's been cut up and carted away, and even though I'm sad it's gone, the patch of churned-up dirt at my feet feels symbolic of a new beginning, not just for me, but also for Morgan and for Gabriel. Tonight, the three of us are going to Open Mic, and today Morgan finds out what role she got in *Grease.*

Unfortunately, I won't be seeing Gabriel this morning because he's missing school to help his mom with something. I'm not sure what, and he seemed uncomfortable talking about it, so I didn't press him. I take out my phone. Its screen is cracked, thanks to Scott hurling it across the room, but it still works, and while I wait for Morgan, I send Gabriel a text.

Hope everything's going ok with your mom.

He texts back:

Thx. I'll tell u about it when I see u.

Then another text:

U doing ok?

So far so good. 🙂 Waiting for Morgan.

Ok. See u at lunch.

Across the courtyard, Morgan is heading my way, but she stops when Josephine runs up to her. They start talking, probably about the play, and even though I feel the old pang of jealousy, I also know Morgan would never ditch me. I told her last night we'd go together to look at the cast list, but seeing her with Josephine makes me think she'd probably rather go with someone who's actually in the play with her, and maybe she didn't want to tell me that because she didn't want to hurt my feelings.

I start walking toward them so I can tell her it's okay if she wants to go, but before I get there, Josephine hugs her goodbye and offers me a cheery wave before she leaves.

"Oh my gosh, your eye!" Morgan grabs my hand. She knows what happened, but I guess seeing it for the first time is kind of shocking. The swelling's gone down, but the bruising's gotten worse.

"It doesn't hurt," I tell her. "Not unless I touch it."

I can tell Morgan wants to hug me, but she knows I have two fractured ribs. "At least you're away from *him*," she says. "How is it, by the way? Still bearable?"

She's talking about Circle of Hope. "Honestly," I say, "it's a lot better than I thought it'd be."

"Really?" She's peering at my face like she's not sure I'm telling the truth.

"Let's just say it's been a long time since I woke up *not* feeling anxious."

"That's amazing," says Morgan, taking my arm, and together we walk toward the school.

○ ○ ○

Maybe I *should* feel anxious, though, and maybe I do, just a little, but only because kids are doing double takes as Morgan and I walk down the hall. They're staring at my black eye, and I remind myself of Gabriel's philosophy to not measure myself by what other people think of me. It's a good philosophy, but people's stares still have a way of making me feel less-than.

Morgan leans into me. "You okay?"

"I'm good. How about you?"

"Nervous," she says.

"You got this." I squeeze her hand, and she gives me a tight smile.

There's a crowd gathered outside the drama room as everyone jostles to get a look at the cast list taped to the door. Girls are hugging each other and either squealing or crying. Guys are fist-bumping and either cursing or laughing. I glance at Morgan, who's biting her lip.

"No matter what," I tell her, "you are amazing."

She hangs onto my arm while we push our way to the front. The cast list is printed on two sheets of neon yellow paper. The first sheet lists the lead and supporting roles. I scan it for Morgan's name. Nothing. But I see that Josephine got Marty, one of the Pink Ladies. I scan the list again. Still no Morgan. Then I notice how hard she's gripping my hand. She's staring at the second sheet and trying not to cry.

"I got Girl One," she says.

"Morgan, I'm sorry."

"I worked so hard."

Suddenly Josephine is beside her, helping me lead her away. "It's only because it's your first musical," she says. "Hardly anyone gets a good part if it's their first musical."

"I shouldn't have got my hopes up."

I try to think of something comforting to say, but I can't think of anything that doesn't sound useless. Josephine's still talking to her. ". . . take that part and run with it. Make yourself stand out."

"It sucks that you didn't get a speaking part."

The voice comes from behind us, and all of us turn to see Gigi blinking her big blue eyes at Morgan, as though she's actually sympathetic. Kendra is right beside her, looking bored as she munches from a bag of Doritos.

"Oh my God, your eye!" says Gigi, and the faint look of disgust on her face combined with her fake sympathy for Morgan makes me want to slap her.

"I didn't see *your* name up there," I say.

"Well, maybe you should get that eye looked at."

"She got Rizzo," Josephine mutters from Morgan's other side. "No surprise there."

Now I remember seeing the name *Gianna* up there. Gianna Jordan, a.k.a. Gigi.

"Look on the bright side," Gigi says to Morgan. "It probably has nothing to do with whether or not you have talent."

If anyone else had said this, I'd think they were trying to be nice, but there's always an edge to Gigi's compliments. So I say to her, "What's that supposed to mean?"

Gigi leans closer. "Maybe you don't know this, but *Grease* takes place in the 1950s."

Kendra's still munching on Doritos, but I see her wince.

"And I'm not racist, but let's face it," says Gigi. "No one really believes there could have been a Black girl in the Pink Ladies."

My mouth drops open as Morgan stiffens beside me.

"Don't get all mad," says Gigi. "Schools were segregated back then."

"Not all of them," says Josephine. "And there was a Black Marty in the live TV version."

"Right," says Gigi. "But that's, like, an alternate fact. Most people prefer reality."

"Wow," I say. "You really don't get it."

"Because I'm not politically correct? Maybe you should worry more about yourself and less about me."

"What's that supposed to mean?"

"What do you think it means? Aren't you living in a car or something? Where do you even shower?"

All the old embarrassment comes flooding back, but Morgan squeezes my arm, and I feel better. "So what if I am?"

"Nothing. It's just, some people would call that mooching off society."

"You're a bitch," says Morgan. "You know that?"

Gigi rolls her eyes. "Calm down."

"You want to see calm?" Morgan gets right up in her face. "This is calm. This is me not slapping the crap out of you."

"Go ahead," says Gigi. "See how that helps your cause when a Black girl—"

SMACK!

Josephine slaps Gigi's face, and yeah, I'm stunned, but not as stunned as Gigi.

"What the hell?" Gigi's face is scrunched up like a troll's. "You just hit me!"

I almost tell her she deserved it, but then I think of Scott beating the crap out of me and I stay silent.

"I can't believe she hit me!" Gigi looks around. "Did you guys see that?"

We're far enough away that no one's paying attention. They're either celebrating their success or bemoaning the fact that they didn't get the part they wanted.

Gigi points a shaky finger at Josephine. "I'm going to report you. Don't think I won't."

"Go ahead," says Josephine. "Get yourself banned from the musical for fighting."

Gigi turns to Kendra. "You saw it, didn't you? She attacked me, so it's not my fault."

"Honestly?" Kendra crumples her empty Doritos bag. "I wasn't paying attention."

"Well, I'm telling you . . ."

Gigi's voice fades to a hum as the three of us walk away.

When the crowd is behind us, Morgan stops walking and turns to Josephine. "Thank you," she says. And all I can think is, *I should have done more to defend her.*

"Believe me," says Josephine. "It was my pleasure."

"I hope you don't get expelled," Morgan says.

Josephine sniffs. "No one saw anything. Remember?"

"Still . . ." Morgan hugs herself. "You didn't have to do that."

"Someone had to." Josephine shrugs, smiling brightly. "I should go."

"Congratulations on getting Marty," says Morgan.

"Thanks. We'll talk later."

Morgan nods, and as Josephine bounces off, there's an awkward silence between us. Morgan's still hugging herself.

"I'm sorry you didn't get the part you wanted."

"It's okay."

"If I'd practiced lines with you . . ."

"Layla, it's not your fault."

She starts walking, and I stay beside her. "Is there anything I can do?"

"You're doing it."

"Am I? You must be so disappointed, and then all those things Gigi said. I should have done more."

"Like what? It's not like you didn't defend me."

"I should have been the one to slap her. I wanted to. I wanted to scratch her eyes out."

"And I'm glad you didn't," Morgan says. "That's not who you are."

Honestly, I'm still confused about who I am, still afraid of who I want to be, but as I link arms with my best friend, I'm sure of one thing. Morgan and I have each other's backs, and nothing in the world is going to change that.

CHAPTER 42

Drink drops of me with every meal
Though salty, swallow them with zeal
With every taste, a fear I'll heal
I'm made of stone, but I can feel
—from "Statue" by L.F.

It's funny how when you're attracted to someone, it controls your whole body. Your heartbeat, your breathing, especially your thoughts.

I don't even taste my lunch because Gabriel is sitting next to me in the cafeteria, close enough that our legs are almost touching. Morgan's sitting across from us, and he's just told us that his mom got a promotion at work, but I'm having a hard time concentrating. The Nirvana T-shirt he's wearing covers his tattoo, but as his arm brushes mine, I'm hyperaware of how his skin is branded, not just by a defunct sobriety date, but also by burns. He could have died in that fire, and as much as I want to be with him, I can't put his sobriety at risk. I won't.

"That's great," says Morgan. "Does that speed up the timetable for moving out of the shelter?"

My brain rewinds. His mom got a promotion. I should be congratulating him.

"Yeah, actually, it does." He glances at me. "The thing is . . ."

He doesn't finish his sentence as Felix walks up to our table.

"Hey, Freeman." Felix's gaze flicks to my black eye, then away. He seems uncomfortable, as he should be. This is the guy who blabbed about me living at the shelter.

"What do you want?" I ask.

"Just to make sure you got home okay." He flushes. "Not home. I didn't mean that."

"You mean to the homeless shelter."

"Right."

"I did, as it turns out. Thanks for asking."

He nods, starts to turn away.

"And thanks for spreading it around."

"Huh?"

Is he really that clueless? Maybe he's playing dumb. "Someone told Gigi about me being homeless."

"And you think it was me?"

"You're saying it wasn't?"

He holds up his hands. "The only person I told was my brother. And only because you wanted him to drive you there."

I look at Morgan, who shrugs. Maybe he's telling the truth.

He lowers his voice. "I didn't figure you'd want people knowing."

Now I do believe him. He may have used his charm to get me to write his poem, but at least he didn't throw me under the bus.

"Okay. Sorry for accusing you."

"Hey, I've been accused of worse."

"Why doesn't that surprise me?"

He grins. "I know a way you can make it up to me."

Beside me, Gabriel's shoulders stiffen.

"Let me guess," I say. "You want help with an assignment?"

"Well, since you're offering."

"I'm not."

"Here's an idea," says Gabriel. "Why don't you get a tutor?"

"A tutor?"

"You know . . . Someone who helps you study?"

Felix looks confused. "I don't need help studying. I just need—"

"Someone to do it for you," I say.

"Are you offering?" Again with that grin.

"No, I'm not."

"Which means you can go," says Gabriel.

"But . . ." Felix doesn't move.

"Never mind. We'll go instead."

Gabriel gets to his feet, and I do too. Morgan stays sitting.

"Aren't you coming?" I ask.

"No way." She grins at me. "You two need alone time."

I'm not so sure that's a good idea, but I turn to Gabriel, who avoids my eyes as he shoves his hands in his pockets. "I actually need to tell you something."

I don't move. Whatever it is, it has him nervous.

"Jeez, Freeman, go with him," says Felix. "Can't you see he likes you?"

o o o

Gabriel likes me. I knew that. But what does he want to tell me? The hallway is empty except for the occasional stray kid. Gabriel leads me to a row of lockers and stops. "Would you rather go outside?"

"That depends." I lean against the lockers so we're facing each other. "What's this about?"

"The promotion my mom got. It involves moving to Miami."

My heart sinks. Miami's only an hour away, but still . . .

"I should have told you sooner, but that's where I was this morning, helping her look at apartments."

"Did you find one?"

"We did actually."

I nod, letting that sink in. "When do you think you'll leave?"

"We're moving on Friday."

"But . . . What about the deposit? The first and last month's rent?"

"Her company's helping us out."

"Oh."

"I'm sorry, Layla."

"No, it's good." Of course it's good. He'll be out of the shelter by the weekend.

"I know that's election day. I wish I could be here for you."

"It's okay."

"I want us to be closer."

"Me too."

"And I feel like, before I move, we should at least . . ."

"What?"

"Kiss."

"Oh." He's looking right into my eyes, and as he leans closer, my breath catches. "Gabriel, I—"

Whatever I was going to say gets lost when his lips touch mine. Soft, almost searching, and without thinking, my own lips respond. Not just my lips. My hands as I pull him close. My body as I arch into him. While his lips explore mine, his palms glide down my waist, and suddenly my whole body is one live wire, pressing against him as his tongue lightly traces my lips. My sore ribs are aching, but even so, a moan wells up inside me—I want this so bad—but I also want him to stay clean, and I'm scared, terrified really, that he'll relapse. And worse, that he'll relapse because of me. The kiss is amazing—my first kiss! But this isn't right. It takes all my strength, all my willpower, to freeze my body, to push him away.

His eyes open. "I'm so sorry."

"Don't be."

"I should have asked your permission."

"I'm glad you didn't."

"Because you would have said no?"

I shake my head. "I would have said yes. And that's the problem."

"Okay, I get that."

"This can't happen again."

"It won't."

"I mean it, Gabriel. It's easy for me to forget you're an addict because I've never seen you that way. But I've seen my mom. I've seen what alcoholism did to her, and the last thing I want is to put you at risk. So you're going to do what they tell you in order to stay clean. And if this happens again . . . Gabriel, it can't happen again."

The whole time I've been talking, he's been staring at his feet. Now he looks up, meets my eye, nods. "You're right. As much as I hate it, I know you're right."

Part of me wants him to argue, to press his body against mine so I can feel his breath, his touch, his longing . . .

"I just need to know one thing," he says.

"What's that?"

"Was the kiss okay? I don't have a lot of experience, so . . ."

Heat rises to my cheeks. "Yeah, Gabriel." I start walking before I do something stupid. "The kiss was perfect."

CHAPTER 43

My knocking will not cease until I'm freed,
For here outside the world is what I heed.
—from "In Search of God" by L.F.

I'm mad at Gabriel. I let him talk me into coming to Open Mic, and what does he do? He bows out at the last minute. I still have his text on my broken screen.

> Being around u is too hard. When I'm around u I want to kiss u and that's not fair to u. I forget ur going through stuff too.

And then another text.

> Both of us need time to heal.

That was an hour ago, and I haven't texted him back. I thought about calling up Morgan and telling her to forget Open Mic, but by then Phil was on his way to pick me up, and I didn't want to piss him off since he's the one who persuaded Circle of

Hope to let me come. Apparently homes for at-risk kids don't just let you leave the premises whenever you want. You have to get permission, and they don't give permission for just anything. Phil convinced them Open Mic was a wholesome church activity that helps build character. Score one for Phil.

So here I am with Morgan in the crowded rec room of her church, sipping Dr Pepper and trying my best to be invisible.

It's hard to be invisible when you're sporting a black eye. And when you're wearing a shirt that people automatically try to read. I should have changed out of my poetry shirt, especially because I don't want anyone to remember me from last week, the girl who froze when called to recite a poem. At least there's no pressure this time. I made it clear I'm not performing.

"Excuse me." Someone taps me on the shoulder, and I turn to see the guy who recited "Yet Do I Marvel" last week. His mouth drops open when he sees my black eye. "Sorry to bother you. I just wanted to tell you, I really like your shirt."

"Uh, thanks."

He thrusts out his hand. "I'm Michael, by the way."

"Layla."

"Nice to meet you, Layla. I remember you from last time."

"Well, that's embarrassing."

"What? No, I remember you because Morgan said you wrote poetry, and I write poetry too. Anyway, you should have seen me the first time I got up there. I literally had a panic attack."

"Really?"

"Well, not literally. But I was pretty terrified. Maybe you'll do something tonight? It gets easier, believe me."

"I kind of doubt that."

"But you'll never know till you try, right? Mind if I read your shirt?"

"Uh, no. Go ahead."

So I stand like a statue while he circles me. Not until he zeros in on Edgar Allan Poe's "Annabel Lee," which happens to be right on my chest, do both of us realize where his eyes are. He backs away, looking mortified. "Sorry. Didn't mean . . ."

"It's okay." I'm embarrassed, but it's also kind of funny. "When I put it there, I wasn't expecting anyone to actually read it."

Behind me, Morgan snorts.

"That's one of my favorites." Michael points to a verse from "My Papa's Waltz" by Theodore Roethke. "I can totally relate."

Is he saying his father beats him? Maybe he's trying to make me feel better about my black eye. "The poem you did last week," I say. "I liked it a lot. I wish there was room for it on my shirt."

"Maybe you can squeeze it right here." He points to a tiny blank space near my sleeve. "I think the rhyming couplet would fit."

I smile.

"What?" he asks.

"Nothing. I'm just impressed by anyone who knows what a rhyming couplet is."

He smiles too. "Not many people are impressed by that."

"Yeah, well, not many people like my poetry shirt either."

Morgan takes my arm. "Hey, how about we get another soda?"

Before I can answer, she's leading me away.

"Did you see that?" I ask. "Someone liked my shirt."

"Don't get any ideas," Morgan says.

"What are you talking about?"

"I know Gabriel's moving, but you guys are perfect for each other." She knows about our kiss, of course, and she's not a fan of our decision to keep apart. In fact, she's taking every opportunity to remind me how great Gabriel is. As if I need reminding.

"Just remember, Gabriel likes your shirt too," she says.

I smile and shake my head.

"What?"

"Nothing. I'm glad you're my friend."

Feedback from the microphone grabs our attention. Jasmine is at the front, signaling that it's time to get started. Morgan and I take our seats, and I check my phone in case Gabriel texted me again, but it's the same words, frozen on my screen.

Being around u is too hard.

Maybe he's right. Maybe it's better that he stayed away.

Demetrius is the first person to perform, and just like last time, his guitar playing is way better than his singing. Still, I'm impressed. After him, there's a girl doing stand-up. She's obviously nervous, but we all laugh at her jokes. The next performer is a guy playing the trumpet.

Morgan fidgets beside me, and when I look over at her, she's biting her lip. Not getting a good part in *Grease* was a huge blow to her confidence, and I kind of know how that feels. In the car on the way here, I told her how Mr. Kidd had dissed my poems, finally realizing how stupid it was to hide that from her.

"So that's why you don't think they're good?" she asked.

"That's part of it, yeah."

"Well that's crap. He obviously doesn't know what he's talking about."

"My point is," I said, "you can't let other people define you. You know you're a good singer, right?"

"Maybe."

"You are. Believe me."

She gave me a tiny smile.

Now, as Jasmine calls Morgan up to the front, I whisper to her. "Remember, you are insanely talented."

That gets her to smile, but she still looks nervous.

As she walks up there with everyone clapping, my heart is pounding as though I'm the one about to perform. I just want her to do well, to know how good she is. Once she's up there, she almost drops the microphone when Jasmine hands it to her.

"You got this!" someone calls.

After a short pause where she bows her head, my amazing friend starts singing "Amazing Grace." There's no music, but she doesn't need it. Her voice is clear and sweet, powerful and filled with emotion. Near the end, she gets choked up and can barely finish, but that makes her performance more powerful. When she sits down, I'm grinning with tears in my eyes, so proud of my friend, so happy for her because this is what she does, and she's really good at it.

Michael gets up next, reciting "Dreams" by Langston Hughes. I've read the poem a million times, but as he's speaking, the message moves me in a way it never has. Hold on to your dreams. Don't let them die.

It's a short poem, and he's done in less than a minute, but I swear it's like a driving force has scooped me up. As Michael takes his seat, he catches my eye and winks.

Did he choose that poem for me? Surely not, but I think about what Morgan always says, that everything happens for a reason.

Flustered, I stare at my hands while something like courage sneaks into my chest.

Jasmine is at the mic asking if there's anyone else who wants to perform, and if so, now is the time. As she talks, I imagine she's speaking directly to me, but that's stupid.

Or maybe not. Because something compels me to stand up. Something compels me to go forward, and the next thing I know, I'm standing beside Jasmine at the front of the room.

She leans close to me and whispers, "Way to be brave."

I'm not brave, but I am hopeful.

Hopeful that maybe my poetry's not as bad as I think. Hopeful that maybe, just maybe, God is giving me an opportunity, and all I have to do is take it.

"Everyone, this is Layla," Jasmine says. "And I think she's doing a poem?"

I nod, not trusting my voice.

"And it's something you wrote yourself?"

Again I nod, aware that everyone's looking at me. As she hands me the mic, my hands are shaking. I hold the mic to my lips. "It's called 'The Murky Swell,'" I say. Or at least that's what I try to say, but an earsplitting whine of feedback drowns me out.

Jasmine grabs the mic and lowers it an inch. "Now try."

Everyone's quiet, faces turned toward me. My heart is literally beating out of my chest. What am I doing up here? What was I thinking? I find Morgan in the audience. Her face is earnest, her eyes encouraging.

Maybe I can do this.

Swallowing hard, I lean into the mic. "I wrote this not too long ago, after my mom and I had to move to a homeless shelter. At the time, I was feeling pretty lost, but things have a way of working out. My friend Morgan would call it God working in my life, and maybe she's right. I'd like to think she's right. Anyway . . ." I smile nervously. "This is my poem.

> "I choke and splutter for a breath
> of love and charity

of how I long to be
in this, the murky swell.

"A longer spell without a breath
will kill me in the end,
a flaw I can't amend
in this, the murky swell.

"So desperate am I to breathe,
to crest the smothering waves,
to close the open graves
in this, the murky swell.

"My flesh was made to float atop,
but only when I choose.
I'll drown if I refuse
in this, the murky swell."

As the words leave my mouth, I remember how I felt when I wrote them—lost, afraid, yet still hanging on to hope. By the end of the poem, I'm trying to control my shaking voice, wondering how much of a fool I've made of myself, not looking at anyone as I step down and blunder to my seat.

Vaguely I hear clapping, cheering. Someone pats me on the shoulder. Morgan grabs my hand. "That was awesome," she says. "I'm so proud of you."

I'm proud of me too. Proud for putting myself out there. Proud for how far I've come, though I still have a long way to go. Gabriel was right. Both of us need time to heal, and even though it's painful, I'm grateful the healing's begun.

CHAPTER 44

The cries I have heard are unreal to my mind.
Never shall they stop me from being what I long.
Don't turn around, Mother, leave them behind.
The sobbing will cease and you'll sing a new song.
—from "Sonnet for My Mom,"
by Layla Freeman

The days that follow pass in a blur. Seeing Gabriel at school is hard, but Morgan is a good buffer between us, and it's kind of nice to get to know him better without the distraction of being his girlfriend. At least that's what I've been telling myself.

But now it's Thursday after school, and this is the last time I'll see him before he moves to Miami. Both of us are waiting near the car line for the Circle of Hope van to pick me up. Gabriel offered to drive me, but it's against their rules. Plus, us alone in the car? I keep imagining what it would be like to kiss him again. Maybe he's imagining it too because he stands about two feet away while all around us kids are talking and laughing, cars are pulling up and driving away. I'm trying to be happy for him, but my heart is breaking.

And we're running out of time. *Say something!*

"The weather's supposed to be nice tomorrow."

He smiles faintly. "Yeah, I saw that. Good day for a move, I guess."

"You nervous about starting a new school?"

"Maybe a little."

"Just think," I say. "No more homeless shelter. You'll have your own room."

"I'm definitely stoked about that, but, Layla . . ."

As he moves closer, my heart races. Slowly, he reaches out and touches my hair.

"Gabriel, don't."

"Can't I just . . .?"

At that moment, the van from Circle of Hope pulls up. Gabriel steps back from the curb, his hands in his pockets. I open the door, look back at him. "Bye," I say, but he doesn't answer. I start to get in the van, but then I stop, and just as I'm turning back, he's stepping forward. He pulls me into a hug, and it's like every cell in my body comes alive.

"I'm going to miss you, Layla."

"I'm going to miss you too."

As we pull apart, I can't look at him—it's too painful to look at him—but as I climb into the van, his scent lingers, and I find myself smiling. He smells like soap and lemons.

○ ○ ○

The next day is Friday, election day, and in between moping through classes and crying on Morgan's shoulder, I keep checking election results, even though a winner won't be declared until late.

That evening, when I'm lining up for dinner at Circle of Hope, my phone jangles from my pocket. We're not supposed to use our phones during meals, but I've never heard it make that sound, so I pull it from my pocket to see who it is.

Celeste is FaceTiming me.

I haven't seen her at school, so I duck out of line to accept the call. Her face appears on my cracked screen.

"Hey," she says. "Have you seen the latest?"

"Election news? I haven't had a chance."

"It's not over yet, but it looks like Dad lost."

"Thank God!"

"Actually, it's thanks to you."

"Yeah, well, I'm happy to do my part."

"He's losing by a landslide," she says.

"That's good."

"And child services is really up his ass."

Which is also good, but I'm worried about her and Tanya. I lower my voice. "I guess things are pretty tense there, huh?"

She looks behind her. "That's the other reason I called."

I'm distracted for a second when Olivia, one of the girls I share a room with, comes up beside me. "You'd better put that away," she says. "The Ice Woman Cometh."

I follow Olivia's gaze to where Mrs. Deetz is heading my way as she patrols the cafeteria.

"Celeste, let me call you back."

"No problem." She hangs up.

"So what's the news?" Olivia asks.

"My uncle lost the election."

"Well, that's good. And what about your boyfriend?"

"He's fine, but he's not my boyfriend."

"Well, just think. By the time you two can 'officially' date, you'll be out of here."

I hope I'll be out of here, but when I leave depends entirely on Mom. She's reportedly doing well in rehab, but since I won't be allowed to talk to her until Sunday, I don't know for sure. Olivia, on the other hand, has been here for almost a year, and with both her parents in prison, it doesn't look like she'll be leaving anytime soon.

Not that it's horrible here. Even Olivia admits that it's better than staying with a foster family. And she would know. She's been through three of them.

After eating our chicken cutlets and green beans, Olivia and I go back to the room we share with ten other girls. After dinner is our designated homework time. Mrs. Deetz makes sure we're not goofing off, but after a few minutes, I get permission to go to the bathroom. I lock myself in a stall to FaceTime Celeste.

As soon as she answers, I hear yelling in the background. She's walking with her phone, heading upstairs.

"What's going on?" I ask.

"Mom's divorcing Dad."

She says it so casually that I'm not sure I heard her right. "Seriously?"

"That's what she says."

"Are you okay with that?"

"Why wouldn't I be?"

"Because . . . you know . . . the money thing."

"There won't be a money thing. Unlike you, I don't have to sue for child support."

"Yeah, well, I'm not suing either."

She holds the phone close to her face. "You might want to rethink that."

By now she's reached her room. She closes the door behind her.

"Why?" I ask. "What's going on?"

"Mom told Dad she knows."

About him being my father. It takes a second for that to sink in.

"Dad tried to deny it," Celeste says.

"And how'd that go over?"

"Mom laughed in his face."

"Good."

"But there's something else."

Now Celeste looks worried, and that makes *me* worry. "What?"

"As soon as Aunt Shauna can have visitors, my mom's going to tell her she knows."

"Uh . . . Not sure if that's a good idea."

"Mom thinks Aunt Shauna can handle it. She said you were the one who said the secret was eating her up inside."

"I said that, but—"

"My mom thinks the air needs to get cleared, and she wants you to go with her when she does it."

"Okay."

"So if you think it's a bad idea, you can talk her out of it."

Someone bangs on the bathroom stall. "I hear you talking in there!" It's Mrs. Deetz.

"Jeez, sounds like home," says Celeste because, at that moment, someone's banging on her door too. A second later, her door opens, and Scott slumps into the room looking more worn-down than I've ever seen him. His hair is flat, his face drawn, but it's his eyes that get me the most.

They look haunted.

And just as I'm noticing this, Celeste ends the call.

o o o

Sunday is family day at the rehab center. After signing in at the front office, Tanya and I are searched for contraband. Alcohol and drugs are obvious no-nos, but surprisingly, so is chocolate, caffeine, and any kind of shampoo or hand lotion that contains alcohol. That means the skin-care products Tanya brought as a gift get confiscated, but that book *Crank*, which Tanya read after I left it in her kitchen, makes it through.

Once Tanya gives up arguing, we're led to the cafeteria where a handful of families sit talking in pretend normalcy. Mom is waiting at one of the tables. She smiles a little when she sees us, and both of us give her a hug. Tanya first, then me.

"How are you?" I ask.

"Okay."

"Just okay?" She doesn't answer, and my heart sinks. "What is it, Mom?"

"Can Tanya and I have a minute?"

"Sure," I say, but this is what I've been dreading—Mom and Tanya talking alone. I point to the far side of the cafeteria. "I'll be over there."

As I'm getting up, I give a little headshake to Tanya to tell her now's not the time, but I can't tell if she got the message.

There are no empty tables, so I sit at the far edge of one where a girl who looks like she's still in high school is being visited by a woman who must be her mom and a little boy about three years old. The girl is trying to hug the little boy while he's struggling to get away.

"Don't you want to be with your mom?" the girl asks.

"No! I want to go home."

The girl starts crying, and I turn away, trying to give them privacy.

Which leaves me facing the table where Mom and Tanya are sitting. Obviously, Mom doesn't want me spying on them, but since I'm not allowed to leave the cafeteria, I really have no choice.

Mom and Tanya are sitting side by side on the bench, their

heads close together. Even from the back, they look alike, both of them skinny, both with slumped shoulders. Suddenly, Mom starts to get up, but Tanya drags her back and pulls her into a fierce hug. I see Tanya whispering, Mom gripping Tanya's shirt. Even from across the cafeteria, I hear Mom sobbing. Shit. Why couldn't Tanya wait? At least until Mom got stronger.

Tanya turns to face me—she's crying too—and motions for me to come over.

As soon as I'm sitting beside her, Mom lets go of Tanya and throws her arms around me.

"Layla, I'm so sorry."

"I know, Mom."

She pulls away. "I told Tanya."

"What?"

"I told her about me and Scott."

I look at Tanya who mouths the words: *She beat me to it.*

"That's . . ." I want to say *amazing, incredible, awesome.* But none of that sounds right, so instead I take Mom's hand. Tanya takes her other one, and together we sit in silence, each wrapped in our own thoughts.

Mom's hand is warm. That's what I'm thinking. It's warm and she's alive, and I realize in this silence that feels exactly right that I'm proud of my mom, and that's something I haven't felt in a long time.

EPILOGUE—ONE YEAR LATER

Despite all this a beam of light shines through
And leads me on to feelings fresh and new.
—from "Ode to Fifteen" by Layla Freeman

I haven't been to one of Mom's AA meetings since we lived in the homeless shelter, but today is special. Today she's celebrating one year of sobriety, along with a bunch of other people who have anywhere from one year to fifty, but all of them got sober in November. Her AA group does this every month, and Mom says it's her favorite type of meeting.

Looking around, I can see why. All the smiling faces, the handshakes and hugs. I've actually been to an anniversary meeting before, back in June when Gabriel picked up his one-year medallion. Now Gabriel takes my hand—I still get a thrill whenever he touches me—and together we weave our way through the crowd to where Mom is waving to us from behind a hedge of flowers and balloons.

"Mom, you look great!" I say, giving her a hug.

"Thanks. Is the hair too mom-ish?" It's cut in a wedge and blow-dried to perfection.

"No, it looks good on you." It actually makes her look younger.

Or maybe it's the smile on her face. Or the fact that she's finally getting her life together. Next week, she signs the lease on a new apartment, which means she gets to move out of the halfway house and I get to leave Circle of Hope. I'm nervous about living with Mom again, but every time I see her, she looks better, more healthy. I just hope it's not an illusion.

Gabriel looks shy as he gives Mom a hug. "Congratulations, Mrs. Freeman."

"Thanks, Gabriel. How've you been?"

"Great. Busy."

"Layla tells me you're getting ready for college."

"Just Miami Community."

"It's still college. How's your mom?"

"Good. Working a lot."

"She still volunteering at the shelter?"

"Every Saturday."

"Tell her I said hello."

"I will."

A pretty lady with twinkling blue eyes and dangly Christmas tree earrings hands Mom a bouquet of flowers. I've never met her, but I know this is Peggy, Mom's sponsor. "Congratulations, my dear!"

"Oh wow, thank you!" Mom buries her nose in the flowers before adding them to her collection on the table. "Peggy, I'd like you to meet my daughter."

"So nice to meet you," says Peggy. "I've heard a lot about you."

"I've heard a lot about you too." I glance at Peggy's socks because Mom told me she always wears interesting socks, and sure enough, they're fuzzy and bright blue and one of them has a wreath on it, the other a dreidel.

She sees me looking and smiles. "Not exactly fashionable, but I like to be festive."

"They're awesome."

I want to pull Peggy aside and ask her how Mom's doing—like, how she's *really* doing—but then she says, "Your mom's a joy, and I couldn't be more proud of her."

"Told you," whispers Gabriel.

He did. Since he runs into Mom every once in a while at AA events, he sees more of her than I do. But I still find it hard to wrap my head around the idea that she's doing well. Not that I don't see the evidence before my eyes, but since I haven't lived with her for the past year, a part of me thinks maybe I've been imagining it—this transformation in her. And then I think of what happened to James Saint James, how he relapsed after he lost his job and how no one's heard from him since. All the phone calls go straight to his voicemail and all the texts go unanswered, so maybe he doesn't have his phone anymore. Or else he's ignoring us. Gabriel even went by his halfway house, hoping to bring him back to AA, but he'd disappeared. Everyone who knew him is kind of in shock, and I can't help thinking that if James of all people could relapse, then no one is safe.

Peggy smiles at Gabriel. "Hey, kid. How you doing?"

"Really good. How about you?"

"No complaints. You hear anything from James?"

Gabriel shakes his head.

"I sent him a message this morning," Mom says. "Told him it was my one-year anniversary and asked him to come."

"Did you hear back?" Gabriel asks.

"Not yet," says Mom, "but there's still time."

Gabriel nods, but he doesn't look hopeful.

Mom's phone buzzes from the table. She picks it up, her brow furrowed.

"What is it?" I ask.

"Tanya's not coming."

The old fear rises up. Is this going to set Mom back?

Mom reads the text out loud. "*Sorry I can't get there. Scott causing problems.*"

"Probably on purpose," I say. "He probably knows it's your anniversary and he's trying to sabotage it."

"Or she just doesn't want to come," Mom says.

"You know that's not true."

"I guess." She offers me a brave smile, but I wonder if she's really okay.

Because whenever she's feeling guilty about Tanya, or whenever Scott comes up in conversation, I see the change in her. She'll get quiet. Sometimes she'll pick her nails. And I know she's beating herself up. I try to avoid talking about Scott, but with Mom suing him for paternity and Tanya suing him for divorce, that's hard. Mom's lawyer jokes that, by the time Mom and Tanya get through with him, he'll have sunk to a lower tax bracket. You'd think that would make Mom happy, but she still feels a lot of guilt.

"Hey." I lean close to her. "This is your day. Remember?"

"I'm all right."

"You sure?"

"Positive."

She doesn't glance away, so maybe she's telling the truth.

"I forgot to ask," says Mom. "How's Morgan?"

"She wanted to be here, Mom, but her stepdad said she couldn't miss church."

"Well, church is important."

"She really did want to be here."

"I wasn't expecting her to come. She's doing okay? You guys are still friends?"

"Mom, you ask that every time you see me."

"Sorry."

"It's okay."

Peggy taps Mom's arm. "We should sit down before someone steals our seats."

I check the clock. We have five minutes before the meeting starts, but people are still filing in, and the room is getting crowded. I move Mom's purse and sit down. Gabriel sits beside me, and Peggy's next to him. Mom sits on my other side, and there's a seat next to her with her umbrella on it that I guess she's saving for Tanya. Just in case.

My phone buzzes with a text. It's Celeste, who's away at college.

> Tell your mom I said
> congratulations! 🎈 🍰 💕

I show it to Mom, and she smiles. "I'm impressed she's up this early. Tell her I said thank you."

As I'm finishing up my text to Celeste, the meeting starts. Everyone gets quiet as the chairperson introduces herself. Then we launch into the Serenity Prayer.

"God, grant me the serenity . . ."

The door opens, and (I can't believe it!) James shuffles in. He looks beat down, his hair scraggly, his beard patchy. And yet, my heart fills with gladness at the sight of him.

Gabriel and Mom don't see him—they have their eyes closed as they pray. I wave to get his attention, but he doesn't see me. He looks like he wants to bolt, so I get up as the prayer's ending and go to him.

As I take his arm, he looks at me with tears in his eyes. "Layla," he says, like he can't believe I'm real.

"Good to see you, James."

Slowly, because James is having trouble walking, I lead him to our table where Mom hurriedly moves her umbrella. Peggy is beaming, and Gabriel shoots me a relieved smile. The whole room is quiet while I get James settled, and when I sit down, the chairperson starts talking.

"Today we're celebrating a hundred and ninety years of sobriety."

The room erupts with cheering.

"And our first celebrant is Shauna with one year, presented by Peggy."

While Mom's knee bounces, Peggy goes to the front of the room where the chairperson hands her an envelope with Mom's name on it. I know from having been to Gabriel's anniversary that inside is a card that everyone's signed, plus a one-year medallion that says on it, *To Thine Own Self Be True.*

Peggy's smile lights up the room. "Congratulations to all the celebrants," she says. "But a special congratulations to Shauna, who's worked harder than anyone I know . . ."

So proud of you, Mom.

"This is a woman who was homeless, who hated herself and wanted to die . . ."

Thank God you didn't, Mom.

"But thanks to her willingness and her honesty, she's becoming the woman she always wanted to be, the woman she was *meant* to be. Shauna . . ." Peggy looks directly at Mom, whose chin is trembling. "Come get your one-year medallion."

Mom gets up, and the room explodes with cheering. Gabriel whistles. I murmur, "Go, Mom." And even James mumbles "good job" as Mom takes the envelope from Peggy's hand.

They hug, and as Mom turns to face us, I suddenly remember another meeting more than a year ago when Mom picked up her thirty-day chip at the homeless shelter. And I remember how she got up in front of everyone, and I was so afraid she would embarrass me that I didn't hear how desperate she was.

Is she still desperate? Maybe her smile from earlier is only a veneer to hide the darkness beneath. Or maybe her sobriety is so fragile that any little thing—loss of a job, a fight with me—could make her relapse.

"I just want to say . . ." Mom's head is down as she fumbles with the envelope in her hand. "I want to say how much I've learned this past year. It's been tough trying to get back on my feet, and I couldn't have done it without all of you."

Now she lifts her head, and her eyes go first to Peggy and then to James.

"But most of all," Mom says, "I couldn't have done it without my daughter."

Heads turn in my direction, and my heart starts pounding. Gabriel squeezes my hand.

"She could have let me self-destruct," Mom says. "But she didn't, and I'm not sure why she stood by me after what I put her through."

Mom looks down as she fiddles with the envelope, and I think for sure she's about to tell us how hard her life has been and how she doesn't know if she can keep going because life sucks, doesn't it? And while I'm thinking all this, I'm praying to a god I want to believe in.

Please, God. Please let this be real.

Mom finally looks up from the envelope. "My sponsor once asked me what I want out of life, and I told her I want to be a good mom. 'Is that it?' she asked me. 'What about your own happiness?' And I told her, 'Yeah, I'd like to be happy, but I've spent so much time being selfish that I don't think I deserve it, and plus I'm not sure I know *how* to be happy.'" Mom shakes her head. "And you know what she said? She said being happy is a byproduct of doing the next right thing, whether it's going to a meeting or helping another alcoholic or telling my daughter I'm proud of her."

Mom looks at me with tears running down her face, and before I know what I'm doing, I'm stumbling out of my chair and throwing myself at her chest. She stiffens—probably I've shocked her—but then her arms wrap around me and squeeze me tight, and I'm crying because I'm happy, but also because I'm afraid.

That maybe this won't last.

That maybe Mom will start drinking again, and maybe Gabriel will break up with me, and maybe Morgan and I will go off to our separate colleges and never be as close as we are now.

But then I hear James call out in his deep, rumbling voice, "Keep coming back!"

And I remember where my feet are.

AUTHOR'S NOTE

Some authors are chock full of ideas. Unfortunately, I am not one of them, so my stories tend to be based on things I've gone through in my own life. That was the case with my last book, *A Work of Art,* and it's certainly the case with Layla's story.

I guess you could say I was a troubled teen—not that I got in trouble, but my home was often a place of fear. Plus, I was bullied quite a bit in school (for being awkward, ugly, weird, fat), and though I tried to pretend it didn't bother me, I always felt less-than; I always felt uncomfortable in my own skin. As an adult, I realize how much my mom struggled to pay bills and buy basic things like food, but as a teen, I was more focused on the social difficulties of being poor. Getting new clothes was a rarity, and we often couldn't afford to go to the laundromat or to buy what I then considered to be luxury items like hairspray or notebook paper.

My point is, Layla Freeman is based on me. Like her, I wrote poetry as a teen. In fact, many of Layla's poems are actually my poems, written when I was a teenager. And like Layla, I showed them to an English teacher at my high school who told me they were "too filled with teenage angst," which, as you can imagine, was a huge blow to my self-esteem. Even to this day, I have no idea if the poems are good, but I do know they came from the heart of a teenage girl who was struggling, so why not give them to Layla?

What We Wish For also has roots in my own experience with alcoholism. In fact, the seed for this story was planted when I was chairperson for a recovery meeting at a homeless shelter. During my years as a sober alcoholic, I've witnessed firsthand the hope and the heartbreak of men and women trying, and often failing, to get better. Layla's mother Shauna is not based on any one person, but on a mixture of people I've known, including myself. I know what it's like to struggle with addiction, and I know what it's like to find peace and joy in recovery.

And so this story, if it's about anything, is about hope. I look back at the poems I wrote as a teen, how I longed for something better, how I felt in my heart that if I just kept trudging, I'd surely come out the other side. I did emerge into a happier place, but not before alcoholism brought me to my knees. I almost lost myself, but even in the throes of my addiction, I had hope that life would get better, that *I* would get better.

It's a hope that's served me well.

ACKNOWLEDGMENTS

When writing this book, not knowing whether it would ever be published, I used to dream of the day when I could write my acknowledgments, naming all the people who helped me in this journey. Now that day has come, and it's my huge pleasure to give a shout-out to all those who rooted me on and helped in the telling of Layla's story.

A huge thank you to my "Tuesdays" critique group, which includes Joanne Butcher, Cathy Castelli, Stacie Ramey, Jonathan Rosen, and Joyce Sweeney. Each of them brought their own sharp insight to the book, but Joyce deserves a special shout-out for her incredible storytelling acumen. I'd also like to thank Jamie Morris, Tori Kelly, and Nicole Cabrera. Each of these women brought unique and valuable insight to early drafts of the book. Lizzie Poteet gave an incredible critique of what I thought was a finished manuscript, and I owe her a debt of gratitude for connecting me with Blackstone Publishing. My current agents, Julie Gwinn and Cole Lanahan, have been fantastic cheerleaders throughout the publishing process, and I look forward to working with them in the future.

I would be remiss if I didn't mention the many wonderful employees and volunteers at the Broward Outreach Center in Pompano Beach, Florida. Their dedication to helping others get back on their feet has been a huge inspiration. Also, the men, women, and children I came across while volunteering there provided the root of this story, especially a mother and her teenage son who introduced themselves at a community-wide meeting and who I will never forget.

Finally, I'd like to thank Tina Purcell of the Purcell Agency for being such a wonderful cheerleader; Marilyn Kretzer, senior acquisitions editor at Blackstone Publishing, for believing in this story and shepherding it through publication; Editor Madeline Hopkins, who helped me dig just a little deeper; Windy Goodloe, whose sharp eye made the book shine; and Sarah Riedlinger, whose thoughtful cover design helped bring the story to life.

For all this and more, I am filled with gratitude.